brazen
and
BREATHLESS

Brazen & Breathless
Untouchable #6
Copyright © 2020 by Heather Long
Editing: Bookish Dreams Editing
Cover: Crimson Phoenix Designs
Interior Formatting: Sloane Murphy

Brazen & Breathless/Heather Long – 1st ed.

ISBN-13 978-1-956264-07-4

For all the people trapped in this house with me.
This is how I saved your lives.
You're welcome.

Foreword

Dear Reader,

Thank you for picking up *Brazen and Breathless*. If you haven't read the first five in the Untouchable series, I caution you to go and grab those right now and read them first.

Kicking off the sixth book is kind of surreal. At the same time, there's an inescapable joy at welcoming Frankie and the boys back from their vacation. They're in a much better place.

I talked about found family and friends in the last book. It definitely still applies, but this is also about coming into your own. Frankie has been coming into her own for a while, healing, and letting her confidence out to shine once more. A lot of changes have happened over the last few months, but the best one I think is where she's not hiding who she is anymore and she's definitely not afraid to stand up for herself.

It's an awesome thing for me, the author, to explore.

This series wouldn't be complete without the enormous support of Blake Blessing, Rebecca Royce, Alyssa Muller (even if she is #TeamMadAtHeather), and Sara Vermillion. They've been tremendous as cheerleaders (and in Sara's case, cracking the whip), as sounding boards, and sometimes even telling me to take a break because I was pushing too hard. I flove them to pieces.

I'll be honest, I'm always pushing too hard so these folks keep me in check :D You should thank them, too.

One of the best parts of an ongoing series is there are so many more people to thank along the way. Thank you Katrina for the gorgeous covers, you helped me bring Frankie to life. Elisabeth and Stephanie, thanks for reading and all your comments not to mention the pictures, the videos, and the painting (OMG the painting is so awesome). Thank you to Laura, Jenna, and Sloane for listening to me gripe. And thank you Tate for the ending here. Just making sure everyone knows the bus goes both ways.

Thank you to every single reader who has given this series a shot and to those who left reviews. Thank you to the readers who recommend the series to their friends and to every single person who has reached out to me about it. I see and hear all of you. Thank you to the readers who make the beautiful collages and cast who they see as the characters in this series.

I get such a thrill for every single one I see.

Thank you. Thank you. Thank you.

One last thing, for those who are not on my newsletter or in my group, this series is slated to be ten books long. We're just over halfway there.

And as always, the housekeeping notes:

For those of you who have never read a reverse harem before, first let me thank you for picking this up and giving it a shot. Second, a reverse harem means the heroine will not make a choice in this book or any other between the guys in her life. It may take her a while to reach that conclusion, but it's the journey that drives it. There are many ways to frame this kind of relationship, currently reverse harem fits it very well.

Also, this is the sixth book in a series. If you haven't read the first five, I encourage you to pause here and go grab them. While there may be no specific happy endings at the end of each of these books, there will be one to the whole series, that I promise you. Some of these books will have cliffhangers, largely due to the size of the story, but the happy ending has to be earned as part of the journey.

Thank you again for reading Frankie's story and I truly hope you enjoy it!

xoxo

Heather

Chapter One
CRAZY IN LOVE

Being back at school exhilarated me. From the moment we walked into the cafeteria together, to when I gave Ian and Jake quick kisses before heading off with Archie for first period, my spirits remained high. Were people staring? Yup.

Did I care?

Nope.

Archie kept giving me these sideways looks and biting back smiles.

"What?" I asked, raising a brow as my phone dinged.

He chuckled as he slid his arm around my shoulders and took over piloting while I glanced at my phone. "Nothing. Just happy that you're happy."

"Well you need to be happy for you, too," I retorted, giving him an elbow. The text on my phone was from Coop, with pictures of my kisses with Ian and Jake. Well that didn't take long. Only he also sent a pouty face.

I laughed. I'd given him a kiss when he said he had to run to the library before class. Archie snorted as he glanced at my phone. "Next time kiss Rachel, too, then he can really pop a blood vessel."

I elbowed him again, but it barely had any impact as he chuckled and then pressed a kiss to my temple before turning us into class. I fired off a quick text to Coop that promised I'd make it up to him later.

A minute after we were in our seats, Rachel's text hit my phone.

Rachel

Brace yourself. They already hit Snapchat and Instagram.

I scrolled back to Coop's text and the two pictures he'd sent. They weren't bad shots really. I saved them to a file on my phone and then tabbed back over to Rachel's message.

Me

Fuck 'em.

Rachel

That's my girl.

My phone buzzed twice more, both messages to our group chat.

Archie

You snooze you lose, Coop. Don't whine cause you had to go to the library. You could have asked F to go with.

Coop

Jake and Ian piled on, but I just grinned and shut the screen off. It was going to be a great day.

My mood held through calculus and all the way to French. It faltered a little when I realized Mathieu wasn't present. He always beat me to class, but he wasn't there. That kind of sucked. Rachel quirked a brow at me as she dropped into her desk. "Problem?" she mouthed, but I shook my head.

Madame cleared it up when she reminded all of us that Mathieu had gone home, his semester abroad ended in December.

Oh. My. God.

I was the absolute worst kind of friend. I had completely forgotten I wouldn't see him again. I hadn't even said goodbye. Man, I sucked.

Rachel nudged me with a foot, and I shook my head. "Just…I didn't even think about the fact that he wouldn't be back." I'd breezed out of that last class with him with a half-wave, and I was off. Since we'd been able to blow off classes on the actual last day, we hadn't bothered to show up.

She let out a little huff of laughter and rolled her eyes. I flipped her off with my hand hidden behind my book so Madame wouldn't catch it, and Rachel snorted again. Bitch.

But we grinned at each other and then dove into class.

Seriously, though, it kind of bugged me all the way through AP Lit, and I was chewing on the thought when Ms. Fajardo asked me to stick around for a couple of minutes after class. Apparently, I wasn't doing a good job of hiding my concern, because Coop shot me looks all the way through class and then lingered with me as the others left to head to lunch.

With a roll of her eyes, Ms. Fajardo just shook her head at Coop before focusing on me. "I just have a packet for you to review so you can get me any questions you have." She held out the folder, and I stared at her blankly for a minute.

As I took it, I stared at it and then her. "I feel like I'm forgetting something."

"The internship."

Oh. Shit.

Coop snickered at me. The asshole. "Sorry, Ms. Fajardo, Frankie's still recovering from our holiday break. I think she might have had too much Christmas cheer."

I totally didn't wait to flip him off with one hand behind my back before I opened the folder.

Amused, Ms. Fajardo said, "It's fine. You got all the paperwork in, and since you have the temporary emancipation order, we were able to get it all finalized without involving your mother.”

Good.

“So, just take that home and read it tonight. Email me any questions, and we can talk tomorrow. Orientation is next week, so you'll be signing out on Wednesday for that. Then likely Wednesdays and Fridays for the next few weeks.”

“Thank you,” I told her. I really had forgotten all about this. Fuck, that was going to add to the pile I already had.

“And on that note,” Coop said, hooking an arm around me. “I better go feed her before the hamster wheel burns out. I can already see the lists she's typing in her head.”

With another laugh, Ms. Fajardo waved us out, and I hugged the folder to myself as we walked. “I can't believe I forgot about this.”

“I can,” Coop teased. “We had a lot more fun things to think about than…” He cut his head to the side. “Business opportunities. Since when do you care about business opportunities?”

“It's the scholarship and grant money,” I reminded him. “I'd like to keep all my options open.”

He grunted, then pressed a kiss to my temple before pausing in the hallway to nudge me against a locker.

“Coop,” I warned him.

He just grinned, the little shit. “Frankie. PDAs are back on the table.” Then he kissed me with enough ferocity, it threatened to burn right through my clothes.

“Mr. Brennen. Miss Curtis.” The prim voice intruded right through the lustful haze slapping me right back to Earth.

Wearing the cockiest smile, Coop lifted his head and glanced at Ms. Phillips. We'd had her for ninth grade humanities. “Hey, Mrs. P.”

“Good afternoon, you two. Off you go, and I'll pretend there was nothing to see here.” The warning was unmistakable, but so was the indulgent smile on her face. I had to be about fifty-eight different shades of red, but Coop just grinned.

"Sure thing. We're going to be late to lunch anyway." He gave me a mock glare. "You really need to stop dragging me against walls, Frankie. We're *at* school."

Asshole.

I narrowed my eyes, and he waggled his brows.

If he wanted to play that way, game on.

"Sure thing," I retorted as I ducked under his arm. "I'll make sure I just trip you next time and grab Rachel. She won't complain."

I made it all of three steps before he had an arm around me. "I don't know whether to spank you for that or get turned on, 'cause that's kind of hot."

"Keep it up, Cooper. I'll do it."

He laughed. "No you won't, because you wouldn't want to lead Rachel on."

"You and your logic can bite me," I told him as we pushed out the doors to where Jake and the guys waited with the SUV.

"That can be arranged," Coop said with a grin.

"Why are you two *always* late?" Jake asked, glaring at us over the edge of his sunglasses. I slid my own on as our phones pinged.

"I apparently assaulted Coop in the hallway when I tripped him, and his mouth landed on my lips."

"Well," Jake said. "All right then. Asshole can ride in the back, Baby Girl gets shotgun."

"Hey," came the complaint from Archie and Ian, but Coop just laughed as I circled around to the passenger side.

Girlfriend perks.

I could get used to this.

At lunch, I sandwiched between Archie and Ian as we grabbed pizza at Joe's. It wasn't as busy, and we could get all the individual slices we wanted. Ian kept one hand on my thigh the whole time, and Archie wanted to see the folder as soon as Coop told them what it was.

He was flipping through it, with me reading over his shoulder. Most of it was pretty straight forward—we'd be doing internships at different businesses, some would rotate us to give us a feel across the board, but it was all about leadership and negotiations.

"Why are you doing this again?" he asked, giving me the side eye. Ian had begun rubbing my thigh, just gentle circles with little massaging squeezes that did nothing for my thought process except to utterly derail them.

"Like I told Coop, it's about the scholarships and the grants."

"You got that huge one, babe, you don't need to pile more responsibilities on your schedule."

Not that he didn't have a point but…

"It's up to her whether she does that or not," Jake jumped in. "But if you're looking for our opinions. I'm with Arch."

From being my hero to joining forces with the opposition. I wrinkled my nose. "I know I have a lot on my plate already." Four boyfriends were a lot. "But it's a good opportunity, and it might help me whittle down what I want to do."

You'd think I had that all in the bag, but I didn't.

"Is it a good opportunity? That's two days a week you won't be at school, which means you'll have to double up on your homework to keep up with assignments."

Okay, Jake had a point.

"But stuff like this looks great on college applications."

Thank you, Coop.

"And if we hadn't already submitted them, that would be a huge perk." Course, he couldn't resist tacking that last bit on.

Ugh.

"Stop all siding against me."

"We're not siding against you," Archie countered, and Ian gave my thigh a squeeze before he nudged my plate toward me. I'd only eaten one slice. I picked up the second one with a half-pout. "We're all Team Frankie here, right, guys?"

"Definitely." Ian gave me a little pinch when I rolled my eyes at him. "We're all Team Frankie, and you have a lot on your plate. If you want to do this, we'll support you, but cut us some slack. That's two days a week we're not going to see you at school, and then you throw in you going back to Mason's…"

Fine. He had a point, too.

Ugh.

"I would hate to give up on it just because I was afraid of a little work."

"Is it really giving up if you *forgot* about it?" Coop challenged.

"Yes," I mumbled, then took a bite of the pizza, and Jake grinned at me.

"Then, we figure it out." Jake winked, and Archie nodded.

"I'm going to look more into this program though and ask Grandpa…" He flipped to the next page. "Make sure this isn't a lot of dog and pony showing with no substance. If you're going to spend time on it, then they need to make it worth your investment."

It was a done deal as far as he was concerned. "Tell you what," I offered. "If you and Grandpa Ted come up with something that says this is a bad idea, I'll ask Ms. Fajardo to get out of it."

"Sold," Archie murmured, then gave me a kiss before he scooted out of the booth with the folder in one hand and his phone in the other. "Gonna go call him now."

And he was off.

I stared after him a beat, and Ian chuckled as he trailed his hand up to wrap around my nape. "He'll be fine, Angel. He just has to make sure everything is good enough for you."

He really did try to fix everything. "You know, I haven't even finished reading everything in that folder."

"It's all fine," Coop told me. "Before the day is over, Archie will know all the nitty gritty and everything in the small print."

But that really should be me doing that. Still, it was hard to tell them no. At Ian's gentle urging, I turned and met his kiss. The slow massage of his lips against mine and the teasing of his tongue had me sighing, and the tension melted away.

Course, I could just let them fry all my brain cells, too.

He lifted his head and smiled at me.

"You two are adorable," Jake snarked, then threw a napkin. "Stop hogging her."

"Not my fault you called shotgun for her," Ian teased without looking away from me.

I rolled my eyes and he gave my nape a squeeze as I turned back to my pizza, but he curled his arm around my shoulders and it was just nice to be cuddled. Seriously, I loved the girlfriend perks. Across the table, Coop wore a grin as he watched me and I crossed my eyes at him, which only made him laugh.

"So enough about me…" I began.

"Not possible," Jake said with a wink. "But do continue."

Okay, warmth spread through me, even if he was just teasing. "Anyway," I said through a laugh. "How are your days going?"

"Meh," Jake said.

"Not bad," Coop grunted. "But…I always thought senioritis was a myth."

"No myth," Ian agreed as he took a sip of soda. "I keep thinking of all the things I could be doing if I weren't here."

"Yep," Jake agreed, and I stared at all three of them.

"Really?" I turned that over in my head. I mean, I did miss having them around all the time. I'd gotten very used to having them just right there. But I still got to see them in classes.

"I love you, Baby Girl, but yes, really. Not all of us are as enamored of the academic process."

"Or being away from you," Archie tacked on as he slid back in next to me. He offered me the folder back. "Grandpa is going to check the program, but he has heard of it. He'll call back with the details and let me know if he has any concerns."

"Feel better?"

"Yes," he said. "Thank you."

Lunch passed almost too swiftly after that, and we were back at school. But at least it was study hall. Jake dragged me to the farthest corner of the library, where a table had been set up in a little nook between shelves as far from the librarians and the others as we could get. It was also tucked up in the engineering reference section.

One hardly anyone used because according to Jake and Archie, it was hideously out of date and the best resources were online. After setting our backpacks down, he slipped his arms around me and pulled me down across his lap before kissing me soundly. Not that I was complaining, but we were kind of at school.

I didn't get any of those words out around his tongue demanding access to mine, or with how his fingers dug into my hips and urged me to rock forward. The erection he sported had a tangle of lust coiling in my belly.

"Jake," I whispered against his lips when he dipped his fingers beneath the waistband of my jeans. When the hell had he unbuttoned *and* unzipped them?

"Shh," he whispered, nuzzling kisses along my jaw. "No one comes back here. No one can see. And I've missed you."

He had two fingers under my panties and speared into me even as I surged up. I sucked in a breath and tightened my thighs as he worked his thumb against my clit. We should so not be doing this. Mouth on mine, he sucked on my tongue as he plunged his fingers in a series of relentless strokes even as he circled my clit.

The orgasm ripped out from under me, and I damn near drew blood biting down on my own lip to keep from crying out. I was still shaking when he eased his hand out of my pants, his pale blue eyes shimmering with smug satisfaction as he licked off his fingers one by one. "Best post lunch dessert ever," he whispered, and a shudder went down my spine.

I glared at him, but I doubt there was any heat to the expression at all, because seriously. What brain cells managed to survive that pleasurable onslaught were still pinging off each other in some mad dance. Panting, I looked at his watch as he continued to clean his fingers, and little shudders raced through my system at the promise of his tongue savoring the taste.

We had time.

"You're sure no one comes back here?" I asked around the time I found my voice.

"I'm positive, Baby Girl," he assured me. The husk in his voice just did things to me. I wiggled off his lap and fixed the button on my jeans and zipped them up. I couldn't do anything about my now-soaked panties, but turnabout's fair play, right?

His eyes widened as I went to my knees and then undid his jeans. The shock registered, and he darted a look up past me. "Worried?" I teased as I undid his belt. The fact that his ring winked at me as I unzipped his jeans just sent another shiver through me.

I loved that ring.

I loved the meaning behind it.

I loved the fact that Jake had gotten it for me.

I loved him.

"No," he said with a bob of his Adam's apple as he swallowed. He tracked my every motion, and I swore his cock jumped when I ran my hand over it.

"Good."

Then I pushed the where we were out of my head as I swiped my tongue across his slit, catching the drops of pre-cum.

"Just keep quiet," I whispered, and I felt more than heard his groan as I swallowed around his cock. I'd gotten much better at this over the last few months and I'd almost mastered my gag reflex, so I could take him all the way to the root and he bumped into my throat.

He fisted my hair as his muscles went rigid. I showed him the exact amount of mercy he'd given me as I cupped his balls and began bobbing my head with swift, sure strokes as I added pressure with my tongue.

He hissed out a breath, then another, and then I couldn't hear him breathing at all. Slanting a look up, I found him staring down at me, almost red-faced as he held his breath, and then he came so hard and so fast, I nearly choked on his release.

The tautness of his hand in my hair kept me in place as I swallowed every drop, and then he sagged back as I lifted my head. My jaw ached, but nothing could hold back my smile as I tucked him away gently and pulled up his zipper. He could fasten his own belt. Tugging me up, he kissed me hard and sweet, his breath ragged as he whispered.

"That's one of the hottest fucking things you've ever done to me," he said. "I'm pushing you more often. I like this."

So did I.

Smoothing a hand over my hair, I settled into the chair next to his and accepted the bottle of water he offered, even as I preened under the awe in his stare. I'd just recapped the water when a freshman wandered into the row and hesitated when he spotted us. Jake stilled, then glared at the interloper.

It took the kid no time at all to retreat, and I had to bite my lip as Jake glanced at me with a wince.

We stared for a beat, then we both cracked up.

Yep. We were crazy.

But I loved it.

Still, even with how great the day was going, I knew it was coming. It didn't happen until I hit the bathroom between sixth and seventh, but Maria walked in as I washed my hands and our gazes locked in the mirror. There were a couple of sophomores there too, and they had been blatantly whispering when I walked in and silenced as soon as I disappeared into a stall. They lingered at Maria's arrival for whatever happened next.

Yep. Gossip for the mill.

"Hey," she said, and I lifted my chin.

One of the sophomores giggled, and Maria flicked a cool look at them. They didn't seem moved until I joined in staring at them, and then they were shoving each other out the door. With a glance back at Maria, I finished washing my hands.

"So, it's true?"

"Depends on what *it* is." I wasn't trying to be coy. Maria hesitated as I grabbed a paper towel and dried my hands. There was no more putting it off.

I faced her.

"You're dating all of them." It wasn't a question.

"I am."

Surprise flickered across her face. Like she couldn't believe I'd admit it. I had to admit, her floundering amused me, a little. But Maria and I were okay. I felt bad about what happened to her. I was sorry she'd been hurt.

I would *never* be sorry I had Jake.

Or any of them.

They were mine now.

"Wow," she said slowly. "I didn't think you'd just come right out and say it."

I shrugged, then fixed my backpack. "I have nothing to hide."

Not anymore. They could all suck it.

"You know people are going to call you a slut."

The corner of my mouth kicked up before I could even restrain the reflex, and I snorted. "They called me a slut before I dated anyone, apparently. If I'm going to do the time, I might as well enjoy the crime."

With that, I headed to the door, then paused and glanced back at her.

"You could do me a favor though."

"And that would be?" She looked really skeptical.

"If anyone asks, you feel free to tell them the boys are off the market.

They're mine, and I have no intentions of sharing them anymore."

And I had been sharing them, whether intentionally or not.

"Just ask Sharon my feelings on the subject… You know if she's had her nose fixed yet?"

Maria almost smiled at that and then shook her head. "I'll take your word for it." Before I could open the door though, she added, "Hey, Frankie?"

"Yeah?"

"You make sure they treat you right."

"They already do," I told her with a real smile. "Later."

Out of the bathroom, I swallowed the first bit of shakiness and blew out a breath as I hurried to seventh. I'd texted Jake I had to make a pitstop at the bathroom and I'd meet him. Thankfully, he'd taken me at my word and wasn't waiting for me right outside the door.

No, he was just down the hall where he could see it.

Which meant he saw Maria come in.

But all he did was raise his brows. "All good?"

I grinned and tucked myself under his arm. "It's perfect."

Chapter Two

THIS ONE'S FOR THE GIRLS

"**S**o, no go?" Rachel asked as I flung myself down on her bed. We were trying something different today. I'd come to her. She always came to me. My work. My classes. My car. My apartment. I'd been to Rachel's all of twice in the past.

She was not big on her family.

Seriously, I got that.

"Not that bad," I admitted, staring up at her ceiling. There were little stars everywhere. The kind that would glow in the dark, and there were fairy lights strung on the walls, around some of the pictures and weaving around the posters. They were on, but so was her desk lamp and bedside light. Still, it gave the room a cozy effect. "Marsha's great. But the new girl is apparently working out really well, and one way or another, I'm gone after May or at least by the end of the summer…"

"And she needs to train the new Frankie," Rachel guessed. Clearly, she'd been working on homework when I got here, but she twisted the desk chair around to face me. While I was still in jeans, she'd thrown on some cutoffs and a T-shirt. It was a little too chilly for shorts yet. But her place was kind of warm.

The Mannings lived smack in the middle of one of the new developments for our area. New as in it had been built about ten years earlier or so. I was pretty sure Rachel's family was one of the first ones to move in out here. They had a great view of the green belt and a huge backyard, but no pool.

It wasn't like I had a pool either. Archie and Ian had pools. Jake didn't. Well, technically, Coop and I had the pool at the apartment complex, but yeah, we hadn't gone swimming in it since Ian's parents had one built in their backyard.

"Yeah," I said, dragging my wandering attention back to the subject at hand. "So, I can take two shifts of whatever I want, and she'll get the other two. Marsha even offered to let me just be a floater—you know, fill in when someone is sick if I wanted. That way, I stayed employed but I could have my time back."

Sometimes, I thought Marsha must be on the far opposite end of the spectrum from Maddy. Kind of a universal balancing effect.

And now I sounded like Coop.

A smile tilted my lips. Guess he really had rubbed off on me, in more ways than one.

A pillow slapped against my head, and I laughed as I blew some of the errant strands of hair out of my face.

"You went all dewy-eyed. Which one of the assholes were you thinking about?"

"Coop," I admitted. Tucking the pillow beneath me, I rolled onto my stomach and kicked my bare feet up into the air. No one wore shoes in Rachel's house. Her parents would have a conniption. Shoes didn't even come in the house. They were set neatly on a stand in the vestibule. Well, guests did anyway, mine were the only shoes there. The family had a stand in the garage.

"Uh huh."

I glanced past her to where the condom cactus sat in a prominent spot and bit back a smile. I didn't stare at it too long, 'cause I didn't want to draw her attention to it. Especially since she'd added a little flag name tag to it that said

"Asshat."

That was adorable.

"Anyway," I circled us back because the conversation about work was troubling me more than I wanted to admit. "If I'm going to work for Mason's and for Marsha, I want to actually *do* my job."

"And you've kind of missed it." If Rachel was guessing, she was doing an excellent job. Then again, Rachel seemed to get me without a lot of effort on my part.

That was something I planned on changing, which was another reason I'd offered to come over and hang out here rather than invite her back to my place.

Well, that and the four sexy distractions currently occupying my apartment. I loved having them there, but it did make girls' night challenging. Especially a rather spontaneous and unplanned girls' night.

"I have missed it," I admitted. "But not as much as you might think." Guilt stabbed me on that last bit, and I cut a look at Rachel. "I loved working at Mason's because Marsha's great and it can be fun, don't get me wrong. But it was also brutal, and I ran my ass off. I am honestly okay if I never see another shake again, and it really kind of put a crimp in my love of burgers."

"Well, anything that damages your love of food," she teased with a smile that invited me to join her in laughing at me. Which, I could, because yeah, I got it. I liked to eat.

"But I feel bad."

"Girl, anyone ever tell you that you overthink the shit out of things?"

"I don't know, Rach, let's talk about dissecting poetry and planning out a loving campaign with roses and poems and little gifts to brighten someone's day without getting anything in return."

"Pfft, I got to enjoy your joy," she countered. "That was totally something in return."

"Fine, but you still thought an awful lot about it. So I'm not the only one who overthinks, hesitates, pulls back, reassesses, then plans again."

Her nose wrinkled, and she cut her gaze skyward as if debating it. Then nodded. "Fair enough. We are a lot alike that way." The corners of her mouth tilted. "Probably why we could rub each other the wrong way."

"I thought it was because we locked horns over that writing project in seventh grade."

Rachel narrowed her eyes at me. "We didn't *lock* horns."

"What do you call it?" I challenged.

"You're a control freak." She fired off that answer without missing a beat.

"I'm a control freak?" I snorted. "Me?"

"Yes, you, Frankie Curtis, are a control freak. 'Here, Rachel, let me break down the assignment so we can just split it in half. Then we can both work at our own pace and neither of us has to rush.'"

"Is that supposed to be how I sounded?" I debated whether I should be offended or not.

"It *is* how you sounded. Oh my god, Frankie, have you ever listened to yourself? In seventh freaking grade, you had a breathy, soft, butter wouldn't melt in your mouth voice. Now it's a little deeper and huskier, but it's got that bedroom quality to it."

I shook my head. "Still pretty sure I didn't sound like *that*, and we're straying from the point. Splitting it in half was the best way to go, we're too competitive and…"

"And you didn't know at the time if I could keep up, so you figured if you split it in half, you could do both parts and then substitute your work for mine if I sucked." Arms folded, she propped her feet up on the edge of her bed and stared at me, daring me to disagree.

"Well, I didn't have to do that."

Rachel rolled her eyes. "Because I wouldn't let you just send me off to do my half, I made you stay after school every day with me until we got it done."

Oh yes, I remembered. Jake, Ian, and Coop had given me hell about it, too. That, and I ended up having to walk home most days after because the bus had already come and gone. Maddy was always at work, so she wouldn't have time.

To be fair, Rachel's mom offered to bring me home that first night, but she'd made a face at our apartment complex, and after that, I just would rather skip that experience.

"And you argued with me on every single point we researched, even when I had facts on my side."

"That part was just fun," Rachel admitted, and I groaned and flopped on my back.

"You suck."

"Not as much as you, I'd bet."

I rolled over and threw the pillow, but she already had her arms up to block it. Thankfully, we were both laughing.

"Hey," she said. "Seriously…the thing with Mason's. You've got ethics. You don't want to take their scholarship and run, even if Marsha's giving you that option. You love the job…because it gave you independence. I get that. My crappy job is crappy, but I really love having my own paycheck, even if it's a pittance."

"Yeah," I admitted. "And I'm whining about the fact that she's letting me off the hook and that realistically, if I wanted to just blow it off, I could supplement with the delivery. I have money in savings, and it's not like Archie's letting me pay any of my bills."

"Letting you?"

I shook my head. "Let me put it this way, he's paid everything. Like months in advance. The rent, the electric, the water. Everything."

"Wow," Rachel said before she abandoned the chair to flop on the bed next to me. "Sounds like a horrible problem to have. Rich Boy at your beck and call…"

"Rach…"

"I'm giving you shit," she promised, bumping my hip. "You don't want him taking care of everything."

"I don't want him to feel like he has to," I corrected. "I know he *wants* to, because Archie is a fixer—and this is getting off topic. We talk about my problems all the time. I want to talk about yours."

"Well, the topic was Mason's, not my problems," she said with a laugh. "What makes you think I have problems, anyway?"

Too light. Too easy. Brush it off.

"And I like helping with yours. I meant it when I said I was going to be your friend," she reminded me.

"Friendship isn't a one-way street." I rolled onto my side and propped my head on my hand and stared at her. "You focus on me a lot, and I adore you for it. You make me feel good about some really crappy stuff, and you've been there for some even crappier stuff. I haven't been the best of friends, but that's changing. I want to be your friend too."

"You are my friend." With a sigh, she pushed up and moved to sit against her headboard. That put us at opposite ends of the bed. Distance.

Yep, just like me.

It would be almost funny if it didn't make my heart hurt. I did that, too. And next she'd…

"The thing with Mason's, before we get too distracted," Rachel said. "Marsha cares about you, and you're not the one asking for the out. She's offering it to you. Just like Rich Boy wants to fix things for you and I want to be there for you. You're not used to people doing things *for* you, even if those four idiots have been for years."

"It's not the same—then versus now. And at the end of the day, I'm still their friend, too. I help them. At least I hope I do." Yeah, I did. I shook off that thought. "And you're not distracting me. Something's been bugging you since before Christmas. You're usually acerbic, but you've been a little more razor sharp since going to Ohio."

She thumped her head back against the wood of her bed frame.

"And you haven't said anything about Skylar other than it didn't work out."

"Well, it didn't. We wanted different things." A faint smile pulled at her mouth. "I'm not head over heels for her, and she definitely wasn't for me. This isn't apples to apples, Frankie. Skylar and I had fun. Then we weren't having fun."

Pursing my lips, I considered her, then sat up and criss crossed my legs as I faced her. "Okay, if it was that simple, then what was eating you?"

"Well, no one, that would be why I was grumpy." Not even a flicker of expression change.

"Then hang out with Sally Thumb and her four sisters," I retaliated.

Rachel laughed out loud and clapped her hands. "Damn, you didn't even blush. Those boys *are* doing their job."

I rolled my eyes and then glared at her. "Don't start."

"Hey, if you're going to worry about my orgasms, then why shouldn't I worry about yours?"

"Because you started it with your tongue advice, so I'm just returning the favor."

Head cocked, she considered the argument. "I'll give you that one. Fine… you don't have to worry about me or Sally Thumb." She reached over and tugged the drawer next to her bed. "I have an assortment of gadgets for my pleasure."

An assortment was right. Holy crap.

"Wait…" I half-crawled over there and stared down at the dildo and then at her. "I thought you said you didn't like dick."

"I don't like it anywhere near as much as you do," she said with a smirk. "And that one is free of other irritating attachments, like a personality or bossiness. It does what I want, when I want, how I want."

I burst out laughing.

I didn't even have words for it as Rachel gestured from one device to the other. "I pretty much have all my options covered. See…" She held out one that when she turned it on, it made a little waving motion. "Good tongue action."

Hands over my face, I cracked the fuck up. There was no way to hold onto that seriously. "How do you have so many?"

"The internet is a pathway to many things some would consider unnatural. Or at least too kinky. Besides, I like experimenting. Can't know what you like if you don't try." She waved her wiggling tongue vibrator at me, and I made a face. "And it's not that many. Some don't work like they used to, so I probably should clean it all out. Maybe order some new ones. How many do you have?"

I just stared at her.

"Frankie." Her mouth dropped open. "Seriously?"

I lifted my shoulders. "When was I going to go buy one?"

"You could have ordered one."

I gave her a look.

"One, that meant spending money. I never spend money if I can help it." I could get by on a little, and I socked everything into savings. Turned out, I was right to do that, even if I had the guys right there like a safety net trying to make my landing as soft and bouncy as they could.

Yeah, okay, don't think about bouncy and the boys while looking at Rachel's sex toys.

Just...don't.

"And now I'm guessing you think you don't need them," Rachel said as she put her toys back into the drawer. "I suppose with four of them, one of them is probably always ready. Then again, they all talk too, and sometimes a girl just has to scratch the itch and get back to it."

Scratch the lack of blushing from earlier. My face was on fire.

"And law of averages suggests that among that many partners, at least one of them has to have a kink. I mean, having four partners is a kink all its own." Rachel tapped her lower lip. "Even if they're not, sooner or later, multiples are gonna happen at some point. So in that case, sex toys might help ease you into it."

Yep and on that note, I rolled forward to bury my face against the pillow. How did she do this to me? I was talking to her about her, and now we were talking about my sex life.

"Frankie Curtis, you bad girl! You've already double dipped, haven't you?"

I peered at her. "You want to know that, you gotta give me a truth for a truth."

She snorted. "I should never have sent you those books."

"But you did, and I read them, and I loved them. So, truth for truth."

"Fine, what do you want to know?" Her expression locked down some and her eyes tightened, as if anticipating how bad this whole conversation was going to go. I didn't want her to dread it. I mean, I got protecting myself.

"If you don't trust me enough to talk to me about whatever it is, I won't keep pressing." I could offer that much. "Right *now*. But you were right when you said I needed a friend and you decided you were going to be my friend. That meant a lot to me. More than I realized then. But I'm right when I say friendship is a two-way street, and I'm *going* to be your friend, too. That means all the nitty gritty and irritating stuff, like talking about our feelings and listening to each other bitch about everything—boys, girls, parents, college, school—and whether Avery should choose Aodhan or Atticus. I mean it. Everything."

Rachel snorted. "In what *world* does she choose Aodhan over Atticus? Please." It was an out I was offering her and she toyed with it, but the reticence in her expression softened some. "And you're right, a truth for a truth. You are my friend. Even if you don't think you are. You give me something to fight for. You accept me for exactly who I am and don't expect me to change."

"You might be the whole damn cactus, Rachel Manning. But you're my cactus, and I'm keeping you."

She grinned and turned her head away as she shifted as though needing to get in a more comfortable position. I didn't miss how she wiped at her eyes, however. Clearing her throat, she faced me once more and then said, "After the

Halloween party and everything went down, Skylar wouldn't let go of asking me about you. And she decided I was spending too much time with you, and that's why we broke up." A lift of her shoulders tried to make light of something that wasn't. "I'm not going to apologize that you're my favorite, just like I'm not going to turn my back on you because my girlfriend decides that you're competition."

I winced. "Rach…"

"Nope," she said. "I liked Skylar. A lot. We were good, but if she can't accept my friendships, then we're not that good. Even those four idiot boys of yours are okay with it. Or at least working on being okay with it. I get it. I see it. I might almost like them, but I'll deny it to my grave if you tell them."

"Your secret is safe with me, and for what it's worth…I'm sorry. Would it help if I talked to her?"

"Oh fuck no," Rachel said. "The thing is…once we broke up, I really didn't miss her all that much. It's just like before, I miss the sex but…" She motioned to her drawer. "I'm not going to die when I can get myself off." A sigh escaped her. "Just sometimes it would be nice…to be able to trust it, you know?"

"I do and I don't," I told her, but I reached over to squeeze her hand. "I'm the worst at dating advice. Even if I'm getting a crash course in it from the guys right now. I mean, apparently, they were trying to date me and I didn't notice. Probably not the best one to be able to say I get it all the way. But…I really love that they are there for me, and I know they'll be there tomorrow and the next day and the day after that."

I could trust it.

I *did* trust it.

If everything the last few months had thrown at me proved anything, it proved that.

She squeezed my hand. "So, my turn now?"

After blowing out a breath, I said, "Yep, your turn. What do you want to know?"

"So many questions…" Rachel looked thoughtful. "One of those boys has to have a kink…one he's shared with you and you like. So that's what I want to know, which one of them?"

"Rach," I said with a wince. "That's kind of personal."

"I won't tell them I know," she promised. "I'm a vault. Besides, you said a truth for a truth, and I bared my bruised and lonely soul."

Okay, at that, I rolled my eyes. But then again, she did have a point. Huffing out a breath, I groaned and squinted one eye closed. Technically, I thought we were all a little kinky, depending on how you defined it. "How about I tell you the kink but not who?"

"That is an acceptable trade-off," she said magnanimously. *"For now."*

Drumming my fingers against my thighs, I leaned toward one of Coop's kinks. Probably the safest one to mention. Ian loved to restrain me, and I had to admit, I loved it, too. Never thought I'd be into that, but we needed more time to figure that out for ourselves.

"I'm waiting," Rachel said. "I'd offer you a shot, but my parents aren't thrilled when I drink."

"Yeah, and I still have to drive."

"I guarantee you that there are four guys who are more than willing to come and get you and your car, even if I don't mind you crashing here. That said, time's up, Curtis. Spit. It. Out."

"One of the guys really gets off on watching."

She squinted at me, head tilted. "You know that makes sense and isn't even that much of a kink."

"Rachel."

"Well," she said. "It's not. I mean, there are four of them. Unless you guys are punching a clock somewhere, one of them is going to have to see you with the others…"

"You're killing me."

She grinned. "Not yet, but our next girls' night, we're going to Kink on the Hill."

"We're doing what now?"

"Oh, my sweet summer child," Rachel said, reaching over to put her hand on my leg. "There is a lot of kink out there, and I'm going to make sure you know what all of it is. That's my duty as your friend."

"And you really want to know which of them is into what."

"Well…yes, but I'm also curious about what you're into and what you've gotten them to explore for you…"

Yep, this was how I died.

From embarrassment.

"Truth for a truth," I reminded her.

"Ask."

Grasping my courage, I waded in. "Are you really letting your feelings for me get in the way of a real relationship for you?"

It was what worried me. Not because I didn't value her friendship. I don't think I could have handled everything the last few months without her and the guys. Especially when there were times it was hard to talk to the guys.

But I needed to not be the reason she was not happy.

"I like you," she admitted slowly. "I freely admit…if there was even the remotest chance you were interested in me, I'd give those four idiots a run for their money. And I'd win. Because I'm really good."

I bit my lip to suppress the laugh that wanted out so badly. Because this wasn't funny.

"But you're not, and I'm okay with that. Am I comparing other girls to you?" She gave a little shrug. "Maybe I am now, but I think that's a damn good standard."

I winced.

"Girl, you—you're awesome. And I am not the mushy sort, but this friendship thing? It's working for me."

"It's working for me, too."

"Then don't worry about it. You're not letting those boys push me away, and I'm not letting whoever I date do that to you. They accept you, or there's the door, don't let it hit them in the ass on the way out."

"I just want you to be happy, Rach."

"And I love you for it," she told me. "But I'm really okay. Thank you for worrying."

"Will you tell me if you're ever not?"

"I promise." She held up her pinky like we were five, and I hooked mine with hers. "You tell me when you're not."

"I have," I reminded her. So it was an easy promise to make.

"Excellent," she said as we sealed it with a pinky squeeze. Flopping back against the pillows, she eyed me with a sudden wicked grin. "What's your kink, Frankie? What is something you've figured out that you like?"

Yep. Saw that one coming.

But a truth for a truth, right?

Chapter Three
WHAT'S YOUR GAME?

Fifteen minutes into the orientation, and I had to wonder how I got into this program. The guy on the stage was talking about leadership and how it was a choice. One you had to make every single day. Instead of an auditorium setting, we were seated at these oversized round tables. Instead of being at a business, we were at a hotel in a really bland, beige colored room with a geometric patterned carpet that gave me a headache if I looked at it too closely.

There were about thirty altogether in the program. It didn't seem a huge number, but I really didn't look like most of the people here. I'd dressed nice enough, I supposed, but there were a lot of kids here in actual suits, like the kind you wore to go into an office daily. Of those *not* in suits, they were still in slacks, or skirts and looking put together.

I'd worn jeans. Probably not my best choice, but the paperwork said this was orientation. A day to spend on leadership skills and workshops. Who wore a *suit* to a workshop? My shirt was nice, and I'd paired it with a fun patterned vest. I looked kind of sassy.

At least, if Archie's reaction this morning had been any indication. I'd had to talk him out of undressing me, because they had to get to school and I had to go to orientation. Talk about strange. Ian left on his bike, and Coop rode with Jake, while Archie took his own car. And I wasn't leaving with any of them. It was just *weird*.

Not that I minded the very sound and thorough kisses I got from each of them. Those had my toes curling, and thankfully, the thirty-minute drive to the hotel where they were hosting the orientation had given me time to get my hormones under control.

Barely.

Ten minutes into the presentation, a girl slid into the seat next to mine. I'd chosen one of the tables near the side and to the back. Mostly because I didn't know anyone, and while there were six tables, they weren't all full. Mine was me, a guy with glasses and a friendly enough smile who'd just nodded to me when he sat down, and now the newcomer. Weirdly, I didn't mind the fact that all these people were strangers, but I was glad the chick who decided to pick my table had dressed in jeans, too.

Solidarity.

"Hey," she whispered as she hurriedly unpacked a spiral bound notebook and a bottle of water. I still had my coffee from the drive-thru this morning. I'd cheated and gotten two. One I pretty much shot-gunned on the way here, and the second I'd been sipping to keep up my strength. Because based on the last ten minutes, I was going to need it.

Interesting material or not, our presenter was dull as dirt.

"Hey," I answered, barely moving my lips. I'd mastered the talk without looking like you're talking trick a long time ago. Largely because Coop could be annoying if I ignored him too long when he wanted to tell me something in class, even if we weren't supposed to be talking.

Granted, that was elementary school and he wasn't as bad about it in high school since we could text and shit, but still a useful skill to have.

"How much did I miss?" she asked, her gaze almost as steady on the

PowerPoint on the screen as mine was. The sad part, this guy wasn't offering anything beyond the details on each of the slides. Seriously, I could copy it all down and get as much out of it as him telling us.

More maybe. I read faster than he spoke.

"Not much," I told her. "Just introduced himself, said we'd be discussing leadership, then started this on how it's a choice."

Seriously, she hadn't missed much.

"Cool." Then she was quiet as the guy droned on and on and on.

Kill me.

Please.

I was half-tempted to text the guys to get me out of this. But I couldn't, not after Archie checked, then re-checked to make sure everything was legitimate and on the up and up. I doubted Ms. Fajardo would have recommended me for a shady program, but Archie wanted to be sure.

It was only after he'd gone over everything twice with us and even Jake seemed to relax that I got it. Archie wasn't just checking on it to soothe me, he did it to soothe them. The guys worried about me, and after the last few months, I got it. It hadn't been easy, but this was supposed to be a great opportunity, and they wanted me to enjoy it and not have to worry.

After another fifteen minutes of my life slowly bleeding away, the girl next to me shifted in her seat as she stretched her legs and tried to make herself more comfortable. She'd stopped taking notes ten minutes ago.

I hadn't, but old habits and all that…

"I'm Mollie, by the way," she said, and I cut a quick glance at her. She had sandy blonde hair with just a hint of pink on the tips of it. A hint because to be honest, it could be the light in the room. I'd love to be able to color my hair something fun, but school rules said natural colors only. Lucky, her she got to go somewhere she didn't have to worry about that. "Mollie Barragan."

"Frankie Curtis," I answered her intro with my own. "Robertson High."

"West Arbor," she said with a shrug.

I had no idea where West Arbor was, not really. I'd heard of it. But then I'm guessing she probably had no idea where Robertson was either. Didn't matter. It was another monotonous forty-five minutes before he called for our first break, and I leaned back in my chair with a groan.

"This is how I die," the guy said from across the table. "From absolute boredom. Do you think it gets any better?"

I lifted my shoulders with a laugh. "I hope so. But I guess not everything is going to be interesting."

"There's not interesting, and then there's killing people slowly with your delivery," Mollie snarked, and I grinned wider. She reminded me a little of Rachel, not a bad thing. She drained her water bottle and stood. "I'm going to pee. Then hopefully find coffee." She eyed my cup with no small amount of lust, and I curled it closer to me.

It only had a quarter left, but I wasn't going to risk losing it.

"You mind watching my stuff?" she asked, and I waved her away.

The guy across from us stood and stretched. The other students were up and moving, too. I should probably walk around, but I had a feeling that if I got up and started walking, I might head out to my car and go back to school.

"I'm Bryan," he said as he walked around the table and offered me his hand. It gave me my first good look at him, too. He had on slacks and dress shoes with a Hawaiian shirt. I almost wished I could snap a picture of him to send to the guys.

You know, maybe not.

He was a guy, and he was talking to me. Jake might show up, and the day would get a lot more interesting.

Biting back a laugh, I stood so he didn't loom over me. I'd never been a fan of it before, and I was less of one now. I clasped his hand for a quick handshake. "Frankie."

"Awesome," he said and let go of my hand. "Gonna get coffee. You want anything?"

Did I want a guy I'd just met to get me a drink? Let me think about that. How about no? "I'm good," was all I said though. He gave me a little smile and then headed away, and I sank back into my seat.

There were ten minutes on the clock ticking down on the screen, so I pulled out my phone.

Archie

How's it going? You missed nothing in class.

Ian

I got the homework. It's not bad. All good there?

Wow, I'd been here long enough to miss two classes.

Blegh.

Rachel

Your idiots look lonely.

There was a picture attached of the four of them sitting around the table in the cafeteria. They did look a little lonely, and I made a face. It was one day. I could handle one damn day away from them. I had one of them in my bed nearly every night, sometimes two.

Maybe if this were more interesting…

Coop

I'm bored. Sneak into the bathroom and send me some pics.

Eyes rolling, I laughed and just sent him back a middle finger emoji.

His response was instantaneous.

Coop

That was the idea.

The last message was from Jake, and it just made me smile

Yeah. Me, too.

I sent that to all of them, too. I missed them. But…I needed to make the most of it. Orientation was just this all-day thing, and then we had one other day where we would have to have orientation at our 'assignment.' Hopefully, we found out what that was today, too.

Mollie wandered back in with a yawn and a Styrofoam cup of coffee. Bryan followed a minute later, and one by one, the others trickled back to their seats.

As soon as the clock ticked down to zero, we were back to dull as dirt land.

Only, at least we got to participate in this next segment.

Yay.

By the time lunch rolled around, I had decided that if nothing else, this morning had shown me what I didn't want to do in life.

This right here was what I didn't want to do in life.

Lunch had been catered in so we didn't have to go anywhere. Boxed sandwiches, chips, and sodas. Not bad. Mollie and Bryan turned out to be decent conversationalists, and I only texted with the guys to let them know I was surviving. Still hadn't sent them smoke signals to come and rescue me. And we only had another four hours to go.

Bryan went to Spencer. That was a more affluent school district, I knew that for a fact. They were also the rivals for Robertson's football team. Well former rivals, so that little fact would stay out of the notes for Jake and Ian.

They were serious about their dislike for football rivals, and I wasn't getting in the middle of that.

Still, Bryan was funny and had a dry sense of humor. We debated some of the leadership examples we'd been given, and I had to admit, if we needed to make it a choice, could we at least make it a funny one?

While the morning had dragged by in slow motion, the afternoon passed at a steady clip. It proved to be more interactive and a hell of a lot more fun. Each table was given an example of leadership to tackle as a group project. Not my favorite thing to do, and yes, I did shoot Rachel the mental finger on that one, even if she'd have just laughed at me.

So for an hour, Mollie, Bryan, and I debated the merits of the leadership style we'd been given. None of us liked it. So we worked out our presentation based on all the reasons you should never use this.

We were cracking ourselves up.

The following hour, all the groups cycled through their different styles, and I got more out of those presentations than I had the whole morning. Even doing our own, we managed to elicit more than a few laughs, and most of the kids who'd come in suits had taken off their jackets and rolled up their sleeves.

To say we were more relaxed was an understatement.

During the last hour, our presenter went over some key things we needed to know for our internships. They were still being sorted. We would receive an email by Friday with our assignments and all the key contact details. We were expected to show up every day of the internship, but because things did happen, there was a procedure to follow if we were gonna be out sick.

Fair enough.

Then he did the best thing all day, he sent us home early.

Mollie and I traded numbers. I got Bryan's, too. The chances were we wouldn't see each other again, but social media data had also been exchanged along with email addresses.

"We'll just have our own little bitch group," Mollie told me after we said goodbye to Bryan and headed out to the parking lot. "Because after today, I'm not sure whether we should be looking forward to this or not."

"Well, on the upside," I told her as I opened my car door. "At least we should have a good grasp on what we don't want to do."

"True that." She lifted her hand in a wave as she disappeared into her own car.

All the way back to the apartment, I jammed out to Torched, singing at the top of my lungs. I was still tickled that I'd gotten to go to their concert. And while my energy reserves had been at zero after the morning, I was bouncing back. That, and I was going to get back nearly an hour before the guys. I'd sent the guys a text to the group chat that I was finished early and on my way home.

I'd just pulled off my shoes when the backdoor opened and then closed. I'd gone to the bedroom to change, and I pivoted and crashed right into Archie, who had his arms around me and his mouth on mine before the words could even form.

Ferocious was the only word I could use to describe the way his lips massaged mine and how his tongue demanded access. I groaned at the lightning sizzle of heat that every lick and nip sent rioting through me. He walked me back to the bed, still kissing, and then we tumbled down. He caught himself with one arm to keep from landing atop me, but then he settled his weight and I was torn between a sigh and a groan.

There was just something about the way they covered me that truly turned me on and utterly relaxed me in the same breath. I had missed them all day today, and Archie was here and kissing me, and I couldn't breathe as I dug my fingers into his back and then down to tug at his shirt.

He broke from the kiss long enough to sit up and yank his shirt off, and then it was gone before he swooped back down to claim my mouth again. There was no mistake about that. It was definitely a claiming. It scorched right through my system, and I ground my hips up against his.

"You're home early," I managed to pant out as he nuzzled kisses down to my throat. He nipped and sucked hard just over my pulse point, and I arched my back and tried to wrap my legs around him.

Jeans did not help me get the friction I wanted though, dammit.

"You said you were gonna be here," he told me, still licking and kissing until he had me squirming. His skin was so hot under my fingers, and I traced one hand against where his tattoo was. "Ditched last period."

A smile pulled at my lips, and then he sat up, and I groaned as he pulled away.

"Shh, babe, I just need to unwrap this beautiful package. Do you have any idea how sexy this vest is?"

I quirked a brow at him. "How sexy?"

"Not as sexy as it's going to be when I have it off." He popped open the two buttons, then went after the buttons on my shirt. In nothing flat, he had them all open, and he spread it wide as he gazed down at my lacy bra.

I'd found them in my drawer after we got back and I didn't say a word to Archie about it, but the absolutely delighted smile on his face told me I'd been right about guessing who they were from.

"It would have been weird to give it to you in Colorado," he whispered as he caressed me with his eyes, even as he traced a finger along one cup. My nipples had pebbled with his first kiss, and they tightened further under his teasing touches. "Mostly because I wanted to be selfish about seeing you in them. After today, I don't mind if the other guys do…"

Understanding flickered through me. "That was why you tried to get me out of the vest this morning."

He cast a look up to my face and gave me the more adorable grin, so full of cocky smugness, it made me laugh. "I've been checking the drawer just to see if they were gone."

"So when I said I was done early…" I shook my head.

Fingers trailing down to my abdomen, he eyed me. "Too weird?"

"No," I promised, and rubbed at his hip with my leg. "Want to finish unwrapping me so you can see all of it?" Because the panties matched the bra. The scalloped lace was in a sexy red that I happened to know was one of Archie's favorite colors for me to wear.

When his teeth scraped his lower lip, I licked mine. I wanted to bite that lip, too. But there was an intensity to the way he focused on me that I didn't want to interrupt either. His fingers were leaving little paths of fire everywhere he touched me, and I had to bite my lip when he undid my jeans with a kind of reverence, peeking up at me once with a silly little grin before he tugged them open and he could see my panties.

I was so wet at this point, they were going to have to be changed regardless, but all the breath backed up in my lungs when he leaned down and pressed a kiss just above the lace band and murmured, "Hello, beautiful, all dressed up for me today."

After peeling my jeans down, he scooted back off the bed and dropped them where his shirt was before he stripped out of his clothes. I sat up to enjoy my own show, not that he lingered. "Someday," I murmured. "You're gonna have to do that like a striptease."

He eyed me, one corner of his mouth kicking a little higher. "Oh, am I?"

"I think so." I pulled off the shirt and the vest and sent them flying.

"And why would I do that?"

"Because I won't object to you taking a picture of me like this so you can see the set you picked out any time you want." Honest to god, that offer slipped right out of me and it was not what I'd intended to say, but the way his eyes flashed and the pure delight filling his expression made me mean every single word of it.

"You sure?" he checked, already reaching for his abandoned jeans, and I swore his cock seemed to pulse at the offer.

I let my gaze linger on the way his abdominals flexed as he bent to get his phone out of his jeans and then aimed at me.

"You still happy with your purchase?" It was almost mumbled, and his lips twitched, but his eyes were really serious.

"I love my purchase," I told him. "I love you."

His smile grew and he motioned me to lie back, so I slid my hands under my hair so I could toss it up and then I sprawled back on the bed, looking at him. This was so weirdly awkward and intimate, but it was Archie, who had an entire locked file of photos he'd snapped of me over the years on his phone.

This was just for him.

Just like those were.

He angled the phone with a sigh and snapped a couple of pictures. "I love you, too, you know?"

"I heard a rumor," I teased him, and he chuckled before snapping a couple of more.

"Would it be too much to see you roll over?"

I lifted my eyes skyward as if it was such an imposition. There was a kind of fun to the way he watched me, and I said, "I suppose."

He made a little joyful sound followed by, "Yay."

Laughing, I rolled to my side and then over, and I paused at his very appreciative inhale.

"Fuck. Me."

"I plan on it," I told him over my shoulder as I caught him just staring at my ass. Yes, his lovely lace panties left half my ass hanging out. While not quite a thong, it was damn close.

There were a couple more camera snaps, and then his hands skated up the backs of my legs. "I love this on you," he said, kissing the back of one thigh, then the other. The scrape of his teeth over the curve of one ass cheek had me wiggling my butt.

"I bet you're going to say you'd love it off me more…" I didn't even get to finish the sentence before he tugged the panties right off and nudged me back down, then he slipped a pillow under my hips. Ass up.

He massaged my ass, and I could feel his dick prodding just between my thighs, but it wasn't until I looked back at him that he pushed in with one fierce thrust that had my whole body curling upward. "I want to fuck your ass," he said as he groaned and snapped his hips forward. "If we're in a sharing mood."

"Noted," I gasped, because he was stroking deeper with every press. He did this little rotation with his hips as he ground inside of me that had me seeing sparks. Still, he palmed my ass. "We can… Oh fuck…" I pushed back to meet his thrusts.

"That's what we're doing," he teased as he ran his hands up my sides, and then he pulled me upward until I was flush with my back to his chest and he could wrap his arms around me. The angle was different, but every bump and grind edged me closer. He bit against my neck and then dipped his fingers down to tease my clit.

I was right there, dammit, so close, and Archie's hot breath on my neck just seemed to drive me closer to the edge.

The bedroom door opened, and I glanced over to see Coop ducking inside. "Don't mind me," he said quickly as he vanished behind us. Archie never slowed once, drilling into me faster and faster, until I wasn't even trying to hold back my cries. He palmed one hand over a breast, the stroke teasing my already aching nipples, just as he applied pressure to my clit.

Fuck.

"Just needed to grab my shoes," Coop said as he started to close the door. He paused though, and my eyes locked on his for a breathless moment just before I splintered. "Keep it up, man. Great form."

Laughter bubbled up through me as the door closed, then Archie added more pressure to my clit and that was it, I was gone. A scream tore out of me, and Archie gave another few pumps, just pushing me through it, before he followed me.

Panting, we collapsed to lie sideways on the bed, still somewhat locked together, and I let out a long sigh.

"Coop was right," I exhaled the words.

"Was Coop here?" he snarked and bit down on my shoulder lightly.

Grinning, I stroked his hand where it still nestled between my legs. A mistake, because it added pressure to my already sensitive body, and I clenched around him. We both let out a hiss. "Yeah," I admitted after that round of shudders passed. "You have great form."

He chuckled and rolled me over until I was on my back and he was over me again. This time, his kiss was as much sweetness as steam. "And I haven't even gotten your bra off yet…"

Chapter Four
WE BELONG TOGETHER

I'd ridden to school with Archie that morning, but I came home with Jake. Coop was going to get some work hours in, so he'd kissed me at school and promised to see me later. Ian wasn't far behind us, and Archie would be over to scoop me up later for a date. The guys grumbled, but Archie wanted to steal me away for dinner, and being asked with a rose and a cup of coffee first thing that morning made me more than amenable to the plan.

Not that he had to bribe me with coffee. Or roses. Still, it had been sweet. Ian and I had plans this weekend to work on the recording for his demo tape. I still hadn't quite worked out why he insisted I record with him, but the quiet words of praise and encouragement in his eyes made it so damn hard to say no.

True story, I didn't want to say no. He made me sound like I knew what I was doing, so as long as it made him happy, I was there for it.

"I'm going to check the mail," I called over my shoulder as I headed for the front door of the apartment. Jake had snagged my backpack. Another boyfriend perk, apparently, or maybe it was a requirement. They no longer let me carry my backpack, constantly tugging it off my shoulders or snagging it themselves. It was a ridiculously little thing that made me warm and gooey inside.

"You want me to just go ahead and order the pizza now?" Jake called as he paused at the fridge. "I know you and Arch are going out later…"

At the front door, I glanced back and grinned. "But you're hungry and I can always eat. So sure, it's not like we won't eat it. Though…" I hesitated.

"If you say it costs too much, I'll spank you." There was no threat in those words at all, but a shiver went right through me.

"Promise?"

His eyes heated and the fridge door slammed as he stalked toward me.

Laughing, I escaped before he got there. The air had a bite to it, and the wind had picked up. Thankfully, I still had on Jake's jacket, so I huddled into it. Trina was checking their mail, and she threw me a grin.

"Hey," I said with a quick sideways hug that turned into a real one. "You okay?"

"I hate my parents," Trina confessed. "Dad's turning into a real dick. He was supposed to take my side with Mom, but Mom won't even hear a word he has to say." She made a disgusted sound and then slumped back against the mailboxes as she eyed me. "If you and my brother weren't making sex eyes at each other all the time, I'd ask to move in with you. At least you have no parents to have to deal with anymore."

Yeah, no parents to deal with. "You know your mom loves you, right?"

Trina scoffed, and I stared at her a beat.

"Trina, my mom couldn't care less about what I do." I ignored the breeze for a moment. "I get you don't like being grounded or fighting with them. But at least she *cares*."

The younger girl made a face. "It's not the same thing."

"No," I agreed with her. "It's not." I sighed and leaned against the mailboxes. "Seriously, it's not. Maddy's…Maddy's never been there for me. I used to tell myself she was, even when she wasn't. I used to make excuses for her. She was busy. She had bills to pay. She did her best. She just wasn't like that… You don't have to make excuses for Carly."

When Trina bit at her lower lip and chewed on it, she looked a lot younger. "It's just that… Why is it okay for Coop to date and stay out all night, and I can't even look at a guy?"

"Is this really about the guy?" I ignored the breeze sweeping around the mail center and focused on her. "I mean, really."

Slumping with her back to the mailboxes, Trina stared away from me. "I don't know. I get the smoking thing. Fine, I didn't even really like it, I just wanted to be cool."

"Well, I can't say I haven't done things I wasn't all that interested in to get people to like me."

She scoffed. "Everyone loves you."

Not everyone. Maddy certainly didn't. That thought burned a little, but I shoved it aside for now. This wasn't about me. "Trina…"

"I know," she grumped and made a face. "But it's different. You and Coop—it's always been you and Coop. He's my brother and he's gross, but I want a guy to look at me the way he looks at you."

"And you're fourteen," I pointed out. "You literally just turned fourteen."

"So? When you were fourteen, Coop looked at you the same way."

I'd give her that. Even if I hadn't seen it the same way she did. "He's my best friend, has been for as long as I can remember. I didn't see him as a boyfriend."

"Well, that was stupid," Trina informed me with all the sage wisdom one has at her age. Then again, she wasn't totally wrong.

"Agreed," I told her with a wry smile. "But my point is, we were friends first. He never asked me to be anything but what I was and who I was. If you have to change who you are?" I lifted my shoulders. "To get the guy to look at you? Then no, he isn't the guy who deserves you."

Trina frowned.

"And cut your mom a break. I don't live your life and I'm not there every day, but she cares enough to meddle and to keep involving your dad. I'd trade you for that. Maddy might not have cared what I did, but that wasn't because she was *cool*. It's because she just doesn't care unless it gets in the way of what she wants." Erin would be so proud of me. It was what she'd been working on getting me to verbalize for weeks. And I managed it without a stutter.

Go me.

Teeth dragging at her lower lip again, Trina cast me a long look. "So what you're saying is find best friends with benefits?"

I rolled my eyes, but the corners of her mouth quirked into a hint of a smile.

"I'll try," she promised, though it was half-hearted at best. "Dad mentioned I could go and stay with him for a while if it got too tough here."

I winced, but that was not an argument I could weigh in on. She was lucky to have two parents who both wanted her around. "That's your call, but talk to your mom and Coop before you make that decision."

"You guys are gone next fall," Trina said slowly. "Then it's just gonna be me and Mom, and if we're still fighting like this, maybe I should live with Dad."

"I don't know how to respond to that." I spread my arms and then on impulse, hugged her. The fierce clutch of her arms told me it was the right call. "Just don't forget that they love you," I whispered. "Even when you're fighting. Or maybe especially when you're fighting. Try to hear what she's saying even without words. And my door is always open…"

"Except when my brother is there," Trina said with a sniffle. "'Cause I really don't want to walk in on you or hear you. That's gross."

I laughed.

Then I kissed her forehead like she was ten years younger than me rather than just four. Fourteen had been a shitty age. Thirteen hitting fourteen hadn't been much better. But Trina was right, I'd had the guys. I'd had my best friends. Guys who hadn't even complained when I stood in the feminine products aisle and read every box at the age of twelve to figure out what I needed. Coop had called his mom when we ran into issues.

Why I hadn't asked *Maddy*...well, I didn't wonder about that one anymore.

Wiping her eyes, Trina pulled back and then opened her mailbox. "Okay, I need to go home. I'm still grounded."

I frowned, retrieving my own mail. There was a stack of it in there. "I thought you would have gotten off of it over Christmas."

The corner of her mouth tilted just a fraction higher, and mischief sparkled in her eyes. "I might have stayed out all night with friends and forgotten to call Mom."

I groaned.

"Yeah," she admitted. "Probably not my smartest call, but we were having fun."

Dammit.

"Trina, you're not having sex yet are you?"

Her whole face flushed pink, and she dipped those gray-green eyes so much like Coop's, even as her hair swung forward to hide her face. "Not... exactly."

Oh, I hated my life. Were there rules that said I had to tell Coop if I knew? Was there a line? "Not exactly?" I prodded, because yes, I was a masochist.

With a cough, she gave a little shrug. "We played a kissing game. No one did anything, you know, really dirty, but one of the guys kind of...you know, felt me up." She was beet red.

"Did you enjoy it?"

Owl-eyed she stared at me. "Well...yeah?"

"Okay then." I should probably offer other advice. I mean, we'd had this talk before but... "Just don't leap. Wait for the right guy to make it special for you."

"Like you did?" she snarked, and I just met her stare until the rebellion in her expression eased.

"That's exactly what I did. And I'm glad for it." Another shrug. "Anyway,

I gotta go. I'm not going to judge, but if you ever need to talk, you call me, and if you ever get stuck somewhere and want to leave and don't want to call Coop, call me."

She'd gone back to chewing on her lower lip and gave me a little nod. I didn't make it a couple of steps before she said, "Don't tell Coop?"

I glanced back at her.

"About me thinking about moving in with Dad or about making out…?"

"Yeah, I don't think telling him about the making out is a stellar idea." Not if she wanted the boy to live. Just the image of Coop hearing that and then telling Jake… Nope. Just nope. I didn't want Archie to have to get either one of them out of jail.

At that bit of advice, Trina burst out laughing, and some of the gloom in her expression dissipated. The cold added to the pink flush of her cheeks. "I'll talk to him about Dad and about Mom…and I'll talk to you before I make any decisions. I just wish…"

Facing her, I waited and then prodded, "You wish?"

"I wish she trusted me like she trusts Coop. He stays over with you all the time, and I know you guys have to be having sex. Not!" She held up her hand abruptly. "Not that I want any details. Like none. Zip. Zero. My brother does not have a dick."

It took everything in me not to laugh my ass off. Then again, I didn't really want to discuss his dick with *anyone*, so she was safe there.

"Give her a chance," was all I said. "And maybe give her a break. High school is a marathon, not a sprint."

"And you're almost to the finish line."

Yes, we were. "I'll talk to you later, okay?"

"Deal. And, Frankie? Thanks."

"Anytime."

I was shivering despite the coat by the time I got back to the apartment. Ian was already there, and he and Jake both stared at me as I shuddered my way in the door. "I was just about to come looking for you," Jake said. "You okay?"

"Just talking to Trina," I told him as he slid his hands under his jacket and tugged me against him. Oh. Warm. Very warm.

Ian rescued the mail from my chilly fingers and then stripped me out of the coat. It let the heat of the room surround me, and then he settled right up against my back as I tucked my hands under Jake's shirt.

"Fuck your hands are cold," Jake swore, but he didn't move away. Nor did Ian, and I grinned as I snuggled there.

"But this is nice," I admitted. He chuckled, a sound Ian echoed, and the rumble just made me sigh. A hand settled on my hip and squeezed, but Ian made no move to hide the steadily growing erection pressed against my ass. Oh, this would be fun if he would…

A knock at the backdoor had Jake pulling away with a mutter. "Pizza is here." He dropped a kiss on my nose, and Ian wrapped around me and pulled me firmly back against him.

I had been down at the mailboxes longer than I thought. Ian nuzzled at my ear. "Don't think I don't know what was going through your mind," he whispered. Then his teeth scraped at my ear. "I'm not ready for that, Angel."

I shivered and rubbed my hands to his. "I know," I murmured. "Doesn't mean a girl can't dream."

"Or get spanked?" He bit my earlobe, not hard enough to really damage, but I definitely felt the sting. "If you're in need, Angel, we can make arrangements."

I groaned. "You're a tease."

He smiled against my neck and then bit down lightly before whispering, "Then behave next time." The hand on my hip slid over and landed the lightest of slaps to my denim clad ass as he slipped away to meet Jake with the pizza. I laughed. Still, that was a promise he would deliver on later, and I was ready to talk about that some more.

Well, talk and other things.

No longer half-frozen, I toed off my shoes before collecting the mail. The first couple were just statements on bills Archie had already paid. The third was a credit card bill for Maddy. Pfft. I needed to add return to sender on that, since she no longer lived here. Would serve her right if they canceled all her credit cards.

I waited for the sense of guilt to stab at me, but it wasn't coming. Shrugging, I flipped through to the next couple of sale offers, a loan offer for improve your credit blah blah, and as I sat down on the sofa, I froze on the last one.

It had Harvard in the corner.

It was a small envelope. I'd gotten worried at the first small ones I'd gotten, thinking they were automatic rejections, but so much was done online now, they didn't always send more than the form letter.

But this was Harvard.

"Baby Girl?"

"Angel?"

Worry decorated both of their voices, and I glanced up to find them staring at me, plates of pizza in hand. Jake even had a plate with three slices for me.

"Harvard," I said, holding up the letter.

Ian dropped into the seat next to me, while Jake perched on the coffee table in front of me.

"What does it say?" Jake asked, his pale eyes steady as he set the plates aside.

"I'm almost scared to open it." Harvard had been the goal for so long that it became synonymous with getting away from Maddy. From escaping this apartment and this town…but I had gotten away from Maddy, and now this apartment had them in it.

I sucked at my lower lip, torn between looking at them and looking at the letter. It just sat there in my hand like no big deal. It could be a ticking time bomb ready to shred my dreams, or it could be my ticket out. And what if it was? What if it was an acceptance letter? Archie had gotten into Harvard, but no one else had theirs yet. What if we got in, and they didn't?

Then I just wouldn't go to Harvard.

I wouldn't leave them behind.

Blowing out a breath, I said, "Well, let's find out." Having made the decision, it seemed easier to slit the envelope open.

The form letter thanked me for my application and informed me that I had been placed on the waitlist. They indicated that spots do open up later in the semester as students accept their admissions to other schools, but it could be as late as summer before I heard anything more.

The crash wasn't as bad as I feared. A part of me had already thought I wouldn't get in. They were very exclusive and had nowhere near as many available spots as they had applicants. Reality and odds said my chances of getting in were less than three percent.

Three.

But still, it hurt, and my heart sank and my stomach bottomed out. Even as I tried to tell myself I didn't need this ticket out anymore. Any other school would do…

Ian wrapped an arm around me and tugged me close, and then Jake plucked me away and they shifted around until I was sandwiched up between them again. I sniffled and then let out a watery laugh. "It's stupid to be upset."

"It's not," Ian told me. "You've wanted this for so long. The stupid ones are them."

"Damn straight," Jake rumbled, and then pressed his lips against my hair, even as he rubbed a hand along my thigh. Ian had his hand on my back, and I swiped at the stupid tears. "You have been wanting it for a long time, but no one would go there without you, you know that right? None of us."

"You didn't even care about Harvard," I pointed out. "You and Arch wanted MIT."

"True," he admitted. "But I don't care where I go to school, Baby Girl. I care about going with you. I care about none of us making this long distance."

"Agreed," Ian stated, and his tone was so firm, like it was a done deal. "We applied to the same schools, I auditioned for all the programs. If you four get in somewhere and I don't, well, I'll be house boy while you guys go to school and I work on my music."

Jake snorted. "You've got a potential recording contract."

"That too," Ian said with a gentle smile. "A contract I have no interest in chasing if it doesn't have you involved somehow."

I sighed. They were making me feel so loved…treasured. "I don't want you to put your lives on hold for me. You guys have dreams too…"

"Fuck that," Jake said, and his voice went hard, inflexible, and downright stern. He cupped my chin, turning me to look at him, even as Ian lifted me back into his lap and settled my back to his chest. There was no escaping being surrounded by them. Not that I had any interest in going *anywhere*. "We're a team," Jake stated, gaze locked on mine. "The five of us are here because we *want* to be here. I love you. They love you. And you love *us*."

None of those were questions. "I do," I confirmed anyway, even as the feeling tightened like a fist around my heart.

"Then we make the decisions together. We make the best one for *all* of us. One of those considerations is that we're together. If that means we're all in the same town but at different schools, fine, we'll find a way to make it work. But understand this, Baby Girl, where you go, we go. That's all there is to it."

"Jake's right," Ian weighed in. "All of us agree with that. Coop, Arch, me, and him. We don't want to be where you're off somewhere else, and we don't want you to be without us."

I let out a little sigh and leaned my head against Ian's shoulder. "I don't want to go somewhere without all of you or even just one of you."

"Then we're agreed, so no more of this crap about not making decisions that don't include you." Eyes fixed on mine, Jake kept his grip on my chin firm and gentle. "Together. Or not at all."

I licked my lips. "What if Ian gets that recording contract…"

"Then we make that work," Ian promised. "We talk it out, we weigh the pros and cons, together. All of us. We make this something that the five of us agree on. Because it's not just my life or your life."

"It's our lives." Jake skated his thumb over my lower lip. "Dammit, Baby Girl, I thought you got how important this was to all of us. To me."

Tears sparked at the back of my eyes for an entirely different reason, and guilt scraped through me. "Sometimes, it's difficult to imagine that it's not an imposition if you guys were to change something for me." Maddy didn't like rearranging her life for me. Fuck knows whenever she'd been forced, she threw it in my face.

"We're not your mother," Ian said in no less a firm voice than Jake used. "We're not saying we're giving up anything, but if we haven't been clear, you're more important than a school. We'll get the education, the skills, the training, we can do that anywhere. Maybe it won't be hoity toity and cost Archie a new wing on a hospital or something…"

A laugh escaped me, and it was a little wet but it was real, and Jake was still tracing the outline of my mouth, even as Ian kept his lips at my ear.

"You are more important to me than all of that. The guys are more important to me than that."

"This family we're building is more important than that," Jake finished. "We'll find a way to take care of *that*."

I let out a shuddering breath and then nodded. "Okay."

Relief seemed to sag Jake's shoulders, and even Ian seemed to ease up as he rubbed his cheek against my hair. Jake flicked a look above me, and I had the sensation that he and Ian had locked gazes. Some wordless communication passed between them.

I kind of hated it when they did that.

I kind of loved it, too.

Yeah, I know, I was a little weird. But I loved that they were all still friends. Those friendships were so damn important to us.

Not just friends, I reminded myself. Family.

"I think we call the guys," Ian suggested. "Tonight is family planning night. We talk about the schools everyone has heard from, and we work out contingency plans."

"Yep," Jake agreed, and then leaned forward to kiss me. The pressure was demanding and claiming until my lips parted for him, and then it was all sweetness and aching delight. With one last nibble to my lower lip, he said, "Go change, Baby Girl. Get in something comfy. You and Arch can decide on your date later. I'll call him and get Coop to dump his shift. Then I'll order more pizza."

Some of the unease still threading through my system let go. It had been a long week, and the letter just seemed to take all the air out of what we'd accomplished. There'd been push back at school. I'd known it would happen, but I refused to let it get to me, and Rachel and the guys had my back. Still…

"Okay," I said. "Sounds like a plan."

They finally let me up, but Ian followed me back to the bedroom and stood there, leaning against the wall as I stripped out of my school clothes and into one of his T-shirts. I ditched the bra and then just went for a pair of Coop's boxers under it.

Yeah, I was being sappy.

As soon as I'd changed, he opened his arms and I walked right into them. Against my hair, he said, "I know I'm still earning your trust…"

My heart fisted again.

"…but I need you to believe this, Angel. We're in. *I'm* in." Pulling back, he gripped my arms and stared down at me. "I'll say it every time you need to hear it, but if you tell me you don't want me to adjust my life for you or in *any* way suggest I leave you behind…well, I don't know what they're going to do, but I'm going to spank you until that ass is so red, you can't sit down."

A real shiver went through me. His pupils flared, and he shook his head.

"I mean it."

"I know you do," I told him, and the corners of my mouth curled upward. "I'm still getting used to this." I spread my hands against his chest. "And I do trust you, Ian. I promise, you don't have to keep *proving* anything to me. I'm working on it. It's hard to be the one someone puts first."

"I know, Angel. We've done it for a long time though, and it's time you believed it, okay?" Then he kissed me with so much sweetness, my eyes flooded with tears again. The weight of his hands on my ass lifting me even as I wrapped my arms around him settled me even more. I don't know how long we stood locked together like that, but Jake clearing his throat popped the moment.

"The guys are coming, and as much as I'd like to say let's continue wherever this is going, you're not into sharing that far yet," he snarked at Ian. "And I'm not interested in watching television while you make Frankie scream back here."

Another shiver of anticipation went through me.

Ian snorted, then kissed my nose. "To be continued…"

Yes, please.

By the time I was back on the sofa and sandwiched between them again with pizza in hand and the cats coming out to join us, I wasn't feeling quite so melancholy. You know, they were right and I knew it. I'd already made that decision.

Harvard *used* to be the dream.

Chapter Five

COLLEGE GIRL

JAKE

Arch called as soon as my text hit his screen.

"What happened?"

"She got waitlisted by Harvard," I told him and pitched my voice low. I had him on speaker in the kitchen while Bubba took her to get changed. "I ordered more pizza. I know you two have a date tonight, but she needs a plan."

"Fuck," Archie swore. Something crashed on the other side of the phone. "I can fix this."

"Maybe," I agreed with him. "But right now, she needs us and she needs a plan more than she needs you making phone calls and pulling strings. This damage is already done." Coop called while I was still finishing the text to him. "Hang on, I'm going to conference Coop in, just get in your car and head this way."

"I'm already on my way downstairs."

I switched lines. "Hang on, Coop, looping you in with Arch." Then I connected the two. "I don't have much time before she's finished changing. She got the Harvard letter today, she was waitlisted."

"Fuck," Coop's response echoed Archie's perfectly. I felt it all the way to my bones. I kind of wanted to go kick the shit out of whatever admissions flunky looked at her transcript and mine, then decided I was in and she wasn't.

Fuck them.

Fuck them sideways with a rusty chainsaw.

Blowing out a breath, I scrubbed a hand over my face. "Yeah, so, here's what we're doing. I ordered more pizza. You two are getting your asses here and we're working out a plan." The only way she'd let some of this go was to make a plan. That was why I told her I'd call them in the first place.

Frankie liked knowing what was coming. It was what made her crazy about our relationships. I got that. We all got that. She needed order in chaos. Waitlisted by her dream school was definitely chaos.

"I'll drop off this last order and be there in twenty," Coop said. "Need me to bring anything?"

"I've got alcohol already in the car," Archie answered. "We got ice cream?"

I opened the fridge. It had been fully stocked when we got back. And… "Yep, two half gallons."

"Good deal, be there soon." He hung up, his tone as tense and terse as I felt. But Coop was still on the line.

"How is she?"

"She doesn't want us making sacrifices in our choices just because she didn't get in."

He groaned.

"Exactly."

"I'm coming," he said. "We'll figure this out."

Yeah we would. After I ordered the pizzas, I walked back to find Frankie and Bubba locked together. As distractions went, that definitely worked. And fuck if it wasn't hot.

"The guys are coming, and as much as I'd like to say let's continue wherever this is going, you're not into sharing that far yet," I teased, meeting Bubba's gaze. "And I'm not interested in watching television while you make Frankie scream back here."

I got it, he wasn't up for sharing her in bed. Fine. I liked my one on one time with her too, and I'd gotten a hell of a lot more of it than he had. Frankie shot me a smile. Some of the tension had left her face, but there was still a hint of stress around her eyes. The smile didn't quite reach in and chase the shadows out of her green eyes.

We'd make a plan. That would at least go a long way toward helping, even if we couldn't fix all of it. Frankie slipped out to the bathroom, and Bubba shot me a look. "You know it's not…"

I waved him off. "Dude, we're good. Not a discussion we need to have until when, and if, you're ready."

He raked a hand through his hair and then nodded. "Can you answer one question?"

"Depends on the question." Some things were private. Even among us. I knew he got that.

"It doesn't bother you at all when you're right there and Coop's all over her?"

A slow grin curved my lips. "Nope. Doesn't bother me watching you with her, either. Not as long as she's happy. Besides…watching her come? It's pretty fucking sweet. Then getting to fuck her while she's coming apart and can't see straight? Oh yeah." And now I was hard as a stone.

Fucking wonderful way to spend the evening.

Bubba shook his head. "I'm not saying never…"

"I know, man." I clapped him on the shoulder. "And considering what Coop's packing, I get the intimidation."

He jabbed me in the kidneys as I walked away and I laughed, even as the air whooshed out of me.

Twenty minutes later, Coop walked in on the heels of the pizza, and Archie had beers passed around and a bottle of wine for Frankie. She'd gone right to Archie when he'd come in and wrapped him up in a hug as tightly as he gripped her. I snagged the bag from him so she could murmur her apologies.

Yeah, we'd make up for the missed date.

But once we had pizza and drinks, she curled into the spot between Coop and Arch where they sat on the floor with their backs to the sofa, while Bubba and I sat opposite them. We needed to get more furniture in the living room. The big sofa was fine, but we needed a couple of chairs...

You know what, that was a problem for us next week. Not tonight.

Slice in hand, I cut a look at her. "You want to start?"

She rolled her eyes at me, but the flash of humor glimmering in the green depths promised me she rallied. Exactly what I wanted to see and *why* we were all here.

"So, Harvard has waitlisted me."

"Bastards," Archie mumbled, then pressed a kiss to her shoulder. "They need to take the stick out of their ass and see how fucking awesome you are."

"Agreed," I said, but pinned him with a look. He snorted, then took another bite of his pizza. "Just saying."

Frankie tilted her head and pressed a kiss to his chin. "Do not spend money to get me in."

He scowled at her but just kept chewing his pizza. Yeah, none of us were buying that look.

"I mean it," she informed him as she liberated another slice for herself. At least she was eating. When she stopped, that was when things were really wrong. "I want to do this on my merits."

"Your merits aren't in question," Coop said, his tone almost idle, but there was a tension in his hands as he took a long swallow of beer. "Their appreciation for said merits? Yes. And if you really want Harvard, let Archie smooth the way."

Raising my brows, I stared at him. What the hell was Coop doing?

Then her smile grew, and she bumped his shoulder with hers. "Don't be an ass."

"I'm not," Coop said. "The point is, you wanted Harvard. You deserve it. You've worked your ass off. Everyone needs a little help and this is a family effort, so if he can wedge that door open so they can't slam it in your face, I say let him. Where you lead…we'll follow."

Dropping her pizza onto a plate, Frankie twisted and wrapped her arms around Coop. His smile as she buried her face in his throat had me frowning. Why was he pleased about making her cry? When I glared at him, he flipped me off.

I couldn't take her shaking shoulders. "Baby Girl, it's going to be fine."

"I know," she said in a strangled tone, then lifted her head to look at me. There were tears in her eyes, but her whole face creased with laughter. "Coop's just teasing me and being a dick."

Yeah, I didn't get it either, but sometimes those two had that connection where they got it and we didn't. Fine, I waved it off and then lifted my own beer. But her gaze was unwavering on me.

"Do you remember when I first decided on Harvard?"

Honestly? I remembered just about everything about her. "It seems like you've *always* wanted it."

Coop snorted a laugh, even as Frankie elbowed him.

"Okay," Archie said. "Raise your hand if you want in on the secret."

Bubba's hand went up and so did mine.

Coop laughed harder and muttered something that had her whapping him with these little stinging slaps that just made his laughter swell. "You're such a dick. I can't believe you're going to make me explain this."

His eyes positively danced with glee.

And now I was jealous. "Yeah, he's a real fucker. Why don't you come sit in my lap and tell me, Baby Girl?"

Snaking his arms around her, Coop dragged her into his lap—asshole—and buried his face against her hair. "I can tell them…"

"No," she argued, squirming. "You'll make fun of me."

"Only a little," he teased, but her laughter kept me from wanting to punch him.

"Yep, and now I *really* want to know." I drummed my fingers against the bottle like I was annoyed, but as much as I wanted to know, Coop had done the one thing we hadn't quite managed yet.

He'd gotten her to relax. Some of the tension buzzing the air around her dissipated, and she sagged back against him before grabbing her slice of pizza and mumbled, "Rory wanted to go to Harvard."

"What?" Archie asked.

"Rory," she repeated.

Rory. Who the fuck was Rory?

Wait…

"*Gilmore Girls* Rory?" Bubba asked, incredulity filling his expression.

Frankie squirmed again.

"I thought she went to Yale though," Archie countered, and it was my turn to stare at him.

"Dude, your panties are showing," I deadpanned.

"Yeah, fuck off. She loved the show and made me watch it when she found out I hadn't ever seen it." Archie dismissed me with a wave. Of course, he couldn't tell her no. Not that I could blame him. "Besides, she liked to snuggle when she watched it."

And there it was.

Frankie let out a sigh. "So, at the risk of starting trouble, and now because I *want* to know, how many shows did you guys watch with me because I liked snuggling?"

"All of them," I answered.

Bubba snorted, then shrugged as he said, "Yeah, fortunately some of them were pretty good, so we didn't mind."

"Agreed," Coop teased her. "Though, you've always been a cuddle bunny when it comes to shows. It's 'cause you don't like jump scares."

True enough.

"*Anyway*," Frankie muttered as she tried to slide out of his lap, but Coop kept an arm around her and she finally settled again. "Harvard has always been… the dream. But…dreams can change."

I met her gaze steadily, then fisted my courage in two hands. I'd been avoiding this conversation. "I only applied to go with you," I told her. "And I don't plan on accepting my admission if you're not there."

The silence in the room grew thick.

"Jacob Benton. You got in?"

With a shrug, I nodded. "And I should have told you, but until you got your letter, I didn't want you feeling bad."

Then she was wiggling out of Coop's lap and climbing over Archie before she circled the table, and I barely had time to move my pizza before she straddled me. Hands on my face, she scowled at me. "You do not get to keep exciting news from me!"

"It wasn't that exciting, Baby Girl," I admitted. "The excitement of you getting into NYU along with me? Along with the guys? *That's* the excitement I want. Harvard? Nope. Not if you're not there. Pfft. They have nothing to offer me."

"What he's saying in his blunt way," Archie offered, "is that we care less about where we go than who we go with. He doesn't want a long-distance relationship. For any of us."

"True story," I agreed before pressing a kiss to Frankie's forehead. At her gentle urging, I moved to meet her lips, and then I let the guys fall away as her mouth moved against mine.

"Why didn't I get a kiss?" Coop complained. "I'm calling foul."

Frankie laughed against my mouth and twisted to flip Coop off before she wiggled to sit between me and Bubba. Probably better. No way she missed the erection poking at her ass and those boxers were loose enough, I could probably get them off in nothing.

"Because you wanted to give me crap about the fact that I loved Logan."

He rolled his eyes. "You loved Tristan, too."

"Tristan was misunderstood."

"Uh huh."

"And he could have gotten better."

"Uh huh."

"*And,*" Bubba interrupted them, because the two were about to dive down into snarkland together. "Let's talk schools?"

"Fine," Frankie agreed, almost too quickly, before stealing a look at Archie, who wore the most pleased little smile. Fuck, I needed to go back and figure out *why* these dudes were an issue. "NYU is a yes for all of us, right?" She stole a look at Bubba. "Have you heard from them?"

"Conditionally," he said. "But all of my admits are going to be conditional based on the program I get into. The auditions are for the specific musical colleges, so…they are a little pickier." He shrugged. "I'll go where you guys go, and if they don't take it, I can just do general education and audition again the next year."

A frown tightened her brow. "That doesn't seem fair to you."

"It's totally fair to me, Angel. I'm with you guys. Who we're with, not where we go. Besides…there's still the contract. That might keep me busy."

"Any word on that?" Archie asked with the same look he'd had at the cabin when Bubba's music came up. Five bucks said he would diversify and invest in the music business any time now. Because Archie.

"Nope," Bubba said, easily. "Frankie and I have two more songs to record, then I can send them the full demo. They wanted six or seven with a little different styling to check my range."

"And when do we get to hear these?" I glanced at her. The fact that he got her to sing should probably make me jealous. Well, not *should*, maybe could. It didn't though. The pink flush to her cheeks whenever it came up and the surprise she'd shown when we all applauded her singing at the cabin made me too fucking happy.

"When I'm not there to hear how terrible I am," Frankie retorted, but then she made a face when Bubba pinched her. "Yeah, I know, I'm not terrible. It's just…I am more impressed every day that you let me hear you sing, because that's *terrifying*."

He chuckled and reached over to snag her wine glass for her when she finished off that piece of pizza. "You made it easy. Hopefully, I can do the same for you."

"You are," she said with a sigh.

Coop quirked a brow, but I shook my head. This wasn't our fight…*yet*. He nodded, and Archie just tipped his beer back to drain it. "So," he said after setting the bottle down. "Let's go down the schools we're all in, who we're waiting to hear from, and then pros and cons."

She lit right up at that, and I bit back a smile. Did we know our girl? Yes, yes we did.

So for the next hour, we batted them back and forth. We had three schools total that we were all in. NYU was the one we circled back to time and again. But Frankie kept latching onto MIT. She wanted Archie and I to have that opportunity.

Don't get me wrong, MIT was a killer school.

"If you say it's not where but who…" Frankie scolded as she stood with her hands on her hips. We'd dragged out the white board from her room and it was leaning against the TV stand, and we had a list going in different colored markers. NYU was winning by a landslide. "I'm going to kick all of you out and sleep by myself."

"I'll just sneak in after you're asleep," Coop said without an ounce of irony or shame.

"The fuck you will," Archie countered. "*My* date night."

"And we're making it up to you," I pointed out. "You two deserve your night out, but not one where she's stressing about this."

"Fair point, so I'll take the hit for us," Bubba said with a slow smirk. "I'm sure I can keep her distracted."

"Right." I thumped him in the arm, and he flashed a grin at me. "I think it will depend on who gets there first."

"Oh, I like those odds…" Archie leaned forward. "Where are we on the screaming orgasm chart?"

"Boys," Frankie snapped, hands on her hips, but despite her stern tone, her lips kept twitching. "There's plenty of room in there for all of us, thanks to someone. We were discussing schools?"

"We were," I agreed. "But right now, NYU is in the lead. So let me ask you this…" Because I'd been thinking about it. "Do you need this internship if we go there? Or will your current scholarship cover it all?" Because she had the huge one from Mason's. Mental math said the one I'd gotten would cover about eighty percent of mine. I could do the rest with loans that would mean I wouldn't have to lean on Dad's GI Bill benefits and leave it for the girls.

Perfectly fine by me. The less I owed him, the better.

She chewed her lower lip, then considered the board.

"Did you find out where you were interning yet?" Coop asked. "Weren't they supposed to email you today?"

"Yeah, but I didn't get anything earlier," Frankie mused. "I mean, I think it would more than cover the tuition, the books, and probably living expenses. But New York's really pricey. And I don't know about their rules for living on campus as freshmen."

"That we will be working around," Archie said. "Even if the four of us have to get a shared dorm, you just move in with us."

"It'd be cozy," Coop said with a slow grin. "But we can make it work. Though Archie on campus with just a room and a bunch of beds will be hilarious."

"Yeah, fuck off. Grandpa has a place in the city, so we can always just crash there on weekends too. The point is, we have options, on campus or off. If it's on, then you can save on housing expenses by staying with us."

Frankie chuckled. "You guys have an answer for everything."

Bubba leaned back on his hands. We'd all but finished the pizza. Ice cream would be the next thing I grabbed, but she wasn't upset at all anymore. In fact, her mood was far more thoughtful and, dare I say, excited?

"If Rachel ends up at the same school, I need to room with her," she said. "Even if I stay with you guys."

"Right," Coop said. "Because Rachel."

Yeah, deal with that later.

"Where has she applied?" Archie asked, and though he didn't quite grit his teeth, he did look like he'd swallowed a lemon.

"I'll ask," Frankie said after a beat. "She doesn't talk about herself much."

Oh boy. I knew that look. "You'll sort it out, Baby Girl. But I think we're all in agreement *at the moment*, it's NYU?"

That was the question we'd been dancing around for the last three hours.

She chewed her lip again, her gaze going back to the whiteboard, and I split a look with the guys. Coop lifted his chin, but Bubba looked more thoughtful. Archie was plotting. There was no missing it, and I raised my brows at him. He mouthed "later," and I nodded.

Sometimes, it was better for the four of us to settle something before we tackled it with her. She would always have the last word, unless we could persuade her to our way of thinking.

"New York City," she said slowly.

"Manhattan," Archie said. "Washington Square Park. Greenwich Village. We could go ice skating at Rockefeller Center at Christmas."

"They get snow," Coop threw in.

"Broadway," Bubba added.

"Central Park," I tossed up. "The point is, there's options, Baby Girl. And it's not *here*."

There was the barest twinge in my gut over that. Mom didn't like the idea of me going so far away, not that she'd tried to convince me to go to a local university. I knew she'd prefer it, but she wouldn't ask me not to go. Which was good, I never wanted to have to choose between my mom and Frankie.

Ever.

But I would, if she made me.

Shoving that thought aside, I scratched at my jaw and waited.

Frankie let out a sigh. "Do we have any idea of what NYU's colors are?" Laughter spilled over the room as she gave us a wry look. "And we should probably check out the colleges and the classes and make sure they really have what we want."

"Done," Archie said as he rose and caught her hand. When he pulled her to him, I could see what was coming next. "And on that note…"

He swept her up and moved swiftly down the hall with her laughter pealing out behind him. The door slammed, and it was just me, Coop, and Bubba.

"Saw that coming," Coop said with a tip of his beer. Her shriek of laughter climbed a beat, and I cracked up all over again. Fist out, Coop added, "Since he's gonna be a couple of hours, rock, paper, scissors for who sneaks in there later?"

"That would be me," I informed him with a salute from my bottle. "Calling the family meeting was *my* idea."

"Fair enough," Coop said. "I'll just steal her in the morning when your crazy asses go running."

"I was thinking about that," Bubba said, stretching back to snag the game controllers and flip on the television.

"No," Coop said.

"You don't even know what he's thinking," I teased, but I had an idea and I wasn't opposed.

"I don't care if it involves dragging her out at oh dark hundred to go running with all of you. I'm opposed."

"That's just because you want to keep her in bed."

Coop flipped me off. "You like to run in the morning. I can think of more energetic and satisfying ways to kick off her day and mine."

"That," Bubba said, shifting so he could sit on the sofa as he scrolled through our game options. First person shooter was probably where we were going.

A moan filtered through from the hallway, and Tiddles came trotting out, followed by Tory. The black cat had the most disgusted look on his face, but the white one just moseyed over and plopped in Coop's lap. Crazy little cat didn't go out of her way for any one of us except Coop. He just ran his hand over her back as the volume from down the hall climbed. The sharp, piercing cry had Coop checking his watch.

"Not bad, five minutes. Someone's feeling motivated."

I snickered and settled on the sofa as *Call of Duty* hit the screen. That would work. My cock was not thrilled with the audio presentation going on. Then again, he was just a bit jealous it wasn't us making her scream. We'd make up for that later.

"He just likes being ahead on the board," Bubba said with a grin. "Anyway, what I was going to say was we should start taking Frankie to the gym with us. You wanted to work on her punching."

That I did. Punches. Kicks. Scratching asshole's eyes out.

"Agreed." Not that I had any intention of letting some jerk get that close to her again.

"Tomorrow?" Coop asked.

"Maybe," I said. "She has work tomorrow."

Bubba grunted. Yeah, none of us were fans of her schedule filling up again. The internship thing was out there, too.

Snagging the remote, Coop cranked up the sound on the game as she let out another laughing cry. Heh, I wasn't the only one shifting in my seat.

"I want to take her to the studio tomorrow, too," Bubba said. "Either of you have a problem with that?"

"Nope," I told him. "But I'm showering with her in the morning."

Coop swore, and I grinned.

"Shut up, ass. You just said you were going to wake her up. So get her all nice and dirty for me so I can clean her up in our shower."

He rolled his eyes. "If I must…"

Then we laughed, even Bubba. The corner of his mouth quirked a little higher. I gave him two months.

Tops.

He wouldn't hold out forever.

Then again…maybe he would.

I shrugged and focused on the game, because it was damn tempting to go use the bathroom in the hall to get myself off while I listened.

An hour later, they were at it again, and I left Coop and Bubba playing while I did just that.

It wasn't anything close to the real thing, but fuck, it felt good to imagine it was her mouth on me making all those noises.

Archie apparently had something to prove tonight, and Baby Girl was all about it.

Time to up my game.

Chapter Six
HANDS DOWN

FRANKIE

The studio was locked when we got there, but Ian had keys. At my raised brows, he grinned. "I told you, I made a deal with the owners. I'm tutoring kids on the piano and with the guitar, and they give me studio time."

I loved the idea of him teaching. "I may have to come and watch that. I bet you're an amazing teacher."

"We're about to find out, aren't we?" he teased as he let us in, then locked us inside together. After entering the code on the security system, he rearmed it and then caught my hand as he led us down the hallway to the studio we'd used the last few times we'd been here.

I had my guitar this time, though, the one he'd gotten me for Christmas. I was also wearing one of my Torched shirts for inspiration. Ian had given it a grin when I changed after I got home from Mason's. First day back, and it was like being a stranger in a strange land, even though I was intimately familiar with everything. I wasn't sure what had really changed so much, but I felt one step to the right all day long.

"You're quiet," Ian murmured as he opened the studio door and flipped on the lights.

I shrugged.

"Hey." He caught my arm as he set his case down and then curled his fingers over mine on the handle to my case. "If you're too tired to do this, we don't have to."

Blowing out a breath, I gave him a smile and then slid an arm up to wrap around his neck. He shifted immediately, stepping into me, and the hand on my arm dropped to my ass. The weight sent a shiver through me, and I bit my lip before rising on my tip toes. It took no urging on my part for him to pull me into his kiss.

The first brush was gentle, but he didn't linger there long before he curved his fingers against my ass and lifted. I locked my thighs to his hips and leaned into the kiss as his tongue swept inside to stake his claim. My whole body hummed just from that contact. The feel of him squeezing my ass just ramped my temperature and my pulse.

I bit down on his lower lip, a gentle sting, and then I was against the wall as he devoured my mouth and ground his hips into mine. There were too many clothes to get the right amount of friction, but it still felt good and my nipples stabbed at my bra. Sweat dampened the back of my neck, and I half hooked my fingers into his shirt to tug, but he caught my wrists and then they were pinned above my head as he coaxed my mouth wider, and all I could do was squirm in what little room he allowed me.

Shock and no small amount of awe danced through me with every lick of his tongue or roll of his hips. The weight of his chest crushing my breasts just made me ache for more. I longed to touch him, but any tug on my wrists only tightened his grip, and that in turn sent more liquid heat coursing through my system.

When he kissed a path from my mouth to my jaw, then to my throat, I whimpered. An honest-to-god whimper escaped, and I wanted to be embarrassed by the sound.

"Need me to fix something, Angel?" he teased before his lips closed on my earlobe. The soft stroke of his tongue seemed to go straight to my pussy, and I arched my back, but I was thoroughly trapped. I couldn't move much at all.

It was delicious.

"Yes," I complained on a breathy moan. "I want more."

But we were kind of in the studio.

"Do you?" he whispered right against my ear, and his breath sent shivers cascading through me.

"Yes."

His lips curved where they rested, and with his free hand, he rubbed a soothing motion along my side. Each time he came close to my breast, I half-expected him to cup it or shove my shirt up. But he didn't, and the near-misses tore another whimper from my throat. Another kiss just behind my ear, and then he bit down over my pulse point and held still until I quit squirming.

My heart thundered in my ears, and I swore I could hear the rushing of my blood through my system. Heat soaked through me, and my pussy clenched around emptiness. I swore if he told me to beg, I probably would.

"Ian," I whimpered again when he still didn't move. "Please."

"No," he told me against my skin before he sucked another kiss to where he'd been biting. The intensity and sharpness pulled my blurred focus from need to something *more*.

"No?"

Lifting his head, he smiled at me, the gentleness in his eyes and the firmness of his mouth a direct contrast to his denial. "No. I like you squirming and needy. I like that you're so desperate, you want to beg." He licked his lips slowly, and I tracked the motion of his tongue, damn near mesmerized. "You want to beg, don't you, Angel?"

Fuck. Me.

"Yes," I said, even as heat stained my face and sent a flush from my toes to my scalp.

Another kiss. This one infinitely gentler, and he let go of my wrists. "Keep them there," he ordered before he trailed his fingers down, and the soothing strokes along my side seemed determined to bring my racing pulse back under control. I didn't argue, I kept my arms up, even if my shoulders were beginning to burn. They could stay up there for the rest of my life if he kept touching me.

A touch of his nose to mine. Then he slanted his mouth across my lips, and his breath teased me as he whispered, "I want you to use all of this frustration and need on the song we're going to record." A gentle nip. "And if you're a good girl, Angel, I'll give you everything you want and more when we're done."

My heart plummeted and my stomach bottomed out as the anxiety hit, but the desire burning inside of me turned almost molten. "You're mean," I complained, and he chuckled. Two seconds later, I was down and facing the wall, with my hands there and his body pressed up against me. Dammit, now I couldn't even see him.

"I'm mean?"

"Yes," I told him, half-turning my head, only to have him card his fingers through my hair and fist it. The hot weight of him was delicious where he leaned into me, and I swore he was going to burn right through my clothes.

"Do you remember what I said about you being a good girl?" A bite to my neglected earlobe this time, and I full-body shuddered.

"Yes…"

"Calling me *mean* isn't what a good girl would do."

I licked my lips, anticipation trembling in every muscle. "No?"

"No." He bit me again, only it was all scrape of teeth in sharp relief before he sucked another hickey that would definitely be on prominent display.

I almost couldn't wait to show it off.

I swore he melted my brain.

And my panties.

"Not good at all, Angel. So I'm going to let you off with a warning this time, but if you keep being bad, then I'll punish you."

Fuck. Another shudder chased up my spine, and he laughed softly.

"Um…" I licked at my lips, my mouth suddenly dry and my heart beginning to hammer again. "What if I don't want to be good?"

"Do you want me to punish you?" Intrigue filled his voice, and I grinned. If he was going to tease me, it was only fair that I tease him, right?

"Maybe."

He straightened but didn't let go of my hair, and I kept my hands on the wall where he'd put them. Even half-expecting it, the slap to my ass still took me up to my toes. It didn't hurt. Not really.

If anything, it sent a tremor through my system and amped up my need. It would only have been better if the denim and my panties weren't in my way.

Another smack, and I was clenching on emptiness as a soft, longer groan fell past my lips.

"Still want to be bad, Angel?" Amusement and something far headier darkened his tone, and I sighed at having gotten that response.

"Not feeling at all deterred," I managed to form those words, but I barely got them out before he delivered a series of stinging swats that had my ass burning and my clit grinding against the seam of my pants. I swore I saw stars with every well-timed strike.

I was a trembling mess when he pulled me back against him. "Head against my shoulder, Angel." Then he had my jeans open and his fingers curling inside to cup my pussy. He dipped two fingers in for me to clench on and then ground the heel of his hand against my already, aching and swollen clit.

It took almost nothing before I splintered. I was a shaking, shuddering mess by the time he lifted his damp fingers to his lips to clean them one at a time. He studied me with heavy-lidded eyes, and I smiled up at him.

"I'll be good now," I promised. "If you want."

He chuckled. "You're a brat."

"Sometimes," I agreed. Who knew it could be so much damn fun?

Cupping my neck, he let me turn and then kissed me with a kind of savage possession that threatened to turn me into a wild and needy mess all over again. With a groan, he pulled away and then pointed me to my guitar.

"We're working and then we're recording. After that, I'm going to tie you to that bench and fuck you until neither of us can walk. Understood?"

My breath left me in a whoosh. "Promise?"

"Yes, Angel," he told me, his eyes all heat. "I promise. But music first."

"Yes, sir," I whispered, and I swore his eyes flashed and I grinned wider. I could be good.

'Cause then I got to be bad.

Win. Win.

Even if I had to sing for my pleasure.

An hour later, I had the guitar braced against my knee as Ian wrote out musical notes on sheet music. There was just something magical about watching him sketch out the notes at speed like I would a sentence or Archie would a diagram. It made me want to crawl inside and see the music through his eyes.

I couldn't read music, not really. He'd been teaching me, but I could probably write the *names* of the notes out in French and process it easier. As it was, he kept me to simple chords. He played most of it, and then I strummed a light accompaniment.

I'd already earned five swats when I told him he'd be better off just doing all the music himself. My body tingled in anticipation, and he'd given me a wink as he walked me through the chords again. I could do it though, I could play the two-chord exchange like a champ.

The fact that he also had one of the picks with my face on it just made me smile. He stared at the page a minute, then put the pen between his teeth before he strummed out the opening lines and I followed along, counting the measures before I added my two-chords. He shot me another grin around the pen before he pushed on.

Four more refrains, and then he paused to write out more notes. "Okay, I think I have it. We're going to drop a key here, go low when we sing, and then I want you to climb up a half-octave for each line that follows."

"Okay," I agreed. "Walk me through each half-octave so I'm doing it exactly how you want me to." His swift smile flushed me with pleasure. I didn't argue about being the one to sing anymore. I just didn't know how good this was going to sound. I really didn't want to be the reason he didn't get this contract. He was too good to be held back.

Of course, I wasn't going to say that aloud again. The look on his face the last time had less to do with the shiver inducing spankings that led to orgasm and more to do with real disappointment. So, no, we'd do this his way.

Believing in him meant I had to believe in his faith in me, even if I didn't quite share it. Yes, the thought was convoluted, but it made perfect sense to me.

He set aside his guitar, then took mine, and when he set my hand on his chest, I grinned wider. I loved this part, using his heartbeat for a metronome, and he could tap his fingers against my hand lightly when he wanted me to go up a note.

"Remember the scales we've been doing?"

I nodded and exhaled.

"Start in the first note, then work your way up the arpeggio. We're going to do major and minor chords. I'll tell you which ones I want to use for each, okay?"

"Yep."

He cupped my face. "Thank you."

I blinked. "For what?"

"You're not fighting this anymore."

My lips turned down a fraction, I couldn't help it. "I'm still worried this is going to mess things up for you." I held up my free hand before he could scold me. "But I believe you when you say you like how it sounds. So, I'm doing this for you."

That earned me a gentle, breathtaking kiss, and my heart bumped my ribs as he sucked on my tongue with so much care, it sent a riot through my system and made my eyes sting with tears. "That's why I'm thanking you, Angel."

We stared at each other for a long moment, and I worked to get my breathing under control. You couldn't sing if you couldn't breathe. That had been lesson number one. For the next twenty minutes, we ran through the scales, singing them together, then climbing each arpeggio until he decided on which ones he wanted me in, and which one he would sing.

Every time our voices meshed though, I had to admit I got a thrill. It was like his sexy tones drifted right beneath mine and then buoyed it higher. I didn't think I could feel it more if he were lifting me up physically to extend my note above his.

Finally, we were back to the guitars, and we ran through it. The first couple of times we stumbled—more me than him—though he did stop us once and make an adjustment. On the third run through, we sang it clean, and I swore I wanted to cry.

The song had seemed full of fun and verve, but every time he had me go higher, while he dipped into a minor key, it added this haunting element. Like we had all this joy, but life constantly threatened to steal it away from us. Maybe it was the journey, the song seemed to have so many different layers of meaning.

But as the last note trembled in the air, we stared at each other and I wanted to cry all over again.

We sounded perfect.

How the hell was that *me* singing?

Cupping my chin, he gave me another nibbling kiss, then murmured, "We're going to record it now, promise not to freak out on me?"

"Promise to spank me if I do?"

He narrowed his eyes. "I've created a monster."

I burst out laughing. "Maybe."

"Hmm."

But he didn't look remotely displeased at the notion.

While he got the recording equipment set up and queued to where he wanted everything, I stretched my legs. I'd ditched my shoes during our first half hour here. It seemed weird to make myself at home, but since I'd had an orgasm not ten minutes after we got in here, I figured it was fine for me to just be in my socks.

Ian motioned to the water in his bag, and I pulled out a couple of water bottles. "Hydrate," he teased.

"I hope so," I told him over my shoulder in what I hoped was at least a bit sexy and teasing. If the way his gaze stroked over me was any indication, it was close enough. Still, I kept eyeing that piano bench and tried to figure out exactly how he planned to tie me to it.

Fifteen minutes later, we were on another attempt to record the song, following a couple of minor tweaks. I thought we sounded amazing and that was saying something, but Ian pushed for *more*.

I fully intended to give him whatever he wanted, so I followed his directions. This time though, there was just a moment when everything seemed to click and to flow. I forgot that I was playing any of the chords, even as my fingers hit them at exactly the right times.

The twisting of the notes acted like a tease, hopeful and melancholy all at once, until we came together at the end and then it was just filled with life. A tear slipped out of my eye as the last note fell away, and then Ian let out a whoop.

"Yes!"

I sniffed as he did a fist pump and then dragged me to him for a rough and sweet kiss.

"Perfect, Angel. Absolutely perfect."

"It's all you," I laughed in between nipping bites. "Thank you for letting me be a part of it."

"Nowhere else I'd rather be," he reminded me with another fierce kiss, and then he shut off the recording and started packing up the guitars. My heart was full, and my mind a little dazed. A minute later, the song filtered over the speakers, and I stared over at him as he closed the case.

That was us.

Singing together.

He grinned.

"See? What did I tell you?"

I pressed a finger to my lips in a shushing motion. It was one thing to sit there and sing it with him. It was something else altogether to hear how we sounded. Was that even us? The real depth of emotion in Ian's voice always blew me away, but each time I joined in or took over for a line or two on my own, it was like listening to a stranger.

Who was the girl who sounded like that?

How the hell was she me?

When the song wound to the end, Ian caught my hands and pulled me to my feet. "You," he said, "are amazing."

"It just—it's good, right?" I almost wanted to believe it.

"It's better than good, Angel. It's perfect. It's exactly what I was going for, and that's going to be in the first three tracks I send them."

I blinked. "You have two already done?"

At his sly smile, I groaned. "You recorded our other practice sessions."

"Yep," he said, very pleased with himself. "I needed you to believe in yourself, and until then, I was happy to do it for both of us. Want to hear them?"

I was torn between outrage and delight. Embarrassment and pleasure. The level of caring was enough to make me want to cry. "Yes!" I admitted, then he pulled me over to the sound board, and I settled on his thigh as he queued up the songs.

And sure enough, there we were, singing some ridiculous and playful version of one of my favorite Torched songs. It took this moving melody about a lost girl and turned it into a romp about a girl who wanted to be lost, even as he kept trying to corral me back.

Me. Not just some girl.

It was about me. And it was about Ian.

Each of the songs we'd done had some element of an emotional connection. Head tucked against his shoulder, I tried to listen as uncritically as possible, and still, I couldn't stop the warmth stealing through me. Ian did all this because he loved me.

He loved me, and he loved sharing his music with me.

I wanted to kind of just stay right here in this moment forever. The guys kept doing things like this. Little stealth ambushes full of affection and caring. I didn't think I could love them more, and they kept proving me wrong.

After we listened to all three, I traced a pattern against his arm and studied the way the muscles flexed as he turned it off.

"Well?" he asked after a really long moment as I tried to find the words to tell him what it all meant.

"I love you," was the best I could do, and I lifted my gaze to his. "It's… beautiful. You make me sound so beautiful, and you've always sounded amazing. I'm going to be your number one fan. Just FYI, and when girls start sending you their panties, I'm going to burn them."

He burst out laughing and wrapped me up in a tight hug. "Deal. The only panties I want belong to you anyway."

I grinned.

"I'm serious though, you are going to have panties and bras flying at you."

"Don't care," he murmured against my hair. "No one has ever compared to you."

Another flush of warmth went through me, and we just sat there, cuddling. "Can I ask you a question?"

"Always," he murmured. "You know that."

"Yeah, but this is a weird question."

"Ask me anything you want, Angel. For you? I'm an open book."

Chewing my lower lip, I asked, "The tying up and the restraining?"

"Yeah?"

"How'd you know you'd like that?" I stole a look at him. I refused to ask him about his ex. She wasn't welcome in this conversation in any way, shape, or form. But how had he figured this out?

"Imagination," he began slowly, as though he were really giving weight to my question and searching for the real answer. "Fantasies. I read about some of it. Saw some videos. Wanted…wanted it bad. And it was always you I wanted it with."

Surprise flickered through me, and when I looked up, I found him staring at me steadily.

"I took a class over the summer."

A class?

He grinned at my expression, which probably looked like I was strangling back every question I had. "They have *classes*?" What hill had I been living under? Rachel would laugh her ass off at me. Fuck, I was not talking about this with Rachel. Still…

"Yes, Angel. There are places where you can explore kink, safely, with other people who know what they are doing. It was more a demo than anything else. But what I saw I loved, and I wanted to do more." Trailing a finger down my cheek, he said, "And I've never done it with anyone, not like I did with you."

"I didn't ask…" I began, but he shook his head.

"You wouldn't ask, but I know you have to wonder. I made some mistakes with my choices, but I didn't mess that one up. This…this is for you and me, as long as you're still interested."

"That's—yes," I promised without hesitation. "I'm more than interested. Every time you mention spanking me, I get all turned on, and when you restrain me, all I want is more." The words spilled out of me in a rush. I didn't want him to think it bothered me at all. On the contrary… "I just…I need to do some reading."

"Or," he said slowly. "We could go to a demo…"

The word yes burned on my tongue, and at the same time… "What exactly do they do at these demos?"

"There's no overt sex," he promised. "But from what I saw last time, even with her clothes on, the woman was having the time of her life and she was so blissed out."

Okay then.

A shiver bounced through me, and I glanced at the piano bench and back to Ian. "I think you owe me five swats."

He grinned. "I do…but you were such a good girl, and good girls get rewarded."

Yay.

"Here?"

"Hmm-hmm. Unless you can wait until we get back to the apartment."

The guys were at the apartment, and I wasn't quite sure what they'd have to say about all of this and I wasn't ready to share it yet.

"Where do you want me?" It was the right question.

Ten minutes later, I was definitely secured to a piano bench, and the combination of cool wood against my back and hot Ian between my legs had me on the edge of losing my mind. The T-shirts made for loose ties, but I didn't strain against them.

As he sank into me, fingers biting into my hips, I couldn't look away from him except when my eyes rolled back in my head. "This is why I don't want to share," he whispered to me as he pistoned away. "This right here is all mine."

"Yours," I agreed.

And I got it.

He was mine, too.

We were at the studio really late.

Before we left though, I agreed to the class. It intrigued and terrified me, but I wanted to know more because I liked this. I also had no panties when we got back after I threw him my pair, because the only ones he wanted were mine.

Chapter Seven
RABBIT HOLES

Rachel eyed us from the driver's seat of her blue Honda Civic. "You realize he's packing the wrong equipment for a girls' day, right?"

I grinned. "Yes, but he begged to come along and I couldn't say no to this face." Coop snorted at the description, even as Rachel rolled her eyes.

"I can tell him 'no,' no problem," she retorted. "No, this is Frankie and *me* time. Not Frankie's boy toy and me time. See? Easy."

"Good," Coop drawled, utterly unperturbed. "'Cause it's also Frankie and me time, but she said you'd asked her to go shopping and I'm always willing to tagalong on a girls' shopping date."

Nose wrinkling, Rachel stared at me.

"One," I told her, holding up a finger. "I thought he had to work and he didn't. I also don't want to disinvite him." Then I stuck up a second finger. "Two, I thought he could give us a different perspective."

"You mean a perspective with a penis," Rachel mused, and the corner of her mouth curved ever so slightly as she cut another look at Coop. "Do you know where we're going?"

I bit my lip. Well, I hadn't gone that far yet, and I gave a little head shake. Today's date had been an impulse borne out of texting this morning while we'd been doing French homework. Truthfully, I really hadn't known Coop was going to be home this afternoon. Archie had gone to play golf with his grandfather, and he promised to be back after dinner. He'd invited me to go, and while I was curious about 'real' golf, I also didn't think I should be crashing his grandfather time either. Jake had work and dinner with his family, and Ian had music tutoring today with some students. A shiver went through me at the thought of the studio.

Somehow, I didn't think I'd ever look at that recording room the same way again. And on *that* note, I focused on Coop eyeing Rachel with a grin of amusement. "Do your worst," he told her. "I want to spend an afternoon with my girl, and I'm even willing to spend the afternoon with you, Rach. You gotta accept that we're gonna end up being friends by default if nothing else."

Her snort had me biting my lip, but she rolled her eyes and just waved to the interior of the car. "C'mon, but just remember," she said the last two words to me. "You asked for this."

Coop grinned and gave my hand a squeeze before he slid into the backseat and left me with shotgun. "So," he asked as Rachel backed out of the parking spot. "Where are we going?"

"Store called Kink on the Hill," Rachel answered without missing a beat. "I'm getting Frankie a couple of vibrators." The smirk she tossed over her shoulder was full of wickedness. "Still want to tag along?"

"Well, I'm *definitely* going now," Coop said with a drawl before cutting a look at me. My face heated, but I met his grin with one of my own. "Getting daring, are we?"

"Getting?" I dared him, and his grin grew slow and pleased.

"Fair enough," he said, then slumped back in the seat. "So what else do we do on girls' day?"

Rachel snorted. "Hair, nails, sometimes we get coffee and talk about your dick sizes."

"Works for me," Coop said holding up his hand, eyes twinkling. "I could definitely go for a manicure."

"Waxing is an option, too."

And I put a hand over my face. Oh my god. Rachel had to go there.

"Bikini waxes are the rage. Tell me, Coop, are you a fan of the groomed or the wild?"

"I'm a fan of Frankie," he said, grinning, and I bit my lip as I looked out the window. "But you do you, Rach."

"Cool," she said, and they both seemed to settle into the quiet. "Then again, you could get a little trim, make it nice and neat so she doesn't have to pick hair out of her teeth."

"I haven't heard any complaints," Coop replied. "You need me to wax the boys for you, Frankie? Not a fan, but if you'd like it, I'm sure we can work something out."

I died.

Yep.

This was how I died.

Kink on the Hill was an actual sex shop. Rachel hadn't been kidding about it. It looked rather unassuming if you ignored the giant red neon sign flashing *Adult* in the window. Nothing else about it said 'naughty sex toys sold here' but apparently, naughty sex toys were *definitely* sold. It took everything I had not to gawp when we went inside.

Coop held the door for both of us and linked his fingers with mine once we were inside. Lips right next to my ear, he asked, "Do I want to know why you want a vibrator?"

"Nope," I answered in a hushed voice. The people at the counter had greeted us warmly and asked if we needed any help. Rachel demurred, thank God.

Yeah, I had zero desire to ask them about anything, but at the same time, I couldn't help wanting to look at every single thing. Part of this trip was research.

A coffee shop sat right next door, and the scent of coffee teased my nostrils as soon as we were inside. To my shock—and honestly, no small measure of delight—there was an opening to the coffee shop *inside* the shop.

"Okay," Coop murmured, giving my fingers a gentle squeeze. We made it another two steps before my gaze tracked over an entire end cap of rainbow-colored dildos. All shapes. All sizes. Some had ribs. Some didn't. Some had little knobs on them.

"You don't want those," Rachel said. "Those can be fun, but they are more for looks than action. The ones you want are back here." She caught my free hand and tugged, winding us through the aisles toward the back right of the store opposite the coffee shop.

One aisle boasted baskets of rope, leather, and chains. Restraints. There were cuffs, too. I didn't want to linger too long, but I mentally bookmarked that aisle. I needed time to study it. I could always come back by myself, right?

We passed a display of paddles and balls on leather. Yeah, no. Ball gags according to the sign. Those looked *really* uncomfortable. Finally, Rachel halted in an aisle that was nothing but dildos, vibrators, and other *Toys for Feminine Pleasure*.

"Okay, at the risk of sounding incredibly stupid," I said as I tried to take it all in, and seriously, I did not know where to look first. "Why are there so many different kinds?"

No sooner did the words leave my mouth than it hit me—I had sex with four different guys, and they all had different cocks.

"Never mind," I told Rachel, even as I clapped a hand over Coop's mouth. His shaking shoulders and whuffs of breath against my fingers betrayed his laughter. "Just please forget I asked the question." I met Rachel's gaze and crossed my mental fingers she'd go along with it.

She studied me for a beat, then Coop, and finally one corner of her mouth kicked a little higher and she shrugged. "I didn't hear anything."

Relieved, I stole a look at Coop and glared. His gray-green eyes twinkled with mirth, and I leaned forward to whisper, "Blue Bobs." It wasn't enough to let out the secret to Rachel, but no way Coop could miss it.

His eyebrows bounced with some hilarity as he chuckled. Then he covered my hand with his and kissed my palm. "No need to get mean, beautiful. I'm on your side."

Rachel snorted but moved down the aisle as though searching for something, and Coop dragged me back against him as I started to follow.

Lips at my ear again, he murmured, "If you want to get one to play with when it's just you and me, I'm all in."

And heat rushed through me. Dammit. At the same time, I couldn't stop my grin as I said, "Why don't you pick out one and surprise me?"

Shock actually rippled across his expression and delight speared me. Yes. Score. Try to embarrass me. Ha.

"Frankie," Rachel called, and Coop winked at me before I turned away to go see what she'd found. "These are what I'm thinking you start with." She motioned to the selection of small boxed items. "They're bullets. Tiny, great for clit massage, varying speeds, and definitely worth a quick orgasm or three. They're also pretty noninvasive."

She was so calm as she went down the list of what they offered before she picked up a box and handed it to me.

I was half-reading the back of it as she pulled me along to our next stop—vibrators. "They've got a decent set here. Rabbits are popular because they have the clit stimulator to go with the g-spot access. Now that can take a little angle practice to get it right, but definitely worth it. You can also get your range in girth preference. I kind of like these here, but they are a lot pricier…"

Pricier. Holy shit, that one was two hundred bucks.

"But it's got some motion so it curves as you rock it in, I'm assuming like real guys do, and it's definitely got varying pressure so you can alternate speeds.

You know whatever gets you off."

I didn't think there was any blood left to rush to my face, so I just sort of listened as Rachel played the role of cruise director on the Sex Boat.

Dildos. Vibrators. Clit ticklers. Anal stimulators. Yes, I paused to look at those and not once did she hit me with a raunchy teasing remark. In fact, she was more than happy to help me answer questions as we read the backs of the boxes and she pulled out her phone to research. Coop vanished the next time I glanced around.

But we were at sex toys for partners, including wearable vibrating panties that you could give the controller to someone else, when he popped back up with coffee for both of us. "This is thirsty work," he teased.

I groaned, but I couldn't disagree. I was a little bit turned on and a little bit terrified. Okay, I was a lot turned on, but the dizzying number of possibilities kind of made it all overwhelming.

Vibrating panties had the kind of possibilities I wasn't sure I was ready for, but Coop pursed his lips as he looked at them and then slanted a look at me. Yeah, okay, I could see the possibilities. "Maybe next time," I murmured before giving him a kiss for my coffee.

Rachel snorted, but continued on our tour. "Now, we haven't really discussed kink limits, and you're probably still figuring yours out."

Bless her for not bringing up what kink conversation we'd already had. I didn't think Coop would care that I told her about a kink without naming one of them, but I also didn't think she needed to throw it in his face.

"I know some of them," I admitted, and ignored both pairs of curious eyes that latched on me. "I can tell you that some of this stuff is not for me. But…at the same time…"

"I got you." Still sipping her coffee, Rachel guided us over to the bondage gear. "Let's take time to look at everything, maybe give you some privacy? And then if you have questions, you can ask."

"Fine." Coop dragged out the word as though it were such an imposition.

"But we better be getting that mani-pedi after this."

I adored him. I grinned, and he winked.

"C'mon, Rach, you can give me the tongue talk. Apparently, you're full of advice." He hooked an arm over her shoulders and tugged her away. And I wasn't sure what floored me more. That he did it, or that she let him.

You know what, I wasn't going to look that particular gift too closely in the mouth. I *wanted* them to get along. It would make my life a thousand percent easier if Rachel and the boys could all keep building that bridge. They'd all made positive steps, and with a glance after Coop and Rachel, I made my way through the bondage gear, but kept my pace slow and looked at *everything.*

Seriously, I looked at things I wasn't quite sure how they worked and, in some cases, not sure I wanted to know. There was a crotchless body suit though that I did pause in front of it. It was almost all lace, and it was really pretty.

Not practical though, crotchless or not.

There were aisles with games and other items that I wasn't sure what you did with them. And while it took me fifteen minutes of just idle wandering, I finally got to go down the aisle with the restraints. There were fur-lined leather cuffs. Stiffer regular leather cuffs. Chains. Yeah, I wasn't sure what I thought of those, but the silk ropes were nice.

Ian liked restraints, but so far, he'd used his belt, T-shirts, his hands, and more than once, just had me put my hands up and keep them there. Would he like ropes? Oh man, just the thought sent little quivers through me.

Time to get out of this section. I did a quick visual check, and Rachel was looking at something near the counter, but Coop had vanished back onto one of the other toy aisles. Satisfied they were fine, I finished my circuit of the store, but at a wall of books, I had to stop and peruse.

Fifteen minutes later, I had a stack of books next to me and three more to read the jackets of and flip through. My coffee was finished, my ass was numb, and I was pretty sure I was going to spend way too much money.

"Hey, beautiful," Coop murmured as he crouched next to me. His grin was contagious. "Find a few you want to get?"

I made a face and hugged the one I'd just been flipping through. "Nerdy, right?"

"Maybe a little," he whispered. "But you're the hottest nerd I know."

Then he gave me a kiss. I sighed at the brush of his lips and the light weight of his hand on my nape. To be honest, my whole body went electric at the contact. There was definitely something smoking hot about being in this place. I kind of wished Rachel wasn't with us or that we had one of our cars 'cause I could really go for...

"Keep looking at me like that," he warned. "And I'm going to find out how kinky this place really is."

Delight speared me, and maybe the threat of more public sex shouldn't... Okay, fuck it. I kind of liked the public-we-could-get-caught thing that Jake and I had going on, but I wouldn't be opposed to figuring it out with Coop.

"Fuck," he exhaled, and his fingers tightened on my nape. "You're killing me."

I bit my lower lip to try and not grin. It utterly failed. "Think you could carry my books for me?"

"Promise to pick one of those out and read it to me later?"

I considered the question and tilted my head. "Deal."

He palmed his phone as he stood, then offered me a hand up. I let him pull me to my feet as he fired off a text and made no move to hide the screen from me.

The Guys

It was his text thread with all of them

Coop

Frankie and I have plans tonight. No interruptions.

Two middle finger emojis hit the screen one after another from Jake. Then...

Have fun and give her a kiss from me. I'm
stuck with Mom and the girls tonight anyway.
I'm getting guilt for always being gone.

I grimaced, but Coop just rubbed his hand against the small of my back. Ian's answer came next.

I'll crash in the other room. Might be late,
want to work on remixing some stuff at
the studio. Just leave a light on.

I'm having dinner with Grandpa, I was
going to invite Frankie. Tell her she
owes us dinner.

In fact, my phone buzzed before the message even finished hitting his screen. I pulled it out and saw it was a request from Archie for a dinner date on Wednesday with him and his grandfather.

I grinned.

Coop bumped my shoulder as he clicked off his screen and tucked his phone away while I answered Archie. He gathered up my stack of books and raised his eyebrows at the BDSM for Dummies. I shrugged my shoulders a little, trying and failing to not blush.

"I'm curious."

"Okay," he murmured. "I'm just trying to decide which one I want you to read me. Out loud, while naked and sitting on my cock."

And I typo'd the crap out of my message to Archie.

With a playful grin, Coop carried the stuff up to the counter. The tension winding its way through my system was just growing tauter and tauter. It was also getting hard to ignore. Rachel gave me a smirk when I reached the counter, and she added my new "toys" to the stack of my books.

I almost cringed at the total, but Coop handed over his card before I could. He also got a customer card for bonuses, which we earned with how much he spent. I glared at him, and Rachel chuckled before she ducked out of the way, murmuring, "Not my circus and definitely not my monkeys."

"Coop," I scolded him outside of the store. The weather had turned colder while we were inside, and the clouds had darkened.

"Frankie," he mimicked my exasperated tone. Then his expression softened. "I wanted to buy them for you because I intend to enjoy testing them out on you tonight."

"Still standing right here," Rachel said, and I glanced over to where she leaned against the car, arm resting on the top of it.

"Still don't care," Coop answered without looking away from me. "I promise if either of us don't like it, we'll come back and get a different set to try."

I rubbed a hand over my face. "Fine…but do me one favor?"

He just mimed zipping his lips and throwing away the key. "What they don't know, I get to enjoy all by myself."

I burst out laughing and so did Rachel.

As it was, we didn't go straight home. We went to Rachel's favorite nail place, and Coop made me laugh by getting a manicure and pedicure. He sat on my left while Rachel was on my right, and it was relaxing. He even offered to try the waxing, but I promised him that I was more than fine with him the way he was.

Much later, sprawled out on the bed, spent and shaking as Coop studied the vibrator he'd been playing with, I had to laugh at his expression. "I think this was a good investment," he murmured, then studied me almost critically. "But I think we have one last test we need to try."

I gaped at him. "Are you serious? You just…" I didn't get to finish the line before he lined himself up and pushed in, all the while kissing me. Coop was always a bit much at first, but already shaking and swollen from the five different test runs he'd done with the vibrator after insisting he could do better. The stretch had me gasping into his mouth, and then he rolled his hips and I pretty much forgot about the rest of it.

The vibrator was nice.

It was definitely fun.

But as he rocked his hips and kept devouring my mouth, the only thing I could think was that he was so much better.

"That's it, beautiful," he whispered against my lips, punctuating every word with a thrust, until I couldn't see straight. "Clench around me like that. Just like that. I love playing with your pussy. But I love being inside it even more."

Clinging to him, I answered every thrust of his tongue, dug my nails in, and held on as I tumbled toward another orgasm, but he shouted his own release and chased me right over until we were both shuddering.

Hearts racing and more than a little sticky from sweat, we just sort of lay there in a heap. The discarded vibrator lay two feet away from us, kind of lonely and abandoned. A giggle escaped me, and Coop let out a breath where he'd buried his face against my throat.

"One question," he asked in a muffled voice.

"Your dick is way better," I answered, kind of running my fingers up and down his spine. I wasn't sure who I was soothing, him or me, but I was enjoying it.

Lifting his head, Coop peered at me with a lazy smile. "Good to know my dick is preferred over a vibrator, but that wasn't what I was going to ask."

I would not blush. I would not blush. I ran my tongue over my lips. "No? But you were curious."

"Granted," he said, and then settled on his elbows so he could cup my face. "But what I wanted to know was, did you want to pick the book since I got to pick the toy? And did you need a water break before we started round two?"

I blinked for a moment. "Round two?" Wait, hadn't we just…

"Definitely round two, beautiful." His grin spread wider. "Hydration is important. I'll get us some water, so you stay there and decide which of those books we're going to read while you sit on my cock."

A groan stole out of me as he pulled out and stood. Even softening, he was semi-hard still. He ran a hand over his hair as he stared down at me.

"You really are fucking beautiful."

I bit my lip and stared right back up at him. "So are you."

He made a superhero pose, and I burst out laughing. I rolled over to stare at the stack of books he'd set right on the nightstand. Those were so moving before the boys saw them. I had a lot of research to do… He draped over me again and pressed his lips against my tattoo, and I closed my eyes at the wave of feeling that went through me.

It happened any time one of them traced it or kissed it. It grabbed me when I saw theirs, too. I loved this new link between us. Right now, it was just for us, but I didn't give a damn if the whole world saw it. Not anymore.

I glanced over my shoulder at him as he reached the door. "I love you, Coop."

He fisted his hand and touched it to his heart. "I love you too, beautiful. More than you know."

Yeah, I was pretty sure I did know. Especially after the last few weeks, if any questions had lingered, they'd all been answered. He strolled out of the bedroom naked and headed for the kitchen. I had no idea if any of the other guys were back. One thing we'd made work for us since we'd gotten back from Colorado was that if one of the guys called for private time, the others left us to it.

Even the day Coop wandered in to get his shoes, he hadn't stayed, he'd just wandered in and out. And they didn't seem to mind. Excitement threaded me as I glanced at the stack of the books. I finally pulled out the first one I should probably read.

Learning How to Discover Your Flavor of Kink: A Newbie Guide to Alternate Lifestyles and Sexual Discovery

I set it on the bed and then grabbed my phone. There was a message on the screen. Mollie.

They finally sent the assignments. I'm going to a law firm. Why does this *not* excite me?

I made a face and tabbed over to my email, and yep, there it was. My internship assignment with the day and time of my on-site orientation. I clicked it open and skimmed all the information reminding me to dress professionally, show up on time, and be prepared to learn and have fun, but that the internships were about work so we needed to be prepared for that.

The actual name of the business and the location didn't pop until the end, and I stared at it. Then I read it three times.

"Hey, I grabbed some snacks, too." All the lazy smiles abandoned his voice though when he asked, "What's wrong?"

I met his concerned stare. "I got my internship assignment."

"And?" He frowned.

My heart thudded painfully against my ribs. "It's at Standish Enterprises," I told him, handing him my phone, "with Archie's dad."

"The fuck?"

Chapter Eight

BOYS WANNA FIGHT

ARCHIE

The guys at the security desk straightened up the moment my foot hit the tile of the lobby. I didn't bother stopping or signing in. They damn well knew who I was, and while I didn't make it a habit of showing up here, I had learned from an old pro that when you asked for permission, you gave them the chance to say no.

Standish Enterprises had my name on it, and I didn't have to ask for shit when I was here.

Blood still boiling, I jabbed the button on the executive elevator then swiped the blank white security card. The only concession I'd made to this ambush was the suit jacket Jeremy insisted on. It looked fine over the Torched T-shirt and jeans.

Better than fine, if Frankie's expression when I dropped her at school this morning had been any indication.

"Please don't go pick a fight."

"Babe, I didn't pick this fight, but you're damn right I'm going to wade right into it." Hand on her nape, I'd locked eyes with her. *The other guys were outside, leaning against Jake's SUV and waiting for her. "I don't fucking want him messing with you or anything you do. I don't trust him, and I don't know what he's up to. This is a bad combo. So, yes, I'm dealing with it."*

"I don't want him to hurt you. I'm sure this is one of those things where I'll be interning at some grunt level, and his name is on it because he's the head of the company or something." It was weak and we both knew it was, but she wanted to protect me. Fuck, was it any wonder I was crazy about her? She wanted to protect me.

I was fucking fine. Archibald Edward Standish the Second had proven what an absolute fuckhole he was as a parent to me a long time ago. Not much left to disappoint to be honest. But Frankie was not an option for his goddamn games. "I'll be fine, babe, pinky swear."

The tease worked, and she hooked her pinky with mine. "Call me?"

"I promise. Have a good day." I kissed her. *"If I can make it back by lunch, I'll be here, otherwise, I'll see you after school."*

She wrinkled her nose, then leaned over and kissed me so soundly, I debated saying fuck it to heading to the office and just taking her back to the apartment. After she bit my lower lip, I chuckled and stroked my thumb along her nape. I got it. Frankie wanted to protect me. It was so damn adorable. "Take care of you," she informed me. *"I mean it. I'll kick that man in the balls if he hurts you."*

I'd pay money to see that. "I know you would. I love you."

As much as I hated leaving, I trusted the guys would look after her. There was a perk to sharing her I hadn't really considered before. One that had proven beyond soothing after Homecoming. We never had to leave her alone.

Of course, our stubborn girl had begun pushing back, and I was—strangely maybe—okay with that. I liked it when she reminded us she could stand on her own two feet. That she wanted to protect us, and that maybe, just maybe, she wanted time to herself. Or Rachel time to do girl stuff.

But after the bomb of her internship dropped? Yeah, I wanted one of us with her in case her cunt of a mother pulled something. She had been quiet for weeks.

Maybe too quiet.

As the elevator sped its way to the executive floors, I checked my phone. I'd put a call into Wittaker, but he hadn't gotten back to me yet. Jeremy would be following up while I tackled Edward. I'd managed to avoid him completely for the last few weeks. While he hadn't moved out of the house, no matter what Frankie's idiot mother thought, he had taken a couple of bags and not returned as far as I knew.

The elevator doors opened to the senior executive floor. The whole space was luxurious, from the premium carpets to the wood paneled walls, huge plants and works of art hanging prominently. Susan sat at her desk. She was about sixty-five if she was a day, and she'd been among the senior secretaries for as long as I could remember. Slipping a hand into my pocket, I pulled out the candy bar and set it on her desk as I smiled at her.

"Good morning, Susan. You look fantastic as always, when are you dumping these assholes and running away with me?"

Her eyes lit up with fond laughter, and she shook her head. "You never forget."

"And I never will," I told her with a wink. When I was three and stuck at the offices whenever we were between nannies, Susan had been tasked with looking after me. On days when I behaved, she always gave me a full bar of chocolate. On days when I didn't, I just had to split it with her. "Is he in?"

"In his office," she told me, tapping the candy bar. "Am I going to have to share this one today?"

I chuckled. "You're always good, so I very much doubt it."

For me? I made no similar promises.

Without another word, I strolled down the hall. There were only three offices on this floor.

Edward's corner suite, easily occupying about three thousand square feet. Grandpa's, which he only used when he was in town, though they both had similar offices in other corporate buildings in other cities. And mine.

To be clear, I'd never used mine.

Janis glanced up from her desk. She was Edward's private secretary of the most recent variety and occasional fuckbuddy. I'd walked in on her blowing him behind his desk enough that it rather surprised me to find her at her desk. She'd offered to blow me more than once. Not in so many words, but at least intimated it.

Hard pass.

She stood at my arrival and leaned forward. "Archie," she greeted me in that breathless voice that made me wonder if she had asthma or something. Then again, it could have more to do with how tight her top was and the fact her breasts—handsomely paid for by Edward—threatened to spill out of her too deep for the office neckline.

I gave her a nod as I continued forward. Unlike Susan, I didn't expect Janis to be around all that much longer. Then again, maybe she didn't care about being the office squeeze while he plowed Maddy. What the fuck did I know?

Except now I had that damn mental image, and it turned my stomach.

She hurried out to catch my arm, and this close, I drowned in the scent of her perfume, but not even the power of it could erase the smell of sex. Clearly, still the office fuckbuddy. I gave the hand she put on my arm a cool look, then stared at her until she removed it.

Her tongue flicked out nervously to wet her lips. "He's on a call."

"I don't give a fuck." At her startled look, I raked my gaze over her. "You know, you could do better than him, right?"

A blush stained her cheeks, and she gave me a coy look.

"And I can definitely do better than you."

Outrage flooded her eyes and she reared that hand back, but I caught her wrist. So predictable.

"Tsk tsk, that will get you fired." I winked at her and she flushed a deep red, more furious than flirty. Good. I didn't need to fend her off. I'd never been interested and that was saying something, because there was a time when all a girl needed to have was boobs and she had boobs. But she couldn't hold a candle to Frankie.

Not to mention I wouldn't touch a woman Edward had with a ten-foot pole.

Walking away, I pushed open one of the double doors to Edward's office and let myself in. The man in question stood behind his desk, hands in his pockets as he faced the window, a headset on, and he spared me a glance before he answered a question in near flawless Italian.

I helped myself to the French press coffee and didn't bother with anything to sweeten it. I wanted the bitter brew on my tongue. It definitely fit my mood. The call lasted another five minutes, and as he ended it, Edward faced me fully.

"Archie," he greeted me in a chill tone. One that warned I'd already irritated him by showing up in the first place.

Too. Fucking. Bad.

"Edward. You want to explain me to what the fuck it is you think you're doing?" I didn't waste any time on pleasantries. I had none to share.

Removing the headset, he crossed to his desk and took a seat, not bothering to answer me before he pressed a finger to the call button on his phone. "Janis, move my next call back fifteen minutes, and the next time I tell you I'm not to be interrupted, make sure it happens or find a new job."

That done, he leaned back in his chair and studied me. I didn't twitch, just met him gaze for gaze. These little power plays were old hat for me. I could make some scathing remark about his secretary, but she mattered so very little to him, it wouldn't even make a dent.

But I had collected a few nuggets of information along the way that definitely would.

"Perhaps you'd like to clarify that question with some actual information, or is this just another teenage tantrum? I'd have thought you were over the hormonal stage by now." The faint smirk used to enrage me. It was like he'd throw that in my face, bored with me and my so-called tantrums.

Of course, I used to long for his approval, too.

I got over it.

"Frankie." I said her name in the same dry tone he'd affected when he'd opened his mouth. "What the fuck do you think you're doing with Frankie?"

Oops. Not so unaffected, but his faintly puzzled frown wasn't anywhere near as convincing as he might wish it.

"I'm doing nothing with Frankie."

And fuck if I didn't *hate* hearing her name on his lips.

"It's my understanding that she and her mother are having some issues, but they will work them out." A careless shrug, like it had nothing to do with us.

"Right, and you didn't pull any strings to get her assigned to Standish for an internship."

One corner of his mouth quirked a little higher than the other, the barest hint of pleasure in his expression. It made me want to punch that smirk right off his face. I'd experienced any number of feelings where this man was concerned over the years, but being incited to violence was new.

I could see every detail in sharp relief. We were the same height, roughly the same build, but he didn't work out with near the frequency I did and I could make it fucking hurt if I belted him.

But first, I needed answers.

Business before pleasure and all of that.

"Archie, my boy," he said, almost laughing as he pushed his chair back and stood. "Are you jealous? You shouldn't be. You have an office just down the hall. You could come to work here, the offer has been on the table for years."

"Let's not pretend this is about me," I told him before knocking back the rest of the coffee then setting the empty mug on the table as I tracked Edward's passage from behind the desk to where I stood near the coffee. "This is about whatever game it is you're playing with Frankie and her slut of a mother."

Edward spared me a look. "There is no game, Archie. You need to grow up. Maddy and I are engaged, I'm going to be a fact of Frankie's life. There is nothing wrong with me trying to make things easy for her. The program is a solid one, she's an excellent candidate and she'd do well here."

I shook my head. "Engaged. You're still married, and your little fuck princess outside can attend to your needs. So, one would think you're busy enough at the moment to not mess with a girl who's more than half your age."

"More than?" Edward raised his brows. "Barely. But that's not the point." He took a sip of his coffee, then added, "I owe you no explanations. I'm doing something nice for the young lady, and if you'd stop poisoning her mind, maybe I could fix some of the things going wrong. Like a rejection from Harvard. Clearly, she is the better candidate."

"What she does or doesn't do is none of your business. Leave. Her. Alone."

"Oh, but I take it she's your business."

"Yes. She fucking is. And I'm not letting you drag her into whatever sick little game you are playing. Buying her clothes. Trying to get her a car. Now you want to bring her to work here? She's not a toy."

"Are you quite finished?" Edward's glacial stare had dropped several degrees. Well, well. I touched a nerve.

"Hardly. I want you to leave her alone."

"I don't care what you want." Oh, there was just the barest hint of a snap in his tone. Definitely hit a nerve.

"Clearly, I've never entertained the illusions otherwise." Not since I'd been a kid. "But you're going to do this."

"Or what?" he challenged. "I'm going to do what you want or what? Because let's be clear, *son*, in business and in life, you don't make a threat you're not prepared to back up."

I slugged him.

Verbal chess was our thing. We'd done it for years. But the smug superiority in his tone coupled with the smirk on his face, and I took that last little nugget he'd shared to heart. The blow landed on his jaw and caught him unawares as he toppled onto his ass. My knuckles screamed and my fist ached, but fuck that felt good.

"Great advice, Edward," I told him with a stare of my own. "So let's get a few things cleared up, shall we? You're going to leave Frankie alone, or I'll tear you a-fucking-part. I'll come for you, for your company, and everything else you hold dear. You think I'm fucking with you?" I raised my brows. "Try me."

Blood decorated his lip and began to run from his nose. He had a hand to his face, and I wasn't sure if he was more startled or in pain. I actually didn't give a shit which. I just wanted him to fucking listen.

"If I cut her loose from the internship," Edward warned, "she might lose her place in the program. They've already placed all of them."

"Then you just stay the fuck away from her if she's here. Delegate it." As fine as I would be if Frankie was out of that program, it wasn't my damn decision to make. "You're a damn expert at that."

Slowly and warily, Edward rose to his feet. I admit, I enjoyed knocking him off his game almost as much as knocking him on his ass. "I'll see what I can do."

I nodded once, then pivoted and went to the door. But before I stepped out, I glanced back at him. "Don't push me. You want to fight with me? You want to come after my shares in the company?" I didn't flinch from his stare. "Fuck, you want to come after my trust fund? You come for me. I'll take that fight, but you leave her out of this. Forget her name. Forget she exists. Run off into the sunset with Maddy, leave Frankie alone. This is the only warning I'm going to give you, and it's a hell of a lot more than you deserve."

I didn't wait for his response to that and just left. I strode past his little fuckbuddy pouting at her desk and didn't slow my pace. If I hesitated, even once, I'd walk back in there and punch him again. It felt really fucking good to hit him in his lying, arrogant face.

Anger seethed through me all the way to the elevator. Susan glanced up at me, and her smile faltered. Without a word, she held up the candy bar I'd brought her, and I shook my head. It took some effort to muster a smile, but I managed.

She sighed, then cast a glance back the way I'd come and then at me again. "Take care of yourself, Archie."

"You, too," I said as the elevator opened, and there, I got another smile out for her as the doors closed after I punched the lobby button. You needed a keycard to go up, but nothing to go down. Dropping my chin, I stared at my battered knuckles.

Frankie wouldn't be happy with me. Fuck. I should have kept my cool.

Should have.

Would have.

Had.

So many times.

I wanted him out of her life before he fucked up everything. It was what he was good at.

Downstairs, I crossed the lobby and exited without a glance to anyone else. My car waited for me right out front. Perks of the last name. They existed, even if I could have wished I'd been born a generation earlier.

Course, then I wouldn't have gotten to know Frankie, so maybe I could live with the shit lottery I won in getting Edward and Muriel. At least I'd always had Grandpa and Nana.

In the car, I started it up and the music started pouring from the speakers. Raking a hand through my hair, I pressed my mouth against my abused knuckles before I pulled out my phone. A quick text to Jeremy to find out where he was.

Home.

Well the house, anyway. I wasn't sure I really considered it home anymore.

I sent him an on my way and then pulled out. It was another forty-five minutes back to the house, and it gave me time to stew. I'd been stewing since

Coop texted us the night before and I got home to read the email myself.

Jeremy was working in his tidy little office just off the kitchen when I got there. "There's coffee brewed, Mr. Archie, and some sandwiches. I suspected you might not have paused for breakfast." He glanced up, then removed his reading glasses to give me a stern once over. Yeah, I didn't think he'd miss the hand.

Rising, he set his reading glasses down, then motioned me back into the kitchen. I settled at the island while he poured the coffee and set the platter of sandwiches along with some chips in front of me. He stepped out, only to return a moment later with the first aid kit.

He didn't ask and I didn't offer, just sipped the coffee and stared out the windows toward the garden. Only when he finished and had put an ice pack in place, did he give me a hard look.

"We've discussed your new-found penchant for leading with your fists," he scolded, disappointment in his voice. "You will win far more battles with words and wits, than with fists."

"True," I agreed. "But sometimes, you just want to knock the fucker on his ass. Or at least I do."

"Should I be calling your lawyer?"

"Doubtful," I said, though that would be an interesting twist if Edward decided to have me charged with assault.

Worth it.

"Did you get a hold of Wittaker?"

"I did," he said. "He's tied up in court this week with a case, but so far, there has been no movement from Ms. Curtis on the matter, nor has any counter suit been filed. They do, however, have another ten days to answer that suit. They may be running the clock out."

"That seems like an exercise in futility, right? She turns eighteen in three months." This all presupposed that Madeline Curtis *planned* to contest the emancipation hearing. Still, would she be petty enough to fight over three months?

The bite of my sandwich settled like a hard lump in my stomach as though answering that question for me.

"Perhaps. I wouldn't want to hazard a guess in either direction at this point. I'm afraid Ms. Curtis' motives seem a bit of a mystery to me."

What a polite way of calling her a crazy bitch. My phone buzzed, and I glanced at it. It was the group chat. Jake was teasing Frankie about something, and she kept sending him flip off emojis, which was kind of flirting. My name flashed across the screen. Frankie wanted to know if I was doing all right. Just checking in.

"That seems to be going rather well," Jeremy commented as he studied me.

"It is going well," I admitted. "It was easier in Colorado, even with all of them there and knowing she's with them, too. It worked and yet..."

I frowned and then shook my head.

"Nothing."

"I would say your feelings are hardly nothing, Mr. Archie. While this relationship you have involved yourself in is hardly conventional, one truism to making all relationships work is open, honest communication. If something is bothering you, you should not repress it. Your feelings have merit."

I chuckled. "I'm okay, Jere. Seriously. It's just that some days, I want her all to myself and I don't want to share. I want to be the reason she smiles or she flirts, and it's not always going to be me. I'm glad she has them. I am..."

"But you want her to want you the way you want her." It wasn't a guess. "You have been in love with that young lady for years. She's exceptionally good for you."

"But...?" Because there was always a but.

"But you are in a unique position, and one I am familiar with."

Excuse me? I leaned back and stared at him. "Did I miss something, Jere?" Did he even date? I should know this, right?

Jeremy chuckled. "Well, perhaps not the exact same position, but I serve this household and I have for many years. You. Ms. Muriel. Mr. Edward. My position has always been clear. I worked for a short time for Mr. Ted, before Mr. Edward married Ms. Muriel. I moved to working for Mr. Edward because you were coming along."

Yeah, I really should have known this. "Okay, but I'm not seeing the similarity."

"My job is to look after all three of you, to see that your needs are met and that you want for nothing. I am not, nor have I ever tried to be, your father. That wasn't my place. Nor have I tried to be Mr. Edward's friend or Ms. Muriel's confidant."

But he…he had been all of those things.

"When you were younger, you desperately wanted Mr. Edward's approval. It's a natural thing. But his distance and his traveling, they often resulted in you coming to me. I did my best by you, but I admit, I preferred it when I was the one who made you smile or could give you that bit of encouragement you needed. That said…I wish Mr. Edward had done more. You deserved more. So while I might have been…envious of his relationship, should he have taken advantage of it, I would have been far happier that you were happy."

I rubbed the back of my neck, a little touched by the confession, and at the same time… "So me being aware of how it makes me feel sometimes is okay? Me wanting to be a little selfish sometimes is okay?"

"Mr. Archie, you are easily one of the most selfless young men I have had the privilege to know, particularly with the people you care about. So yes, it is quite all right for you to be a little jealous sometimes and a little selfish. However, I would recommend that you continue to be honest with Miss Frankie. I've noticed, and rightly so, that the majority of your issues with her stemmed with keeping certain pieces of information to yourself. She cares about you, I dare say almost as much as you care for her. She would want to know."

Heat crept up the back of my neck. We didn't really do the touchy feely, Jeremy and I. This was a pretty damn big declaration. "Have I thanked you for always looking out for her?"

"Actually," Jeremy said, wearing the faintest of smiles, "you have. Many times. Particularly when you trust me to look after her."

I really did trust him to look after her. He made me feel a bit better.

It helped.

It all helped.

"So," I said, trying to give us both a breath from too much emotion. "Do you have any cat videos you didn't send her?"

"She does have a birthday coming…"

That she did. "And you have some ideas."

"Well, if one were inclined to hearing a few suggestions?"

I grinned. "I'm listening."

True Colors

"So, it's been how many weeks since you spoke to your mother?"

"Not since before Thanksgiving," I told Erin. This was our first real session since I'd gotten back from Colorado. She'd been on vacation the first week. "I actually can't really recall the last time we spoke. We argued…that day at the park, and then she moved in with Mr. Standish and we changed the locks on my place… Okay, *Archie* changed the locks on the apartment so they couldn't get back in, and that was that. I haven't spoken to her directly."

"How do you feel about that?"

"Is it wrong to say I feel relieved?" I'd been turning this one over in my head for the last few weeks. "When we were in Colorado, it was…" I licked my lips. How did I say this without sounding like a complete lunatic? Talking to Erin had grown easier, but she was still a therapist and it was still weird to tell her things like, *Oh, yeah, I'm definitely dating four guys, and they are all okay with it. More than okay. We're practically living together.*

She didn't push me or supply any words to finish the thought, just sat there and waited me out as I wrestled with the verbiage. You know, fuck it.

"It was freedom. I didn't have to be on my guard. I don't think I've ever realized how much time I spent *waiting* for her to get mad at me or to react to something. Like I wanted her to *notice* me and what was going on. Not just ask, but *see* me, and even if she did, I don't feel like she ever cared except in how it reflected on her. And when we were there, that fear was just…I don't want to say gone, but diminished? I guess that's the right word."

I was rambling, but it was like the floodgates opened.

Leaning forward, I clasped my knees and stared at her, but I wasn't really seeing Erin or her office. It was like I was staring back at the lodge at the five of us just hanging out. No pressure. "They listen when even I don't know I need to be heard. Sometimes, they hear the things I'm not saying. Don't get me wrong, they're not perfect. Far from it. And neither am I, but they are perfectly imperfect and I love them, flaws and all, and they love me."

That thought ballooned in my chest.

"They care about me, and not just because of how I make them look or how I make them feel. My feelings are important to them. Archie got us tickets to see one of my favorite bands. I've never been to a concert before, but he wanted us to all go and he made it happen. We went skiing and played video games—okay, they mostly played because I can only play so many shoot 'em ups, but… we could just be together in the same room, and it was good."

I licked my lips.

"And I didn't miss Maddy, not once. I was *glad* she wasn't a part of it. On Christmas day, Coop, Jake, and Ian, they all went to call their families and have some time with them, and there's me and Archie and we're cuddled up together on the sofa with a fire in the fireplace and the Christmas lights on the tree twinkling with snow in the window. It was a fucking Hallmark movie moment…" I winced. "Sorry, it was like something out of a fairytale, and it was perfect. She's not tainting it."

Erin smiled at me, the encouragement in her quiet relaxed manner. "Do you think you'll be able to make your peace with your mother?"

"I don't have to make peace with her." Before the words came out of my mouth, I hadn't realized how true they were. "I didn't do anything wrong. I was the kid. I might not have been perfect, but if the guys can love me? Even when I'm sometimes blind or silly or obsessed with my schedule and my homework… If they can love me, then I'm lovable. So why doesn't she?"

"Do you love her?"

I exhaled, and my grip on my knees tightened. I wanted to say no. I wanted to say I didn't give a damn about her. That she didn't deserve it.

"I wish I didn't, sometimes. I really do. Coop's sister is fighting with her mom right now, and she's so angry with her and so hurt and she's really obnoxious about it." I licked my lips and shook my head. "But she can be because Carly is never not going to be there for her. She doesn't see it, not like I can. She looks at me and seems to envy me the freedom I have. But I'd trade it for a good mom, someone I could trust, who would have my back and care enough to fight with me, to fight me for me, but…Maddy is never going to be that woman and I still love her. Because as much as I hate her sometimes, I don't want to hate her. I just want her to love me."

Chapter Nine
ON THE CLOCK

The butterflies in my stomach had butterflies. It didn't help that Archie fumed in the hall as I pulled my hair back into a braid and up. Quiet fury churned the air around us and turned it positively electric. I almost didn't want to breathe too hard in case it set him off. I was supposed to be interning in an actual office, so I'd gone for business casual as per the instructions.

"I know you're not happy," I said, trying for the third time to broach this discussion with him, but since he'd taken the day to go see his father, he'd pretty much seethed any time the discussion came up. He'd also asked me to drop out of the program if they wouldn't change my assignment.

No, they wouldn't change it—I had, in fact, asked—and I'd wrestled with whether to just drop the program altogether. No, I didn't want to disappoint anyone. I also didn't want to work with Mr. Standish on anything. But at the same time…

"Not happy is an understatement," Archie said as he shoved away from the wall and crowded into the bathroom until he was pressed up against my back. "I hate the idea of him being anywhere near you."

He settled his hands on my hips and then leaned in to press his cheek to mine. I'd gone with a dark green blouse and a pair of black dress pants rather than the skirt I'd originally planned. One, skirts just made me uncomfortable, and two…well, the fierce look on Archie's face when I'd pulled it out just made me *not* want to have that argument.

Since he'd gotten home and we'd shown him that email, he'd been in a rage. The fact that his knuckles had been bruised and split when he came by after school on the same day also worried me. All he would say was that he was working on it.

"Babe," he murmured. "I need you to be aware and on your guard. If you're going to do this, then I support it, but if anything, and I mean *anything* feels off, you text me. I also want you to rely on that list of allies I gave you."

I met his worried gaze in the mirror. "I love you," I told him simply. There were any number of other words on the tip of my tongue, but those leapt out. "I will do everything you asked."

"Except cancel and drop out of the program." He ground his teeth, then closed his eyes as he seemed to wrestle with his temper.

Turning slowly, I faced him. "I get it," I told him. "I get that you don't want me there and I get you don't want me working with him. I can't imagine I would be…and at the same time, I wouldn't put it past Maddy or him. But…do you think I'm in real physical danger from him?"

Archie had been against anything to do with *Eddie* from the beginning. Even when we were younger and before the whole joke of bad meatloaf, we just hadn't really had anything to do with him except in passing.

Head tipped back, Archie stared at the ceiling. A muscle ticked in his cheek, and I waited him out. If he said there was a real threat, then I'd take the hit and ask to withdraw from the program. My biggest concern right now was if it would affect my temporary emancipation. Maddy had been quiet, but there was a little over ten weeks left until my birthday.

If she pulled anything and it got taken away from me, I'd survive those ten weeks, but I didn't want to just *survive.*

"No," Archie said slowly. "I sure the fuck hope not. He…he likes women." Those dark brown eyes held so much pain when he focused on me. "And he seems a little *too* interested in you. So, avoid being alone with him. If you have to be in his office, keep the door open. Just…"

I rubbed a circle against his chest. "I'll rely on the people on the list you gave me. You told me Susan works on his floor, right?"

"She does."

"Then I'll check in with her before I go anywhere near his office, but all the schedule says for today is to show up, check in and I meet with someone from HR who will get my security pass, show me where I'll be 'working,' and then do an orientation on Standish." I smoothed down his shirt. "Who knows, maybe I'll never get anywhere near his office, and they'll stick me in some back corner doing something like coffee and copies."

He snorted, hand coming up to cup my face. "Don't hate me, but I love the idea of you never being anywhere near him."

"I know. If I think for even an instant that something is wrong or even a bit uncomfortable…"

"You'll text me," Archie said. "I'm going to apply at school so I can leave and come up to the office as often as I can. I might see if I can work out ditching my afternoon classes on the days you're there…"

"Arch."

He shook his head and then pressed his forehead to mine while threading our fingers together. "Let me be paranoid and overprotective. Okay?"

I made a face. "As long as you trust me to handle myself." Because this was a test for all of us really. None of the guys were particularly happy about it. Coop had damn near bitten his tongue in half when the others had been around, but he made his thoughts on the subject very clear when we were alone. Ian had done much the same thing.

"We trust you," Jake said from the hall. "It's bad meatloaf we don't trust."

He and Archie shared a look, and I sighed.

"Okay, we have to dial this back some. I know you guys are worried, but my nerves have nerves…"

"C'mon," Archie said with a kiss. "We got you something."

Jake paused us in the hall with a hand to my waist, then pressed a kiss to my cheek before he tugged me from Archie and gave me a proper kiss. Thankfully, I hadn't bothered with cosmetics beyond the absolute bare minimum that I'd snapped a pic of and sent to Rachel. She'd given me a thumbs up and suggested a nude gloss. I'd put that on *after* I left so the guys wouldn't kiss it right off me.

The faint clearing of Archie's throat didn't slow Jake's deep exploration of my mouth, nor did it quiet my sigh as he dug his fingers into my hips. At this rate, I would not only not be going into the office, I was going to be naked and back in bed.

Not that I was complaining.

But still…

I groaned as Coop whistled. "Yo, we need to give her a present."

"I'm giving her a present," Jake murmured, and I cracked up. He smiled against my lips, then waggled his brows playfully.

Coop gagged, then socked him gently. I say gently because Jake still had a hold of me. Archie tugged me away, and Ian ran interference when Coop and Jake started shoving each other.

They stumbled into the living room and right into the coffee table.

"Don't wreck the table," I said at the same time Archie snapped, "Watch the table, guys."

The table shuddered and slid a few inches, but they did not, in fact, break it again.

So, win?

In the kitchen, Archie tugged me over to the table where we'd had breakfast a little earlier. They'd all insisted on eating here rather than at school, since I wasn't going in with them. There was a lunch bag on the table and a travel mug with a photo of all of us from Colorado printed on the side of it. It was from skiing and we were in the snow, all grinning like idiots.

Opening the bag, Ian showed me an apple, a sandwich, a bag of chips and a couple candy bars.

"There's also a few twenties because you need a real lunch," Archie murmured against my ear. "Or at least money for coffee. Don't hit the coffee shop in the lobby, they suck at steaming milk properly, go outside and across the street and less than a block down. There's a great place, and I know they make fantastic pastries and hot sandwiches, too."

"Also," Coop said, sliding his arms around me. "We got you this." Then he held out his palm in front of me and there was a briefcase charm.

I burst out laughing, and they all grinned. Yeah, Archie didn't want me to go, but he was also being amazing about it, too. "Thank you," I said, kissing each one of them, and Archie scooped up the briefcase charm. I didn't have my charm bracelet on today, but I did have my ring and I had tucked the charm necklace on under my blouse.

"I'll get it added for you," Archie offered. "Knock 'em dead, babe."

"Love, you," Ian told me.

"Love you more," Jake murmured.

"Love you most," Coop said. And then we were all walking out. It was a little ridiculous that they all walked me to the car, but Jake even made me wait while he slipped me into my coat. My last sight of them was waving to me as I pulled away.

I didn't even make it one block before my phone buzzed.

Archie

Love you best.

My grin didn't falter once on the drive.

The butterflies, which had quieted during the farewell, roared back like helicopters as I pulled into the parking garage. Instructions told me to collect the stub and take it in for validation. I'd finished my coffee on the way to the office, and I pressed a kiss to the mug and left it in my car. I didn't want to risk losing it.

Then I collected my stuff, including my backpack, and headed inside. I checked my phone.

Archie

> Tell me when you're there. Also ask for Steve or Jim when you get to security, that has to be your first stop. I asked them to look after you.

Jake

> Archie's losing his mind, Baby Girl. Don't worry, we'll look after him.

Jake

> Or knock him out. Whichever works.

I groaned.

Coop

> Ignore Jake, he's being an ass.

Ian

> Angel, you're going to be great. We can't wait to hear how the first day went.

Archie

> Don't forget to give Susan a candy bar when you meet her. Trust me, she'll get it.

I bit back another smile, and then fired off several quick responses to them and one last one to the group text.

Me

Boys, be good. I'm fine. I'll check in, like I promised. I'll even eat all my veggies at lunch. I'm putting my phone away now because I have to go inside. Do not freak out if I don't text or read your texts for a few minutes. I love all of you.

Then I snapped a picture of myself blowing a kiss. It looked stupid as hell, and I sent it along with the message.

Then I texted Rachel.

Me

Can you keep an eye on them?

Her answer was an image of all four of them.

Rachel

If I must. Though whatever you just sent must be good because Jake had to adjust himself. Boy seems to be packing.

I groaned.

Me

You're terrible.

Rachel

And you love me for it. But not as much as what he's packing.

Me

You keep talking like that and you're totally gonna flunk the Bechdel test.

I was almost to the main doors when I got her response. It was just a picture of her middle finger, and I grinned.

At least it changed the subject.

Inside, all the jitters were back in full force as I checked in at the desk and they directed me to a set of elevators to go to the third floor, where I would meet with someone from human resources. The lady was actually waiting for me when the elevator doors opened.

Linda was a friendly woman, probably in her forties with a hint of gray sprinkled through her dark brown hair. She had pale brown eyes, but they were filled with mirth as she introduced herself. "You're one of our two interns this year," she told me with no small measure of excitement. "I'm a huge fan of this program."

"Oh?"

"Yes," she assured me. "We don't always get our first picks, but we lucked out this year. So let's get you set up, and then we'll go up to the conference room. You'll be with us most of the day. We have some basic materials to introduce you to Standish Enterprises and what we do here, as well as a full overview of each division."

As she spoke, she moved at a fast clip, and I had to stretch my legs to keep up with her. Considering she wore four-inch heels and I was in flats, I wasn't quite sure how she managed that stride.

"First stop is here, Francesca?" She paused a beat and gave me a glance.

"I'd prefer Frankie." Not that she'd given me time to introduce myself.

"No problem, Frankie," she told me with a warm smile as she knocked on the first door before opening it and ushering me into what looked like another larger office with four or five desks. "This is the security office on our floor. "Steve Madison, this is Frankie Curtis."

Steve was easily six and a half feet tall. No exaggeration. He'd tower over Jake and Ian both. He was also built broad with thick biceps that seemed to strain, even in the cut of his suit. The man offered me his hand and smiled. "You're a friend of Archie's, right?"

"I am," I said.

"Fantastic, come on over and let's get you your security badge, while

Linda hurries off to the fifteen other things she has to do."

"You're a lifesaver, Steve. When she's done here, can you show her to the blue room?"

"Yep."

Before I could say another word, Linda was gone. Soon, I was sitting down to get my photo taken and filling out the information to get a security card printed. He added the card to a lanyard before he held it out to me. Then we went over security procedures, including never letting anyone surf in behind me. If they didn't have their own ID card, they had to have an escort.

I wasn't sure if I was supposed to fend them off with a stick, but I promised to make sure the doors closed. Steve just chuckled at me, then had me bring up my phone and download an app. Archie hadn't mentioned that Standish had an app, and I had to clear my screen of messages before I loaded it.

The app would also double as my security card *in an emergency*, but Steve stressed that I would have to get them to authorize it and that would mean reporting where my card had gone.

Note to self, never be that person.

After that, we went over a few other things—layout of the building, different floors where I had open access, and others where I would need an escort. My head was already hurting and we still had material to cover.

Before he took me to the blue room—which by the way, *wasn't* blue— he also made sure I had his number and texting information, along with the assurance that if I needed anything to let him know. He said the next time I was there and Jim was on, he'd find me and do the same.

Good to know.

Apparently, Archie really had gone overboard. If it wasn't so sweet, I might want to throttle him.

Steve showed me where the water was and there was a coffee urn in the corner along with some snacks. Apparently, we rated because the coffee was fresh and there were croissants, bagels, and more fresh treats. Seriously, my stomach growled, even though I'd had breakfast, but I should probably wait to stuff my face until after we finished whatever was next.

I'd just set my bag down on a chair and shrugged out of my jacket when the door opened to let Linda in, along with another familiar face. A faint grin pulled at my lips as the guy with her gave me a startled look.

"Hey," he said and winced. "Frankie, right? Frankie."

"Hey, Bryan," I said with a laugh, and took his hand as he crossed toward me and we shook briefly. Almost as briefly as we had at the first orientation. "I didn't know I'd be seeing you today."

"Ditto," he answered, and we both glanced toward Linda, who grinned at us.

"Like I was telling you both, we don't always get our pick of candidates, but this year, you two made the top of the pile and we're thrilled to have you here. I'm glad you've already met, because you're going to spend the day on orientation here."

She turned her back to us, and Bryan rolled his eyes at me and I had to bite back a laugh.

"Make yourselves comfortable," she told us, and Bryan pulled out a chair near mine as she set up and then typed something into her laptop.

I automatically reached for my backpack to get out my laptop and notepad. Bryan had his bag, but he didn't crack it open so much as flash a grin at me.

"I don't think there's gonna be a test."

I shrugged at him. "You never know. There might be."

"She's right," Linda agreed with me, and Bryan made a face. "There might be, but the only tests you're taking today will be strictly inventories for human resources that we will keep on file. So, let me go over your day for you real quick."

Our day, in a nutshell, was going to involve multiple video overviews of the various areas of Standish to give us a good feel for what the company handled. There would be the inventories we filled out. Lunch would be catered in, and Bryan made an ooh-la-la face at me when Linda turned to pull out some menus that she offered us. Next came folders with packets of information.

We weren't expected to memorize it, but even though we were interns, we would be getting the full employee treatment to give us a real look at the work.

"And once we're done, we'll do a quick introduction to the heads of the departments, who've all expressed interest in you shadowing them. Ideally, you'll work in four to six different departments over the course of your internships, because we want to give you maximum exposure and experience. That should take us up to about four or five this afternoon. I would also advise you to not make plans most evenings immediately after your internship days, because we often go into overtime, so I need you both to be prepared for that." Then she gave us a warm smile, as if that would make up for what sounded like incredibly long days. "We'll try not to overwork you, but again, the best way to learn is to do."

I'd heard that phrase before. Plenty of times.

"Would either of you like to grab something to eat or a drink?"

"Absolutely," Bryan said. "You like coffee, right, Frankie?"

"Yeah, I can get it though."

Linda's phone rang, and she gave us a little finger wave. "I need to take this. Get set up and give me five, and then we'll get started." Then she was out of the room.

"How much coffee do you think she drinks?" Bryan asked me as he cracked open a bottle of the spring water and offered it to me.

"I'm good," I said as I filled a cup with coffee. "And I have no idea, but she probably has to do this a lot for new employees and she has other things to do, too."

"Point," he said, unperturbed at me turning down the water. Bryan was a nice guy, but I didn't think I was taking water from anyone ever again.

Just…my guys.

That was it.

I sipped the coffee and then set a couple of the croissants onto a plate and carried them back over to the table, before I added what looked like cheese and cherry danishes. It was like someone had added all my favorites.

The coffee was fantastic, too.

"Is it just me, or is this a lot swankier than you were expecting?" Bryan asked as he settled into the chair next to mine again.

I gave him a little shrug. "I'll be honest, I didn't know what to expect. At least so far, it's not boring."

He laughed. "True story. And we have each other, so that counts for something right?"

I grinned. "I hope Mollie got a friendly face wherever she ended up." I needed to text her at the end of the day. She'd been happy about her law firm, I thought. Linda returned before Bryan could wind up to say anything more, and he settled back as she dimmed the lights and the first video started.

She was serious about us watching a lot of videos.

Holy crap.

They had a video for everything.

Videos on the company, and okay, the parts on the history of the company were kind of interesting. Especially the bits about Grandpa Ted. He even appeared in a few of them. I tuned out on the Edward parts. Just, no thanks. I kind of hoped Archie would be in one, but I only caught a glimpse of him in the background when they were talking about the future.

There were videos on each department. Then there were videos on sexual harassment and on behavioral expectations in the workplace. I actually caught myself zoning out on a couple of them, until they began discussing Standish's work on the environment when it came to land development. The company was huge with sprawling and diverse interests.

I was the worst girlfriend on the planet. I literally knew nothing about what this company did, so I tried to take mental notes and real ones. All of this was going to be Archie's someday, and that thought just froze me in place.

Seriously, when he talked about the company, he couldn't sound more disinterested, but it would be his. My stomach bottomed out, and I forced myself to focus. Maybe this internship here was the best plan. I'd at least know what he had to deal with, and maybe I could be helpful.

How?

Well, I'd figure that out.

By the time we got to lunch, my head was swimming with facts and figures. At lunch, I shot off some texts to the guys so they knew I was alive, and that I'd just spent four hours watching videos about the company and my brain hurt.

Archie

Sorry, babe, it doesn't get more interesting.

I didn't say it wasn't interesting, but I didn't argue with him for now.

Bryan looked about as dazed as I was, and he spent as much time on his phone as I did while we ate and we didn't talk. I took a quick bathroom break, and then we were on to the afternoon portion of the day.

I didn't die of boredom.

But I did think I strained my brain trying to store all the facts and figures. I was so screwed when it came to meeting the department heads. I was never going to remember their names. Hopefully, I could check out their profiles on the corporate website.

We made it all the way to the end of the day before Mr. Standish put on an appearance. I steeled myself for the interaction, but I wasn't sure what stunned me more—his brief welcoming smile and firm handshake before he left Bryan and I, or the black eye he had.

Well, that explained Archie's bruised knuckles.

Holy crap.

By the time I got into the car to go home, I just wanted to go to sleep right there. Thankfully, Rachel talked to me on the phone all the way back in traffic, 'cause I was dying. My guys were all waiting for me when I got home with food, foot massages, and questions.

I managed to answer about half of them before I fell asleep, and the next morning, I had no idea who tucked me in, just that I was sandwiched between Coop and Archie, warm and safe, and my head still hurt when I woke up.

And that was just our first day. We hadn't even done any real work.

Chapter Ten

LOOK WHAT YOU MADE ME DO

"Rach?" I called as soon as I was in the bathroom.

"Last stall." Aggravation vibrated in her voice. I slid right up to the door and then squatted to pass my emergency pack of pads underneath. "I am so annoyed right now." She took them from my fingers.

"I'm sorry," I told her. It definitely sucked when the period started out of nowhere. I did a quick glance around and then asked, "Are you good with panties? I actually have a new pair with me."

Dead silence from the other side of the door.

I could almost picture her facial contortions. "Put away your dirty thoughts, Manning. I keep a clean pair with my emergency pack *just in case.*" I'd been caught unawares a couple of times, and there was very little that was worse in my opinion.

"My reasoning was *so* much better." The tartness in her tone was so much better than the earlier aggravation. "Also, the temptation to say I have a pair of your panties is really doing my mood wonders."

I rolled my eyes. "Keep it up, and I'll rescind the offer."

"You won't," she teased. "You love me."

"I do love you," I said. "I also spoil you and let you get away with too much teasing, and it would do you good."

Her laughter made me grin. "Fair point," she admitted. "Yes, please, can I borrow your panties?"

"You can keep them," I teased and tugged the little pack out of my backpack and slid it under the door. "Don't say I never gave you anything."

She snorted, but the smile in her voice was unmistakable. "Thank you, Frankie. You're my favorite."

And just because smug could be fun, I said, "I know. I'm the best."

The door to the hall opened and let Sharon in. The blonde made it two steps before she froze and stared at me. I'd seen her here and there, but I hadn't been looking for her to be honest. Her nose looked all right. She'd had plenty of time to heal from our last encounter.

Me too, as it happened.

The flushing of the toilet broke through the impasse, and Sharon jerked her gaze away from me. Yeah. Blink, bitch.

Any residual sympathy I'd held for her had long-since died. If she stayed in her lane and away from me and the guys, I'd leave her alone. Crossing to the sink, I turned the water on to wash my hands, but I tracked Sharon in the mirror. She made it two more steps to a stall and then glanced at me again.

"So you really are a slut," she muttered.

Shutting the water off after rinsing my hands, I reached for the paper towels and turned to face Sharon again as Rachel's stall opened.

"Excuse the fuck out of you?" she demanded, but I held up a hand.

"I got this. You go ahead and finish," I assured her, and Rachel cut a look at me, eyes glittering. "Seriously," I told her. "I got this."

Sharon snorted. "You got something."

I glanced back at her and smiled. Her brow tightened, and my grin widened. It was unnerving as fuck when you were trying to piss someone off and they grinned at you. It made it harder to get under their skin.

Archie proved that time and time again.

"You actually think I give a fuck about your opinion," I said. It wasn't a question. "What's even more impressive is you think your opinion has value. Though now that I think about it, it's more sad than it is impressive."

"I think you're fucking four guys," Sharon spit out. "That's kind of the definition of a slut."

"I think you're jealous, because you wish it was you and you've pretty much shot yourself in the foot with them even bothering to look at you, much less piss on you if you were on fire."

"Damn," Rachel mouthed as she washed her hands.

"I also no longer have time for meaningless friendships, forced interactions, or unnecessary conversations. You used me. You wanted me out of the way. You participated in trying to terrorize me. You failed, spectacularly, and it blew up in your face, along with your broken nose."

Sharon flinched. Tears actually welled in her eyes. "I hate you."

"I don't care," I said, and the rage and hurt in her voice rolled right off of me. Once upon a time, I felt bad for her. I couldn't find it in me anymore.

With a strangled scream, she pivoted on her heel and slammed out of the bathroom, damn near knocking over two freshmen on her way out.

Rachel slung an arm around my shoulder. "That was hot as fuck…"

I rolled my eyes. "Come on, we're gonna be late to French."

"Did I ever tell you you're my hero," she sang as she followed me out, and I laughed. "Everything I would like to be…"

There was a freedom in being pushed past the point of compassion with people who just wanted to use it to hurt you. Coop had given me the biggest grin when I got to lit and then leaned over to whisper about how sexy me being a badass was. I didn't ask him how he knew, but I thumped him when Ms. Fajardo wasn't looking and he laughed.

At lunch, I handed him my backpack so I could take the helmet and climb on the back of Ian's bike. We were all going to eat, but it was a relatively nice day with sunshine and in the mid-sixties. And I wouldn't freeze my ass off on the back of the bike.

Soon as I had my arms around Ian, he glanced back at me. "Ready?"

"Yep."

We led the way out of the lot and blew right past Sharon and a couple of her friends. I'd invited Rachel to come to lunch, but it was her half-day and she had a date with chocolate and a shower before she had to go to work. I promised to call her later.

Cramps sucked.

Surprise cramps sucked worse.

One upside of the implant, my periods were moderately better. I still got them, but they weren't trying to kill me and they were shorter. I was calling it a win.

At the stop light, Ian put his hand over mine where I'd tucked them against his abdomen. No words, just a soothing rub, and then we were off again. Lunchtime traffic was a little heavy, but nice weather in January always brought people out. It was supposed to drop back below freezing this weekend.

When we reached the barbecue place, Jake pulled in right behind us. He really did like to follow when I was on Ian's bike. After I climbed off, Ian said, "You busy this weekend? I know you have a date with Archie tomorrow to make up for last week."

"No plans yet. I mean, I have to work at Mason's on Saturday."

"Save your evening for me?"

"I can do that," I teased as I backed up a couple of steps. "What did you have in mind?"

"You'll see," he winked, taking my helmet and his to set inside Jake's

SUV before sliding an arm around me. If we hadn't been close to the school, we'd have left them on the seats, but he didn't risk anything since the incident with my car. Then he pressed his lips right to my ear as we followed the guys. "Dress comfortably but in loose clothing. We might be out late."

A full shiver raced up my spine. No complaints here. "Sounds good to me."

Archie eyed us as we got in line with them. "What sounds good?"

"Just staking my claim on Saturday night," Ian told them. "We'll be late. No one wait up."

Coop snorted. "That doesn't mean no one sleep over."

"Actually," Ian said, "it does mean that. Thanks for the reminder."

"Nice," Jake said with a laugh as he elbowed Coop. "If you'd kept your mouth shut, we could have just been there."

Clasping my free hand in his, Archie murmured, "We're gonna stay at my place tomorrow, if that's cool with you?"

I grinned. "I have to work Saturday morning, so just don't let me oversleep."

"Don't let you sleep," Archie agreed. "Done."

I laughed, and then we were giving our orders. Jake paid for mine before Archie could, and I stared up at the ceiling as Coop laughed at me. At the rate we were going, they were never going to let me pay for anything and it was sweet, but…

"Don't make that face," Coop cajoled as he tugged me away from Ian and followed after a bickering Archie and Jake. "We like spoiling you. Besides, boyfriends pay for food. It's a rule."

"Where is it a rule?"

"It just is," Jake informed me. He also *had* my food since he'd filled a tray, and he started offloading it and putting my food in front of the chair right next to him. Coop stole the seat on my other side as Archie and Ian glared at them.

"No teaming up," Archie snarked, and Jake snorted.

"Too late, that ship has most assuredly come and gone," Jake said with a wicked grin.

"And come again and again," Coop threw on top, and my face flamed.

"Funny," Archie tossed out there.

"Hilarious," Ian added dryly.

Almost as one, Coop and Jake grinned and made mock bows. "Thank you," Coop said. "Frankie definitely enjoyed it."

That earned him an elbow in the gut, and he grinned at me.

"Now, Frankie," Ian said in an almost soothing tone. "You have to cut them a break. We all heard about how you staked your claim today. I gotta say, it was hot."

"You heard?" I picked up a french fry and debated just eating the fries and the ribs. If my mouth was full, I didn't have to answer any questions.

"Oh yeah, Baby Girl," Jake said, stretching an arm along the back of my chair and knocking Coop's off. "We heard you were *badass*."

"Remind me to kill Rachel," I said with a half-smile.

"Wasn't Rachel," Archie informed me. "Besides, she's a vault about you most of the time. She only brings stuff up to smack us back to our place."

"She does do that," Ian mused.

"But she gives excellent advice," Coop informed us as he scooped up his sandwich. "And she knows the best places…"

"Feeling blue?" I asked him, even if my ears were still burning, and Coop gave me a teasing grin.

"Aww, I was just playing." He raised his eyebrows as if daring me.

I picked up a fry and bit it in half, emphatically, and his eyes danced. We could play chicken, but I had him, blue bobs and all.

Leaning forward, he kissed my nose. "You're adorable when you get all riled up."

"We're missing something," Archie mused.

"Yep," Jake said. "They have their own language sometimes. We just need to tickle it out of Frankie later."

"Ha." It was Jake's turn to get an elbow, and he made a mock *oof* sound, then nuzzled my ear with a kiss that tickled like hell.

"It could work," he added, still laughing. Across the table, Ian studied me for a long moment and the expression in his eyes intrigued me.

"Good to know," he murmured, then picked up his own sandwich and another shiver danced up my spine. Jake pulled my chair a little closer as if I were cold, and I liked leaning into him, so I kept the why on that delightful bit of anticipation to myself.

After that, lunch switched to debates about spring training that would start up in a couple of months and various players on the baseball teams. I liked baseball. I was not married to it and I couldn't quote stats. But I liked games.

I really liked stadium food and hot dogs.

It was also really nice to just listen to them while I leaned against Jake, and I then switched to leaning against Coop when Jake had to hit the restroom. As we were getting ready to leave, Coop snapped his fingers. "That reminds me, I still have your mail."

Oh. I made a face. "It's probably just bills. I can get it later."

"I got it," Archie said with a grin, and I glared at him. "What?"

"You can't keep paying for everything."

"Sure I can," he grinned. "It's in the boyfriend rules."

"Who said?"

"Everyone," all four of them answered, and I rolled my eyes.

"See?" Archie spread his hands. "It's done. Don't worry about it."

What was I supposed to do with them?

On the way out, Archie wrapped an arm around my waist and tugged me against him. "Don't be mad…"

"I'm not mad."

"Yeah you are," he continued, lowering his voice. "You're a little mad, and I'm being a little pushy."

I shot him a look.

"Okay, I'm being a lot pushy. But I like taking care of you."

"I have to be able to take care of myself."

For the most part, Coop, Jake, and Ian all lagged behind us as we headed out. I guessed Archie was supposed to take this hit for the team.

"You do," Archie agreed. "Just like you look after us, too. So…maybe a compromise?"

"I thought that was a four-letter word with you," I couldn't resist pointing out, wrinkling my nose but having a hard time fighting a grin.

"In business. You are not business." At the SUV, he wrapped both arms around me, and I leaned into him as he tilted his head. "We'll open them up together, and if it's bad, I'll take care of it. If it's nothing that makes you freak out…you take care of it."

I squinted at him. "So if it's like a couple grand, and I don't have a heart attack…"

He made a face.

"Rules are rules," I pointed out. "This was *your* compromise."

It was Archie's turn to look skyward. "In all fairness, you're right. I'll probably still try to take care of it and then do some significant groveling to earn your forgiveness afterward. I mean…since we're compromising."

I laughed. "You're impossible."

"Not for you," he said, then cupped my face and kissed me. I sighed right into the contact, everything else just falling away.

"Man, he can talk himself out of just about anything," Coop admired. "Boy has skills. I say we keep him."

Jake laughed, and I giggled.

"You guys suck," Archie complained, then gave me another kiss before letting me go to grab my helmet. I was bouncing and ready to get back on the motorcycle.

"Actually," I teased as I buckled it on and Ian got the bike started. "They don't."

"No?" Archie inquired, and I swung my leg over to climb onto the bike behind Ian.

"Nope, they don't suck," I said with a wink. "I do."

His eyes flashed, and I blew him a kiss.

Ian was laughing as he backed the bike out, but not before Coop and Jake both groaned.

I missed whatever they called out, but I laughed all the way back to school.

Jake and I spent our study time in the library exploring all our options at NYU. Then he let me dig into MIT and Harvard for him and Archie, even as he reminded me that they weren't going to Boston unless we all went to Boston.

And just like that, we started checking into other Boston-area colleges. Sure, Harvard and MIT were huge, but they weren't the only schools in town. Jake's sisters kept blowing up his phone, and when I asked, all he said was they were fighting and wanted him to choose sides.

"And who did you pick?"

He grinned. "You."

I laughed, but it was sweet.

My TA period flew past, and Mr. G had more timed writing and sample tests for us in the AP Euro. I flew through the exam easy peasy, and I was feeling pretty good about it when I beat Jake by a solid minute on turning it in.

I was pretty sure my smug grin said it all, but he mimed tickling and I flipped him off, discreetly of course. Mr. G was cool, but probably better not to borrow trouble. Ian texted as we were heading out to the car. Jake and Coop were both working tonight, while Archie promised to be over later, but he had to spend some time in his workshop for whatever his and Jake's new project was.

They were being cagey and not telling any of us what the *secret* project was.

Which I had to stay ahead on because beginning the following week, I'd be spending two days a week at Standish. Couldn't wait.

Really.

I grinned at that, and Jake gave me a squeeze as we headed for his SUV. Coop had brought his own car because he'd planned to work right after.

"You want to come with?" Jake offered. "We can hang out and maybe make out in between orders."

I laughed. "The last time we said we were going to do that, there was never a lull."

"True," he said with a grin. "Still can't hurt to try."

"I'd love to, actually, but…don't take this the wrong way, but I'm kind of looking forward to a little me time tonight."

I loved that I never *had* to be alone, but sometimes, I missed having the quiet time when it was just me.

"Not taking it the wrong way at all," Jake murmured, before he gave me a kiss. "I'm still coming back after work though, yeah?" He brushed my hair back behind one ear.

"Yes, please," I said. "Not going to lie. I do not like sleeping alone anymore."

"Well, you don't have to and I get it. I'm not a huge fan of it either." Neither of us made any move, either me getting out of the car or Jake pausing in twining one lock of my hair around his finger. "Want me to bring you dinner when I come back?"

"Nah, there's still Chinese leftovers from last night. I'll heat up some moo goo gai pan after I feed the cats and get in my pajamas, then I'm going to do all the homework."

He gave my hair the gentlest of tugs. "Text me if you change your mind, okay?"

Cupping his face, I leaned over to kiss him again. This one longer and more lingering, until he huffed out a little growl.

"Time to go, Baby Girl, or I'm going to skip work and you're not going to get any time to yourself."

"Not sure if that's a threat..." I teased him as I slid out of the car and hooked my backpack over one shoulder, "...or a promise."

Unsurprisingly, he waited until I had the backdoor unlocked and open before he backed out of his spot. I turned on some music, fed the cats, and then grabbed a quick shower before I changed. I liked having the time to just let my hair dry and not have to blow it out. Out of the shower, I nudged the heat up because the warm day had given way to the very chilly late afternoon and evening.

Tiddles trotted after me as I padded into the kitchen, and I got my plate of leftovers ready and in the microwave before I carried my backpack to the living room. There were signs of the guys everywhere. Coop's jacket—or one of them anyway—over the back of a recliner. It was new and had just mysteriously showed up here this week, along with the new loveseat.

I loved it when they all played dumb and innocent. Except Archie, he totally threw Jeremy under the bus. His logic was I couldn't say no to Jeremy, right?

Sometimes, they were too cute. Probably a good thing.

For the next couple of hours, I focused on getting through as many assignments as I could. One of the best parts of this semester's syllabi was they included nearly all of our homework, and while we couldn't turn it all in early, I could get it done early.

The more I did, the less I had to worry about, and the guys still filled in a lot of hours, but I also had work and now the internship. I checked the time. I had another hour, at least, before Coop would be done. Though he might work later. He and Jake sometimes did a long shift so they didn't have to go out every evening.

I had time to knock out the last book on the AP reading list, and I could curl up with ice cream while I did it.

I'd just opened the fridge when the door lock jiggled but didn't open. I paused and stared at the door. Then it did it again. Locking it was automatic, especially since the guys all had keys. I doubted it was one of them, since they usually texted me when they were on their way. I closed the freezer and headed for my phone.

No messages.

The hard knock as I glanced at my screen made me jump. My heart hammered, even as the knock turned almost violent, like a fist hitting the door.

"Open this damn door, Frankie, I see your car out here."

Maddy's voice had me sagging in relief. Not that I wanted to see her, but the last thing I wanted was the sudden vision I had of Mitch being the asshole knocking on my door.

Blowing out a harsh breath, I walked over to the door. I could just ignore her. She couldn't actually see inside and her keys didn't work. Another hard knock, and I debated it.

My phone buzzed in my hand.

Maddy

We need to talk.

No, we really didn't.

Maddy

I've given you more than enough time to indulge this tantrum.

Tantrum.

Just like that, I retreated from the backdoor, opened the freezer, and pulled out the pint of ice cream. That and a spoon in hand, I walked away from the door and headed for my bedroom. I fired off a text to the group chat about her being outside the door and that I wasn't answering.

Archie

I'll wrap up and head there. Definitely don't answer the door.

Jake

I've got one more order to deliver and I'm coming.

Coop

I just dropped off an order. I can head there now, but I'm 30 minutes away.

Ian

Coming, Angel.

I smiled at the near instantaneous responses.

Me

I'm fine. Just do your thing. I'm not answering the door. I'm in bed with ice cream and a book. It's all good.

There was a beat, then my phone vibrated madly with several texts.

Archie

Definitely coming now.

Ian

Wouldn't miss it.

Jake

Killing me, Baby Girl.

Coop

Fuck all three of you for being closer than me.

I cracked up and rubbed a hand over my face. They wouldn't change their minds, and I didn't mind the backup, either.

Maddy

You can't hide from me forever.

Maddy

We have a lot to discuss, you and I.

Maddy

And if you insist on using lawyers, I can do that.

Maddy

Eddie told me yours is one of his. I can ask him to put a stop to that.

Maddy

I'm trying to cut you a break.

One text after another hit my phone, and I could almost hear her spitting the words out.

Maddy

Frankie, you could at least talk to me. You owe me that much.

I stared at the phone screen as I spooned out another bite of ice cream. I didn't owe her shit.

Maddy

Call me. Don't make me do something you'll regret.

Nope.

I took screenshots of the messages, then sent them all to Mr. Wittaker. He didn't answer, but it was evening and the man probably had a life. Still, I didn't get a single word read or relax while I sat there eating my ice cream, until the sound of the backdoor opening made me jump.

"It's me," Ian called. "Arch is right behind me."

Yes.

Much better.

Chapter Eleven
BOOM CLAP

The guys may have speculated amongst themselves about Maddy's surprise visit, but through unspoken agreement, they didn't discuss it with me and I was glad for that. Avoidance and denial weren't positive coping techniques. Erin would not approve.

But ambushing me was also seriously *not* cool.

Everyone stayed over, but Jake and Coop won rock paper scissors to sleep with me, and I had never been so amused in my life when they wanted rematches over and over. Still, Coop crowded me right into Jake, and I slept soundly.

Jake left super early and retrieved donuts for us, and they were in the kitchen when I came out from my shower. Coffee and donuts here was kind of nice, and the fact that my apple fritters were hot and fresh had me kissing Jake enthusiastically enough that all the guys were adjusting their jeans. I never thought about the idea of affecting them as crazily as they did me, and it was a heady kind of power.

"Oh," Coop said around the donut he held between his teeth as he dragged his backpack open. "Before I forget." It came out a lot more unintelligible than that, but I could speak Coop. He dug out a stack of familiar, if slightly crumpled and thoroughly beaten up envelopes.

Archie went to snatch them, but Coop yanked them away and scolded him, his voice muffled by the donut between his teeth. When Archie cut a look at me, I grinned.

"He said, you and I had a deal."

With a roll of his eyes, Archie pinned Coop with a look. "Boyfriend tax. Hand it over."

Boyfriend. Tax.

I spluttered and the coffee came out my nose, then I was coughing and my eyes were watering. Ian rubbed my back gently and gave me an amused albeit sympathetic smile. "It's part of boyfriend privileges," he explained, his eyes practically dancing as I tried to quiet my gasping for air.

At the distraction, Jake snagged the envelopes and then grinned. "What will you give me for them, Frankie?"

"I'll give you a fat lip," Archie threatened, but the absolute lack of violence in his voice promised he wasn't serious.

"Right," Jake said, his grin growing. "That's why I'm not asking you."

"Let me guess," I managed to say, no longer spluttering, and at least I'd managed to not get coffee all over myself. Score. "You want a kiss."

Wearing a sly look, Jake cocked his head. "I'm open to negotiation."

Ian shook his head as I scooted around the table and Jake grinned. Planting one hand on the table top, I leaned in close. Jake's pale blue eyes flared, and his lips parted. "Negotiation?" I murmured.

"Negotiation," he agreed. The clean fresh scent of him was aftershave free. He didn't always wear it. That was a good thing.

"Good to know." I closed the distance, then licked him from the corner of his mouth to near his eye. He let out a bark of laughter as I snatched the letters and danced backward.

Amusement rolled around the table, and Archie caught me with both arms around my waist and pressing up against my back. "Well played," he said.

"Thank you," I laughed, but wiggled when he tried to get the mail.

"At this rate, we're never getting out of here," Coop said, grinning almost wickedly. Heat licked its way through me at the suggestion, and my nipples stabbed at my bra. Damn. Just spending the day together and playing like we had in Colorado? Yes, fucking please.

At my sigh, Archie stopped trying to pluck the letters from my hand. "You want to just call it and skip today, babe?"

Ian grinned at my expression. "I'm going to say the answer to that is yes. The real question is…"

"Will she be able to do it," Jake finished for him. "Do you have any tests today? Any projects that you haven't already turned in? I mean, technically, you won't be at school on Fridays from this week for the next six or seven, right? So you could just get started early."

"No tests," I admitted, then chewed at my lower lip as I leaned back against Archie. Skipping wouldn't kill me.

"GPAs are locked, Frankie," Coop reminded me. "Colleges have already seen them. How are you on homework?"

"I got a lot done last night, and I've got one book left for lit." Still…

"No tests. No projects due. No more Fridays with us for a few weeks…" It was that last wistful comment from Archie that clinched it.

"Sold." And just like that, the twist of guilt in my gut vanished, and I tilted my head back to find Archie giving me a slow smile.

"Really?"

"Yeah, you guys are right. I'd rather spend the day with all four of you than bouncing from class to class. I need to text Rach so she isn't looking for me…" Fuck, there was the guilt again.

"Tell her she's more than welcome to come hang out," Coop offered, even as Jake and Ian swung their heads to half-glare at him. Unperturbed, he spread his legs as he sprawled back in the chair, donut in one hand and looking quite pleased with himself. "She's almost as much of an overachiever as you, but she'd appreciate the invitation."

"And if she accepts?" Jake asked dryly. "There goes some of our plans for the day."

I grinned. "Only some?"

"Well, for them anyway," Archie said with a grin. "I'll still be taking you out tonight."

True.

When he tapped my fingers, I let him have the letters as I twisted to press a kiss to his jaw. "Open them here where I can see them."

He grunted, but gave my waist a squeeze as I retrieved my phone. Back at the table, I grabbed my next apple fritter and then perched in Ian's lap when he gave me a tug, while I sent the text to Rachel before biting into the fritter. Multi-tasking win for the day.

Jake grabbed his keys and headed for the door. At my questioning look, he grinned. "Going to get coffee for our girl." He dropped a kiss on my lips. "I might even get something for these guys—"

"What the fuck is this?" Archie muttered, and Jake pivoted even as I glanced over to see the paper in his hands. He had the first two envelopes open, and he set them on the table. Then the third.

Grabbing one of the sheets, I stared at…*lab results?*

No one said anything.

There were identification numbers listed for samples. Two samples to be exact. At the bottom of the page, it read *No Match*.

DNA reports.

Ice seemed to slick over my skin as I stared at each sheet as Archie set them out.

Four pieces of paper.

Four innocuous, wrinkled pieces of paper.

Each one with sample numbers.

One sample number was the same on every sheet.

The other was always different.

No Match.

No Match.

No Match.

Match.

The lab where the work was done was the same. All in New York. That was why none of the letters had return addresses. They were anonymous, I supposed.

"We don't know what this means…" Coop had begun, but even he couldn't quite make the words work.

Archie hadn't even waited to speculate. He'd picked up the sheet with the words *Match* and pulled out his phone. Currently, he stood in the middle of the living room with his phone to his ear, snapping out something to the person at that lab. I kind of felt sorry for them. He was pissed.

Rubbing his chin gently against my shoulder, Ian tugged me back against him. Jake hadn't left yet, he kept dividing his attention between me and Archie. Coop studied one of the pages and then asked, "What's the date on those?"

I turned them around so he could see them. Honestly, there wasn't enough information on there to make out anything.

Maddy's name and information was in the report's "requested by" field. She was also listed as a maternal match to the sample that had to be me, unless she had some hidden fucking kid out there. Hey, maybe that was what she wanted to talk to me about…

"Think Maddy had a kid she didn't know she had?"

"Yeah," Jake said flatly. "You."

Okay. So, not really a joke. All the playfulness in the day kind of deflated.

"…then get someone on the phone who possesses enough of a clue to answer the question," Archie snapped, and I winced at the frosty level of his tone. "No, I don't want your apology or a call back. I want to speak to someone in authority about unauthorized samples and their analysis. You can find someone to answer those questions in five minutes, or you can expect to hear from my lawyer and government inspectors. Tick. Tock."

"How long before Archie tries to buy the lab?" Coop asked, and my gut bottomed out.

"He won't." Ian rubbed a slow circle against my abdomen. The gentle, rhythmic action soothed some of the disquiet looking at the tests triggered.

I mean, you didn't have to be a rocket scientist to recognize paternity tests or at least DNA matches that suggested paternity.

Four tests.

Four candidates for my father.

Gentlemen, come on down. You're the next contestants on Who's Your Daddy?

Wow, Maddy needed tests to figure it out, because what? She'd been with them too close together to know for sure?

My stomach sank all over again, and I reached up to tug on my ponytail.

"Good," Archie snapped suddenly. "Then you can answer my questions. I have a test here with the following sample numbers… I need the identities to go with the numbers, as well as when these tests were requested."

A beat of silence then.

"You absolutely can if you're authorized by one of those who was tested. Or are you in the business of invading someone's privacy at the whim of another? Because I can assure you, she did *not* consent to have you analyze her DNA."

"You know," Jake mused. "I really kind of like it when he gets all arrogant and issues orders in his *obey me or else* tone."

"Me too," I exhaled. That was much nicer to think about over the actual content of the call or even the reasons behind it.

Three sets of eyes focused on me with such intensity, I had to smile. "I think you're all sexy as hell, too. Don't be hating."

They all laughed, and Coop's eyes warmed as he covered one of my hands with his and squeezed. Beneath his amusement—well, all of theirs really—was a thread of relief and tension. Ian's arms tightened where he held me, and Jake cupped the back of my neck and I tilted my head obediently for another kiss.

"I'll get the coffee. You still want it, right?"

"I'd kill for it right now," I admitted.

"You want to go with me?" The offer was light, but I saw it for exactly what it was—a lifeline to get out of the conversation if I wanted it.

I had thought I couldn't love him more.

I was wrong.

"I'll always want to go with you," I told him. "But I want and need to stay here too. Especially if Archie needs me to tell someone that I didn't spit in a cup or give any samples for this."

"Could have been hair," Coop speculated. "Could have been—"

"Let's not." The sharpness in Ian's tone silenced Coop, and I found myself wanting to soothe them.

"Yeah," Coop agreed. "For now." But he didn't seem remotely bothered by it.

"I'll be back," Jake said, but I didn't miss the way he glanced at me and then gave Coop a hard look. I would assume he did the same to Ian, but I got it. They were worried.

Me too. The door closed behind Jake, and I chewed on my thumbnail, staring at Archie as he paced. Tiddles sat right in the middle of the coffee table, tracking his motions as his tail lashed. I wanted to be on that call and nowhere near it.

I wished we'd never opened the stupid letters.

And I wish I'd never let them sit there for months.

Did she not care about them? I mean…they'd come in when she was still semi-around. Technically speaking. So, why not do something with them? Why keep them…?

"When were the first results sent?" Archie's question had me shifting again. I was still nibbling on my thumbnail when Ian gripped my hand and tugged it away from my mouth. Dammit, I'd stopped chewing my nails years ago. I squeezed his fingers, and he tightened his grip on mine. Whatever the people on the phone said to Archie, he quieted, because his response didn't carry.

I should be the one calling and raising holy hell. I was still processing the fact there were DNA tests in the first place. I glanced back at the three not matches sitting on the table. "Do you think…" I didn't know what to think.

"Not gonna speculate," Ian said quietly. "We don't know enough, and the minute we start speculating or assuming, we invite a lot of assumptions. We have no idea what all this means, Angel."

"Don't borrow trouble?" It was pretty good advice.

"More or less," Coop said, agreeing as he pulled out a sprinkles and chocolate covered donut and held it up to me.

"I'm good," I said with a shake of my head, ignoring his askance look. Yeah, I didn't usually turn down food. Turning down chocolate and sprinkles was worrisome, but the two apple fritters I ate earlier—savored really—sat like hard lumps in my stomach.

I glared back down at the papers again. Fucking Maddy. It had been a good day right up until we opened those letters. Letters I'd been carrying for months, so yeah, maybe I should have opened them, but I kept forgetting they were there.

There were so many other more important things. But fucking Maddy kept destroying everything she touched.

I picked up my phone and tabbed over to the text messages from her the night before. One after another, I scrolled through them, and then I scrolled up to the handful—bare handful—we'd shared over the last few months.

We'd talked so little, it took almost no scrolling to get to last summer and the messages canceling our trips back east to see colleges because she was "working."

The empty promises.

The excuses.

The lack of interest.

"I want the names," Archie said as he walked back into the kitchen, his shoulders squared and his eyes blazing. "I'll give you until Monday, but consider you and your entire lab on notice. I will be contacting my attorneys today, and if it takes filing suit against you for invasion of privacy and damages, you can be damned sure I'll do it."

He didn't look away from me once when he gave a mirthless little smile at whatever the man on the phone said.

"Maybe," he conceded without any kind of concession. It was a marvel how he did that. "But let's put it this way, I can afford to make your life and your lab very uncomfortable. Can you?" He didn't wait for an answer, he just ended the call and then stared at me. "Jake go get coffee?"

"Yep."

He nodded and shoved his phone in his pocket before holding out a hand to me. I clasped his hand and let him pull me to my feet.

"Let's go, boys. You guys are dressed fine, but Frankie needs to change."

"I do?"

"Yep," he said, tugging me toward our room—well, my room really, but it had grown to be ours more and more. "We're not doing this… We're not sitting around and staring at those letters. We know they're DNA tests, and we're assuming that you're the donor being matched with a paternal sample."

In my room, he opened the closet and then eyed me before looking over what was in there. Curious, and a little bit amused, I folded my arms and waited. He still hadn't said *what* we were going to do.

"Without more data, we're going to be chasing ourselves in circles." He slanted a look at me. "So, we have two choices. We can sit here stewing about it all, which is not my favorite choice, but I will if you need it. Or we can get changed, wait for Jake to get back here, and go do something fun." He glanced past me. "All of us. Tonight is still mine, but I can share today."

"Generous," Coop said with a smirk, and flopped onto the bed. Tiddles leapt up to walk over and flop on his chest, motorboat purring until Coop began petting him. "So what is the plan then?"

"WeFLY."

"Excuse me?"

"WeFLY," he repeated, and then pulled out one of the Torched long sleeve sweatshirts I hadn't gotten to wear yet. The rose on fire had always appealed to me. At the drawers of my dresser, he pulled open the second on the right and lifted out a pair of my yoga pants. "Indoor skydiving."

"Holy shit," Coop said, bouncing upward, and Tiddles leapt off the bed with a note of disgust.

"Seriously?" Ian gaped at him, but there was absolutely no disguising the thrill on their faces or the wide grins they suddenly sported.

Almost instantly, they were peppering Archie with questions and warmth suffused me. Even as Archie answered them with this adorable little smile and indulgent look, he kept glancing at me. Oh, I needed to change.

I stripped hurriedly to swap outfits out. I had to toe off my shoes before peeling down my jeans, and once I was dressed again, I sat on the edge of the bed to pull on my shoes. "I didn't think there was a place close by."

"There's one close enough," Archie said.

"When did you plan this?"

"Multi-tasking is an art," he told me with a wink. "Trust me?"

"Yes." No hesitation at all. Not that Archie couldn't still pick on me sometimes or tease me. I'd hate it if he ever thought he couldn't play with me. But no doubt existed in me. I could trust him. Even when he drove me crazy trying to take care of everything… "Boyfriend privilege."

"Yes," Coop cheered with a fist pump before he high-fived Ian, and I laughed. "Told you she would come around. Boyfriend privileges rock."

Ten minutes later, Jake was back and we headed down to his SUV to meet him. They'd briefed him on what we were doing, and I sat in the back with Coop and Archie while Ian rode up front. It took us ninety minutes of driving, but we sang along with the music, laughed, teased, and played.

You know what we didn't do?

We didn't discuss the letters, the results, none of it. It kept trying to creep back in, and then Ian would smile back at me, or Jake would switch the song right in the middle of one we liked that he didn't, or Coop would decide to randomly tickle me. They were all looking after me.

When we got to the place…

I got to fly.

For real.

I forgot all about Maddy and the rest as we spent two hours learning how to ride the wind, and I even managed a couple of tricks. I might never dance in the air like Emersyn Sharpe or be an aerialist or super hero—and I was never, ever jumping out of a perfectly good airplane for real—but I could fly.

It was awesome.

Even better…

I was still humming when we hit an all-you-can-eat sushi place for lunch.

The buzz carried us on the drive back, and to the apartment. Someone had put the letters up before we left, and I didn't look for them. I just went to get changed for my date with Archie, but he caught my hand and pulled me back.

"We're going to do simple tonight," he said. "So just grab what you need to spend the night?"

Simple was lasagna and garlic bread, followed by huge ice cream sundaes with Jeremy, who actually deigned to join us for fifteen minutes so we could talk about colleges with him before he told us to enjoy our "date" and leave him the clean-up.

In his room, Archie insisted we had to be naked to enjoy popcorn and the movies he'd picked out. For atmosphere…

"It's *Jurassic Park*," I argued as he queued up the first one. "Why do we have to be *naked*?"

"It's a mood, an aesthetic. Our ancestors in the caves didn't wear much either."

"There weren't humans in the Jurassic era."

He paused to eye me, then reached up and pulled his shirt off. It hit the floor. Followed by his belt, then his jeans and his boxers. "Your point?"

I grinned. "You're still trying to distract me."

"No, babe, I promise. Right now, I just want you naked so I can hold you for all the jump scares and see how excited you get. Then we're going fuck for an intermission before we kick off the next movie."

"What if I want to do something during the first movie?"

"Then we're not watching *Jurassic Park* because I will never turn you down, but it's a sacrilege to ignore the movie."

That did it. I cracked up, and he grinned. It was exactly what he meant. So I got naked—not like it was a hardship—and Archie nudged up the heat in his room so we didn't freeze, and we curled up on the bed with the popcorn and drinks.

We made it about halfway through the movie before he proved to both of us that he was no longer as invested in watching the movie. Of course, the fact we could *pause* it didn't hurt. We finished the last bit in a boneless heap, and I was almost too relaxed to jump at the velociraptors.

Almost.

But later, after we finished the second movie and curled up, my mind circled back to the results…

"I'm going to have to talk to her," I murmured, and he sighed before pressing a kiss to my shoulder blade right over my tattoo, and my heart squeezed.

"I know, babe. But not tonight, and not until you're ready. You set the terms and you decide when." He tucked his face against my throat and snuggled my back to his chest. "Then we'll ambush the bitch and see how she likes it."

Ambush her.

"I like it."

"Good. Now sleep, I'm right here."

I sighed, and I tried to go to sleep. I really tried, but the one thought kept niggling at me. "Archie…what if she tells me something really horrible? Like my father is in prison or he didn't want me or whatever? I mean, she doesn't seem to have known who…"

"One, we don't know why there are multiple tests. We are assuming she needed to determine paternity out of a list of possible candidates, but we're not sure."

Fair. We were probably right, but fair.

"Two, I don't care if your father is a boring accountant from Akron, Ohio or the leader of some gang of thugs. He's a sperm donor, and who he is has nothing to do with you."

I liked that.

"Three, her decisions aren't yours, Frankie. She's an adult. Those choices have been and always will be about herself. It's not on you to excuse it or understand it. You don't owe her the time of day, much less a thought process considering her behavior."

Someone had thought about this. I turned my head a little, seeking him in the dark, and he rubbed his cheek to mine.

"And four, most important of all, I love you. We all do. You're not alone. I'll have your back every step of the way. I promise, I'm not going any-fucking-where."

Interlacing my fingers with his, I pressed a kiss to his lips. It wasn't deep or passionate, more a brush and hold, a token and acknowledgement. "I love you. Thank you."

"Always, babe." Another kiss. "Always." After a beat, he asked, "Think you can sleep now?"

Yeah. I absolutely could sleep.

And I did.

Every time I jerked awake from a dream I couldn't remember, he was right there.

Just like he promised.

Chapter Twelve
LOVE ON TOP

Saturday dawned dreary and wet. I woke before Archie, but I didn't try to sneak away. Instead, I curled up there, aware of his heartbeat, the way he held me close, even in sleep, and the fact that our legs were tangled together. It was comfortable as fuck.

The dull spatter of rain against the windows held my attention as I traced little patterns on the back of Archie's hands. The calluses on his fingertips always made me want to play with them. I almost wanted to turn over and stare at him asleep—not creepily—but because I loved how relaxed he'd get in the early hours of the morning. Sometimes, even in sleep, he wore the most consternated little frown. Other times, he looked just like that boy we met in ninth grade.

Every once in a while, I wished I could go back and slap myself. There was a clarity that came with *knowing* how they felt. He had absolutely been trying to date me, and I never fucking noticed. They all had, in their own ways. Knowing what I knew *now*, I could see it.

A brush of lips against my tattoo made me smile. I loved tracing theirs, too. I'd spent part of the movie last night lying on his back and just tracing it over and over. At least until he'd flipped me over and we forgot all about the kids and the T-Rex for a little while. We definitely focused on the screen for the raptors.

Couldn't miss those.

A giggle eddied up through me as I wiggled around to face him. "Good morning," I whispered, and his eyes opened halfway.

"Still early," he murmured. "Go back to sleep."

I curled my fingers against his face, teasing the blunt cut of my nails against the stubble on his cheeks. His breathing softened, and I smiled as I pressed a kiss to his jaw, then to his throat and worked my way down his chest to the very interested cock waiting for me.

Archie's groan answered me as I wrapped my lips around him. Pausing for a moment, I stole a look up, and a flash of lightning from outside illuminated the naked lust on his face. So much for sleepiness, right?

"Go back to sleep," I teased. "It's still early."

The fact that he fisted my hair and thrust with his hips was all the answer he gave me, along with a drawn out, "*Fuck*!"

Fifteen minutes later, he returned the favor.

Yep.

Definitely a good morning.

I was in a good mood when I got to Mason's, full of French toast from breakfast at Archie's. We had a lazy morning before I had to get ready for work. I was super proud of him for not trying to talk me out of my job. Maybe I didn't have all the hours here I used to, but Marsha was good people and I had loved the job. Maybe I didn't love it as much anymore, but I also didn't want to give it up before I absolutely had to.

He dropped me off because Ian was picking me up. The guys had all texted, and Coop sent me pictures of the cats, spoiled as hell. Coop had plans with Trina today. Apparently, he was going to try and talk some sense into his sister. I wished him good luck. Jake and Archie were meeting to work on their super-secret-we-can't-tell-you-just-yet project. Ian had a couple of students to work with at the music studio.

Busy days. Jake's sisters started blowing up my phone at some point.

Becca

Okay, we need a girls' day. We've decided.

Blake

What she means is she decided.

A series of laughing out loud emojis followed it.

Louisa

Girls' day would be fun. We haven't in a couple of years.

I winced at that reminder. Louisa's birthday was coming up.

Me

How about I pick the three of you up next Sunday?

Blake

YES!!

Becca

OMG, would you?

Louise

No Jake?

I chuckled.

Me

No Jake. I promise.

My phone vibrated madly.

Jake

Yeah, that's not working for me, Baby
Girl. The four of you together…

Me

Hush and go work on your secret project
that you don't want to tell me about.

Jake

Heh. Don't let them drive you nuts.

Me

They really don't. I love them.

Jake

Me too, doesn't mean I don't want to
smother them occasionally.

I laughed.

The rest of my shift, any time I checked my phone, there were new messages from the girls. I'd actually suggested we invite Trina, too. Blake hesitated and so did Louisa, but Becca said she'd talk to her. It was always kind of weird that the girls hadn't been closer friends, considering how tight Jake and Coop were, but…I couldn't really say much on the subject.

At least not yet. Even if they didn't end up inviting her, I'd make sure Trina and I went and did something. I hadn't checked on her in a couple of days. Probably time to do that.

The stormy weather worsened throughout the day, and the temperatures plummeted. I'd brought a change of loose-fitting clothes for our "date" as requested. Ian showed up in my car rather than the bike, and I grinned when he pulled up and then I darted out the front door and right into the passenger seat.

"I was going to—"

I didn't let him finish the sentence before I kissed him. My cheeks were damp from the ten seconds it took me to get from the door to the car. There was a hint of ice in the plinking against the windshield, and I had a feeling Mason's would be closing early.

One hand cupping the back of my neck, Ian took over the kiss and tugged me into him. Even leaning over the parking brake couldn't have dislodged me. The sweep of his tongue demanded entry, and I was more than happy to open to him.

He smelled fantastic. The smoothness of his cheeks was almost baby soft, and a little thrill chased up my spine over the idea that he had showered and shaved before coming to get me. That he spent the time to get ready before coming to get me. Ian tightened his grip a little, then slid his hand from my nape to my throat and tilted my head back so we could break the kiss, but I didn't move away.

"You interrupted me," he said with a definite lick of heat and warmth.

"I did, but I blame that all on you," I informed him with a sigh. My pulse thudded like a happy puppy whose tail wagged frantically.

Amusement flared in his eyes, despite his stern expression. "Me?"

"Yep. You. You smell good. You feel good. You're here to get me. It's all your fault I interrupted you—"

I gave a little mental fist bump when he claimed my mouth this time, stopping the flow of words. I didn't care where we were parked or where we had to go, I was thoroughly enjoying this right here. When he nipped at my lower lip and then dragged his teeth over it, I sighed.

Yep, this was a good spot to be.

Chuckling, he stroked his thumb in circles over my pulse. "Hi, Angel."

"Hey," I greeted him with a smile. "I hope what I'm wearing is okay for tonight."

He didn't once look away from my eyes. "It's perfect. You good? Not too tired? I know Archie probably had you up half the night."

I laughed. "No, we did actually sleep, I promise. And I feel pretty good.

We weren't busy today, not really. I'm also kind of excited about tonight, even if I only have the vaguest idea of where we are going."

He slid his hand up to cup my face, then to my hair, where he tugged the ponytail holder gently. "May I?"

"It's going to be a little poofy," was all I warned. I'd braided it for work and it had come out of the braid in a wild kinky array, which kind of fit the theme for the day, now that I thought about it. With a delighted smile, he tugged the tie free and then combed his hand through my hair.

"I love it when it looks like this. You look like you just rolled out of bed."

I wrinkled my nose, and he kissed the tip of it.

"Also," he said, "you look perfect. But you always do."

"That is so not true."

"Uh uh. Tonight has rules, Angel, and the first rule is you don't get to disagree with me."

I leaned back a little and stared at him. "Seriously? Have you met me?"

He grinned. "I have and I love you, but that's why we're discussing it here. Tonight, I want you to trust me. Let me make the calls and the decisions just for tonight. I want you to watch, to listen, and absorb every piece of the evening, then we can discuss what we like and don't like after."

Not an unreasonable request. Excitement fluttered through me. "Can I ask a question right now?"

His eyes softened. "Yes. It doesn't really start until we get there, so we have time to discuss anything you think I need to know."

I let out a little squee and did a bouncing dance in the seat. Ian leaned back, laughing at me. Maybe laughing with me.

You know, it didn't really matter. I'd been reading, a lot. I had all kinds of questions. "We don't get to talk about this as much."

"I know," he said. "Thank you for not bringing it up around the guys."

"I don't mind protecting our privacy." Some things were just for us, just like some things with the others were just for them. Not once had Coop really gone for truth or dare with Jake there, so I got it. We each had our moments.

This was for Ian and me.

Especially since he hadn't shared it with anyone else. No way I'd betray that trust.

"It's not that I care if they know eventually," Ian promised, and when a car honked behind us, he grunted and shifted to move us so we left the parking lot of Mason's as he added, "By the way, I meant to get out and let you drive," he told me. "This is your car."

"I don't mind if you drive it," I promised. "If you're making the decisions tonight and I'm trusting you with me, then I think I can trust you with my car."

His smile warmed me from head to toe. "Hit me with your questions, Angel."

"Can we get coffee?"

"We can get anything you want."

"Tell me about where we're going?" I asked after I had my hot mocha and he had his own.

"We're going to a gathering. There's a fetish club in Dallas that I've gone to a couple of times."

Wait… "Didn't you go with your dad to Dallas?"

Ian burst out laughing. "I promise, Angel, I went to the club when I was there with him once, but not *with* him."

Relief had me sagging, and I shot him a grimace. "Sorry."

"It's fine," he soothed, rubbing my thigh. "I'd done some research and it was far enough away, I thought it was a good place to go and see. They don't allow sex during open hours at the property, and they have to act as a private club so that they can vet anyone who joins. Membership means agreeing to their rules, particularly privacy. But one of the perks was I found out there was another club a lot closer to us."

"Seriously? I mean we have Kink on the Hill…" My face heated. I hadn't really confessed the sex shop visit yet, though I had wondered if Coop told anyone.

Jake had found my books, and I knew that because he left me a sticky note that said he'd borrowed one. He'd been returning them and borrowing the next one for the last week or so. But we hadn't discussed it.

"So, Rachel, Coop, and I went to Kink on the Hill," I told him. Then I admitted to the books and the reading and maybe to the sex toys. It took us a bit to get back to where we were going, but as it turned out, we were there. Just forty-five minutes away from where we lived in a little industrial park. There were a few cars, but everything around it was closed. The club, Ian told me, was for members only, but he'd gotten me in as his guest.

I'd need my ID and my order of emancipation, which explained why he'd checked about whether I had both in my wallet.

"We're going to observe," he told me as we parked. "They have viewing rooms, and there are some where we can sit by ourselves. Though, this is more of a class, so I thought it would be better if we sat somewhere you can hear the questions others might ask. But that one is up to you, Angel. And…" He reached into the backseat and brought forward a small bag. "We can wear masks once we're inside. But I promise, everyone agrees to protect the privacy of everyone else, and they aren't going to stare at you…"

"I don't care if they do," I admitted, even if my face heated in evidence to the contrary. "I'm going to be there with you, and since you're making the decisions tonight…what do you want me to do?"

He grinned. "I want you to be comfortable. This is one where you do make the call, Angel."

"Then I just want to go with you."

Anticipation curved through me. To be honest, even with all the reading, I still wasn't one hundred percent sure what to expect. I'd half-considered checking out some BDSM fiction books. I actually had a few of those on my Kindle. But I decided against it, because from what I remembered of a couple of them I read, it was more like the kinds of things you'd find in a fantasy and not a real place.

I wanted the reality of it.

Weird maybe, but it worked for me.

Hand in hand, I walked with Ian inside. The icy rain was still coming down, and he'd checked his phone before he shut it off and we'd tucked both phones away in the glove compartment. No photos were allowed. No recording devices of any kind. They also had lockers if we decided we wanted to play where we could secure our stuff inside, and a shop if we needed items we hadn't brought with us.

They really had thought of everything. I didn't think I was going to be up for playing *here*, but I hadn't totally eliminated the idea either. There was paperwork to fill out inside, just a short sheet with my pertinent details, and then they examined both my ID and the emancipation order. When they asked to make photocopies of both so they could attach it to the sheet, I agreed.

I got it. They wanted to protect themselves for any legal repercussions. Sex might sell big time, but we lived in a nation of bizarro prudes, where they wanted to be titillated while also holding on to some moral high ground to punish people from. Slut shaming, adult style.

Either way, I didn't mind. Once we'd done everything, Ian took a pair of dog tags from them and hung one around my neck and the other around his own. I glanced at it out of curiosity and found his name on it and grinned. It wasn't quite military style, but it did have his last name and first initial, then a date pressed into the metal.

"Membership," he murmured against my ear. "They check for these when you're coming in, not your ID, so on those nights when we just come to play, we can leave everything we want outside the door."

That made a lot of sense.

Whatever I was expecting, the next room was not it. It was like walking into someone's well-used and loved dining room and sitting room all rolled together. There were drinks and snacks set along one counter, and there were people at the table chatting. A few glanced up and gave us welcoming smiles or a hello and then went back to what they were doing. There was one guy who had to be in his forties and looked like I'd pictured every biker, ever.

There was another guy with more tattoos than skin visible. Older. Younger. A girl with pink tips on her hair and six small piercings in her eyebrows, another lady who reminded me of the librarian at the high school right down to her silvery-gray hair and way too much blue eyeshadow, but her grin was so warm, it was hard to feel uneasy.

Ian kept me tucked right under his arm, and I had an arm around his waist as he guided me through. "This is where people can socialize or rest in between sessions." There was a couple on one of the sofas, a woman who sat with a man's head in her lap. His expression was kind of far away, and she just kept stroking his hair as she murmured to him.

Sessions.

Okay.

There was so much to take in, and it was so utterly…normal. A woman came through another door, and she looked like someone's mom. Not that she wasn't pretty, because she was. But she seemed so…ordinary, and like someone I would see at Mason's ordering burgers with her family. It was *weird* and *normal* at the same time. She made her way around the room introducing herself to each person there, and then it hit me. A few were just like me—they'd never been here before.

When she got to me and Ian, she greeted Ian with a squeeze to his arm and then a warm smile for me. "If you have any questions," she told me, "we ask that you save them for the end of the demonstration. Then we'll take the time to address them. It's important that you listen and absorb. The Master and his sub who are doing the demo tonight have been doing this for over a decade. They are very experienced, but they also like to focus on each other so you can benefit from the full power exchange."

Oh. I had questions, but I nodded. I could make a mental list. I also gave myself a mental pat on the back for doing the reading. There was so going to be a test.

I gave a little excited nod, despite my determination to keep it cool, and

Ian pressed a kiss to the top of my head, even as he huffed with laughter. "I love you, Angel," he whispered, and I grinned up at him.

It turned out the lady who warned us to hold our questions until the end was the sub in the Master and sub who were doing the demonstration. The Master, a man they only introduced as Richard, specialized in silk ropes. For the next forty-five minutes, I sat glued as he created the most intricate pieces of art with his ropes and the sub.

The ties eventually held her suspended, but the more he bound her, the more she seemed to relax, and I had to admit, I wanted to know everything about it. He explained that there was more to this experience than just tying someone up. For he and his sub, they shared a Master and sub relationship, but not everyone would have that. But for them, it meant simply that she trusted him to give her what she needed—in this case, to be erotically bound.

It was definitely erotic. Despite the fact that she was dressed, her peaked nipples showed through her shirt. The shorts she wore were super tiny and her thighs were damp whenever he threaded the rope between her legs, and yet nothing he did was overtly sexual. We were six feet away, so there was no missing anything, but at the same time, it was probably one of the most sensual things I'd ever witnessed.

Beyond the simple power exchange, his job was also to monitor her condition. Subspace—I'd heard that one before—could pull a sub deep, and sometimes, the sub could faint from the over stimulation and rapid heart rate.

That explained all the little checks he did in between different tying moments. For her part, she looked so blissed out, it left me a little breathless. By the time the demo ended, I almost whimpered that it was over. Ian had been holding my hand for the last half hour, tracing his thumb over the inside of my wrist, even as he kept his other arm around me.

Sighing, I leaned back while Richard slid the ropes off of Lyssa, his sub's name, and cuddled her close. He'd mentioned aftercare being something important, and then nodded for us to return to the little sitting area and dining room before he walked away with her.

"How you doing, Angel?" Ian asked me, and I stole a look up at him. His pupils were a little large, but his whole expression was so intent and focused on me, I warmed.

"That was amazing," I admitted, a little breathless. "Is that what you want to do?"

He curled one lock of my hair around his finger. "I'd like to experiment with it. I want—I could picture doing that to you. I still have to learn the ropes and it takes some time, but they have teachers. If you'd be willing to learn with me."

Oh, that didn't even take me a moment to think about.

"Yes."

His eyes flared, and so did his smile.

We didn't leave right away, though it was seriously tempting. Instead, Ian wanted to ask some questions and he wanted to give me time to ask them. Eventually, Lyssa and Richard joined us, and she looked so completely at peace, I envied her.

Most of the questions that were asked, including the ones Ian asked, satisfied my own curiosity. I thought I'd want to ask more, but the questions I had were a lot more personal. I wanted to know how it felt. How did you know it was the right choice for you? I was all kinds of turned on from watching *them*, and I couldn't imagine the level of pleasure if I'd actually been the one being bound.

And that part made the most sense to me. I didn't want to be the one doing the tying. I wanted to be bound. But not just by anyone. Ian.

I trusted Ian.

By the time we bid them farewell, I swore my head was swimming with questions and ideas, and not even the icy chill of the air outside could chase them away. I huddled into him as he got the car started and warmed it up.

"Talk to me, Angel," Ian ordered in a soft voice, and I grinned.

"I don't even know where to begin," I admitted. "I want to do it all. I want to hurry, I want to go slow, I want to go back home and play…" I licked my lips.

The relief on his face was obvious, even in the dark of the car. "So it doesn't scare you at all? No turn offs?"

"No," I rushed out. "I mean, I thought it would be weird or maybe I didn't know what I thought it would be. But they were all so nice and relaxed, and they made it seem so normal that it would even interest me. Which makes me sound all kinds of judgy and strange. But before all of this… I mean, Jake has spanked me a little. But not like you did, and I never knew that would make me feel so much."

I was pretty sure my face had to be flaming red, but I didn't care. The words just spilled out.

"And now it…it's like there's so much more we can do and try and…I want to."

He let out a little groan before he kissed me. "This is going to be an agonizing drive back."

Chapter Thirteen
YOU'LL BE THE PRINCESS AND I'LL BE...

ME

IAN

Frankie's excitement thrilled me, no lie. I'd been hesitant about even admitting my more adventurous interests. Not because I was ashamed of them, but I really didn't want to scare her off. I'd already fucked it up trying to make things easier before, trying to protect her, and to insulate her against the bullshit.

All that succeeded in doing was thrusting her away from me. Then Thanksgiving happened, and I had not a single regret. Even more, when she responded to everything I asked again and again, the need to tie us together even more firmly wedged its way inside of me. But I would never react to her from a place of fear again.

If I wanted that control—needed it—if I wanted to be that strong for her, then it started with me. And the day I made that call, it hadn't gotten easier, but

I had a roadmap and I'd fucking stuck to it at home, at school, in the studio, and with the guys. Frankie first had been our unofficial and sometimes our official motto for so long, it fit me like a glove.

She fit me like a glove.

Tonight had been about exploring our options. There were so many things I wanted to do with her, but I wouldn't without her consent or her understanding. Still, my cock had been hard as a stone from her first breathy exhale during the demonstration, and it showed absolutely no signs of diminishing. I'd been half-hard since she kissed me when she got in the car after work, but now that I could practically taste her anticipation and eagerness?

Fuck.

The drive back took forever and not even a blink of an eye, because we talked about *everything* on the way.

"One of the things the book said was we should make a list of hard and soft limits," Frankie said, and I had to bite back the smile stretching my mouth. The book. What the book said. She'd done research. But of course she'd done research—she was Frankie.

She was so fucking perfect, it hurt.

"Also, like what you're curious about. I started making a list, and I thought we should talk about that on our way home, you know, if that's okay, since you're gripping the steering wheel like my car offended you or something."

Yeah, I white-knuckled the steering wheel, but that was more to keep from reaching over and cupping her pussy to see how wet she really was, or if her nipples were as hard and tense as they looked in the way the shirt hugged her. The jacket she'd worn had come off not five minutes into the drive. It was freezing and trying to ice storm on us, but she was too warm to wear the coat.

Fuck, I tugged at the collar on my shirt, like I was in a button-down and not a T-shirt. "You're right, we need to make a list," I murmured. "I know some of what you like but I want to know all of it, and if you're curious, then I want to be there with you when you figure it out."

Some of her curiosities weren't going to be answered by me. The reality of that settled into my soul, but even as I searched for some sense of resentment, nothing was forthcoming. Archie introduced her to sex, Jake and Coop stretched her limits, and me? Well, we were doing our own exploring, and it was all…it was good.

"You're smiling," she murmured, and I caught her studying my profile.

"I love you," I told her.

"And that's why you're smiling?" Someday, the surprise in her voice would vanish and leave only the warmth. We just had more work to do.

"Definitely one of the reasons."

She laughed, but she also bit her lower lip, and I shook my head. "I was thinking about the list of hard and soft limits," I added. "And how much I adore that you're making yourself comfortable by learning everything you can. I wanted to bring it up with you…" It was part of my plan for tonight, honestly.

"Oops?"

"No oops, Angel." Never where she was concerned. "You have to trust the experience, too. I want you to have control over it."

"I'm still working on that part," she admitted. "The power exchange. The fact that the sub has control at all when she's supposed to be surrendering it."

"But that's the point," I said with a soft exhale. Seriously, the conversation was doing nothing for the stone hardness in my pants. Nothing. Except making me harder, if that were possible. "It's your control that you're gifting to me. You're *allowing* me to take care of you the way I want to and to see to your pleasure and give you everything you need."

And if that wasn't sexy, I didn't know what was.

She squirmed a little in her seat, and when I got a look over there, her face was flushed and her lips parted. I grinned a little wider. "You like that idea."

It wasn't a question.

"I do," she admitted. "Probably way more than I should."

"There is no should." It came out far sharper than I intended, so I relaxed a little. "Angel, where we are concerned? There is no should. There's what feels good. What we want. What we can give each other."

"I like that," she said after a few moments of soft silence. "I really like that."

"Good." I relaxed my grip on the steering wheel and settled a hand on her thigh so I could offer her a comforting squeeze. Part of taking care of her meant making these conversations easy. I didn't think I could be any more thrilled with her enthusiasm.

"Do you want me to just go down the list for you?" The frank openness in her voice threatened to mesmerize me. "You'll answer, too?"

"We can do that," I agreed. "I know some of the answers already, at least for me. I'm definitely more dominant, but the whole Master and slave thing isn't for me."

"She wasn't a slave tonight though, was she?"

"No, Lyssa is a sub, she's very comfortable in her skin." She was actually one of the first people I'd talked to about all of this and the one who gave me advice on how to approach it with Frankie in the first place, but that was not a conversation we were having right now. Mostly because Lys hadn't known who or what I was looking for when I'd talked to her.

Honestly, I wasn't sure what I'd been looking for.

"I am not a slave, at least not by any measure I've seen in the reading, but I don't mind being submissive. It's actually kind of nice."

That sent a wholly decadent sensation up my spine, and at the same time, I relaxed. She was inviting me to share this, to understand her better, and I'd be able to take care of her better. That really was all I wanted. "If you ever think that changes…"

"I'll tell you, but you're not submissive at all, are you?"

"No." I could admit that. "But I think you could talk Coop into it for you if you need it." Jake and Archie probably not, but Coop had the kind of flexibility with her that all of us lacked.

She laughed. "Not a conversation I'm ready to have with him yet."

Yet.

Good. Maybe not yet, but possibly in the future. "And I'll be honest, all of you are a little on the dominant side with me."

Not a little, but again, we could leave it there. "Go on down the list, Angel."

"Bisexual?" she read off her screen.

"If you were, you'd make Rachel's day," I told her. "And definitely no for me."

"Is that why you don't want the other guys there?" She'd never asked me that directly. "I mean, you were there when Archie and I had sex that morning."

"Kind of hard to miss, Angel, I was sleeping less than a foot away." Not that it hadn't intrigued me, but there'd also been a thread of violence weaving through me and I'd wanted to rip his hands off of her. Not conducive to what we were all building, so better to avoid those situations. "And it's not being hetero that makes me not want to share you with the guys at the same time."

I had to consider this, how to phrase it.

"I like the control," I reminded her. "When I'm with you, I want to own every single inch of you. I want to own your pleasure. I want to be the only one touching you and making you feel things."

She gave a little shudder, and I squeezed her thigh. When she covered my hand with hers, I relaxed. I knew how I sounded.

"That said, I know you need and love them, too. They give you so much, and I'd never deny you that. So I can share your time and I can share your love, but some things I want just with you. At least…" I could concede this much. "At least right now."

"I love you," she whispered as she rubbed the back of my hand, and I smiled.

"Love you, too. Keep reading."

She laughed, and some of the tension cording her thigh muscle seemed to ease.

"That also answers whether we have multiples. I'm okay with it, but you're not," she told me, and there was no censure in her voice. "The next page is this really long list, so if I don't know what it is, I'm just going to say no for now."

"That's fair." And she should really know. "I don't know all of it either, Angel. I meant it when I said I'd only gone to a couple of classes and they were a lot like tonight. Demonstrations where they talked to us about what they were doing and why and giving us a feel for what's possible."

"I thought the ropes were gorgeous," she admitted.

"So did I." I cut her a look. "And I want to learn how to do that to you. To put art on you."

"Okay."

Just like that. I grinned. "It could take us time to get that good."

"Kind of like singing, right?" Was that a note of teasing? "I trust you with that, I think I can trust you with this."

And if that wasn't a punch in the feels, I didn't know what was. My heart fisted so tight, I almost forgot how to breathe.

It took a good fifteen minutes to go through them. Anal, blindfolds, biting, breast bondage, and soft bondage were all yeses. Ropes and silk ties were a definite yes. Chains and leather cuffs, she was a little iffy about. Though, she had liked my belt.

Good to know.

No branding or abrasions. Caning was right out. Breath play worried me, but she said she'd trust me with it. So for now, that was a no. She didn't care if I chose her clothing, depending on what we were doing. Like if it was for our date or our play, not necessarily everything else.

That was another thing, this was play reserved for us and privacy. I was definitely comfortable with that. I would never put her on the spot in public. Though…she didn't mind if I wanted to keep a swats counter. The fact that she'd grinned when she said that also told me that impact play was on the table.

Again, we would be careful. Period. Spanking her was one thing. I'd seen enough bruises on her to last me a lifetime.

Anything that sounded like actual torture or a medical exam was just an instant no. Exhibitionism—not shockingly, Frankie had no problem with it in front of the other guys. The surprise and hint of wonder in her voice made me grin. "So if I told you I wanted you to sit naked with us one night while we played video games, you'd be okay with it?"

"I don't think you guys would get much playing done," she pointed out, but the corner of her mouth curved higher. "But I'm totally game to try it."

Laughter swelled up through me. We were almost home, but there were still more things on the list. The sheer volume of things other people found sexually stimulating astounded and intrigued me. Fisting was right out for both of us. Fire play sounded cool, but that would take me time to learn and to build confidence and skill before I brought anything like it near her skin.

The same with wax and electric. We might be in classes for years, and wasn't that a heady thought? Orders and control, already established. Face slapping was a firm hell no. Flogging had her biting her lip. Guess I'd need to study up on that.

I'd seen some really soft leather ones that might feel good.

Humiliation, hell no. Forced anything, no. Orgasm denial, well sure, massages—getting or giving—both yes. Nipple clamps, Frankie frowned. Maybe. But we might have to work up to that. That definitely went into the later folder.

The question of kneeling made me smile, and she grinned. Over the knee spanking? Privately, she didn't have an objection, but she didn't want to just be punished.

"I'm not into just causing you pain," I told her. "Ever. If it hurts and doesn't feel good, then it's a hard and fast no. Period."

Roleplay? "I'm not ready for that," she told me. "Maybe after we figure out what works for Frankie and Sir Ian."

"Sir Ian?" That gave me a little jolt.

I didn't miss her secretive little smile over it either.

Suspension intrigued us both, but that was going to have to wait until we mastered ropes.

We had barely finished the list when I pulled into the apartments. The rain had turned to full on sleet, and I'd had to crawl us home the last few miles. But the conversation kept us fully engaged.

"Can you imagine if we had to do all of these as part of our psych inventories? Erin's had me do a few of these question and answer things."

I didn't say a word as I put the car into park. She didn't bring up her psychologist or her sessions. We didn't ask. They were for her, period. If she wanted to tell us, then we'd listen. This was a hard and fast rule between the four of us. Especially when some sessions left her so drained and ragged, I wanted to kill something, and others left her almost giddy.

So I focused on the question and not the part about Erin. "No, I'm good with being this open with you. It's not anyone else's business."

She grinned.

"Come on, let's get you inside." I helped her back into her coat, and we made a run for it, albeit a careful one. The last thing I wanted was for her to fall.

"It's brr fucking cold out here," she said around chattering teeth as I got the keys in the lock. Inside, I let loose with my own shiver, but she was already burrowing into my chest as I kicked the door closed. The quiet interior promised me the guys had left us alone like I'd asked.

Hoisting her up, I walked us through the apartment to her room. "Before I forget to say it, Angel," I murmured against her hair, "thank you."

"For what?"

"For being curious," I told her as I settled her on the bed and helped her out of her coat. Then her shoes. "For all the research you've been doing. For going with me tonight… For being you."

"I'm not done," she informed as she wiggled her toes when I stripped off her socks. "I have more books to read."

"And more classes to take."

With only the light from the hall illuminating the bedroom, her smile looked even softer. As I hooked a finger under her shirt, I asked, "Do you need anything? Water? Restroom break?"

"You."

Her nipples were every bit as peaked as they'd been earlier, and I smoothed a hand over her cheek. A droplet of water fell from her hair. Yeah. We needed to take care of that. First, the wet clothes. At my urging, she stood, and I peeled her pants down, along with her panties. I pressed a kiss to her bare abdomen and then to each of her hips. She gave a little laugh, and I rubbed my cheek against her skin, just savoring the touch. This was another reason I'd shaved. I didn't want there to be any whisker burn on her.

As if to prove my point, I drew her close so I could lave a kiss over her nipple. My cock had half-given up on me and just seemed to be painfully pointing right at her, but he could damn well wait. This was about her.

For me, it would always be about her.

A breathy little gasp escaped her and she brought her hand up, but seemed to hesitate about touching my hair. Releasing the nipple with a little pop, I said, "You can touch me. We're not quite to the *obey* part of the evening." That, and I loved having her hands on me, even if it shredded my control. I ached to have her touching me.

She sank her fingers into my hair and caressed my scalp lightly with her nails. Lips pursed, I blew against her damp nipple, and it tightened more. After another loving kiss, I moved to the other. She sighed as she stroked her fingers through my hair, and I was tempted to just keep going until I wrenched every lovely sound out of her.

But I also wanted to take my time, and I had some plans. Before I could get carried away, I patted the bed. "I'll be right back." I tossed her damp clothes toward the laundry and stood. I was out of my shoes and shed my own jacket on the way to the bathroom. I stripped off my shirt and ran a fast towel over my damp hair before returning to the bedroom.

When I walked back in, she was on her knees, and all the breath backed up in my lungs. Her hands were on her thighs, palms up and open, her chin down and her shoulders back.

"Jesus, Angel…" That…definitely was more than I expected.

She glanced up from beneath her lashes, and she smiled. "You like?"

"I love." It did all kinds of things to my system for her to do that so openly, and at the same time, I didn't want her on her knees. Not all the time, but also… "I am going to ask for this again."

"You don't have to ask," she told me. "You can want it anytime."

That was an open-ended permission. We had been talking about what we liked and didn't in the car. Reaching her, I used the towel to chase away the droplets still in her hair. One fell against her chest, and she let out a little breathy gasp. Seriously, I wanted to capture that sound forever and only for me.

I was greedy like that.

"You ready to play?" I asked, squatting down to where she knelt. Not going to lie, it lit all kinds of possessiveness in me.

"Yes."

"You know the rule, right?"

"If I need to stop, I just say stop. I trust you," she told me, and I leaned forward to press my forehead to hers while I got my emotions under control. I wanted the control, don't get me wrong. I needed it like I needed her. But when she trusted me with it, it turned me inside out.

Eyes closed, I calmed my breathing and steadied myself. I needed to be steady for her. That was how we both got what we wanted. With one last brush of my fingers, I rose and stepped back. "Get on the bed."

The corners of her mouth curved at the command, and her eyes tracked my every motion as I reached for the belt on my jeans. She rose so damn gracefully and walked backwards to the bed and sat on the edge. Curious, I raised my brows. I hadn't been specific about how to get on the bed or even what to do once she was on it.

When her teeth sank into her lower lip, I had to bite back a groan. I wanted to bite that lip too, but she curled over and brought her legs up onto the bed, until she was on her hands and knees and giving me nothing but that gorgeous ass to look at, with little peeks of pink when she crawled forward.

A playful smile hovered on her lips as she settled on her side and propped her head up with one hand as though she waited for me to entertain her.

God was I lucky guy. Luckier than I deserved. Aware of her staring at me, I stripped out of the rest of my clothes. My cock was still rock hard, but I didn't rush forward. I kind of wanted to just drink in the sight of her. She'd been so into the demo, even more than I expected, and I wished I had something here to drape over her or even play with the idea of tying her up.

Definitely needed to pick up some items going forward.

When I stood at the foot of the bed, she curled the toes of her foot in a silent invitation, but when I didn't move right away, she lifted her leg enough to give me a better view of that perfect pussy. And it really was perfect in so many ways. Perfect to look at. Perfect to taste. Perfect to sink into as it wrapped around me.

"The things I want to do with you, Angel," I told her. "Roll onto your stomach." She didn't even hesitate as she rolled over, and I fixed my gaze on her tattoo. Crawling along her, I paused to press a kiss to where my name was inked into her skin. I never forgot for an instant that she had her name on me. I wanted her name there, and I wanted my name on her. Tracing the lines with my tongue, I smiled at her shudder. "I want to make love to you tonight," I told her. "I want to think about all the things we're going to explore and discover together, but right now, I just want you."

"You say that like you're worried I'll be disappointed," she whispered.

"Just don't have all the things here I want to play with," I admitted, then stroked a hand down the length of her spine to her ass. She clenched her butt under my fingers.

"You have your belt."

I did. Though this bed didn't quite…well… I eyed the headboard. It was solid, but the mattress had give to it and there were slats below.

Easing away from her, I retrieved my belt and wrapped it around her left wrist, careful to keep it from being too tight, then I drew her arm back to the small of her back. When I pulled her right arm to join it, she went all pliant and soft. With her cheek pressed against the cover, she looked back at me with absolute trust in her eyes. I secured her wrists to each other, not so tight she couldn't get free, but still tight enough to keep her arms where I wanted them.

Stretching over her, I pulled a pillow down and then stuffed it under her belly until it tilted her ass up, then I nudged her legs apart. Her teeth grazed over her lower lip again, and her nostrils flared as she let out another one of those fucking gorgeous sighs.

"This good?" I checked as I smoothed my hands up her thighs. There was dampness along the inside of them, and her pussy was soaking when I traced my fingers over the slit. My cock jerked in anticipation, but I ignored its demands.

"Hmm," she said, and wiggled her ass invitingly. "It's a little awkward." She had no leverage.

"Only a little?" I gripped the belt where it joined her wrists.

"Yes," she said. "But it's not too bad. I kind of… *Fuck…*"

I pushed in with one smooth thrust, and she took every inch of me in a vise-like grip that threatened to blow my load right then and there. Her gasps echoed the ones inside me as I balanced my grip on the belt and rocked my hips back and then thrust forward again, even as I pulled her back.

She snapped her head up and let out a little cry. Oh, I liked that. I repeated the motion, and she clenched down on me with every deep thrust. I controlled every part of this dance, and I stroked my fingers over her tattoo and kept my gaze fixed on the way her head tilted, the muscles straining in her shoulders and her throat.

When her head fell forward with one of my thrusts, I gathered a handful of her hair and pulled her head back. I needed to see her, I needed to know she was all right. Lips parted, eyes closed, and her expression taut with pleasure, and I thrust harder and deeper. I didn't think I could get any deeper, and at the same time, I wanted to pound myself into her skin.

"You can come for me anytime you feel it, Angel," I told her through clenched teeth. I'd been holding back my need all evening, and I had a feeling so had she. She writhed in my grip, and I caught her rubbing her nipples against the covers as we matched rhythm. I could live here, feeling her taking me over and over.

The clamp of her inner muscles only increased the friction, and I let go of her hair to reach around and tweak her nipples. The cry tearing from her throat dragged my balls up tight. She was so close.

"Fuck, fuck, fuck…" She chanted it like a litany, and I grinned as lightning seemed to gather at the base of my spine. Need was like a raging fever in me, but I needed to be in her as deep as we could get and I needed to feel her come around me. Sliding my hand down to cup her pussy, I tested the stretch where she took me, and she gasped again.

No more teasing. No more prolonging it.

Faster, slower, and then fast again, until she thrashed around me. Then I found her clit, and with three hard, swift circular strokes, she let out a cry. The ripple of relief that went through her was matched only by the fierceness of her response, and I released that last bit of control as she orgasmed around me. The hard clamp of her muscles fisting around me coupled with the harsh loss of control in her breath shredded my control.

The delicious combination had me gasping in turn as I came with a fierce shout and a rush of pure heat. She bucked back against me as I ground into her and teased that clit. Another sharp cry, too much or maybe not enough, and I kissed her damp shoulder and moved to nuzzle against her throat as I tried to keep my weight off of her.

With care, I pulled the belt free and eased her arms before rolling onto my back and bringing her with me. She trembled against me, and I cuddled her close, aware of the spreading dampness of cum spattering her thighs and running down her legs onto mine. I didn't care about that, I just cared about soothing her until she was boneless and soft against me.

"Sir Ian," she murmured, and a thrill curled through me. "That was very nice."

"Nice?" I teased. "I need to step up my game."

"And I am here for it," she told me with an almost drunken laugh, and then she smiled up at me and I met her kiss as she rolled over to curl against my chest. I drank down her laughter and breathless little sighs, and kept running my hands up and down her back, until all the tremors quieted.

"What are you going to do when I tie you up and make you wait to orgasm for hours?" I whispered, and she gave a delicious little shudder.

"Have the time of my life," she admitted, and I grinned.

She really was perfect.

Chapter Fourteen
WHEN YOU SAY NOTHING AT ALL

FRANKIE

The single best part of the guys sleeping in the same bed with me had to be them waking me up. Or in this case, Ian waking me with his fingers buried inside of me, teasing me as my hips writhed, and his mouth already latched over a nipple. Heat licked me right out of sleep, and my skin was on fire as I opened my eyes. A sound escaped my throat, and he glanced up with the most delighted grin.

"I wondered how long it would take you to join me." Sleep-roughened, his voice had a hoarse and delicious quality. He chose that moment to crook his fingers and it scraped sparks through my system, and I went to reach his face, only I couldn't move my arms.

Sleep fading rapidly, I twisted to find them tied quite securely with some extra sheeting. Then he'd looped it around my wrists so I could almost twist them a little, but nothing was coming free. We'd gone to bed naked and wrapped around each other, so there was nothing hiding me from him. My ankles were tied too, and I let out a little laugh. Apprehension slid into excitement, and I bit my lip.

Stilling all of his movements, Ian studied me for a long moment. I hadn't expected to wake like this, but I wasn't complaining either. He rolled his thumb around my clit in a gentle circuit, enough that it had my hips lifting, desperate for more pressure.

"Uh uh," he said in a soft voice, and all at once, his hand abandoned me and I let out a little whimper. "Stay still, Angel. Can you do that?"

Was he serious right now? I stared at him, mouth open. I'd been asleep and he woke me up with all these loving touches, and now he wanted me to be still? Outrage curled through me, but there was a quiet kind of delight in his eyes and an adoration that had me swallowing the words unspoken.

We were still playing. That was why he stopped touching until it all registered with me. I shifted a little, testing the sheets, and then glanced at him. "I knew there was going to be a test," was all I said, and his sudden smile and huff of laughter was totally worth it. Leaning forward, he kissed me with such deep caring and utter sweetness, he had me gasping back the emotion. The sharp pinch of his fingers on my nipple jolted me from one extreme to the other, and though I wanted to buck, I tried to stay still.

"My perfect angel," Ian murmured. I didn't know how perfect I was, but for the next what felt like forever, he petted, stroked, and teased me right up to the edge and then backed off, until I swore sweat dripped off me and my heart hammered so loud, he had to hear it. I wanted to scream from frustration.

When he nuzzled a kiss to the corner of my mouth and then pressed a path to my ear, he whispered, "So good for me…"

I kind of wanted to preen for those words, but he backed off and I bit my lip to keep from crying out, only to have him loosen the sheets around my ankles. I dragged my eyes open to find him kneeling between my thighs.

I was a mess.

A mess he seemed to be thoroughly enjoying, but the moment he began to stroke his cock teasingly along my slit, it took everything I had to not arch my back. Another little tortured sound escaped, and a part of me knew if I said anything, if I begged him to stop or if I just said stop, it would be done and he'd give me that orgasm he kept taking away.

But the rest of me wanted to ride this all the way out, and desperate and panting as I was right now, I didn't want to lose. We'd made it this far.

The warmth of his hands skated up my chest to cup my breasts, and I let my eyes close as I wrestled with the need to arch something to stretch closer. I dug my toes into the covers, even as my knees wanted to pull higher.

"So, so good for me," he whispered as his breath feathered over my lips and he pushed inside of me. I couldn't stop it. The orgasm rattled over me, and he caught my cry with his kiss. I gripped at the sheets holding my arms wide and almost laughed when Ian wrapped my legs around him as he began to rock into me.

I splintered, everything going to white noise and bliss. Somewhere in the middle of that, I exulted to his words of praise and loving touches. I wanted to say something. Anything. Thoughts kept fading off, incomplete.

"Shit." Coop's voice penetrated the decadent haze. "Sorry." The door closed abruptly. "I didn't see anything," he called, and Ian let out a groan and a laugh where he nuzzled against my throat. Oh, he sounded nice and relaxed. I tingled from head to toe. "But we're going to talk about what I didn't just see," Coop added.

"Fuck off," Ian answered, his voice calm and measured.

"Fucking off."

I tried to drag my eyes open, but Ian had my wrists free and he cuddled me against his lap, and I sighed. Right there was where I wanted to stay. Nothing else mattered except that I was safe and warm and loved.

It was another hour before I opened my eyes all the way again. The pleasant floating haze coupled with being deliciously wrapped up against Ian made me want to just go back to sleep. At the same time, I didn't want to miss anything more.

"Hey," he murmured, stroking my cheek. "Back with me again?"

"Uh huh." Giddiness bubbled through the floatiness, and I sighed as he kissed me. "I'm great."

He chuckled. Though now that I was awake, he had me drinking water and helped me sit up, but I was boneless. It was Sunday morning and almost eleven, and I hadn't gotten out of bed. Wow.

Eventually, I wandered toward the shower on wobbly legs, while Ian promised to go get food started for us. I didn't even realize Jake and Coop were there until I wandered out after the shower to find them both sitting on the sofa, game controllers in hand.

"Hey," I greeted them and wandered over on loose limbs. When Jake opened his arms, I settled right into his lap and curled up to him and tucked my head to his shoulder. I really could just go to sleep. Coop studied me with a small grin, and I wiggled my fingers at him and blew him a kiss.

"Food's almost ready," Ian called.

Right. Food.

I'd almost forgotten.

"What are we having?" Coop asked.

"Frankie and I are having omelets."

"You can make an omelet?" Jake challenged.

"Yes," he sounded almost smug. "I've been expanding my culinary expertise."

I giggled at the description. "I don't need culinary, I just need edible."

"It'll be that, too." The scent of bacon hit me a split second before the plate was in front of me. Oh, fried potatoes. Cheese omelet. Bacon. I squirmed in Jake's lap, and he lifted me over to sit between him and Coop as I accepted the plate. My stomach growled, and Tiddles let out a yodeling meow as he charged out of the second bedroom. The boys' room was what I'd begun to think of it as, and Tiddles had definitely made himself at home in there.

He leapt up onto the sofa and then rubbed against the back of my head.

"This looks amazing," I almost gushed, but I was so freaking hungry.

"It does," Coop said, reaching for the bacon on my plate. Jake smacked his hand, then tried to steal a piece for himself, but Ian smacked him and I laughed as they all glared at each other. Despite what he'd said, he'd made enough for Coop and Jake too, but when they got up to get their plates, Ian slid into Jake's abandoned seat and gave me another kiss before stroking his hand over my hair.

"That was clever," I teased, and he grinned.

"I thought so."

And after food and coffee, I curled up with Ian while Jake and Coop played their way through three levels of their game before Ian joined them. At some point, I'd need to get up and do homework, but I wasn't in too much of a hurry to do anything. As soon as Archie got there, it would be perfect.

"Jake, move your ass," Archie called through the door. "I need to shave, and Coop's still in the other shower."

This was a new one. For the most part, we had the morning routines down. But Jake and Archie had been pulling late hours on their super-secret project that even Coop had taken to guessing what it was.

"It's a space ship," was his latest inane thought. "Or at least a remote control one you fly using VR technology."

My favorite had been an alien encounter because they were going to pull the most epic senior prank ever.

Still, they weren't telling us anything, and I had decided I would not beg for the info. When they wanted to tell me, they would.

"Did I leave my wallet in here?" Ian asked as he ducked into my room. I was sitting on the bed tying my shoes.

"I don't think so," I told him as Archie called out to Jake again and rapped on the door. I pulled back the pillows and then we both ducked to look on opposite sides of the bed. I found Archie's wallet and held it up with a wry smile, but not Ian's.

We split up, and I headed for the living room, pausing to give Archie a kiss and his wallet, just as Jake opened the door to the bathroom. Archie glared at him, but I scratched my nails gently against the stubble on his cheeks. "It's kind of sexy like this," I murmured and winked.

"Yeah?" All at once, Archie's irritation with Jake seemed to fade, and he gave me another long kiss. "I still need to shave, but nice save."

I laughed and actually managed to slap his ass as Jake swatted mine, and then Ian was hustling us all out of the way. His wallet was in the fridge for some reason, and I found Coop's shoes stuffed under the television. No one claimed the socks hanging from the mini-blinds with a resounding chorus of 'not its,' but Jake at least took them to throw in the dirty clothes.

After double-checking I had everything in my backpack, I got to the door first and opened it to let us out, only to frown at the note taped to the door. It was the kind we got from the apartment's main office, usually when they were informing us of exterminators coming or they needed to get in to do some maintenance.

I slit it open and scanned the contents as the guys trailed out one at a time. My stomach sank.

"Babe," Archie said, leaning over my shoulder to stare at the note. "What's wrong?"

It was a notice of intent from the apartment complex. They'd been notified that the lease holder was no longer staying in the apartment. More, that new residents had moved in, a number in excess of those on the lease.

"They can't kick you out," Archie told me flatly. "You're paid up through the end of May. They can try, but they cashed the check."

Panic scrabbled against the inside of my gut and dug its claws into my spine as I read the legalese and warning. They'd been informed.

Maddy's last message.

Call me. Don't make me do something you'll regret.

"Hey," Jake said, rubbing a slow circle against the small of my back. It was cold outside, our breath fogged in front of us, but I barely felt any of the chill. At least not the external one. "What can we do?"

"I'll take care of it…" Archie began, but I shook my head.

"No," I told him, not losing my grip on the paper. "I have to do this one. I need to call Mr. Wittaker, if he's still my attorney."

"What do you mean if?" Archie cut a look at me. "He's your attorney, babe. If he wasn't going to represent you, he would have notified you already." He scowled.

"Maddy mentioned that she knew I was using one of Mr. Standish's attorneys."

"He's your attorney now, and this isn't a matter against Edward," Archie reminded me. "But call him and let him set your mind at ease, then we can tackle the apartments."

I chewed my lower lip and caught Ian and Coop studying me. Coop radiated quiet support right now. He would be right there if I needed him, but Ian looked like he was trying to assess where best to help, even as Jake and Archie both hovered.

Hovered wasn't the right word. They were right there, ready to throw down. But this was also my fight. My fight with Maddy, and this was her way of getting my attention.

"I'm going to take my car today," I said, fully prepared for that to not go over well.

"Why?" Archie and Jake said in damn near the same voice.

"Guys," Ian cut in before I could answer. "If she wants to take her own car, we're not going to fight with her about it."

"We're not fighting," Coop jumped into the fray when Jake glared at Ian, but Archie ignored all of them, even if I was all too aware we were having this conversation just outside the apartment door where anyone could hear us.

"We're expressing concern and asking why. She hasn't taken her car in months, I don't think it's an unfair question."

"It's not," I told Archie. "But I may need to cut out at lunch and go see Maddy."

"Fuck no," he swore, then grimaced as he raked a hand through his hair, disheveling it. A myriad of expressions rioted across his face, and he wasn't alone. I started away from the door to let them work through it, but Archie fell right into step with me. "Babe, can we discuss this before you put yourself through that?"

"I don't know that I'm going, but she apparently wants to talk enough that she's going to pull this with the apartment. I didn't even think about the fact that she's the one on the lease."

"Except the apartment is paid for," Archie reminded me. "And while leases matter and names matter, money also matters. They couldn't throw you out as long as it's all paid."

"Do we know that for sure?" We were now standing between Jake's SUV and Archie's Ferrari.

"I'm about eighty percent certain," Archie assured me. "But it doesn't matter what she does, we can fight her and we will."

"Agreed," Jake said, and Coop nodded. "You don't have to see her."

I didn't want to see her, that was the difference. At the same time, avoiding her wasn't a long-term strategy, at least until my emancipation was decided.

"What do you want to do, Angel?"

"Dude, you have got to stop being Mr. Super Reasonable now," Archie informed him. "That's Coop's schtick. He gets through when none of us can."

I bit back a smile when Jake snorted and Ian just rolled his eyes. "I'm not being super reasonable. I'm trying to figure out what Frankie needs us to do based on what she wants to do before we all bulldoze through this and make it worse."

My heart squeezed. "You're not going to make it worse," I told them, all of them, and I put a hand against Archie's chest. "I love you for wanting to just dive in and take this on for me. And I may very well need your help. But I also need to know why Maddy has suddenly declared war again." Could it have something to do with the DNA tests? They'd been here all along. So either she already knew the answers, or she didn't care about them.

Knowing her, it could be both.

"And I may call Erin and see if she can squeeze me in today before I talk to Maddy."

"That's a good plan," Coop said. "Do you mind if I ride with you?"

"Subtle," Jake said. "I can ride with you too."

Ian chuckled softly, but it was Archie who grunted, "If she wants privacy, us riding with her isn't going to give her that."

That was a concession. He did not want me fighting this alone. To be honest, I didn't want to fight it alone either. But I needed… "I need to establish some boundaries with Maddy and take back some control. Not talking to her the other night was absolutely the right call."

I wasn't ready to deal with her then, not when I'd been in a safe, focused mood. The ambush had unsettled me a lot. Not letting her in had been what I needed then. Taking the fight to her…that was what I needed to do now.

"I'll talk to Wittaker first," I said finally. "Since I am suing for emancipation, I shouldn't talk to her without my attorney."

Archie's smile warmed me inside and out. Which was good, because the cold was starting to sting my cheeks.

I caught Ian's eye and then Coop's, they were both just waiting, but a muscle ticked in Jake's cheek and the sound of his teeth grinding had me leaning into him as I wrapped an arm around his waist. "Drive me to school?"

The minute I asked, the relief draping the guys wrapped around me almost as tightly as Jake did. "You're humoring me, Baby Girl."

"And you're going to let me," I answered him.

It took us a couple of minutes to sort out cars. Ultimately, we all rode with

Jake, which meant the five of us would have to stick together.

"And if you can get an appointment," Jake said, "I'll take you, or we can ask Rachel. Deal?"

I fired off a text to Erin and another to Wittaker.

"Deal."

As it turned out, Wittaker was not in the office that morning because he had court, but he did answer me in brief that he would like to speak to me *before* I spoke with Maddy and he asked for a copy of the letter from the apartments. I sent it over, and he promised to call later that day.

Erin couldn't fit me into an in-office appointment, but she did do a phone consult over lunch that I took in Jake's SUV with the heat running, because the temperatures had continued to nose-dive below freezing. It wasn't perfect, but it did help. More, Erin asked me a couple of important questions that I didn't know the answers to.

Not anymore.

What did I want out of any conversation with Maddy? Besides telling her to leave me alone, since that was what she'd been doing before anyway, I didn't know if there was anything I could get out of that conversation. But Erin challenged that answer and told me to think about it.

Think about it, and we'd discuss it at our session on Thursday.

The second question was a lot harder.

If Maddy wanted to work on our relationship, would I be willing?

I scoffed at that second question. I couldn't imagine Maddy changing her mind after all this time. But had we ever had that kind of communication? No. Did I want it?

Now?

No.

I spent a long time wanting her attention and being left without it.

"I'm not that kid anymore, Erin, I might still be a kid…but I want other things. I want the things she can't give me and has never tried as far as I can tell."

"That's fair," Erin told me. "So you know what you want to do about her getting in contact with you."

"I want it to stop. But…" She went silent and let me figure this out, because we'd danced around the DNA tests. I'd told Erin about them but in short form, because we didn't know much more about them. "But she has answers that I want, too. At the same time, I don't know if I'd ever be able to trust a word she said."

"Yet, there is always the possibility that she will reveal something."

Fuck me.

"Yeah. But could I trust it? Could I rely on that word? Or is it just going to be something else to hurt and undermine me?"

"I don't have those answers either. So let's dig deeper into this on Thursday. Do you think you'll talk to her before then?"

"God, I hope not," I admitted. "I'm not ready to fight with her."

"Then don't fight, you choose how you feel and how you act. You. Not her. You choose how to treat her, not her. You choose your ground. If she can't respect that, then you can choose to end the conversation and walk away."

True.

I could do those things.

It just sounded a lot easier than it felt.

I promised Erin I'd think about it, and I took a few minutes to pack some of the emotion away, but when I got back inside, none of the guys asked me anything, even if they all searched my face. I loved that they never asked. They were there for me, if I wanted to tell them or if I just needed them. Otherwise, they said nothing. In the library for study hall though, I threaded my fingers with Jake's and leaned my head on his shoulder and I didn't look at a single note.

Chapter Fifteen
A DAY IN OUR LIFE

Mr. Wittaker couldn't see me until the following day, but Archie and I ducked out at lunch to go and talk to him.

"Your mother has retained a lawyer," he informed me as soon as we were seated in his office. He spared Archie a brief look. "And from this point forward, Mr. Standish, I am going to suggest you step out as well, in the interests of protecting attorney-client privilege."

"You're still my attorney," Archie reminded him. While they debated the point, I turned the idea of Maddy hiring an attorney over in my head.

"Why?" I interrupted Wittaker's explanation of the complications of attorney-client privilege. That wasn't my primary concern right now. "Why has she hired an attorney? Is she counter-suing, or trying to stop me from getting emancipated?"

"I only received a call from him today," Wittaker informed me as he removed his glasses and pinched the bridge of his nose. His eyes were tired, and the lines around them deepened as he studied me. "He and I will be conferencing this week to find out what Ms. Curtis' goals are, but with that in mind, do you want to be present for that meeting?"

I'd sooner drill my own teeth. Except… "Will she be there?"

"There is a solid chance, yes." Wittaker folded his hands together. "The trick here is we have the temporary emancipation order. They are down to less than a week to file their contest."

A week? Really?

"So it's a natural game to push it to the last minute. There will likely be threats and intimidation. You have the information and the evidence in your corner, enough that a judge granted you the temporary order while we waited out the filing." The confidence in his voice comforted me. Archie reached over and slid his fingers through mine, and I squeezed his hand in response. "But the fact that she has retained a lawyer says she wants negotiation or, quite possibly, she wants something else from you to not fight the emancipation."

Oh.

"That fits," Archie said, grinding his teeth.

"Maddy tried to see me the other day… I sent you the texts."

He nodded. "Yes and I want to assure you that even though I do handle a great deal of Standish business, on this matter, I am your attorney and there will be no conflict of interest."

"At all?" Why had Maddy seemed so certain?

Wittaker favored Archie with a look, then opened a folder on his desk and removed two sheets of paper. He slid both across to me. Archie and I both leaned forward. They were waivers releasing him from a conflict of interest—one was signed by Grandpa Ted and my eyebrows climbed. I hadn't even been aware that he would do that, but the second one floored me.

"Edward signed a release?" Archie stared at Wittaker.

"He did, and I am not at liberty to discuss any of the details of it, other than he released me from any conflict with Standish in representing Frankie, here. I can also tell you the attorney Ms. Curtis has retained is not one retained by Standish typically. As the retainer young Mr. Standish here paid me to represent you was not taken from corporate funds, it relieves us of certain burdens with regard to the family.”

“Huh,” Archie grunted, then set the page back down with the release from his grandfather.

“This doesn’t feel like a good thing, but it is a good thing, right?” So why was my stomach in knots?

“It is neither a negative or a positive,” Wittaker assured me. “It’s merely crossing a t and dotting an i. However, it does remove one threat from her arsenal, and I’m not going to speculate on whether she was aware of the release or not.”

“When did he sign it?” Archie asked, running his thumb over the heel of my hand as though he was trying to smooth away some of the tension cording every muscle in my body.

“Late on Friday…”

Archie snorted. “So after Maddy’s threat.” He cut a look at me, his jaded smile softening some. “Sorry, babe.”

“It’s—it is what it is,” I managed without trying to make light of it. I had no idea why Mr. Standish would make that call or if he had done so in spite of Maddy’s demands or… I blew out a breath. “When is the conference?”

“Wednesday.”

I had my internship at Standish then, and when I told Wittaker, he nodded and then checked something on his laptop screen.

“If you want to be there, I’ll reschedule it to Thursday.”

Did I want to be there? Not really. However… “What would you advise?”

Leaning back in his seat, Wittaker studied us both. “As your attorney, I can represent you in this conference with no issues. It will likely be their issuance of expectations and possibly announcing their intention to file. Then we’ll have time after they file to counter it. Arguably, we can just run the clock out on this until your birthday.”

“But you don’t think that’s what I should do.”

Archie squeezed my hand, but I kept my focus on Wittaker. The older man shook his head slowly. "No, I think this is very much Ms. Curtis' way, via her attorney, of getting you both in the same room. Clearly, she has things she wants to say to you."

I snorted, but I didn't disagree. "Convenient," was my only comment.

"Be that as it may, your presence could mean she will step back from her protest once you've spoken. That would be the ideal situation, yes? That the two of you could resolve the issue, you get your emancipation and your freedom, and you are within your rights to cut her out."

He wasn't wrong.

"She could also use it as a chance to lash out at Frankie," Archie cut in. "Since she seems to thrive on pointing out the flaws in her choices as everyone else's fault."

"That is also a possibility," Wittaker agreed. "And why I'll be there. If it descends into name calling and accusations, then we end the conference and you step out, Frankie. The goal here is to get everyone's cards on the table and manage the situation so that you get what you want. We have a strong case and we can run the clock out until your birthday, so you never have to see her if you don't want to. It really does come down to how you want to handle it."

Leaning back, I stared at the ceiling. "Can you put it off until Thursday and give me a day or two to decide whether I want to be there?"

"Absolutely," Wittaker said, giving me an approving smile. Hey look, I made my lawyer happy. "I'm going to caution you, however, that you shouldn't bring any of your gentlemen friends, including Mr. Standish here."

Archie glared at him. "We can wait for her if we can't be in the conference room. I don't trust a single thing that woman does, and I want Frankie covered on all aspects."

If Wittaker thought that was overkill, he didn't reveal it. After another ten minutes, where we went over how the conference would work and he called the other attorney to leave a message for rescheduling the conference, Archie and I were alone in the elevator on the way down to the garage where he'd parked.

"I'm not going to tell you what to do," Archie said, hand firm in mine.

"But you don't want me to see her."

"No," he answered, tone firm and unflinching. "She hurts you. No, I don't want you seeing her or giving her the chance to get her digs in."

"I don't want to be afraid of her anymore," I said slowly, chewing my lower lip. "I don't want her choices to dictate mine." As much as I wanted to say that her choices didn't impact mine, they did. "That said…" I blew out a breath as the doors opened and we headed for the Ferrari. "I'm not interested in her opinions, and at the same time, I have questions."

"About the DNA tests."

I nodded. "About that. About her mother. About a lot of things… I don't want to blow it all up in my head as something much bigger than it is, and at the same time…"

"You want to know."

He opened the passenger door for me and waited for me to settle inside before he closed it. Once he settled in the driver's seat, he got the engine started and looked at me.

"Then meet with her. See what she wants, but don't let her control the narrative. You have goals when you walk in there. You can choose to ask the questions or not, no judgment either way."

I laughed. "And you'll be outside waiting for me?"

"Hell yes. Probably have to bind and gag the other guys to keep them away." He shook his head, and I bit back another smile as he backed out. I didn't think he meant more by that statement than what he'd said, but Ian was more likely to do the binding and gagging than be the one bound and gagged. "Wanna blow off the rest of the day and go home? Or anywhere else for that matter?"

"I would," I said with a groan. "I really would, but I need to keep up my attendance as much as possible with going to my internship twice a week starting this week."

He made a face. "I'd rather keep up with you naked and getting our time in that way."

"You boys wouldn't bother with letting me get dressed if you had your way. Ian already suggested I just spend a day naked while you four played video games."

Archie snorted. "We wouldn't be playing games for long. Though I could go for a little sudden challenge play."

I groaned. "Do I want to know what that would be?"

A wicked grin curved his lips. "You bouncing on my dick while I kicked the crap out of the game."

"Wait, how is that a sudden challenge if you're playing a *video game* while I get you off?" Not that I was wholly opposed to the idea.

"Babe, if you're on my dick, I guarantee you, my mind is *not* going to be on the game."

"Good to know," I said with a laugh. At his suggestive look and grin, I flicked his ear. "I'll think about it, drive the car."

"I'm driving…"

At least I wasn't thinking about Maddy. Not even a little bit. No, I was too busy fighting back the giggles every time Archie shifted gears and shot me a playful look.

Coop rode with me to do deliveries that night after we discussed our meeting with Wittaker and worked out a schedule for not only homework, but chores. The guys were getting messier week by week, and even Archie was willing to tackle some of the chores, though he'd rather just have Jeremy swing by or hire a maid service.

Thankfully, the guys helped me shoot it down. As I headed for my first pickup, I glanced over to find Coop staring out into the darkness. At least it wasn't raining.

"You're quiet," I told him. The restaurant for my first pick-up was fifteen minutes away, and there was a second order there, too.

"Just thinking," he murmured with a wry grin.

"Well spit it out before those thoughts die of loneliness."

His snort echoed through the car's interior. "If I ask you some personal questions, would you answer?"

"Probably," I said after considering his question for a moment. "I think it would depend on the type of personal questions. If it's about me, sure. But…I don't want to betray any confidences from anyone."

"Fair," he said with a sigh and leaned back in the seat, tapping his knuckles against his lower lip. "The dad thing."

"You mean my sperm donor?"

"Fair," he said slowly. "If we find out who it is, do you want to meet them?"

I shrugged. "I don't know anything about having a dad. The closest were Maddy's boyfriends over the years, and the ones she let get close enough to meet me weren't that many. And after Kenny…" I sighed and shrugged again. "I just didn't want to get attached. Now she's attached to the one I wish she wasn't."

"Yeah, I guess I didn't think about it that way." Coop raked a hand through his hair. "I just…I just wonder if your dad—your sperm donor," he self-corrected without me saying anything, and I loved him for it. "I gotta wonder if he even knows whether you exist or not. Because if he does know you exist and he's ignored you this whole time? Well, fuck him. But if he didn't…you deserve a good parent in your life."

"One," I said. "It's way too late for me to even want a parent rolling in to try and take over my life. I pretty much know how to take care of myself."

He scoffed. "You overdo everything, and yes, you have been looking after yourself for years. *That* is why you deserve to have someone care and look after you."

"Two," I continued, reaching over to rub his thigh lightly. "I have you guys. You care about me enough to fight for me and to work together while we figured all of this out. I have you, Coop. I don't need a 'dad' mucking it up."

He chuckled. "Worried we'd have to declare our intentions to him?"

I cut him a look. "First, that's a little on the patriarchal bullshit line. He's a sperm donor, and whether he knew or not, he hasn't been a part of my life. Why would you have to explain shit to him?"

"Woah," Coop said, raising his hands then covering mine on his thigh. "Not looking to put down your feminism or your independence, just thought trying to explain four boyfriends might be fun."

I snorted. "You'd send Archie and Jake in first."

"Damn straight," Coop said with a grin. "That's how this boyfriend thing works—we all rely on our strengths. Archie can talk his way out of damn near anything, and Jake's just got that *this is what's happening so suck it* thing going on."

"But all of that aside…it's still my life. Not his, whoever *he* might be." I shook my head. "Where is this coming from? You having issues with your dad again?"

"Yes and no. Mom and Sis have been going round for round on the subject, and I'm just not—I don't want to be in the middle of it. Sis is just fighting this fight without having all the facts. She wants to blame Mom for everything, and Mom's not correcting her assumptions. It pisses me off, because she gives Dad a fucking pass and he's the one who fucked up."

I made a face. "I'm sorry." Did I admit it? "I talked to Trina the other day. Not for long, just catching up at the mailboxes and she was…she was upset about being grounded."

Coop let out a growl. "Because she spent the night away from the house without cluing Mom in that there would be boys at the sleepover."

Yeah, okay, so not touching that one.

"Anything could have happened."

True. Except… "Nothing did though, right?"

"So she says," he grumbled. But we were at the restaurant and I had to run inside.

I pressed a quick kiss to his cheek. "I'll be right back."

It didn't take me long at all to pick up both orders and put them in the insulated sacks. Back at the car, I stowed them in the backseat and tapped the phone to get the directions for where I was dropping them off.

"Coop, she's curious and she likes boys. She wants to date. To have the chance to figure out what she likes."

"She's *fourteen*."

"When we were fourteen, we crashed at each other's houses, and yes, it was different," I hurried on before he could jump on that. "Because we've known each other forever. And I was oblivious to you guys wanting to actually date me. That said, Trina doesn't see the differences, 'cause all she sees is that we were together all the time and now we're dating."

"Don't hit me with your logic, Frankie," he grumbled, and banged his head against the seat. "Just be on my side."

I grinned. "I am on your side. I told her to cut your mom a break because I'd trade Maddy for your mom in a heartbeat. She thinks it's cool that Maddy never seemed to care what I did or where I went, but she doesn't get it, and in a way, I'm glad she doesn't."

"Yeah," he said with a sigh. "I wish you didn't have your mom, too. You deserve so much better."

The pall kind of hung over us until I dropped off the second order. Back in the car, I glanced over to find him staring at me. Running my hand over his cheek, I said, "How much of this is you being mad at Trina for not knowing what's happening, and how much of it is resenting that you are aware of it all and feel like you have to choose?"

"A little bit of both," he said quietly, and my heart squeezed for him. "Dad keeps calling me, too. He wants us to go have dinner with him."

"I'll go if you want," I told him. "Whatever you want."

He sighed. "I don't know if I want to see him that much or have you have to deal with our drama.”

It was my turn to scoff. “You deal with my drama every damn day, turnabout is fair play.”

He grinned, then pressed a kiss to my palm before releasing my hand so I could drive. “I like being there for you,” he said into the dark of the car.

“Then you understand why I want to be there for you, too.”

“Because you love me best,” he teased, easing some of the darker tension in his voice, and I laughed.

“Totally.”

“Holy shit,” he said and fumbled for his phone. “Hang on, we gotta do that again. I want that on tape.”

I laughed.

Even if I couldn’t fix everything, I could brighten his day a little. By the time we were done with deliveries for the night, he was still trying to get me to repeat that little gem, but I held it hostage.

Sometimes, it was fun to make them work for it, and his sparkling eyes promised he agreed.

Coop walked me up the steps to the backdoor while kissing me. The fact that he actually picked me up when we got to the steps themselves made me, honestly, want to swoon a little. Yeah, I said swoon, but I loved how easily he just cradled me to him while I had my arms around his neck and his mouth devoured mine.

The heat of his arms chased away the chill, and he pressed me right into the door as he continued to suck on my tongue and alternately nibble at my lips. The sound of shouting behind the door made me pull back a little, and Coop lifted his head.

“Ugh, who told them they could be here?” he muttered, and I made a face. “I vote we sneak back down to the car and leave, then… Well, I’d say get a hotel room for the night, but that would kind of defeat the purpose of all the work you've been doing."

I stroked the hair at the nape of his neck. "We'll settle them and then go curl up and watch something together, yeah?"

He cocked his head to the side. "Just you and me?"

"If you want." Coop didn't demand time with me like the others did. He was as often happy to hang out with the others or share me with Jake, which I adored. But he deserved time too, and I loved it when it was just me and Coop, too. "I'm kind of fond of you, you know."

"I know, I'm your favorite," he murmured, then gave me another kiss without waiting to see if I agreed or not. Then, he added, "Truth or dare," right against my lips.

I chuckled. "Don't make me regret it," I answered, sinking my teeth into his lower lip, even as I raked my fingers through his hair. "Dare."

Head back, he closed his eyes and grinned like a maniac. "Yes, you love me."

I pinched him. "What horrible thing do you want me to do?"

Eyes dancing, he brought his hands up to cup my face. "I dare you to saunter through there, stripping on your way to the bedroom, and say something sexy about me. Preferably dirty sexy."

"Something dirty sexy about you?"

"Yeah, you know…stroke my ego." He waggled his brows, and I snort-laughed.

"I see," I said. "Got it." I slid the key into the lock and glanced over my shoulder at him. "Just remember, you asked for this."

"I know," he said, wearing a grin that probably rivaled my own.

Inside, the wash of voices hit me.

"Fuck you, Arch," Jake snarled, though it lacked the real bite of heat. "I had your ass, and you fucking surrendered."

"What was I supposed to do?" Archie countered. "Just let you pound my ass flat? You won. I let you win when I surrendered, and now we get to play another game."

"You let me win the damn game," Jake growled, and it took everything I had not to laugh aloud at the absolute incredulous look on his face. They were so intent on each other, they hadn't even noticed me or Coop yet.

I shed my jacket and slipped off my shoes before stowing my keys on the table. I also left my wallet there. After the mad-cap race we had hunting everyone's stuff down, I wanted it to be where I could find it. Coop followed suit and rubbed his hands together as I dragged my shirt up and over my head and wandered into the living room.

The argument stopped abruptly, but I was already unhooking my bra. Leaving the shirt and bra in my wake, I freed my jeans. "Excuse me, boys, I need Coop's massive cock. We'll see you guys a little later. Archie, you should let Jake beat you. It's only fair." And I glanced over my shoulder to find both of them staring at me with heated eyes. "And, Jake, don't be so hard on Archie. You know he hates losing."

I winked at both of them.

"Come along, big cock boy."

Coop chortled. "Don't worry, I intend to."

There were thumps behind me, but I made it all the way to my room and was down to my panties when Coop rushed in and closed the door with a slam. Then there was a thump as Jake hit it from the other side. "She said my big dick, Jakey, go beat the pants off Archie again."

"You are so terrible."

"Just you wait," Jake said with a growl through the door. "Also, Baby Girl?"

I grinned. "Yes?"

"You're hot as fuck, and I wouldn't mind you doing that for me next time."

I laughed. "I promise."

Pushing off the door, Coop scooped me right up and tossed me on the bed.

"But right now, she's getting my cock so, buh bye."

Jake's snort carried through the door, but he headed off. Leaning up on my elbows, I stared at Coop as he stripped off his clothes. "What are we watching?"

He raised his eyebrows, and I stopped his forward progress with a teasing foot against his chest, even if it left him with a bird's eye view of my pussy.

"You dared me to say something dirty sexy about you and to strip. That doesn't necessarily equate sex."

Eyes narrowed, he stroked my calf. "No?"

I grinned. "Truth or dare?"

He let out a happy little sigh. "Fuck, I love you."

"I know. But that doesn't answer my question."

He chuckled. "Dare me."

Oh, I planned to.

Chapter Sixteen
CRAP MEET FAN

COOP

It was funny, Frankie didn't so much lock the other guys out as lock herself in with me. I didn't usually care if Jake was there or, fuck, any of them really. Archie and Bubba weren't necessarily on board for the active sharing, but I'd caught Archie watching more than once and the flare of interest, even if he kept it to himself. Dude was allowed.

Bubba?

Yeah that was a whole other hole to dig in later when it was just us. I had questions, but I wasn't putting Frankie on the spot. Especially when she seemed so deliriously relaxed.

We hadn't unlocked the door before we fell asleep. Apparently, a couple of the cats were in the room, and they emerged to find their spots after Frankie wrapped herself around me. I only woke when one of the little bastards stepped on my bladder. With careful disentangling, I slipped free of the bed and unlocked the door. I didn't bother with clothes because it was late.

When I got back from peeing and grabbing a glass of water, I caught sight of Jake on Frankie's other side. I bit back a laugh and set the glass next to the bed before sliding back into my spot. She was already tucked up against Jake, which had her facing me. I threaded our fingers and closed my eyes.

"You good, man?" Jake's sleep-hoarsened voice said he needed the water as much as I had.

"Yeah," I told him. "I just needed her for a while."

"We all need her." True enough. "But I'm here for you, too."

I grinned. I appreciated the sentiment. Except… "She's just prettier."

"Fuck you," Jake muttered. "But I accept that logic."

I chuckled, and Frankie made a little sound of protest that had us both humming little soothing sounds that were so damn identical, a snort escaped me and Jake had to strangle a laugh. When her breathing deepened again, I lifted and glanced over at him.

"We good?"

"We're fine," Jake said, yawning. "I get it."

"Cool."

That was that.

Frankie had her internship hours at Standish today, and Archie hadn't stopped twitching all morning. I was pretty sure Jake was going to slug him. Even if Arch was doing his damnedest to dial it back, there was no missing the way his gaze kept jumping to her or that his mouth would flatline as he conjured up some new scenario. For her part, Frankie kept running her hand over his, soothing him or leaning into his side.

When she headed back to finish dressing, Jake blocked Archie from following, and even Bubba—who had come by early after not staying the night—eyed him. "You gotta chill the fuck out," Jake informed Arch.

Yeah. Diplomatic. That was Jake.

Archie glared at him, and I ran a hand over my face. I still needed to shave, but I probably wouldn't bother before school. No Frankie to give beard burn to meant I didn't care as much.

"I hate that she's going there," Archie gritted out between his teeth.

"We know," Bubba told him, almost the soul of patience. The ease in his voice was at odds with the clench in his jaw. "But you're going to make her nervous, and you're worrying her."

Which was also true.

"She's not unarmed," I reminded them all, but I kept my focus on Archie. "She's also very aware of how this is affecting you, and Bubba's right, she's worrying about you. So dial it back, deep breaths, man. We know where she is, and you've covered a lot of bases and put support in place for her there…"

With a groan, Archie tilted his head back. "I hate this."

"We know," I said before Jake could thump him. He got his attention. Now we just needed to let him know he wasn't alone. "We're all on her side and on yours." Because Archie's dad pulling this crap wasn't just about Frankie. What we couldn't shake was that this was some kind of power play where Arch was concerned.

He glanced over his shoulder toward the doorway. Frankie wouldn't be long, and there were some things we didn't discuss where she could hear. It was just better to be on the same page and not put her in the middle, at least not in a negative way. At Jake's quirked brow and eye roll, I wiped the smirk off my face.

Right idea. Wrong time.

"Let's talk at lunch."

Archie nodded. "I need a minute with her before she goes."

"You got this?" was all Bubba asked.

"Yeah." Rubbing the back of his neck, Archie let out another sigh. "I got this."

Hands raised, Jake stepped out of his way, and Archie vanished back toward Frankie's bedroom. "He does not have this."

"He's doing fine," Bubba said before I could answer. "Let's face it, none of us like this, and he and his parents have a contentious relationship. Throw in Ms. Curtis…"

"It's a clusterfuck," I agreed. "But we can't tell him how to feel." I leveled Bubba with a look.

"Not trying to tell him how to feel." Not flinching, Bubba met my gaze steadily. We hadn't discussed what I'd walked in on, and I had a feeling he was waiting for me to say something. Actually…

"Ride with me?" I said as I grabbed my bag. "It's supposed to rain again today, and you don't need to be on the bike."

Bubba chuckled. "Sure."

"Am I missing something?" Jake asked, eyeing both of us.

"You miss lots of things," Frankie murmured from behind him, and Jake curled around to give her a hug as she stepped into the kitchen. I had to say, Frankie in business casual clothing was pretty snappy. Today, she'd put a colorful vest over a button-down shirt, and she'd pulled her hair up into a bun that I immediately wanted to free. The fact that Jake's hand twitched up toward it said I wasn't the only one.

"You look amazing," I told her, and she grinned at me.

"Thank you."

"He's right, Baby Girl, you look fantastic." Jake dragged her in for a kiss, and I grinned as I drained the last of my coffee. I rinsed out the mug and set it in the sink, then paused to rinse the others sitting there, and Archie grimaced and mouthed an apology. I shrugged it off. He'd learn.

He was getting better at it. Then Frankie turned to me, all flushed and bright-eyed. I gave her a kiss and murmured, "Check in, yeah?"

"I will, I promise."

I couldn't very well fuss at her when I was telling the others to dial it back. But she searched my gaze for a long moment, and I raised my eyebrows. Yesterday had been a little tough, and I'd dumped some things in her lap. But she'd picked them right up and today was better. Apparently, that translated, because she pressed a hand over my heart and gave me another kiss before she went to tell Bubba bye.

On my way past them, I squeezed her ass, and she laughed. That was a sound I would never get tired of. It'd been the soundtrack of my childhood, my teenage years, and would be for the rest of my life. I believed in having goals.

Bubba didn't keep me waiting long. I had the car on and the defrosters on to get rid of the slick of ice off the windshield when he dropped into the passenger seat. Jake was right behind him, but he just waved and headed to Frankie's car.

Heh. Smart guy. "He's warming it up for her while she and Arch talk?"

"Yep," Bubba answered, leaning his head back against the seat. "It's not a long drive, so ask what you want to know."

I cut him a look. "What I want to know, or what I need to know?"

"We'll see. Some things you don't need to know," he answered, and while the tone might be mild, there was a distinctive core of steel in his words.

Turning that over in my head, I backed the car out and sent Jake a wave before accelerating. "We getting coffee since they're gonna be longer?"

"That sounds like a plan," Bubba said and pulled out his phone. "Gives you more time to talk."

"Shockingly clever, I know." But I gave him a sec to send the message before I asked the first question that came to mind. "Is the tying up why you were really pulling away from her? 'Cause I didn't know you were into that."

A shrug. "I've always been interested, just never had someone I trusted enough to share it with. No offense."

"None taken." But I waited.

He blew out a breath, then tapped his knuckles against his knee before he said, "I pulled back because I wanted to protect her. That hasn't changed. I want her to be able to trust me to handle whatever gets thrown at her and to put her ahead of myself. I handled it badly. But it hasn't changed my feelings. The rest…

the rest is just exploring what we enjoy together."

Enjoy… "Don't take this the wrong way, but you're not hurting her, right?" I didn't think he was or would, but she'd been tied to the bed. I hadn't missed that part.

"Everything we do is consensual," Bubba said, his tone flat. "Don't ever suggest otherwise to her. You want to talk to me about it, fine. You'll leave her alone."

I cut him a look. "Dude, not accusing you of anything. But I care about Frankie the same way you do, and if I think something is wrong or you do, what are we going to do?"

"What you're doing right now," Bubba answered without looking away, and there was a stoniness to his countenance that I'd rarely seen there. "You're expressing concern, and I'm telling you, we're fine. Nothing I do with her will ever be anything other than with her informed consent, and I'll never engage in anything I don't understand enough to protect her. She's trusting me to take care of her, and I'm going to be worthy of that trust."

"Fair enough," I said slowly. Jake had definitely slapped her ass more than once around me, and I'd done a little of that and she'd never complained. Not once. If anything, there'd been a flare of excitement. Then there were the books she got at the shop… "I have so many questions."

Bubba chuckled. "Ask."

I cut him another look. "You sure? I don't want to intrude."

The fuck I didn't and the look he shot me said he knew that, but at the same time, this was Frankie we were talking about.

"You want to know if there's something she needs that you're not doing," Bubba said. Succinct. To the point. "And you're curious about what all of what we're doing is."

"Not going to lie," I told him as I pulled into the long fucking line at the Starbucks. "I always want to make sure I'm giving her what she needs, and the idea of pinning her down isn't alien to me." We didn't quite talk this bluntly about our sex lives with *her*. With others? "And it's weird as fuck to have this conversation."

"Agreed." Bubba rolled his head from side to side. "I told her what I needed. What interested me. What…what I wanted to explore with her. I never wanted this with anyone else. Never trusted them with this part of me."

I could see that. "I trust Frankie with everything."

"So do I," he said. "And I think somewhere in the middle of that clusterfuck, when I was listening to Dad and worried about what I wanted to ask from her and seeing all the turmoil she was in because of her mother…I forgot that I trusted her with me and I needed to trust her with her."

I snorted. "That last part is harder than it sounds." It shouldn't be hard at all.

"Agreed."

We inched forward as one car after another placed their order.

"But one of the things I've learned and then nearly fucked up was communication is everything. I *need* to take care of her. That's not just something that I want to do, it's like a physical drive in me. I don't want to be in charge all the time, but when it's just us and we're alone? Yes, I want her to give me that power to be in charge of what makes her feel good. I want to take all those worries and stresses and the crap that life pours on her, and I want to be the wall between that and her for as long as she'll let me."

When he put it that way, it was hard to disagree. Hell, I *wanted* the same thing. But did I need it the same way?

"One of the first things I learned when I went to a class…"

"Hold the fucking phone." I twisted to look at him. "There're classes?"

Bubba smirked at me. "Yes, and I'll give you the information and even take you to one if you shut up and let me finish. This is hard as shit to tell you without the interruptions."

"Done."

He laughed at me and then scrubbed a hand over his face. "Fuck me," he muttered. "Probably easier if I just start at the beginning, but some of that is none of your business."

"Accepted." Because yeah, I wasn't sure I needed to know the whole history of it. "That said, Bubba. I'm not going to judge. I know I sounded like I was…"

"You didn't," he assured me. "You sounded like you wanted to protect her, and we all do. We all agreed to talk to each other when this shit bothered us before we dragged her into it." To avoid dragging her into it went unsaid.

He blew out a breath and paused 'cause it was our turn to order. After I pulled forward again and closed the window, I glanced at him. His gaze was out the window and not on me at all.

"Bubba…don't tear yourself up. Tell me. Don't tell me. I just wanted to make sure you two were fine."

He smiled faintly. "You'd think this would be easier, but it's pretty personal. Communication, though, is the key. I can't demand she let me protect her and take charge, she has to let me do it and I have to earn the right. It's easy to try and put my stamp on everything, but at the same time, there's so much I don't know that I want to learn because I want to be the best for her, and the fact that she wants to learn and is discovering stuff about herself?"

When he glanced at me, there was a look of wonder on his face, and that decided me more than anything.

Whatever they were learning, I wanted to know, too.

Even if I had to do my own research.

"Coop, she's the best."

Yeah.

I grinned.

She was.

"And on that touchy-feely note," I teased. "Tell me about these classes and where I sign up. Might be easier if I do some homework and keep you from opening a vein with me."

His laughter eased some of the tension in the car and the raw emotion on his face.

"And definitely clue Jake in before he walks in on you tying her up, 'cause while I think he'd be fine if he understood it…"

"His first reaction would not be as easygoing as yours."

And we really didn't need to add anything more to that topic.

School fucking dragged, though Frankie checked in a couple of times. She sounded alternately bored as fuck and intrigued. I wasn't sure what I wanted for her more. Though, it also sounded like she didn't have to deal with Mr. Standish, and I was all for that.

Archie almost looked sane at lunch. We'd gone off campus and gotten Thai. Frankie wasn't a fan of a lot of different Thai options. More because she'd eaten Jake's five once instead of her one, and the fact that it set her mouth on fire and turned her beat red and left her sweating had been a kind of trauma.

The funny kind, but trauma nonetheless.

"They aren't keen on letting me skip two afternoons a week for the next five to ten weeks," Archie admitted with a scowl. "Grandpa is gonna work on an angle that gets me educational credits."

"Or you could, I don't know," Jake mused aloud, "trust Frankie to tell us or call us if she needs us there."

The glare Archie shot him was just asking for Jake to punch him, so I just said, "Or we can keep taking her temperature. She wasn't worried about going today, was she?"

"No, she actually seemed pretty at ease. She's more worried about that fucking meeting with her mother tomorrow."

I rubbed a hand over my face at that one. 'Cause yeah… "Then maybe ease back a little, Arch." I raised my hands when he glared at me and kicked Jake when he started to open his mouth. The first quieted Archie, the second pulled

Jake's attention to me and not jumping Archie's shit. "You know your father better than any of us. No one disputes that."

"Agreed," Bubba threw into the fire, but he wasn't attacking the topic so much as listening. I had a feeling he leaned more in Archie's favor than against. So did Jake, but Jake was also actively trying to dial back his own overprotectiveness.

We didn't always succeed, but we had to try.

"But Frankie has already made her feelings clear," I continued. "This internship is important to her. Succeeding on her own merits is important to her. And us having her back is important, and sometimes—as shitty as it feels—having her back means letting her do it her way. If I had my way, she wouldn't be anywhere near him, and I know you feel the same way. The thing is…you keep pushing her, and she's either going to fold to protect you at the cost of her own ideas or she's going to lose faith in herself, which is a thousand percent worse."

"Oh fuck you," Archie grumbled. "Why do you have to have a fucking point?"

"Because he's an asshole," Jake offered up with a wry smile. At least I wasn't getting punched for kicking him now that he'd heard why I wanted him to wait. "But he's our asshole. And he's right."

"It's really annoying," Bubba supplied helpfully.

"Thanks guys, I'm feeling the love."

Archie was still grumpy, but his shitty mood lifted some. Especially when Frankie sent us pictures of her lunch which included the biggest damn cupcake we'd ever seen and the message, *Sprinkles makes everything better.*

I dropped Bubba at the music studio for the lessons he had to teach, and I'd swing by and get him later or Frankie would on her way back after the internship. Unlike the week before, she didn't get done early. Jake and Archie were off to work on their project. Secretive bastards.

Parking at the apartments, I planned to go up and feed the cats and maybe do a little housekeeping. We were getting messier, and that mess had begun extending past the bedroom and the kitchen. Not that I hadn't noticed Jeremy had come by and picked up all the dirty clothes. I was pretty sure Archie hadn't clued Frankie in on that, but since I hadn't pressed a shirt since choir in the fifth grade and Frankie would rather pull off her own fingernails than iron, it had to be the magical butler.

All my plans slid to the side, however, as I saw Dad waiting in the lot leaning against his car as I pulled in. Crap.

The last person I wanted to talk to today. Son of a bitch.

Sucking it up, I pasted on a pleasant expression and climbed out, backpack in hand. "Dad."

"Coop," he said, a smile on his face that didn't quite reach his eyes. "I was waiting on you."

Fuck a duck, really?

"Yeah?" I swung the backpack up onto my shoulder and locked the car. "What's up?"

"Think we can go in and talk?" It was freezing out here. I blew out a breath.

"Yeah, come on up to Frankie's with me," I told him. "Mom might be home, and I don't want to bug her."

Dad hesitated, and I glanced back at him.

"No one's home right now and I gotta feed the cats."

He frowned, but then followed me. He didn't comment when I used a key to let us in, and I could tell immediately Jeremy had been there. Arch was gonna get so busted if Frankie figured out Jeremy was still coming by to clean up after all of us, and man, I was there for that particular conversation.

It would be worth some popcorn.

I dropped the backpack on the table and toed off my shoes since I didn't want to track dirt anywhere.

"Have a seat," I told him. The kitchen was far enough. "Let me feed the cats, and you can dive into whatever you needed."

Tiddles trotted right out to see me, but the other pair made themselves scarce. They probably wouldn't come out while Dad was here, so I only put down part of a can for Tiddles so that I could save the rest for the girls. When I turned back, Dad hadn't taken a seat.

If anything, he looked more uncomfortable and his gaze focused on the fridge. There were pics of the five of us on there. Some old, and a couple of new ones from the trip to Colorado. "You good?"

Dad snapped his gaze to me and shifted "I'm fine, just…not all that comfortable being in Maddy's place."

"Well, Ms. Curtis doesn't live here anymore, so you're safe." I opened the fridge and pulled out a soda. When I offered him one, he shook his head and his frown deepened.

"What do you mean she doesn't live here anymore?"

"I mean, she moved out."

"And Frankie's living here by herself?"

"Not that it's any of your business, *Dad*, but yeah, and she's fine."

He shifted his stance again and shot a glance past me to the other room.

"You want to tell me why you wanted to talk to me? Or maybe what's got you so…"

I stopped, drink halfway to my lips.

"You're fucking kidding me right now, aren't you?"

Dad locked his gaze on me. "Don't say it like that. You said you knew—"

"That you fucked around on Mom. Do not tell me you fucked around on Mom with Maddy fucking Curtis the cunta-fucking-saurus?"

Pretty sure that was the moment my brain exploded.

Chapter Seventeen
HOLD YOUR HAND

On the drive home, I listened to Torched the whole way. I needed the upbeat music. I kind of needed the emotionally dark pieces, too. I didn't want to examine that part too closely. Not yet.

While the day at Standish hadn't been quite as grueling as orientation day, it had been packed with challenges. Bryan and I were assigned to the marketing team for the day, which meant meeting after meeting, a review of the company public relations, and the upcoming campaigns on two major projects I'd never heard of.

One was the rebranding of an airline that Standish now apparently owned. The diversity of the company portfolio was dizzying. Apparently, they enjoyed absorbing other companies and then folding them into the umbrella of the corporation itself. Those new companies became whole divisions with their business practices streamlined.

Translation, whole departments could be eliminated if Standish already had something that could cover those areas. Which meant while the company grew and added labor and specialized divisions, those unfortunate companies they took over as often as not, also had to lay off their workers.

It was a kind of gut punch.

Not that they covered what they did for all those people they let go in their efforts to streamline. Pretty words for an ugly practice. Bryan hadn't seemed discomfited by the knowledge, which didn't really endear him in my book. All I could think about were the people who had to feed themselves and their families. Maybe the folks here hadn't ever gone to bed hungry or worried about how they were going to pay the bills.

I might be seventeen, but I had more than a passing familiarity with that. Good business practices didn't always make for good human ones.

The second project was a lot more interesting to me, personally, and I found myself wanting to focus on it. It involved grants for students in specialized fields, whether it was arts or engineering. Standish actually sought out students in need on all levels and offered grants to get them into everything from better private and prep schools to colleges.

It sounded amazing. The kind of program Ian could use. Or Jake for that matter.

Still, when the marketing and public relations executive we were shadowing described it as marketing gold because it gave them good community standing and helped repair their reputations, it left a sour taste in my mouth. Was doing something for a selfish reason that ultimately helped other people, even as it helped you, a good or a bad thing?

This was the landscape where morals and ethics collided. Bryan teased me about overthinking it when I brought it up so I left it alone. I might ask Coop about it later. I bet he'd understand why it bugged me, even if I couldn't fully verbalize it yet.

Twice, I went to text him about it, and twice, I made myself sit on it. Better to wait until when I could talk to him face to face. Who knew? Maybe I'd be less twitchy about it by the time we were all home. It wasn't like I could do anything about it, even if it did make me a little crazy.

Unlike our first day, we were there kind of late. It was well after five when our guide cut us loose, and I was finishing up my notes to send to our program advisor. They liked to get a daily report, not required—their words, not mine—but they also felt it could help us organize our thoughts and let them know what aspects of the program were working for us.

I liked crossing the t's and dotting the i's.

The guys were all tied up at the moment anyway, so it didn't matter if I took an extra thirty minutes to get this done. Bryan offered to walk out to my car with me, but I told him I'd be fine. There was security in both the lot and the building. He left with a smile and a demand we check out one of the restaurants down the street on Friday. I shrugged, because we had to eat and I had gotten the best cupcake earlier that day.

Honestly, the best part of my day.

Once the report was finished, I packed up my stuff and sent a message to the group chat that I was getting ready to leave and head home. Then I asked about dinner. I could swing by and pick something up if anyone was at my place. I'd check their responses when I got to the car.

A stream of people was leaving, so it wasn't like I was alone on my way to the parking garage. In fact, I was almost to the level I'd parked my car on before the last person peeled away, but the sound of footsteps echoed behind me, and when I glanced around, my keys were tucked between my knuckles like I was Wolverine and ready to cut someone.

It was an old trick and one I hadn't felt the need to use in a while, but it was already dark out, save for the lights in the garage itself, and they just cast deeper pools of shadow. The last person I'd expected to see stood there, and he slid his hands into the pockets of his slacks.

"I was just making sure you got to your car all right," Mr. Standish told me, and I let out a breath. Save for that brief moment on my first day, I hadn't seen him at all. My proximity to him on this internship was making Archie crazy, and I'd assured him I hadn't seen his father at all just two hours earlier on a break.

Great, now I would have to tell him about this. "My car is right there," I said and turned away, intent on getting to it.

"Frankie…"

I hit the unlock on the key fob, aware he was following me now, and that was already enough to make me uneasy.

"Look," he said and then let out a sigh. "I'm sorry."

Wait.

What?

I pivoted, one hand on the door, and glanced at him. He was a few feet away, but not closing the distance. Fuck, he looked so much like Archie, it was unnerving. But where there was always a warmth and a playfulness in Archie's eyes, Edward's were a lot colder, even if his disgruntled expression betrayed an unease.

What the hell did he have to be uneasy about? The fact he was having an affair with Maddy? That ship had sailed a long time ago, right?

"What?" Yeah, I could probably have formed that question with a lot more intelligence. But I really didn't have more to add.

"I'm sorry," he began again, the awkwardness there uncomfortable as hell to witness. "I know this hasn't been easy for you on any level, and I'm partially to blame for that."

Where was he going with this? "The internship is fine." Was I playing dumb? Yes, I was. "Maybe unexpected. But fine." Then, because he still stared at me, I added, "I'm learning a lot, which is the point of the program, right?"

"Good," he said with an exhale, and it was awkward as fuck to see the same unease I experienced on the face of a grown man. He pulled a hand from his pocket and ran it through his hair. "I gave specific instructions that you were to be treated well."

Well, that just drained what fun there had been in it out.

"But it wasn't the internship that I was apologizing for." He seemed more collected and took another step toward me. "Your mother…"

"I don't want to discuss her with you." Not even a little bit.

"I understand."

He couldn't possibly, but whatever.

"But I do feel I should apologize to you, not only for the way Maddy ambushed you… I thought you knew we were seeing each other."

Gag. I blew out a breath. "Does it matter? I mean, really? I think the people you should be apologizing to are your wife and your child."

He gave me the slightest of nods that I couldn't even begin to interpret. "But this division between you and your mother…"

"Is really none of your business, Mr. Standish," I told him, and I kept my tone stiff.

His lips flattened, and he slid his hand back into his pockets. Archie did that sometimes when he had to hold himself back or edit himself in front of others. Was that just a trait shared by his father? Or was I trying to read too much into it? "Of course, I'm overstepping."

"You could say that." I popped the door to my car open. "It's not like we have to speak. I know I'm here interning at your company, but if that's a problem for you, I can request a change."

It would make Archie happy.

"No," he said, almost too quickly. "I would like very much to start over, but I suspect the issue with your mother is going to cloud things."

I tossed my backpack inside. "Are you for real right now?" I stared at him, and he gave me a quizzical look. "You treat Archie like crap. You're sleeping around on your wife—and you know what? Fine, that part is none of my business. Trust me, I wish I didn't know. But Archie is your son, and he's a *really* amazing person."

"Archie and I do not have the best of relationships," he admitted.

"No shit." Okay. There went my veneer of trying to be polite. "You treat him like crap, and that makes *you* the asshole. So instead of trying to do whatever this is you're doing with me, because trust me when I say that *nothing* you could say to me is going to change my mind on how shitty you and Maddy have both behaved, you try talking to your son and apologizing to him."

"He's important to you."

"He should be important to you. Granted, maybe that's what he and I have most in common—we won the lottery on shit parents."

I bit the inside of my lip and then shook my head.

"Look, Mr. Standish…"

"Edward, or Eddie is fine."

"Mr. Standish," I repeated. "We're not friends. You doing whatever you're doing with Maddy doesn't make us anything. My relationship with Archie is none of your business. But if you feel some driving urge to make things right, start with your son. He deserves a lot better than you."

I slid into the car, but his next words froze my hand reaching for the seatbelt. "You're right," he said. "He does deserve better. But I can't fix eighteen years in an instant."

"Then maybe you should get started."

"Would that make you happy?" The question was fucking bizarre, and I just shrugged and yanked the door closed.

Engine started, I glanced over to find him still staring at me and my car. Fuck me.

I opened the window. "Archie being happy would make me happy. Me being here and you doing whatever it is you're doing? That doesn't make him happy. You want to fix something, fix it with him."

He dropped his chin a moment, then nodded. "I understand. As for your suit…"

Great, here we went.

"If you want me to testify at any hearing, I will."

Wait.

What?

"Maddy will be furious," he told me. She'd be livid. Was he insane? "But maybe I should start out fixing something small. You want your emancipation. I won't stand in your way, and I'll help if necessary."

"Why?"

He gave a little shrug. "Because I can." He turned and began walking away. "Drive carefully. They are calling for freezing rain tonight, and you need to get the transmission on that car checked."

Then he was gone.

What. The. Fuck.

I didn't even know what to do with that. I picked up and put my phone down three times to text Archie, then I didn't. Because I didn't know even how to explain that interaction. Mr. Standish made no sense. Was there trouble with Maddy? Did he want me to smooth things over with Archie for him?

Define irony. I have a problem with her new boyfriend, and he thinks making up with me will fix something with her.

Wow.

I turned up the volume as I drove and tried to sort out what just happened. I had to tell Archie, because not telling them things to protect them wasn't going to fly. Even if the very last thing I wanted to do was stress him. But no matter which way I looked at that interaction with Mr. Standish, I couldn't explain what he wanted if I tried. I didn't get it.

At all.

Jake

Picked up Chinese earlier. Got your favorite. Come on home, Baby Girl.

Well, at least that saved me having to figure out dinner. Funnily enough, cooking dinner or at least cutting back on how much we ordered in or picked up was a battle I'd been losing. Archie refused to be constrained to a grocery budget.

Ugh. A battle for another day. I was too hungry to worry about it. Especially when Jake, Coop, and Ian were just as bad. Admittedly, when I wanted to cook, they also pitched in, and they each harbored little secrets—like Ian and his omelets—doling them out like these sweet surprises.

The freezing drizzle showed up the last mile of my drive, but thankfully, I was practically home and parked. Ian's bike was there, but covered. So was Jake's SUV and Coop's car. No sign of Archie's Ferrari.

A brief sensation of relief crawled through me. That would give me some time to figure out how to tackle this best for Archie. Definitely not hiding it from him, but softening it somehow so it didn't add to the anxiety already piling on him. He always wanted to fix things for me.

Backpack in hand, I slid out of the car and hurried inside. It seemed even colder out than when I got in the car at Standish. Three things hit me when I let myself into the kitchen.

The photo that hung on the wall next to the kitchen table was gone. We were short one chair at the table. And there was a large bag of trash sitting next to the backdoor waiting to be taken out.

Jake appeared in the entryway between the living room and the kitchen, his expression tight. "Before you say anything..."

My stomach dropped. What had happened?

"I got here like thirty minute ago and found the mess along with Coop."

I dropped my backpack and flipped the lock. "What happened? Is he all right?"

"I'm fine," Coop called, his voice slurring completely, and my jaw dropped. Jake grimaced and curled his fingers toward me. I barely smelled the unopened Chinese food still sitting in its bags on the counter as I went to him. Coop sat in the living room, a bottle of whisky and a full six pack of beer in front of him.

Well, I should amend that to six empty bottles and a half-full bottle of whisky. When did we get the whisky?

"He had a fight with his dad," was all Jake murmured in a voice so low, I barely heard it. Squeezing his hand, I headed for Coop. To be honest, his issues with *his* dad were complicated and had been since Carly and he had broken up. Coop had been pissed at him for cheating. And I couldn't blame him, it was a shitty, shitty thing to do to Carly.

When Coop's fingers closed around the neck of the whisky bottle, I put my hand over his. "Leave it?"

Coop cut his head back to look at me, and his eyes were unfocused, his face flushed, and I swore there were marks of tears around his eyes. More, his knuckles were scraped and raw on both hands. I glanced at Jake, and his lips compressed. Yeah, he'd seen them too.

"He's not interested in reason right now, Baby Girl."

Fine. Then we'd go with unreasonable.

I crawled right onto Coop's lap, and he had to let go of the bottle or risk dumping me on the floor. He clamped his hands on my hips to steady me, and Jake snagged the bottle away.

"Hey," I said, focusing on Coop and threading my arms around him. "Talk to me?"

He tugged me into him as he sagged back against the sofa, and then he buried his face against my neck. I didn't grimace, but holy shit, he smelled like a distillery. Coop was not one for benders. The other guys? Yes, I'd seen Jake and Archie drink each other under the table, and if egged on appropriately, so would Ian. But Coop was always the most level-headed one.

"My fucking father," Coop slurred. "He's an asshole."

"Got that," I soothed, carding my fingers through his hair. "Tell me so I can go kick his ass for you?"

"Not gonna kick his ass," Coop mumbled against my shoulder. "Pretty sure I knocked one of his teeth out."

Jake came back in and sat on the arm of the sofa. He had a glass of water in hand, and he shook his head. "He wasn't here when I got here."

"Nah, he fucking left when he figured out I was serious." Coop sighed. "I can't fucking believe he did that. I mean, I should believe he did that, but how the fuck am I supposed to look Mom in the eye now?" Before I could respond to that, he jerked back and brought his hands to my face. "Your mother is a bitch, Frankie. A raging fucking cunt. I don't want you to even have to breathe the same air as her again, okay?"

My mother?

"Okay," I murmured, just agreeing. It would be easier right now. "Can you drink some water for us? And maybe let me clean up your knuckles?"

He glanced at his hand and then shrugged, but he didn't let go of my face. "Hands don't even hurt. Why are parents so bad at parenting? Mom is great. Mom's been a damn saint. So much makes sense now, and I don't know why I didn't see it. But fuck me, I wish I didn't see it now."

"Hey, bud," Jake said, bumping his arm, and it eased up Coop's grip on my face. "Water, man. Before you puke all over Frankie then have to look her in the eye later."

I slanted a look at Jake. I could have lived without that mental image.

"Dude, you puked on her the first time you got shit-faced," Coop said with a snicker, but he took the glass of water from Jake, and both of us steadied it for him as he took a deep drink. Gradually, Coop slumped back on the sofa. "You remember that, Frankie? Threw up all over your shirt and your shoes. First time I saw you with tits for real. I mean, we'd seen them before, kind of knew they were there, but you had on that pretty pink bra."

Wow. He really was drunk if he was bringing that up.

Jake's shoulders shook. "Do we tell him?"

I shook my head. "Leave him alone. I want to know what happened."

"His dad, apparently." Jake raked a hand through his hair.

"Course, then I threw up on you," Coop said, his voice almost mournful. "And you said you threw that pretty pink bra away, and I felt bad."

"It's okay," I murmured. "Really, there was no getting burrito and beer stains out of it."

"Fuck, why do you even kiss us when we did shit like that?" Coop groaned.

"And there he goes," Jake said, covering his mouth as if he needed to keep the laughter back. "Dude, don't remind her, or she might not want to kiss us."

"Shut up," I told Jake and stuck my tongue out at him. He winked. Then I focused on Coop. "I kiss you because you brush your teeth. You also held my hair back when I got puking drunk. You guys were doing all kinds of things for me with my broken wrist, including helping me in the bathroom." Trust me, there were things about that I never wanted to think about, and they hadn't hesitated.

Not once.

"Why do you kiss me when you've had to do that?"

"'Cause you're fucking beautiful," Coop said. "Inside and out."

"Well, right back at you. Do you think if we put you in a shower, got some more water and food into you, you could tell us what happened?"

He stared at me for a long moment. "I don't want to tell you," he whispered, his frown tearing at my heart. "You'll just get upset, and I'm tired of the whole fucking world trying to hurt you."

"We're not letting anyone hurt her," Jake told him. "But let's sober you up so you can tell us. If you don't tell us what the dick did, you can at least tell me how much damage to inflict on him."

Coop chuckled. "You'd go find him and kick his ass, wouldn't you?"

"Damn straight." Jake cupped my elbow and helped me climb off Coop, and between us, we pulled Coop to his feet. He slung an arm around me and sighed.

"He had an affair on my mom."

"Yeah, man, we know," Jake comforted him as we got him moving. Coop wasn't quite weaving on his feet, but he was definitely not steady.

At the door to the bathroom, Jake left Coop leaning between me and doorjamb while he got the shower started.

Coop turned those mournful gray-green eyes on me, and my heart squeezed at the sadness there. "I'll help him kick his ass," I promised.

"I believe you," he said with a slow sigh. "His affair was with your mom.

I can't believe he did that. To me. To Mom. I thought Archie's dad was a douche, and it turns out my dad is a douche." A humorless laugh broke out of him. "Hey, Archie and I can now form our own little club. Pretty sure Bubba's dad is definitely not in it, and Jake's dad didn't come back…"

"Yeah, he had his own issues," Jake said steadily as the water pounded down in the shower, but my brain was still back at the fact that Coop's dad had an affair with Maddy. Maddy and Carly had been friends, right?

"Sorry, Frankie," Coop told me mournfully, and I rubbed his spine gently. "I shouldn't have said anything. I didn't want to tell you. I can't believe him."

Maddy poisoned everything she touched.

"Come on, let's get you into the shower."

It took Jake and me both to strip Coop, and then I dropped my own clothes and went in after him to help him shower and wash. Jake stayed right there, leaning against the counter and ready to move if Coop swayed too far from one side to the other.

He bowed his head so I could wash his hair and then leaned it back to let me rinse the shampoo out. I got his hands cleaned up and took my time about soaping him down. Bit by bit, the stench of alcohol began to wane.

"I have regrets," Coop admitted in a less wavery voice.

"Yeah," Jake said. "I'll bet."

But once he was washed, Jake took over balancing him while I toweled him off. Then we poured more water and some toast into him, and he was listing heavily. We tucked him into bed and put water, pain relievers, and a trash can right next to the bed, and I crawled in to sit next to him while Jake went for food.

Coop didn't move, not once the whole time we ate, and Jake leaned back against the headboard next to me and said, "I sent Archie and Bubba texts, they're gonna crash at their places. Arch will pick up Bubba in the morning."

"What did you tell them?"

"Just that I needed you tonight, told Arch you were fine and nothing bad happened today." He rubbed my arm. "You haven't told me about your day yet."

"Later," I said. "I'm worried about Coop."

"Yeah, he'll be fine, Baby Girl. He just needed to vent."

"Except…Maddy…"

"That's on them," Jake said firmly. "That's on her, Coop's dad, and Archie's. They're the adults. They make choices, regardless of the consequences. We may end up paying for them, but they aren't ours to own."

"Except Maddy breaks up marriages," I pointed out. "And I can't choose between you guys. Maybe I'm—"

"If you finish that sentence, I will spank you," Jake snapped, and that sounded like less an erotic promise than a real punishment. "You are *not* her. You are *not* sneaking around. You are *honest* and *loving* and *perfect*. Do you understand me?"

It was my turn for my eyes to burn. "I just hate what she does to people."

"On that we agree," he murmured and pressed a kiss to my palm. "I hate what she does to you, too. But here's the difference. You haven't lied to us. You haven't tried to take something that wasn't yours from the beginning. We know who we are and where we stand. We're better with you, all of us, and we're right where we want to be. Don't ever compare yourself to her again, Baby Girl. You're so much better than she is."

He blew out a breath, and I tucked my head against his shoulder. "I love you, too."

After pressing a kiss to my hair, he murmured, "Frankie, not all affairs are the same. Not all relationships are. One of the reasons I got so pissed at my father was that…when Mom couldn't handle them having a third person in their relationship anymore, he chose her over us. He chose that woman over his wife and his kids. I get it, he loved Mom and he loved Klara. Mom and Klara broke up, and Dad decided to stay there. That will never not piss me off, but that choice wasn't about us, it was about them."

Holy.

Shit.

I stared at Jake. "I'm sorry."

I mean, we all knew his dad never came back. More, we knew he and his dad had a massive falling out. But there had been another woman involved.

Jake gave a shrug. "It is what it is, Baby Girl. I never wanted to be in Germany, and I didn't understand the relationship when I was younger. I get it now, in retrospect, and I even get why Mom made her choices and he made his. The point is, what they do with their lives is on them. What we do with ours? That's about us."

Threading my arms around him, I burrowed into his side. "Hurting you guys is the last thing I ever want to do."

"Ditto," he whispered. "But we've got this…"

Coop made a sound and turned. Jake and I sprang apart. I'd never seen Jake move so fast. He got the empty trash can under Coop's head before he vomited, and I helped support him.

I met Jake's gaze, and we both smiled.

"We've got this," he repeated. "But fuck, that smells awful. Thank you for still being willing to kiss us."

I laughed.

Because it was so much better than crying.

Red Flag

Archie

The parts we ordered will get in today. But I want to be there for Frankie's meeting.

Jake

Agreed. Is it right after school?

Archie

Yep. In fact, I recommend we cut out ten minutes early if we can swing it so we can get there ahead of them.

Jake

Archie

Everything good? I tried to text Coop last night, and he didn't answer.

Jake

He was beat.

Archie

Cool. Frankie said she didn't have a bad day but was tired when she got in. Everything good with her?

Jake

Dude, relax. Seriously. You're going to give yourself an ulcer. And I never knew how much of a thing that could be until this year.

Archie

Ha ha. Is she okay or not?

Jake

She is fine. We talked when she got in.
No complaints that she shared.

Archie

K. I'll get coffee after I get Bubba.
We'll see you three at school?

Jake

Arch, if you have a question ask. Don't
do this fishing bullshit. It was a long night.

Archie

If it was a long night, then tell me what happened.

Jake

It's not mine to tell, and before you have a shit fit in
her direction, it's not hers either. Just dial it down
a couple of notches. And maybe grab food too.

Archie

...

Archie

Hangover food?

Jake

That'll work.

Archie

Done. Do I need to pay to take someone out?

Jake

Don't. Tempt. Me.

Archie

Just saying we have options.

Archie

Picking up breakfast and coffee for school. Miss you, babe.

Frankie

We need to work on your aim.

Archie

Ha ha. How tired were you after yesterday? I know you said you were beat last night.

Frankie

My brain hurts. The amount of stuff the company does. How does one person keep it straight?

Archie

They can't. That's why they have teams and reports. I read the yearly stuff, even if it makes me want to gouge my eyes out, since technically, I'm a shareholder.

Frankie

I wondered about that. And I have to tell you that I spoke to your father yesterday. Don't blow up.

Archie

...

Frankie

I would have said something last night, but you sounded like you were in a good mood and I walked into some stuff here that needed my attention. It wasn't bad. I'll tell you everything at school. Don't lose your cool. It's not bad. I promise.

Archie

Were you stuck in a meeting with him or did he approach you?

Frankie

He followed me to my car, but it's not as bad as that sounds.

Archie

I'll take care of it.

Frankie

Archie, don't do anything until we talk. Please. I knew this would upset you. But I wanted to tell you before school. Please don't make me regret that.

Archie

...

Archie

...

Archie

...

Frankie

I'm sorry I didn't tell you last night.

Archie

Is Coop okay?

Frankie

He will be.

Archie

You're okay?

Frankie

I promise. I'm fine. Though I did kind of tell your dad off

Archie

I'm sorry. What?

Frankie

I told him he was a shitty father and he needed to talk to you and not me. Look, I will tell you when we get to school. Promise.

Archie

Can I drive you and pick you up tomorrow?

Frankie

Frankie

Frankie

Frankie

Will it make you feel better? 'Cause you're gonna be late to school if you take me.

Archie

It will make me feel loads better to know he can't corner you in the parking garage. So yes.

Frankie

> We'll talk about it. No promises.

Archie

That is not a no.

Archie

Get your ass out here. We need to go.
I want to be there when they get in.

Bubba

> Coming. What's wrong?

Archie

Just…get in the car. I'll tell you.

Archie

Grandpa. Tell me we have a plan.

Grandpa

> I'm working on it. I have about half the
> board. I only need two more members,
> and then we can remove him.

Archie

What does that do with Frankie's internship?

Grandpa

> Since I'll be resuming my position until you
> can take over, I'll make sure it's fine. Don't
> worry, Sprout. These things take time, but
> once it's done? It's done.

Archie

How much will it cost me for you to just pack up and disappear for good? Think about a number. You have until the meeting today to make a call. You're not getting this offer again.

Chapter Eighteen
A LIFETIME OF (BROKEN) PROMISES

Archie and Ian were waiting when we got to school. Coop's hangover was bad, but we'd gotten water into him on and off all night. That coupled with the morning painkillers, another shower, and some food, and he seemed semi-human. Jake and I'd both told him the exact same thing, we were there for him no matter what. I wanted to apologize for Maddy, but Jake's words from the night before kept rattling in my head.

That and worry about what Archie would do with regards to his dad had me biting my tongue on all fronts, save one. I sent Mr. Wittaker a text to verify that we were still on with Maddy today. She wanted a face-to-face?

She was gonna fucking get one.

If she wanted to screw up and fuck around with my life? Fine. She'd done it my whole life. That she'd gone after Coop's and now Archie's families? Fuck. Her.

Coop still looked a little green around the gills, but he took the coffee Ian had in the tray and plucked a croissant out of the bag, then he was stuffing his face and kind of angled away from us. Even though it was another gray, brr-fucking-cold kind of day, he had on sunglasses. At Ian's quirked brow, I just shook my head.

What Coop confessed to me and Jake would stay between the three of us until…

"Arch, remind me we need to order shirts," Coop said after downing half of the coffee in his cup. We hadn't even left the parking lot. "As the founding member of the My Dad Fucked My Girlfriend's Mom Club, I feel bad I wasn't there for you when you found out."

Archie slanted a look at me, and I gave him a small shrug. Yes, I knew. And no, there wasn't much I could do about it. Everything in me ached for Coop. Humor was one of his natural defense modes. If he needed to make a joke out of it, I wasn't going to stop him.

"We're cool," Archie told him, even as he slid an arm around my waist. Against my ear, he murmured, "How bad is this for him?"

"Pretty bad," I admitted. "Shock and a lot of hurt."

"He liked his dad." That wasn't a question, and I gave a little shrug.

"He loved him. He was always cool, you know…" I mean, Coop's parents had broken up before Archie came into our lives, so maybe he didn't know. "But he didn't know it was Maddy."

A kiss behind my ear didn't hide his quiet sigh. "You okay?"

"I'm fine," I stressed. "I promise." Then I met his gaze. "On everything."

"Come on, it's freezing out here," Coop said. "Sorry, Frankie. I don't mean to be such a drag."

"You're just being a drama queen, Brennen," Rachel drawled as she joined us, and Ian offered her one of the coffees. "This is hardly new."

"Ah, if it isn't Queen Bitch of the Universe. Please take this with all the emotion intended," Coop told her, a faint smile curving his lips. "Fuck off."

"That's Your Majesty, to you, Coop." Rachel grinned. "And I'll definitely take it under advisement." She threaded her arm through mine as we started walking. Archie just shot her a look but otherwise didn't comment. "Did I miss something?" Rachel asked.

I glanced at her and blinked.

Was that a hickey on her neck?

Flicking my gaze to hers, I said, "Just…same shit, different day. High school."

"Ahh," she said.

"Don't have to cover for me, Frankie. Rachel's one of us. The bitchier side of us, sure. But one of us." Coop glanced back at us from where he walked with Jake. Then he looked at Rachel. "My dad had an affair with her mom. Good times, right?"

"Sure." Rachel didn't miss a beat. But Jake wrapped an arm around Coop's neck and dragged him forward a few feet, and Ian lifted his chin to me before he hurried to follow them. Archie slowed a half-pace and so did I, so Rachel had to, or she would have walked in front of us.

"Cut him some slack, Manning," Archie ordered. "This is not good news."

"No shit." She practically leaned around me to glare at Archie, and I got a good look at a second and third hickey. "Credit me with some humanity."

"You love Frankie," Archie said blithely. "I credit you with a lot of humanity. It doesn't make you less of a bitch when you want to be."

She paused to consider it. "I can accept that." With a grin, she squeezed my arm. "Just let me know if you need help with the bodies."

"Know any good pig farms?" Wasn't that what they used in the Hannaford books?

Rachel cracked up. "Speaking of pig farms, I have a new series for you to read. You are going to *love* it. But you'll probably call me a liar and a fake, because you'll hate it first." Then she laughed harder, and I had to bite back a smile.

"Sign me up," I told her. "I could use a new series with someone else's drama."

"Girl, let me tell you, they have *drama*."

In the cafeteria, Coop seemed to be slightly better, and Rachel joined us instead of wandering off. The guys didn't complain. Archie even pulled out a chair for her when I took a seat next to Coop, and then he claimed the chair on my other side. He hadn't let go of my hand.

Jake gave her all of a minute before he asked, "So, who's the new girl?"

Rachel eyed him. "Excuse you?"

"Unless you're dipping your toe in the XY gene pool, there's a new girl." He motioned with his coffee cup toward her neck.

"Jake."

Unrepentant, he winked at me and pressed on. "Hey, she'd be the first one asking us if we showed up with fresh hickeys like that."

"I don't *give* you hickeys like that." Quite the opposite actually, but we were *not* having that conversation here.

"You're making his point for him, babe," Archie said with a slow smile, and even Coop laughed.

"Not really," Rachel said as she flipped through her phone, clearly no longer interested in the conversation. "What she's saying is that if you showed up like that, I'd be gutting you because she doesn't leave hickeys like that."

There was a painful moment where all four of them paused, and Coop lifted his coffee cup and said, "Touché, Your Majesty. Touché."

I was in the bathroom between classes when a few new girls took it upon themselves to remind me that yes, we were in high school. There were three of them, and someone should really tell them that trying to coordinate outfits like they were in some teen flick went out with the nineties.

Though, everything old was becoming new again.

Honestly, though, I wasn't in the mood. Coop still had a hangover. Archie was firmly in silent plotting mode, I could read it in every tense line of his face. Jake and Ian were both keeping a steady hand on the wheel, but Jake was spoiling for a fight. It seemed to vibrate with his every step. Without football to burn off some steam, I was thinking about the offer he'd made over Christmas to work on my punching.

Maybe I needed to suck it up and get him into the gym.

The girls slanted looks at me. Three juniors and one sophomore. Poor thing had two of their book bags slung over her shoulder like she was their personal pack mule.

That told me all I needed to know about these bitches. I dried my hands as the first one opened her mouth. "So you're the girl banging four guys, right?"

"I'm Frankie," I told her as I turned to face her and her friends. They really did look like carbon copies of each other. It was kind of creepy. Same hair style, same lip shade and eye shadow, even the same cats eye shape to their contouring, though apparently, one of them favorited pink, the other teal, and the third one a kind of minty green.

Pack mule apparently didn't get the memo on the matching outfits, but the poor thing had tried. I didn't know that girl, but man, I felt for her. As for these three…

"We know what your name is," Mint Green Accents piped in. "Not that we care. Usually people just call you the slut."

They all tittered with laughter, and I rolled my eyes. So original. I slid my backpack onto my shoulder and glanced over at the pack mule. "If you want to dump their stuff, feel free. No one should make you carry their damage or their trauma."

"Excuse you?" Pink Accents demanded. "Don't talk to her. For all tents and purpose, she isn't in the room."

"For all intents," I corrected. "Not tents, like something you use for camping, or tense, like we're discussing verbs. But intents. As in you're all intent on getting your rocks off by pretending to be the biggest bitches on the campus. Newsflash, you're not, and you won't be next year either because you're trying too hard and you're more than a little fake."

Teal blinked. "That's what she said."

"No," I informed her. "You might need a hearing check or a diction lesson." I really didn't have time for this or for them. "As for you…" I focused on the pack mule. "What's your name?" Their names I didn't care about. The girl letting them treat her like crap, she mattered.

"It's not important," she murmured. Despite the quiet voice, I hadn't missed the flash of humor when I corrected the coiffed terrorists.

"Sure it is, because a name is an identity. Everything else is a label. I'm Frankie," I said, and pushed right between Pink and Teal like they weren't there. Though I never quite turned my back on them.

I wasn't stupid.

Girls were mean.

In third grade, one chick had come after me when someone told her I was making fun of her parents. I hadn't been. But she'd grabbed my pony tail and yanked so hard, I thought I'd lose hair after that. It was one of the few fights I'd ever gotten in with another girl.

The worst part was I smashed my fountain soda against her head in retaliation, and I hadn't even gotten to have a drink of it.

Oh well, not that it was important right now.

Pack Mule cut a look up and met my gaze. "They're my friends."

"No they're not. Friends don't torture each other or treat them like a servant. If they are telling you they'll be your friend when you've earned it, they don't want a friend, they want a pack mule."

"Hey," Mint Green complained.

"If the truth fits, you need to lace that shit up and wear it," I told the other three, and cut a look at them. "I had so-called friends like you. You fucking suck." With that, I glanced at the girl who still hadn't given me her name. "You deserve better, and you can definitely do better."

I'd gotten lucky. Rachel just walked in and decided to be my friend for real. If this chick needed a friend, I'd do my best.

With that, I sailed out of the bathroom. Maybe I just needed to stop using them at the school. Sharon was in the hallway, but as soon as she saw me, she cut and changed directions. I didn't laugh because it wasn't funny.

But it sure was satisfying.

After school, we were converging in the parking lot because the guys were going with me to the lawyer's office. All four of them, though I wondered if it was a good idea to have Coop anywhere near the office. Especially after the revelations from the night before.

"Hang out and wait for me a sec?" Jake said as he headed to the bathroom. I nodded and texted Archie. He was adamant about going. Like Jake, he was also spoiling for a fight. Ian promised he'd try to keep them out of trouble, but he didn't disagree with *why* they were pissed.

Eddie talking to me had come up at lunch, and there'd been no denying how angry all of them had been. Especially Coop, who would normally help me defuse the situation. What a clusterfuck.

I turned and bounced off someone and grunted. "Sorry," I said automatically and glanced up at a tall boy who looked vaguely familiar. Dark brown hair, dark eyes, square jaw—football player. Had to be. I suppressed a shudder and took a step back. I didn't know if he was one of the guys from Halloween, and I really didn't want to know. Not all of them had been expelled, but following their suspensions, none of them had come anywhere near me.

And I preferred it that way.

"Hey," he said, closing the distance I put between us. "Just the girl I've been looking for. Finding you alone is a challenge."

I frowned. "Way to sound creepy."

He almost smiled, then rubbed a hand against the back of his neck as though sheepish. "But true," he continued, and swung a glance around before looking at me again. "Word has it you like variety—"

"You finish that sentence, Reed, and they won't find enough of your teeth to reconstruct your jaw." Jake's flat voice bounced off the lockers around us, and I didn't sag physically, but relief still pumped through me. I could punch the guy, but he was huge and had a very square jaw. I'd probably have broken my hand.

I dropped back another couple of steps, and Jake was already sliding between me and this dude. Hands up, *Reed* shot me another grin before he looked at Jake. "Man, I was just gonna ask her out. Nothing kinky."

"Yeah, you're not asking her shit. You're turning your ass around and walking the fuck away while I'm still willing to let you do it."

Leaning my head out from behind Jake, I added, "But let me also save you the trouble of trying to find me alone again. The answer is no, I don't want to go out."

"Can't blame a guy for trying."

"I can," Jake informed him. "You leave her the fuck alone and you can tell anyone who asks, they don't go near her either. Got it?"

"Sure thing…though if any spots open—"

Dammit.

I winced as Jake's fist plowed into the guy's mouth. Reed deserved it, but I lunged forward and caught Jake's arm before he could keep swinging. He glared at me, but I dug my heels in and held on. He wouldn't hurt me to yank free. "Don't," I said quietly. "You can't afford to be suspended."

"It'd be worth it," he muttered.

"Frankie. Jake."

Shit.

I glanced over my shoulder to find G standing there.

"And Mr. Reed," his voice dipped in disapproval. Reed hadn't quite collapsed from Jake's punch, but he had dropped his bag and half-froze on charging back at us when G stepped out. "I think you and I need to have a discussion, Mr. Reed, on appropriate behavior."

The other guy wiped the blood from his mouth and glared at Jake. "I'd like to file a complaint."

"You could do that," G told him. "Then I would also have to answer that complaint with your overt and inappropriate attention to a female student who quite clearly told you she wasn't interested. In case you were wondering, the first clues were the way she backed away, but the second one, the largest one, was when she said 'no.'"

Reed blinked.

"I thought you might see a little sense. Come with me, Mr. Reed." He glanced at me and Jake. "As for you two, I suggest you go on about your day, unless you'd like to file a complaint, Frankie?"

"I'm good, Mr. G," I told him, still wrapped around Jake's arm. Some of the tension bled out of him, and I relaxed.

"Very well." With that, G said, "And Jake?"

"I know."

"I know you do, son. Don't let me see that again, yes?"

"Yes, sir."

Reed glared at us once more, then he followed G away, and I let out a breath and rested my head against Jake's arm.

"I can handle a suspension. He doesn't get to talk to you like that."

"I know," I soothed him. "Thank you for rushing to the rescue, but beating him up just hurts you."

"Trust me, Baby Girl, it would hurt him a whole lot more." With that, he wrapped an arm around me. "Let's get this shit show on the road."

The drive to Wittaker's law firm was tense and uncomfortable. Archie's bad mood descended as soon as Jake filled them in on why we were late. I hadn't missed the look he and Ian exchanged either. Could people just leave us alone long enough to get done with high school? Then we'd be out of here and it wouldn't matter anymore.

Jake followed in his SUV with the guys while I rode with Archie. "You know," I told him after we went another couple of miles without exchanging a word. "I wanted to ride with you so we could talk."

"I know, babe, and sorry, my head's not in a good place right now. I'm trying to remind myself that we're not going into that meeting with you, and I'm hating it all over again. Then I hate that you even have to see her…"

"I don't." Even at the soft volume I used, it would be hard to miss in the silent car.

"What?"

"I said I don't hate that I have to see her. Not this time." Not when I had more than a few things to say to her myself.

He frowned. "Why not?"

"Because…I have questions. Before you say I can't believe anything she says, you're right. I can't. That doesn't change the fact that I have questions and I want the chance to demand answers from her." As alien as that even sounded to me. I hated rocking the boat with Maddy. A lifetime of broken moments with her trained me to avoid conflict. It never ended well. She could turn every situation to her advantage.

Something Erin and I had discussed during our last session when I told her about the craziness with the tests and the fact that I would have to talk to her eventually. Maddy turned everything around to make it about her, my words not Erin's, but I didn't have to accept the premise of her statements. Erin suggested I reframe them every single time to rob her of the power she wanted to take.

Sounded good, right?

My phone buzzed, a message from Rach, but I'd check it after. I needed to keep my focus on where we were and where we were going.

"Why ask? If you know you can't trust what she says, why ask?"

"Because I deserve better," I told him. "Just like you deserve better from Eddie, and I told him that."

For the first time today, a real smile creased his face, and he reached over and tangled our fingers together. "Babe, you're too damn kind sometimes."

"No, I'm not," I argued, leaning my head against the seat but keeping my gaze on him. "I'm protective. He treats you like crap, and I'm tired of it. You have been blowing off their behavior for years and acting like it's normal. Just like I pretended it was normal with Maddy and never wanted any of you to see the cracks, because if you did, I had to admit they were there."

Then because he didn't need to be on the spot, I squeezed his hand.

"Maybe they don't see you or can't, but I do. I know you deserve a lot better."

"I've got you, I've got Grandpa and Jeremy, and the guys," Archie said, his smile growing without an ounce of mockery in it. "I'm not doing too bad, babe, I promise. I'm used to Edward and Muriel being less than interested in me. I was a business transaction, an investment. Probably one they aren't thrilled with the dividends on."

I made a face. "I don't promise not to tell your mother off the next time I see her. I felt so fucking bad the last time…"

"You don't have to feel bad for Muriel. She was a bitch to you, and you didn't deserve it."

"And you don't either. So you need to agree with me, or I'm just going to be as annoying about this as I am about mini-golf."

He burst out laughing. "The horror."

I grinned, thrilled at the sound dislodging some of the darkness in his voice. "I bet you I can infuriate her. Have you ever gotten her to cuss at you?"

An amused, if thoughtful look crossed his face, and he glanced at me when we stopped at a light. "You don't have to fight my battles for me."

"Someone I adore told me they weren't just my battles anymore. That I wasn't alone. And that they would always have my back."

His eyes softened, and he relaxed a little more. "You're not going to back off on this are you?"

"'Fraid not. Love me. Love my stubbornness."

He chuckled and leaned over to kiss me. It wasn't long or deep, but it warmed me because he took a deep breath before he leaned back.

"Just remember, no matter what happens, we'll be right outside that conference room, and there's nothing she can throw at you that I can't fix or block."

"I believe you," I told him. "And you remember that I'm a lot stronger than I look. I'm going to protect you, too."

"I believe you," he said, his smile soft. "But, babe, you're going to have your hands full."

"I wouldn't have it any other way."

Twenty minutes later, Mr. Wittaker's secretary led me away from the guys to the conference room where he was waiting with Maddy and her attorney. They'd arrived early, apparently, and he'd only walked into the conference room after we'd arrived.

My stomach was in knots and sweat dampened the back of my neck, but I refused to let *her* get to me. Staring across the room to where she sat and seeing her for the first time in months, I hadn't been sure what I was going to feel when I got here.

"Francesca," Maddy said in a cutting voice. "How kind of you to join us finally. One would expect a little more appreciation for those of us with busy schedules."

"Do married men only keep banker's hours? I didn't know you had to punch a clock for being on your back, Maddy. My bad."

Her face flushed and her eyes flashed as she started to stand. The man with her put a hand on her arm, and Mr. Wittaker stood smoothly. "Ms. Curtis, you will address all of your comments and questions to me through your attorney. Miss Curtis is here only as a courtesy so we can settle this matter as amicably as possible."

"You call that amicable?" Maddy snarled, and it took everything I had to keep the smile off my face. Shots fired?

Today was not that day, and I was not that girl anymore.

I pulled out a chair and dropped into it, trusting Wittaker to take it from here.

I probably should have let him handle it in the first place, but it felt good to clap back at her.

Real good.

Chapter Nineteen
GETTING WHAT YOU WANT ISN'T ALWAYS WHAT YOU NEED

The weirdest thing happened after I took my seat. I was still pissed, don't get me wrong. Pissed as hell. Maddy had fucked up Coop's parents' marriage. Now she was after Archie's parents. Had she hit on Ian's dad at some point?

Oh, that was a horrifying thought. Maybe that explained some of his attitude toward me and why he'd leaned on Ian to take a step back. Or maybe that was me reading too much into it. Really, really hard to tell. Jake's dad might be safe from this particular nightmare. Then again, apparently, there had been three people in that marriage and that was still blowing my mind.

Not once had Jake ever mentioned it. I had a lot of questions. Ones I would never ask unless he wanted to share. That he'd trusted me with that information was a big deal. I intended to respect that. Which brought me full circle to the woman at the other end of the conference table. I'd taken the chair the farthest away from hers.

Mr. Wittaker now stood, nominally, between us. Though his attention was on the other attorney, whose name was…something. I honestly didn't listen. Maddy glared at me, and I just stared at her back. The weird thing that happened though, was I didn't really care what her response was. The fury in her eyes, the way her lips compressed, even the flush to her cheeks—those were all warning signs that told me to back off, retreat, change the subject, or at least try to placate her.

Fuck. That.

Instead, I just focused on her. Everything about her was put together, smooth, and professional. I'd bet every dime in my savings account that those were new clothes and probably designer. They looked expensive. I'd never even looked up the address for their new place, but I would imagine it was pricey, too. Didn't know. Didn't care. Never intended on living there.

But Maddy had on a skillful amount of makeup. The hair style hid it, but she'd gotten it cut. There were layers. Her nails were perfect. They were also the exact same shade as her lips.

Fuck, she looked almost like a Stepford wife, and that was creepy enough. It was worse that she was me in twenty years. We had the exact same eyes, nose, and chin. In so many ways, she was my distorted mirror. At least I wouldn't be bad looking?

Ugh, it was enough to turn my stomach. That pretty face housed a really not pretty person, and I wanted to be nothing like her.

Ever.

"Frankie?" Mr. Wittaker said, and I glanced at him. He and the other attorney looked at me expectantly, and I hadn't heard a word they'd said.

"I'm sorry, I was gathering my thoughts, could you repeat that for me?"

He gave me the kindest of smiles as he pulled out the chair next to mine, but that would also keep him between me and Maddy. "We just went over the terms of how this conference would go. Both Mr. Stevens and I would prefer that all communication be conducted between the two of us. Our job is to facilitate this interaction so that both you and Ms. Curtis can have all your concerns addressed. Does that seem reasonable to you?"

"That's perfectly reasonable to me. I'm happy to let you do the talking."

"I'm not," Maddy snapped, and she shook off her attorney when he put a hand on her arm. "I came here to speak to you, not your attorney."

I probably shouldn't smile, but her aggravation at being blocked amused me. It was petty and small. But it was still funny. I leaned back in my seat and kept my focus on Mr. Wittaker. His eyes held the faintest twinkle to them as he raised his brows at me.

"You are aware of my goals, and I think you have a grasp on the big picture here."

His eyes warmed, and he inclined his head. A split-second before he turned from me, all the warmth drained from his expression, and he favored Mr. Stevens with a look. "In that case, Mr. Stevens, do you need a few moments to confer with your client? She seems to be expressing some difficulty with this situation."

"I'm not experiencing difficulty," Maddy snapped at him. "I have a right to speak to my child. Mine, by the way, not yours. Not his. Mine. She's not eighteen. She shouldn't even have an attorney without my permission."

"Ms. Curtis," Mr. Stevens began, but she glared at him.

"You're my attorney, you're here to do what I want. Not what they want."

"Of course," her attorney attempted again, and I chuckled, I couldn't help it. Of course, Maddy didn't want rules or restrictions. They were getting in the way of what she wanted. "However, this conference is to discuss the fact that you plan to file an injunction to end the temporary emancipation. It would be better if we discussed that before we got into more complicated and emotional matters that might lead to an unfavorable resolution."

Maddy glared at him.

"Frankie," Mr. Wittaker said. "Let's go to my office while they sort this out."

"Sure thing," I said and stood.

"Don't you dare," Maddy yelled as she rose to her feet and slapped her hand against the table. "I won't be ignored like this or set aside while you let others do the talking for you. That apartment is not in your name. Nor is that car. I can take both away from you just like that." She snapped her fingers. "You wouldn't have anything without me. This tantrum of yours has gone on long enough. I am not changing my life just to make you happy."

"Ms. Curtis," Mr. Stevens tried again.

"When I want you to speak, I'll tell you," she snapped at him, and I almost felt sorry for the guy.

Almost.

"Mr. Wittaker?"

My attorney glanced at me, and I said, "Could you please express my regrets to Mr. Stevens, and I really do hope he's charging her through the nose for every hour he has to put up with her."

The twinkle was back in Wittaker's eyes, and he inclined his head. "I can take care of that. Why don't you head to my office?" He motioned to the door, and I nodded.

"If you walk out that door, you're going to regret it—"

"Ms. Curtis," Wittaker interrupted. "That will be quite enough. Understand that while Mr. Stevens may be your attorney and I am Frankie's attorney, we are both sworn officers of the court and I will not stand idly by while you threaten or try to intimidate my client."

I didn't leave, I probably should have, but I kept my back to them as I listened. I wanted to hear this.

"How dare you?" Maddy demanded.

"I dare because I have ample evidence of a lifetime of gross neglect and emotional abuse. The case for abandonment can and has been made."

"Excuse me?"

"Ms. Curtis." Mr. Stevens must really want to earn those hourly fees. "This isn't doing your case any good."

"If you're not going to help me then why are you here?"

I bet he had to be asking himself that question.

"As I was saying," Mr. Wittaker continued. "I've given Mr. Stevens a copy of our brief that was filed with the court. The evidence was compelling enough for the judge to grant the temporary emancipation order. We have received a court date for the first week of March."

We had?

"If you have a brief you intend to file in opposition, you can file that at will and have this office served. I believe it would be in the best interest of my client to limit all contact with you…"

"Well, in that case, I'll just have my car retrieved and notify the apartment complex that an unattended minor is living there and that I have moved out. Granted, I'll have to pay the breaking of the lease fee, but that's a small price to pay if it encourages my child to speak to me." She let out a wet little choked sound, and since my back was safely to them, I rolled my eyes. "I understand I've made mistakes, but how can I begin to fix them if she won't even speak to me?"

"I'm sorry," Mr. Stevens said. "Maybe give us fifteen minutes, and we can try again?"

"Of course." Wittaker turned, and he touched my back lightly as he motioned me ahead of him. Voice low, he murmured, "Just keep walking…"

Maddy's voice rose and an actual sob broke from her.

"Oh for fuck's sake," I muttered as I got to the door. "Everything has to be a damn drama. This isn't about me," I told Wittaker, and fuck her if she heard me. "This is because she can't get her way. Everything she accuses me of is what she's doing."

Wittaker gave me a razor-thin smile and an approving nod, but his tone was almost conciliatory. "I understand, but that's why we're going to give her attorney time to get her under control. Perhaps we should look into some psychological evaluations."

I loved this man. It was official. I think next to Jeremy, he was my favorite person ever to work for Archie.

"You wouldn't mind going to see one just for the purposes of the case?" He knew damn good and well I was seeing a psychologist, but I got it.

"Not at all, though I should warn you…" I turned to glance back at him ostensibly as we reached the door, but I met Maddy's gaze and ignored the well of artful tears. "Curtises don't do therapy. Though, I'm beginning to think it's because they'd put us on psych holds."

With that, I strode through the door, and Wittaker followed me. The guys were just down from the conference room and Archie was on his feet as soon as he caught sight of me, but I shook my head. "I don't think we're done yet."

"No," Wittaker said as he glanced at them. "Gentlemen, I'm going to ask all of you to move into the other conference room. Beth, please get them drinks and make them comfortable. Frankie…" He motioned to his office, and I blew the guys a quick kiss and what I hoped was a reassuring look before I followed Wittaker.

Once inside his office, he closed the door and blew out a breath.

"Should I apologize to you?"

"Not at all," he said. "I'm impressed by how well you held it together. You showed great poise and maturity. Though you definitely landed some well-placed verbal hits."

I shrugged as I dropped into a chair. I couldn't find a scratch of guilt within me. "She deserved it."

"I don't disagree." Instead of sitting, he leaned against the desk. "Real talk. Can you handle going back in there? It's clear she's not going to be satisfied with our refusal to let her speak to you. I have no problem with you leaving now and I'll take care of it from here. I can also take care of the apartments, since young Mr. Standish has paid your rent in full through May, I won't have to work too hard at it so you'll still have your house. The car…"

"I don't care about the car." Actually… "I mean, I do because I've been paying for it."

"That's what you told me. You've been making payments for almost two years. How close to paying it off are you?"

"I owe another three thousand. I've been paying only two hundred a month, and it had a six-thousand-dollar trade-in value, so that was what I agreed to pay her for it in installments." It would almost serve her right if I let her have the car and then took Mr. Standish up on his offer, but even making a joke of that thought made me a little sick. I really didn't want anything from him.

Archie wouldn't let me go without a car, even if I barely drove it except for work. Not that I wanted him taking care of any more than he already had.

"I have more than enough in savings, I could dip into my college fund."

"I would rather you didn't," Wittaker told me, his expression calculating. "I have your receipts for the last several months, including all the times you purchased groceries without her contributing, the payments for the household bills that you've had to take care of in her absence, as well as any other expenses. We've got the list. That comes to considerably more than three thousand dollars."

It did?

"You also pay for the pets from your account, correct?"

"Well yeah, but I always did that."

"It doesn't matter," Wittaker told me. "As your parent, she is legally obligated to all of those responsibilities until you reach the age of majority. That you've had to do so much on your own and you've been successful at it, that's a credit to you, but it will not do her any favors in court. Frankly, I rather hope she has this same type of incident there. It will solve a lot of our problems very quickly."

"I appreciate your confidence. And truth talk…I have questions for her that I desperately want to ask, but they may not get us anywhere."

"What do you want to ask her?"

So I told him. I'd mentioned the DNA tests, but I hadn't gone into detail before. I couldn't tell him about Coop's dad, that was Coop's story. Not mine, but it was out there. "There's so many things she's lied about. The affair with Archie's dad, the tests, and I don't even know who they were for. Does she actually not know who my biological father is? Is there a reason she's suddenly trying to figure it out? What is so damn important that she needs me involved now when clearly she's spent the last two years pulling further and further away? What's her endgame?"

That was it in a nutshell. What did she gain if she had me back? It was all about Eddie. She wanted to look good in front of him?

"I thought it was Mr. Standish, but…he signed that release and he told me he would testify if there was a hearing."

Wittaker frowned. "When did he tell you this?"

So then I had to explain that incident to him, and he frowned before he checked his watch.

"If Mr. Standish approaches you again on this subject, call me as soon as you can and direct him to speak to me as well."

"That I can do," I said.

"All right, let's go back in."

When we reached the conference room this time, Maddy was on her feet with her arms folded and a tissue in her hand.

Oh, kill me.

Her eyes were faintly red-rimmed, and there was the faintest smudge of dark under her eyelashes, like her mascara had run.

Wittaker pulled out a chair for me, and I sat without saying a word. He stood there, one hand on the back of my seat. After the last couple of times at Standish, I was starting to recognize the power plays for what they were.

In this room, Wittaker was in charge. I focused on Maddy's attorney rather than on Maddy.

"Have we reached an agreement?"

"We have," Mr. Stevens said as he pulled out a chair, and Maddy took a seat. "We're ready to begin. Ms. Curtis would like five minutes with her daughter at the conclusion of this conference. It can happen right here and she would prefer it in private, but will not object if you and I stay as long as we agree to keep the information revealed confidential."

"I'll take that under advisement," Wittaker said before moving back to the seat at my left. "Let's discuss what if any objections you have to Frankie filing for emancipation…"

The next thirty minutes were alternately dull as fuck and interesting. Interesting because Maddy didn't seem to pay a lick of attention to anything the attorneys said. Her expression alternated between distant and impatient.

Watching her from the corner of my eye took some effort, so did trying to keep my face blank. I had no idea how people did this in books. They always made it sound easy. Maddy might be good at keeping her secrets, but she didn't have a blank face either. She kept shooting me these little looks I didn't want to try and interpret.

But I got it.

She wanted me to pay attention to her. The more I seemed to ignore her, the more it pissed her off. Or maybe it made her sad.

Ugh.

Whatever.

"To clarify, your client's only objections to the emancipation is that she is not eighteen yet?" Wittaker said as though summarizing, but there was a distinct note of disbelief in his voice.

"It's a consideration of maturity and on focusing on her schoolwork rather than trying to meet the parameters set forth in an emancipation claim. After all, it was Frankie's wish to attend college, or at least that is the impression Ms. Curtis has. If that plan has changed, she has not informed Ms. Curtis of any changes."

"I'm afraid I don't understand what you think will change significantly between now and April," Wittaker stated. "In a little over nine weeks, she will be eighteen and an adult. In the grand scheme of things, she will have her independence at that point, regardless of your client's manufactured concerns."

Maddy's lips thinned. Oh, she didn't like that.

Mr. Stevens seemed unperturbed. "I could in turn, ask you the same question. What is the sudden hurry? If she turns eighteen in nine weeks, this whole situation resolves itself."

"Except her age didn't factor into the choices Ms. Curtis made when she abandoned Frankie, nor did they factor into her decisions to move out and leave a minor to fend for herself."

"I'm afraid I don't—"

"Yes, I know," Wittaker cut him off smoothly. "You don't agree with the characterization, but shall we examine some key incidents of the last year? Or if those aren't enough, perhaps we could call Mr. Standish in. I understand Ms. Curtis' fiancé has offered to testify on Frankie's behalf at any hearing to grant her emancipation."

Wittaker shot and Wittaker scored.

Maddy gave a jerk, and she leaned forward abruptly. "Excuse me? When did Eddie get brought into this?"

"Why don't we invite him to join us to find out?" Wittaker didn't blink. "I'm sure you can speak to him privately elsewhere, but he's been very cooperative to our efforts."

Some of the color drained from her expression, and I couldn't help it, I faced her now. She actually looked ill. Maybe there really was trouble in purgatory, or whatever it was they were doing was called.

"We don't need to do that," she mused and then focused on me. "I want five minutes with you, and then I'll withdraw my objections. Well, we haven't actually filed it yet, but I'll withdraw it."

No, I did not trust that offer.

I cut a look at Wittaker, and he gave me the barest of nods. If I wanted to speak, then he was all right with it. "Why?" I asked her.

Maddy frowned. "Because I want to talk to you…"

"Why is five minutes worth not fighting the emancipation?"

Did I want her to fight it? No.

Would it have been nice if she wanted to fight it because she actually cared about me? Yes.

I wasn't fooling myself though.

Not anymore.

"You want it, don't you?" she asked. "Does it really matter why?"

"You'd be surprised. Kind of like those DNA tests. Why did you have to try and track down my sperm donor? Did you lose track?"

Neither attorney moved, but Maddy straightened in her chair. "Opening my mail, Francesca?"

"Checking for bills, Madeleine. After all, you left them behind, so apparently, they didn't matter to you anymore than I did." Sitting forward, I stared at her. "Four tests. Four potential matches. Only one actual match. Were you planning on sharing this information, or was there some other purpose you've failed to mention? Apparently, you have a thing for married men…"

"Would you gentlemen excuse us?" Maddy glanced at her attorney then mine.

"I'm fine if they listen," I told her, threading my hands together on the table. "Let's be clear, Maddy. The only thing you gain by them leaving the room is no witnesses to you verbally or emotionally assaulting me. You won't be hitting me again, because I will return the favor. I'm done being your punching bag. You've told me plenty of times you could have gotten rid of me or given me up for adoption, so let's not pretend, you and I, that I was ever anything more than a means to an end."

"Those words were said in anger…"

"Sure they were. That might even be true the first time you said it. I mean, the first time I recall it, I was seven. So maybe you were pissed. Maybe even the second time. But that's just an excuse to try and pass off your shoddy fourth-hand parenting skills. I suppose if I were a married man myself, I might have gotten your attention."

She glared at me. "That's uncalled for."

"But is it?" I tilted my head. "I don't think so."

"You always do this. You start twisting everything," she snarled. "I think you're a spoiled child."

"And I think you're a manipulative bitch." I spread my hands. "Are we done here then?" This really was a pointless exercise. "You know what? Actually, I do have one question. My original one. Why?"

"Why what?" She almost sounded tired.

"Why keep me? You never wanted me. I was always a burden. One you were all too swift to abandon at every opportunity and to blame when things didn't go your way. So why keep me?"

"Because you're mine," she said without an ounce of emotion. "You'll always be my daughter. My blood. My legacy."

I might vomit.

"Well, good to know that those things don't mean much to you."

"For fuck's sake, Frankie. What do you want from me? Your father left me for another woman. I did the absolute best I could. Am I a perfect mother? No. Are you the perfect child? Of course not. No one is. But you've been angry with me for the last year. Angry that I'm trying to move on with my life and—"

"Don't," I said holding up a hand. "Don't even start that shit. You started your affair with Eddie out of sight and out of mind of me. You didn't *want* me to know. You slunk around the shadows with your dirty little secret and disappeared on so-called business trips, all the while you were trying to sabotage another woman's marriage. You know what, maybe my sperm donor did leave you, but that doesn't give you carte blanche to go after other men who are already taken. I know it takes two to tango, but it takes a special kind of greedy bitch to repeat that pattern."

"Why do you keep saying that?" She almost looked upset. Almost.

"Well, I suppose you already forgot about Coop's dad. Out of sight. Out of mind."

She flinched.

There it was.

"Yeah, that's what I thought. Look," I said, standing. My stomach hurt. My eyes burned. I was alternating between hot and cold. I wasn't sure if it was a panic attack, fury, or disgust. Maybe all of the above. "The only thing I want from you is for you to go away. I know you can forget about me. You're very good at it. I'd ask for the guy's name—the sperm donor—but I don't think I could believe you, and I don't honestly care. He's only been slightly less involved in my existence than you have."

The silence stretched in the room, and I nodded. Maddy actually looked a little lost.

No worries, she'd rally. Then get mad at me.

It was a cycle.

One I was getting off of.

"Thanks, Mr. Wittaker," I told him. "I'll see myself out. I can call you…"

"I'll call you," he said, rising smoothly and walking me to the door.

"Frankie…"

I paused, but I didn't turn around.

"You will receive a tidy sum on your eighteenth birthday. It's a trust from my parents. I'll leave the details with Mr. Wittaker."

I pivoted. "Excuse me?"

She gave me a tight smile. "You have trust. I've never mentioned it because I didn't want you counting on something that could be taken away, but you're well on your way to meeting the conditions of it. So I'll leave the details with Mr. Wittaker."

"Great. Bye."

I had a trust?

At the door, Wittaker stepped out with me and pulled the door mostly closed. "Are you all right?"

"I have no idea," I told him. "I still think she's lying about something, maybe a lot of things."

"Possibly, and she never got to whatever point she wanted to make with you."

No, she hadn't. And I really didn't care.

I couldn't.

"Let me know about that trust thing?"

"Of course, leave it in my hands. Go on and have Beth take you all to the executive elevator to go down. I'll keep them busy for a few minutes."

"Thank you."

"Of course."

Another small smile and he returned to the conference room, and I just stood there.

That was that.

No more Maddy.

Right?

Chapter Twenty

EVERYTHING I DO

ARCHIE

As tempted as I was to stay and have words with Maddy Curtis, I couldn't do that. Not when Frankie walked into the conference room where Jake paced, Bubba strummed his fingers against the table like he played some imaginary piano, and Coop stared off into space. The latter worried me more than the first two.

He was taking the news of his father's betrayal *hard*. I felt for the guy. I felt for him because I'd had a front row seat to Edward's multiple betrayals over the years. Honestly, I'd always wondered why Muriel and Edward married. The fact that I arrived six months to the day after their wedding pretty much secured the answer.

Coop wasn't me, which meant I had to dig deep and find that empathy for his situation. Even if I couldn't quite experience it the same. He was right about one thing—both of our fathers had fucked our girlfriend's bitch of a mother.

That was not the kind of bonding we needed.

"Baby Girl," Jake said a second after she slipped into the room. The secretary—Beth—was with her. Frankie had her arms folded around herself. Defensive posture. Her eyes, so lit with fire earlier, were tired and more than a little shadowed.

I hated that cunt so fucking much.

"We, um…we need to go," she said. "Wittaker is going to keep Maddy and her attorney in the conference room so we don't have to deal with them on the way out."

Her voice came out a lot stronger than she appeared. All of us were up, and Ian got to her even before Jake did. I hadn't even seen him moving. Wrapping an arm around her, he tucked her to his side, and we followed.

On the way to the private elevator, I glanced toward the conference room where Maddy Curtis waited.

Jake's hand landed on my shoulder. The force in his grip kept me firmly locked into place. "Trust me," he said, "I'd be right behind you, but this isn't the time."

"Reason from you, Benton?" I cut him a look.

"Sometimes, Standish, even I know when to wait to throw the punch. You want to do the most damage, right?"

Damn right I did.

Nodding once, I turned and followed him into the elevator. Frankie gave me a pained little smile, and I just added the discomfort in her expression, posture, and eyes to the list of payback I planned to extract from the bitch who gave birth to her.

The single decent thing she'd ever done—give us Frankie.

Still not enough to forgive her for treating her so fucking badly. Despite being alone in the elevator, Frankie wasn't talking and none of us were pressing. As it was, we had a plan, and Ian kept her wrapped up close. There was an itch between my shoulder blades urging me to pull her away. I wanted to run my hands over her and make sure she was in one piece. But at the same time, she had that distant look in her eyes and leaned into Ian like she needed to be there.

In the lobby, I took point, with Ian and Frankie just behind me, and Coop and Jake just behind them. We'd parked side by side in a parking lot across the street. Call it instinct, but we wanted to park away from the attorney's office if Maddy was going to be there. Force of habit had me scanning for Edward's car.

After his ambush of Frankie at Standish and his offer to testify on her behalf at the emancipation hearing, every warning alarm I possessed kept ringing. We were all missing something. Some key piece of information. I wouldn't relax until I knew what it was.

The air had a distinct bitter bite to it, and the darkness seemed almost smothering. "You riding with me, babe? Or you want to go with the guys?"

She squeezed Bubba, then curled her arms around Jake. They each held her carefully as hell, though Jake picked her up off the ground and whispered something into her ear before he settled her back on her feet. Coop tugged her to him and kissed her. I actually glanced away from the sweetness in that.

When she headed toward me, I got the passenger door open for her, but Frankie just wrapped her arms around me. I pulled her close and locked her up to me tightly.

"We're going," Jake said quietly with a nod toward his SUV. "We'll grab something."

I nodded to him and just stroked a hand over Frankie's hair while keeping a wary eye on the lawyer's building. We weren't directly across from it but we weren't that far, and the wind was getting colder the longer we stood there.

"C'mon," I murmured against her hair. "Before I have to take you back and put you in the hot tub to warm you up."

"I wish we had a hot tub at our place." The muffled words against my throat made me smile.

"Might take a little finessing, but I bet I can get one installed. We'd have to gut one of the bathrooms out."

The rough choke of wet laughter just added another log to the pyre of anger at that selfish cunt. "You'd do it for me, wouldn't you?"

"In a heartbeat," I promised. "I could take you back to my place, too. Whatever you want, babe. Seriously…but can I get you in the car so you don't freeze?"

She let out a little sigh and lifted her head. The passing lights on the road flashed against the dampness beneath her eyes. "I'm being melodramatic," she confessed. At my snort, she sniffed and wiped at her eyes before she added, "I could be. You know, I can be girly and emotional."

"Absolutely," I agreed. "Car, babe. C'mon." With care, I steered her into the seat and then closed her inside. She was rubbing her face with her hands as I climbed into the driver's seat. I should have warmed the fucking car up while we were waiting. Engine started, I glanced over to find her staring out the window. "Do you want to tell me about it?"

"She said I have a trust or something. She's going to give the details to Wittaker. She pitched a fit in there, but Wittaker shut her down." She sniffed and shook her head. "I adore him, by the way. He is worth every penny you paid for him. I feel like I should get him a fruit basket or something."

"Noted," I said, enormously pleased he'd shut that bitch down.

Frankie cleared her throat. "Anyway, she's not going to contest the emancipation, and the court date is set for the first week of March. So it looks like I'm gonna get an early birthday present. She did try to say she'd get me kicked out of the apartment and repossess my car, but Wittaker didn't think she'd be able to do it. I just need to pull some money out of my savings and pay her off and make sure that part is done."

"How much do you owe?"

She glanced at me. "I don't want you to have to pay for it. I have it. I mean, it's college money, but I have the internship and I've got the scholarship and we're looking at going somewhere cheaper than Harvard." She gave a little shrug, and I flexed my hands against the steering wheel, my rage akin to acid in my system.

"We'll talk about it, okay?" I wasn't going to press it. If she pulled it from her savings, I'd figure out a way to replace it. I already had some ideas about how to offset the college tuition for all of us. Housing expenses I'd take care of, and boom there was huge chunk.

"Okay," she said with a sigh. "I did get a few verbal shots in, and I didn't give her what she wanted. But she wasn't fighting for me, she was fighting because of her image. Which I don't get, she called me her legacy…"

A headache pulsed behind my eye, because I'd heard that crap when I was growing up, too. I had to carry on the family name. I had to prove myself. I was the legacy.

Backing out of the spot, I glanced over at her. "Frankie, I promise, I'll always fight for you."

Her smile might've been wan, but it was there again and somewhat brighter. "I'll always fight for you, too."

"That's what matters," I said, then cut a look toward the building in the review mirror. Maddy Curtis exited with her attorney.

She should have taken my offer.

"Let's get you home," I said, keeping it light. "Then I'll have Jeremy bring someone in to look at getting a hot tub installed. Probably increase the value of the apartment."

Her groaning laughter was perfect. "I'm so glad I never told you I wanted a pony."

"A pony?" I perked up. "Does my girl want a pony? I can definitely do that."

JAKE

We swung by for tacos, burritos, chips, the works. We also debated calling in

Rachel. Seriously, when the fuck had she become one of us? Didn't seem all that long ago I couldn't stand her. To be fair, she still irritated me. But more like my sisters irritated me. My phone kept buzzing while we were at the drive-thru.

"I say we hold off," Coop said from the backseat. "Rach would show up in a heartbeat, but I don't know if that's what Frankie wants right now. She looked like she'd been through the wringer."

"Fair," Bubba agreed, and I grunted as I dug my phone and wallet out. "Also, you totally just ordered a dozen bean burritos. Pretty sure that breaks the boyfriend rules."

"It'll make her yell at me," I said, thumbing out my bankcard and then checking my phone. If she yelled at me, it would distract her, and then I could tease her out of the bad mood and have to make it up to her. Archie wasn't the only one who planned.

Mom

We need to talk.

Mom

I've heard some things that I'm not altogether comfortable with.

Mom

Don't blow this off, Jacob.

I raised my eyebrows.

Me

What's up? Was tied up with Frankie.

Mom

I need you to come home this evening.

Me

I can swing by, but I'd rather be here. Coop and Frankie have both had a rough time of it.

Arguably, Archie had too, but he seemed less off-center by it.

"Problem?" Bubba asked, and I shook my head.

"No, Mom wants me to go home tonight, but I'm not leaving her. Hopefully, whatever it is can wait until tomorrow."

Coop groaned. "I haven't fucking looked at my mom since I found out. I don't even begin to know how to look her in the eye. Did she know? She's never once acted badly toward Frankie. Not once. Thank fucking God."

"Fuck," Bubba said. "I didn't even think about that. That would have been awful."

"Right?" Coop said, then rubbed at his face as we pulled up to the window. "So did she know it was Maddy? Did she not? They used to be friendly, but honestly, I can't remember the last time they had a conversation."

"I'm sorry, man," Bubba said over his shoulder. "That has got to suck. I can't…I can't imagine my dad ever doing that to my mom."

"Be fucked up if Maddy hit on him," I mused aloud. Had she just targeted our dads because she was jealous of Frankie? What kind of warped Freudian shit would that be?

In the backseat, Coop gagged and punched my seat. "Seriously, man. That's fucking disgusting."

"My dad would never do that," Bubba said with a shrug. "Though, considering his attitude toward her, I gotta wonder if you're right."

I wasn't the only one staring at him. Coop groaned, and I shook my head. "Ignore me. I'm in a bad mood."

"Nah, it's fine."

After I paid the cash and got the food passed over to Bubba and back to Coop to store, we headed out. "No, it's not. Coop, we're gonna drop you at the apartment by the way and run a quick errand."

"You're going to go kick the crap out of Reed." Of course, Coop wasn't surprised. He'd been incensed when it came up earlier, despite the hangover he'd been fighting all day. The tacos should help with that. Frankie would help most of all. "Thanks for the invite."

"Nothing personal," Bubba said over his shoulder. "It's a football thing. Besides, you aren't the biggest fan of fighting."

"I can make exceptions. Douches who make her uncomfortable and suggest she's a slut are definitely worth the exception."

"You want to go with us?"

"Not particularly," Coop groaned. The paper crinkled in the back, and there was the distinct smell of tacos in the air. Unsurprising. He needed to eat. "Just make sure you nut punch the asshole for me."

"Done." My phone buzzed again. Mom. I waited for a traffic light, then scanned the screen.

Mom: *Tomorrow. No excuses.*

I blew out a breath and turned off the screen. Great. Something had her fired up. Hopefully, it wasn't Dad and Klara. We didn't discuss Klara at home, at all. Dad? Yes. Klara? No. Fuck, I was still a little surprised I'd brought it up with Frankie. After we came back, Mom wanted that part of her life over. Done. Finished.

She asked me not to ask the second time I brought Klara up, and I'd honored the wish. The girls were all too young, except for Becca, and she'd figured it out the same way I had. Whatever went down between them hadn't been pretty. The arguments had been audible and intense, but I'd never actually *heard* the whys of it, and honestly, I hadn't wanted to ask.

Telling Frankie had been a bit of a relief though. I hadn't missed the surprise on her face or the element of shock. But my baby girl just rolled with it, and I was glad I'd told her. The situation we were in wasn't all that alien to me, and even if all I'd wanted was her and I'd been determined if she did pick, she'd pick me, I was glad she didn't have to.

Weird as that might be to some folks, it was perfect for us.

The Ferrari wasn't there when we pulled in.

Coop gathered up the food, but left us one bag, including most of the bean burritos, and he grinned when I flipped him off. "Don't take too long. She won't buy the errand excuse. We all hover when shit like this goes down."

"Yeah, but I'm working on dialing back that overprotective streak."

Coop snorted. "Yeah, that's why you're going to kick the crap out of Reed."

"Well," Bubba said with a shrug. "In fairness, past Jake would have kicked the crap out of him right there this afternoon and we'd have been mopping up a bloody mess. Taking a few hours to think it over and bring backup is an improvement."

"Fair point," Coop conceded. "She's still going to worry, so be efficient and don't get arrested."

Assholes.

Both of them.

I took the longer way around the parking lot to avoid passing Frankie and Archie on their way back in. Better for her to get in and let the guys distract her while we took care of business.

"Did they pick him up?" I glanced at Bubba.

"Yep," he said. "He's at the old gym, and they'll keep him there until we get there."

"You don't have to do anything," I reminded him.

Bubba chuckled. "Oh I know I don't have to, because you're going to beat the hell out of him. I'm just there to be a witness and say it's a fair fight." He glanced at his hand. "And if he stumbles into my fist a couple of times, he should probably learn to watch where he's going."

I grinned.

The old gym had a boxing ring and gloves. It was also under no rules or regulations, so bare knuckles were also acceptable. I might go for the gloves just to give the asshole a sporting chance. But he was getting his ass kicked. It had been a while since I'd had to make a point, but Frankie was off-limits.

Period.

"You know, when you smile like that, you look a little psychotic."

I smiled wider. "Good."

COOP

In the apartment, I set the food in the microwave to stay warm while I stripped out of the jacket and shoes. Then I just changed into softer pajama bottoms and a T-shirt. I had zero intentions of going anywhere else tonight.

A text to Trina to make sure she wasn't giving Mom hell had elicited the response of *fuck off* from my little sister because she was busy. Well, that wasn't all that new, but I was ready for this phase of hers to be over. I loved my kid sister, but I didn't like wanting to strangle her.

I hadn't spoken to Mom since the day before—before Dad dropped his fucking bomb on me. Falling onto the sofa, I flipped the TV on and skimmed Netflix until I found some series of docs that Frankie had been watching and left it queued up. It was that or bad comedies. Maybe an action flick. It would really depend on how Archie handled her mood before they got back here.

Tiddles yowled at me, and even Tory poked her head around the corner and glanced around the room before the white cat hurried over to leap into my lap. She purred immediately and started kneading my thigh. Tiddles, on the other hand, yowled again.

"Right," I said. "Fuck. Sorry, guys."

I dislodged Tory and headed into the kitchen to put out their food. We were all late tonight because of the meeting, and they were definitely put out at the delay. Tabby wandered out as I served up the wet food. Then I checked their dry and water. I'd taken care of the litter box and washed my hands by the time the door opened to let Frankie and Archie in on a wave of cold air.

When she slid her icy cold hands under my shirt and onto my back, I dragged her closer and chuckled. "Frankie-pop. You need a hot shower."

"That sounds amazing. Archie is offering to get a hot tub installed here." She laughed, but it wasn't quite a humor-filled one, more like a sad one desperately looking for some real humor.

"Is he now?" I eyed the man in question. "Well, as long as he understands that there will be shenanigans in said hot tub…"

"I'm pretty sure he can handle it," Archie rumbled dryly as he settled his jacket on the back of a chair and dropped his keys next to mine. We'd all started just leaving them in the dish in the center of the table. At least we'd done the dishes that morning, or Jake had.

"How's your hangover?" Frankie asked, leaning back to search my face. Worry crinkled her brow, and I pressed a kiss to the tip of her nose.

"Don't you have heat in that expensive damn car?" I asked Archie. "Why the fuck is she so cold?"

"Because," he said, arms folded and a faint smile on his lips, "we had to wait for the train, so she opened the window and screamed at it until it was past."

I raised my brows and glanced down at her. Her eyes were bright with a hint of unshed tears and her face red. "Okay," I said, then picked her up. "Naked and in the shower with you." She let out a laugh as I carried her down the hall.

"I'm starving."

"Right, there's food. But you're half-frozen, and we don't want you to get sick." In the bathroom, I set her on the counter before I got the water started. "Hey, Arch, there's tacos in the microwave."

Frankie's stomach rumbled, and she glared. "I want tacos."

Before she could hop off the counter, I blocked her in and cupped her face. "I need you to take a shower and warm up. Just in and out if necessary, I won't even try to pin you to the wall until I have you screaming…" Fuck what was left of the hangover. The best cure in the world was sitting right in front of me.

"You won't?" She fisted my shirt and dragged me closer, and I grinned. "What if I want you to?"

"Well," I said, making a face and squinting at her. "I mean…if you insist…"

When she skated that icy hand down into my pajama bottoms and wrapped it around my poor, unsuspecting dick, I yelped.

"You have a cruel streak."

"Awww…" She stroked me slowly, and I clamped my hands down on the counter to keep from bucking into her touch. It might have been cold as fuck when she got started, but her hand was a lot warmer now. She whispered a kiss along my jaw as she gave me a careful squeeze at the base and teased my semi into a raging hard-on in nothing flat. "Blue Bobs are our thing."

The heat gathering around my balls and the tension in my gut let go at the same time as I laughed my ass off and then kicked the door closed. "That's war." It took me less time than anything to strip us both, and then I dragged her into the shower with me. Two fingers hooked into her, I groaned at how wet she already was, and she fisted me as I lifted her, then I pushed in as she sank down.

Fuck.

Right there.

Eyes closed, I savored the warm fist of her pussy wrapping me up tight and her low groan as she had to stretch for me. Never a complaint, and I knew better than to rush it, but I just wanted to be in her all the way, and she let out a half-scream when I thrust deep.

"Blue Bobs…" I whispered in a strained voice as she squirmed against me. The brush of her hardened nipples to my chest was a distraction, but she dug her fingers into my back as though she wanted me closer, so I gave another little thrust that had us both hissing. "Was a one-time thing… I didn't know the candy would do that."

"You didn't know…" she groaned and bit down on my ear lobe as she rolled her hips, and I dragged back, only to slam into her again. Fuck, I could do this all night. "That if you jerked off with blue candy that it would turn your dick and your balls blue?"

"I was thirteen," I hissed as I curled my own fingers against her ass and dragged her out a little so her shoulders rested on the wall. She braced one arm out as I spread my feet and tucked her legs a little tighter around my waist. "I'd been masturbating for all of about five minutes when I tried it. I didn't know it would stain my skin."

Frankie laughed, and the shadows in her eyes eased. Dragging myself out to the tip, I grinned and thrust in again.

"Fuck," she cried, then bit her lower lip. God that was sexy. Her breasts bouncing as I began to rock into her, increasing the pace until we were both shaking, distracted me almost as much as her litany of curses. I needed her to come, desperately, because my balls were about to explode. I pressed a finger right up to her ass and her eyes rolled back in her head, and she squeezed me so tight, it was hard to pull out and push back in.

The liquid rush poured through me, and I sealed my mouth to hers as she wrapped her arms around me, and we stood there under the steaming water, panting.

"I thought there was something wrong, which is why I asked for your help," I admitted softly. And she'd looked, then even done some research to see if blue balls and blue cock were an actual problem. It had taken me forever to own up to the candy, but she'd been so damn serious and worried. Then when I explained, she'd stared at me like I was an alien for about three seconds.

But she hadn't laughed at me for like three months.

Right around the time the damn dye finally all vanished.

Smurf balls.

I never ate another damn Blue Bob again, thank you very much.

"Coop," she whispered.

"Hmm?"

"You can give me your Blue Bobs anytime."

Laughter cracked through me, and I slid my hand to her knee and squeezed. Her shriek of laughter filled the bathroom. And we made a fucking mess with the water.

But I did end up pinning her to the wall again and making her scream a second time.

Only after the shower and she was pulling on clean pajamas while I finished soaking up the mess and squeezing out the towels, did she ask, "Did Jake go after Reed?"

I sighed.

"Pretend you don't know?" I suggested. "Jake's going to do what Jake does. And that asshole deserved it."

Frankie considered me for a long moment, then said, "I hope he punched him in the balls for me."

I grinned. "Oh, I promise you…he did."

"Yay. Now…tacos." And then she skipped up the hall, and I chuckled. Maybe kicking asses to keep them away from her was okay as long as she knew about it.

Good. To. Know.

I'd have to tell Jake.

Chapter Twenty-One
I DO IT FOR HER (AND US)

IAN

Archie's text hit my phone and Jake's after we reached the gym. I had Jake's phone in my pocket as he stripped down to shorts and gloves. They were both going to be barefoot in the ring. Reed smirked at our arrival. The fool already sported one bruise from his earlier encounter with Jake. The fact that he didn't see the danger he was in just made the lesson Jake was about to deliver that much more critical.

And sweeter.

There were about twenty-three guys at the gym. Most of us had keys, since we used it for training on and off season. As seniors, we'd be surrendering ours at the end of the year, but there were a handful of juniors amongst the guys who'd picked up Reed and made sure he was here. Rogan Reed was not a half-bad player.

On Halloween, he'd been right there to back us up against Mitch and his boys. The team had pretty much split down the middle, with a little more than half falling on the asshole's side of the line and earning their permanent suspension from the team.

"Cameras are off," Darrin told me as he checked the doors. Reed was already on the other side of the ring, waiting. The fact that Jake strapped on gloves sent a rumble through the crowd. There were enough guys here who'd gone to school with us since junior high who probably thought the gloves were a concession.

What they didn't realize is Jake wanted Reed to last a while so he could do maximum damage.

I nodded. "What about Zeke?"

Zeke was the old guy who took care of the gym, made sure it was stocked and cleaned up. Coach liked that we used this place rather than one of the higher end gyms in town, because it kept us focused as a team. The boxing ring was also there for settling disputes, usually with Coach acting as referee to keep us clean.

"Offered to buy him dinner," Darrin told me. "Sent him to Joffrey's, so probably gives us a good couple of hours still."

Perfect.

"Thanks, man," I said, then tucked my phone away. There would be no phones out, no secret recordings, and no photos. The rules were basic and simple.

Jake had an issue. Reed had been called out.

Now they were in the ring, and that was where they would settle it.

"No prob," Darrin said with a wry grin. "Dude shouldn't have fucking talked to her like that."

At least some of them got it. I patted him on the shoulder and headed over to the ring. Chris finished securing Jake's gloves and glanced over at Reed. "He just wrapped his hands. You sure you don't want him in gloves, too?"

Jake grinned, a malicious kind of glee in his eyes. "Nope. Let him be comfortable. It's not going to last that long for him, anyway."

And it definitely wouldn't give him any kind of advantage.

Chris leapt down as Reed made his way to the center and Jake stalked out of his corner. Unlike Jake, Reed hadn't bothered to change. He was still in jeans. He had shed his shirt and his shoes. But the jeans would slow him down.

"You're serious about this?" Reed asked, as though he still couldn't quite believe it. Or maybe he just wasn't taking it seriously.

Dumbass.

Blandly, Jake met his stare. "You should have listened to her. You don't talk to Frankie that way. We've made it clear for years, no one talks to her that way."

"Fuck, man, I've got no beef with her. She's hot."

Wow. The stupid on him just didn't seem to brush off.

"Listen up," Jake said. "What are the rules where Frankie Curtis is concerned?"

"Hands off," one of the guys called.

"Eyes off," another said.

"Keep your fucking mouth shut," Darrin drawled from a few feet away. "She's protected. No one touches, looks, or bothers."

"What rule did you break, Reed?"

"Fuck, man, I thought that was because she was frigid or something. She's hot and she's funny and she likes variety. Everyone is talking about…"

Darrin groaned and shot me a look like, *is this guy for real?* I shook my head. If Jake didn't just break his face open in the next thirty seconds, I'd be shocked.

"Seriously," Reed said, spreading his hands wide. "I get it. She's your girl, and you get to decide who taps that and—"

Yep, I almost wished I could video that just so Archie and Coop could see how fast Jake's uppercut landed. Reed was on his ass, and blood poured from the cut to his mouth.

"Good talk," Jake said. "Now you're listening. You don't talk to Frankie. You don't look at her. You don't approach her like you think you have the fucking right to ask her shit that isn't a thousand percent respectful. Hell, you take the long way to avoid her from now on. You're not a bad guy, Reed, but you are stupid. Now get up. You broke the rules, now you pay the price."

Pushing to his feet, Reed glared at Jake. "You're a real asshole, you know that?"

Jake cracked a smile at that. "Should have figured that part out a lot sooner."

"Man," Darrin murmured from where he'd fallen in next to me. "Stupid never hurt me so much. Dude is not a bad guy…"

Yeah, I didn't disagree. Fuck, Jake didn't disagree. Normally, Reed was all right. But he crossed a line he should have known better than to cross.

The others had circled the ring. No referee, but that was what I was here for. I'd keep Jake from killing him. I wasn't too worried about Reed. If he made it to five minutes, I'd be impressed. Even with Jake's gloves on.

Reed made it four and a half minutes before Jake dropped him. Again.

Only instead of staying down, Reed lunged to his feet and charged at Jake. The savage grin on Jake's face only grew as he dodged the next two wild hits and landed a one-two series of jabs to Reed's kidneys. The gloves would spread out the force of the hit, the gloves cushioning against the force of bone hitting bone.

But what Reed didn't get was how much he'd be hurting the next day, and the day after that.

Light as hell on his feet, Jake danced around him, and I sighed. When he cut into him again and his gaze met mine, I made a slicing motion with my hand. Time to end this. He lifted his chin and then stepped into Reed's hit, and I winced. Reed got cocky, exactly what Jake wanted.

"Fuck," Darrin said with a laugh. "Nice knowing you, Reed."

Three swift punches later, Reed hit the mat and he didn't get back up. Rolling his head from side to side, Jake swung a look around the room.

"Anyone else need a reminder?"

"No, man," Chris said, holding up his hands. "We're good. Reed just got brave, but we got it. Doesn't matter what the rumors say, she's still off limits and we'll make sure everyone knows."

Which was the final point of this exercise.

Reed still hadn't gotten up, and I ducked into the ring as Jake stalked away. Flushed and sweaty, he was too wound up to be the one to deal with whatever Reed popped off with next. The guy had a mouth on him and apparently zero common sense filter.

Crouching, I checked his pulse. Not dead. That was good. The guy let out a groan and squinted one eye open. "How fucking hard did he hit me?"

"Hopefully, hard enough you learned your lesson," I said as I stood and offered him a hand. He clasped it, and then I hauled him upright. Reed swayed a little on his feet. His jaw was swollen, and there were red marks on his cheeks, jaw, and around his eye that were already puffing. Blood trickled from his mouth.

There were worse marks on his torso. If he iced that shit, he'd probably be fine, but it would still hurt.

Good.

With a wince, Reed glanced down at his hands and then over to where Jake was pulling off his gloves. "Look…can you tell him I get it?"

"Do you though?" Because if Jake had to deliver this message again, it wouldn't be anywhere near as a pleasant.

"Yeah, I get it. In fact, probably better not to mention anything about her or whatever the deal is you guys have."

"How about you don't try to scare any girl, much less her again?"

"How the hell was I scaring her?" He frowned. "Chicks like to feel important, and I had been wanting to ask her out."

Closing the gap between us, I gripped his shoulder. The guys had already begun dispersing and heading out the doors. "You're a hard guy to get alone," I mentioned in a quiet voice, and Reed's eyes widened. It took a second, but I caught the moment reality sunk in. It was just me and Jake left. "Think about how you feel right now…" I let him go. "Then remember she's shorter than you are, and Mitch already attacked her, you idiot."

The other guy had the grace to wince.

"But just in case I haven't made the point…" I punched him in the nuts, and he dropped with a soundless wheeze. "That's what it feels like when someone is made powerless." Bending down, I murmured, "That's also from a friend. I could give you a couple of more, but I'll save them for if there's a next time. Clear?"

Still cupping his nuts, Reed bobbed his head. "Done…man. Fuck, I won't even think her name again."

"Excellent. Glad we had this chat." I dragged him back up to his feet and helped him to his corner. "Take a deep breath, then get dressed. We gotta lock up."

Turning away from him, I found Jake dragging his shirt over his head and smirking as he shook his head.

"What?" I asked when I reached him. "You think you get to be the one to have all the fun?"

He chuckled.

It took Reed another ten minutes, but then he could walk out the door under his own power. Granted, he walked awkwardly and you could see the pain, but he was moving. Instead of leaving right away, Jake leaned against the SUV, head tilted back and eyes closed.

I could wait him out…

"Need to run?"

He shook his head. "No, it helped. But he didn't offer much of a fight back, you know?"

"You pretty much played with him instead of just putting him down."

"He needed to learn a lesson," Jake answered with a shrug. "Lesson delivered."

I nodded. "And you're still wound tight."

"Because a part of me wishes I could drag Frankie's mother into a ring like that and school her on how she treats our girl."

I grinned, it wasn't funny and yet… "If only it were that easy."

"Yeah." Finally, Jake turned and looked at me. "What's eating you?"

"Nothing," I said with a shake of my head. "I'm actually…probably in the best place I've been in a while. I just wish I could make it easier for everyone else."

"You kept your head today. I seethed. Archie plotted. Coop's…nursing a hangover and trying to sort out how do you react to finding out your dad is a bigger bag of dicks than you already thought." He shook his head. "Frankie was…"

"Amazing," I summed it up. "She was definitely hurting, but you saw her in between, right? When they went to his office. There was fire in her eyes."

"Yeah, and I saw her after when she looked so damn tired."

"She's going to be fine," I promised him, and pulled my phone out to check the messages. There were three. Two from Archie and one from Coop. "And she knows where we are."

"Fuck," Jake swore and tilted his head back.

"Nah, it's good." I held out his phone so he could read the message himself.

Archie's messages were short and to the point. They were home, she and Coop were currently battling it out in Mario Kart. He was still in a mood, but he had a plan in place. That probably helped.

"Hey, Jake…before we go back, we should talk about something."

He glanced up from the phone. "This isn't another problem, right?"

"Nope," I told him easily. "But Coop had a point, and I want you aware before you walk in, since no one knows how to knock on a closed door."

With a snort, he shook his head. "It's not about knocking, it's Coop wanting to watch. You know he likes watching, right?"

No. I mean, I guess I had known that but… "Huh."

Jake chuckled. "I mean, don't get me wrong, I don't mind watching when it's her, but I'd much rather play. Coop likes both. Closed doors are a temptation to see, and yeah, unless you don't want him wandering in and out, lock the door."

"Noted," I said slowly, then let out a little snort of disbelief. Coop had been damn curious about all of it and a good sport, too. But maybe that was why. He wanted to watch. I still had a lot to learn, but it wouldn't hurt to have backup…though I imagine it would suck for him if I told him all he could do was watch.

Then again…

"Whatever evil idea you just had," Jake said with a laugh, "count me in. But now I'm fucking cold and our girl is at home and waiting for us, so let's take this show on the road."

Once in the SUV, I told him about the ropes. The club. The training. And what I liked to do. Oddly, the more I talked about it, the easier it got.

Jake took the news well.

Better than well.

He just grinned. "I've been reading her books," he admitted. "And I'm down for whatever she needs."

"It's not just about her," I admitted slowly, then grimaced.

"Nah, I get it. Don't open a vein." He waved me off. "But count me in for the classes. I want to know. We better tell Arch, too."

I laughed. "If we all knew something he didn't, he'd kill us."

"Nah." Jake laughed. "He'd pay someone to kill us."

"Justifiable."

"Yep."

After a beat though, Jake cut a look at me, and I'd seen the same look on Coop's face when he brought it all up in the first place. "Ask."

"Just…how did you know? Don't get me wrong, the books intrigue me and there's…a lot of temptation there. But how did you know it was your thing?"

"Same way I knew she was."

And the best part of all.

Jake got that.

JAKE

With Archie taking Frankie to her internship and picking her up, the meeting with her mother done, and Reed and any other idiots entertaining similarly stupid ideas where Frankie was concerned put in their place, Friday should have been a cake walk.

And was, for the most part, until I got home to find Mom waiting for me. The girls were conspicuously absent, and Mom had texted me three times to make sure I was coming. As soon as I was inside, she frowned.

"You've been fighting again."

"A fight," I admitted. "Singular. No big deal. We just had some things to settle."

At her aggrieved sigh, I held up my hands.

"Seriously, Mom. It's all good."

"Jacob Elijah Benton, do not tell me it's all good and just dismiss my concerns. How many times have you nearly been arrested? You have gotten off light, but sooner or later, they are not going to be so forgiving."

"I know," I told her, and since she was already pissed off, I kept a firm grasp on my temper. "I promise I do know." I kissed her cheek on my way past to grab a drink. "And this wasn't like the last set of fights. We were just boxing at the gym."

Which was all true.

Her harsh exhale held so much relief, I frowned and glanced at her as I got the soda from the fridge. "Do you want anything while I'm in here?"

"I want you to come sit down and talk to me."

With the way this week had been going, she probably wanted to tell me Dad wanted to come to my graduation or he and Klara wanted the girls for the summer. I popped open the drink and followed her out to the living room. The fidgeting as she sat and clasped her hands wasn't her, and it put my teeth on edge.

"What'd he do now?" I didn't mean to snap it out like that, but I couldn't help it. Every single time she talked to Dad, she got like this. Dad spoke to the girls weekly, but I'd made a habit of not being around for it, and I thought she had mastered it, too.

"This isn't about your father," she said with a wave. "As far as I know, he is very happy where he is. Or as happy as he can be." She gave a pained shrug and then waved me off. "No, I need to talk to you about Frankie."

"What about her? I know you've been wanting her to come back over for dinner, but it's just been really busy and she has that internship—"

"It's not about dinner," Mom said. "Jake, is she dating all of your friends as well as you?"

Lowering the soda, I met Mom's gaze. Her eyes were a deeper gray with a faint hint of blue, depending on the light. Right now, they were storm clouds. "Not sure how that's any of your business."

"That's a non-answer answer, the kind you use when you don't want to confirm or deny anything."

"It's also the kind you use when you're trying to be polite about telling your mother that your girlfriend and her life are none of her business."

Mom pursed her lips. "I had coffee with Sara earlier this week. Then a very interesting conversation with Carly."

"Okay." I put the drink on the table and kept my gaze on hers.

"Jake, they both believe she's dating *their* sons."

I shrugged. "Mom…I'm not going to have this conversation with you." I'd thought about it. What I'd do if she asked. But the simple truth was, I didn't want to discuss Frankie with her. "I get that you're upset, and I even get why. Things with Dad and—"

"*Don't*," Mom cut me off. "Don't do that. Don't dismiss my concerns. This isn't about her or your father." The fact that she couldn't say Klara's name told me it very much was.

Pushing up from my chair, I moved over to sit next to her on the sofa and then covered her hands with mine. "Mom, I'm sorry things didn't work out for you. I get that you might be gun-shy, but I'm not you. Frankie's not Dad. Right now? I'm happy and exactly where I want to be."

"Jake you have no idea, you're still a baby. *She's* a baby. What sounds so erotic and enticing when you're younger doesn't always stay that way. The naughty factor can be exciting, I get that..."

I grimaced. "Okay, I really don't want to think about *any* of those words in relation to you or Dad or Klara, if you don't mind. I've made it this far without needing therapy, I don't think I need to start."

She slapped my arm, but she laughed, even if her expression remained troubled. "You know that's not what I mean."

"Maybe, but would you want me to give you any details about what I find erotic and exciting?" It about fucking killed me to say those words to my mother, and her moue of distaste told me she was as fond of the idea as I was.

"I'm worried about you."

I put an arm around her. "I know, but I'm happy, Mom."

"You say that now, but what happens when you pick a college with her? That's what you're all doing right? You're all trying to go to the same school?"

"To be fair, we wanted to be at the same college town, if not the same college, from the beginning. We weren't dating when that became the subject."

"But you *wanted* to date her," she argued with me.

I shrugged. "What do you want me to say? I've been crazy about her for years. That hasn't changed."

"And what if you make all these decisions and it does change? What if she picks one of those other boys? Likes him more? What if you get an opportunity to do something, and she won't go with you or support it because it would mean leaving them? What if you're..."

"Mom," I gave her a squeeze, then let her go so I could turn sideways and face her. "Stop."

"Baby, I worry about you. You feel good now and things are great, but they can go so wrong so fast. You can find that everything you thought you knew… People grow. They change. Sometimes, they grow apart."

"Yeah, then you fight to get back to each other," I said. "I don't know what happens tomorrow, I know what I'd like to have happen. I know what I want next week. The month after that. And next year. But none of it happens without a lot of work and time. From me. From her. There's no such thing as a guarantee. It's all work."

With a sigh, she covered her face with her hands and shook her head. "And you're all right with her seeing the others?"

I sighed. "I'll talk to you about this once, exactly once, because you're upset. But we're not having this conversation again, and I'd very much appreciate it if you didn't bring it up to Frankie…*ever.*"

She took something of a shaky breath and lowered her hands before she glanced at me. "That seems…reasonable…if a little harsh."

"Take it or leave it, because I love her, Mom. I love you, too. I don't want either of you to hurt."

Her eyes glistened. "You really love her?"

"Yeah. She's the one. Maybe I'm only eighteen and settling down is still a few years away, but it's always been Frankie. I don't want anyone else. She's not Dad, Mom. I'm sorry about what went down with the three of you, I know you were hurt. But we're not you."

She sniffed. "I'm just scared for you. Because it can seem like everything, and it could go so wrong."

"Name me a single relationship that can't go wrong, even if it's just two people?" I hadn't been able to make a single relationship work because I hadn't wanted them to work. They'd all just been placeholders and barely that. "I know it won't always be easy. It's not easy now."

Her frown deepened.

"But it works. What we have works. I don't want to change it or her. And I get it, if you're not comfortable with it, I won't force us on you."

"That's not what I meant by this," she said, then leaned sideways against the sofa and propped her head against her hand. "You all need to tell the other parents." When I would have argued, she held up her hand. "Baby, there are things that I know without a shadow of a doubt. When you keep secrets from your family, you're telling them you're doing something wrong. I didn't tell Sara or Carly about you dating Frankie, but they are both crazy about her and…while I admit to some reservations about the idea she's dating the three of you…"

Fuck it. "Four," I corrected.

Mom closed her eyes and turned her face skyward, like she had to ask for patience, before another sigh escaped her. "The four of you then. I at least have some context for a less than conventional relationship. They don't, and there could be blowback if they find out accidentally. Your father's parents never forgave him. I swear, your grandmother still prays about it, and she calls me more than she does him, which I tried for a long time to fix it, but she is convinced she did something wrong where he's concerned. And… Look, that's neither here nor there. The point is…don't hide it from them. Give them a chance to understand."

"We're not hiding it." Then it was my turn to hold up a hand to stave off her comments. "We're not. Just…Frankie's working on her emancipation to get free from Ms. Curtis. We're all eighteen, except Frankie. She will be in a couple of months. After we graduate and our college plans are locked in…"

"Dear God, Jake, you planned to ask for forgiveness once it was a done deal? What, drop it on everyone at the going away party?"

"Well…" I made a face. "We hadn't discussed it specifically. We just have a lot of stuff to do. Honestly, I don't want to have to defend what we have. I don't want them to have to, and I sure as hell don't want Frankie in that position."

"I may regret asking this, but how firm in this relationship are all of you?"

"Are we having sex?"

She made a face, and I laughed.

"You're the one asking."

"I am… I just want all of you to be safe."

"We're being models of safety. Everyone has had health checks. We know what we're doing, and we're all talking to each other. No one is under any misconceptions or being kept in the dark."

"Except your families…"

"And I would remind you that it's none of your business." I tried to keep it gentle, but I needed Mom to get this. "You love me. You want to protect me. I love you, too. But this is my relationship. I'm good. Trust me? If you trust nothing else, trust me? Please?"

Chapter Twenty-Two
I HATE EVERYONE (AND THEY HATE ME)

FRANKIE

After the meeting with Maddy, the next week kind of flew by. Archie took me to my internship on Friday and picked me up. I never saw Mr. Standish if he was in the building. Not that I was complaining. After the showdown at Wittaker's office, I was fine with a break. As it was, Friday night we spent at Archie's place, and then I worked Saturday. Sunday, I had to pick up the girls to go shopping.

Trina had been invited, but she blew off my text. Becca, Blake, and Louisa were all excited when I got there, but Jake had followed me in and they scowled.

"I'm not going with you," he said. "I'm taking Mom out to lunch, and you three are not going to drive Frankie nuts. Got it?"

"We're not going to drive her nuts," Louisa countered with a roll of her eyes. "She likes us, and we're not boys. We know not to fart in the car."

I probably shouldn't have laughed as hard as I did, but Jake's eyes flashed amusement. Alicia surprised me with a hug and a kiss on the cheek. Then she admonished the girls to behave and told me she'd given them their own money. They were not to ask me for anything.

After a few more eye rolls and hugs, we were off. The next four hours were hilarious and busy. Becca had a list of places she wanted to hit. Blake complained at every single one of them, nagging her sister until we moved on, and Louisa basically hung out with me, particularly when we got to the clothing stores.

"You don't want to try stuff on?"

She had her phone in hand and snorted. "I'd rather go to the dentist than do the clothing swappity doo. I'm kind of hoping Blake bitches Becca out about the hair and nails thing."

"Pedicures are kind of fun."

Louisa shrugged. "I'm gonna be trying out for a soccer league in a couple of weeks. I don't need to worry about pretty pink toenails when I need to kick the ball."

"That's new. I thought you were more into gymnastics and dancing."

"I am," she said, "but I like soccer. I like sports. More than they do. And I think with Jake finished with football, Mom won't mind if I shake things up. She already said I could try out and then we'd discuss it. 'Cause, it's a commitment you know."

"Yes it is…" Then I laughed. "You wanna know a secret?"

"Sure, I know how to keep one. As long as it isn't something about my brother, because that's just gross. I still can't believe you kiss him."

I chuckled. "I promise, it's not about Jake. I'm not big on all the girly froufrou stuff either. I can barely do my makeup."

"You're not wearing any." The sage wisdom of being eleven years old.

"Nope," I said. "So go for it with the soccer, and I want to hear all about it. If you don't want to do the pedicure thing, what do you want to do?"

"There's a Wide Event place here," she glanced up, her pale blue eyes filled with animation for the first time since I picked them up. "They have everything from batting cages to hoops to places where I can practice my kicks."

"Sold."

She froze and glanced toward the changing rooms, where Becca and Blake had vanished to try on new jeans and shirts. "It's expensive. I don't know if I have enough…"

"Between you and me, I'll cover it. It sounds like fun, and I suck at shooting hoops. But I've never been that good at kicking a soccer ball. At least when your brother and Coop weren't around to make fun of how bad I am at it."

Snickering, she glanced at the changing rooms, then back to me again. "Well, if you really don't mind…I probably have enough for most of a ticket."

"My treat," I offered, and pulled out my phone to check the place. "We can drag them with us and make them do something we want. After all, girls' day should be for all of us."

"You rock," Louisa said with a little fist pump. "I swear my brain cells are dying the longer we do all this girly girly crap."

I probably shouldn't have laughed, but I did. "You know, some of that girly stuff is useful to know."

"But not all of it, right?" Louisa said, and we shared a look. The girl was taller than me already, but I didn't care. We fist bumped.

"Right."

Twenty minutes later, accompanied by a harried Blake and Becca, we paid for a few rounds in the soccer arena. Bless Louisa, she beat the pants off of all of us, but I hadn't laughed that long or hard in a while. Especially when Blake humdinged a ball at the goal, and it bounced off and hit her back. I managed two goals, so I'd call that a win. Becca managed three, and I was pretty sure the third one was purely from her need to beat Blake.

"You know…" Blake said when we got back to the car. "We took a vote before we came out today."

"Blake," Becca snapped. "Don't."

"Nah, Frankie's cool." Blake leaned against the backdoor of my car,

Becca had already claimed shotgun, and Louisa had her door open but she stared at her sisters with a resigned look. "We know about the dating all the boys thing and we weren't sure we were cool with you doing that, but you're cool. Just… you gotta promise to pick Jake if you have to pick any of them. 'Cause he's way less a pain when he's with you."

Louisa stared at the sky, and Becca sighed.

Sucking on my upper lip a second, I studied them. While the sun was out, the air was not balmy. If anything, the wind had just grown more bracing. "I love your brother," I told them, and didn't even mind when Louisa grimaced, but Becca grinned.

With a knowing nod, Blake said, "We figured that out."

"Shut. Up. Blake." Becca pushed each word out between her teeth while still smiling. Impressive technique.

"I'm just saying that I love him and I have no intentions of ever hurting him. I like all three of you, too. And I suppose…" I paused to consider them. "You're all right, too."

Becca snickered, and Blake grinned. "See, I told you she was cool."

Overall, the day had been a blast. My only regret was Trina hadn't come with us. I'd like her to be friends with Becca and Blake. The idea that Coop and I were leaving her behind when we went off to college had begun to nag at me, especially after that last conversation.

Maybe next time.

The whole drive back, we turned up Torched, and I was thrilled that they liked the music almost as much as I did. When I admitted we'd gone to a concert while in Colorado, I winced at their yowls of disbelief.

Oh, I was gonna owe Jake an apology. I had a feeling his sisters would be blowing up his phone. His SUV wasn't at their place when I dropped the girls off, so I fired off a text to the guys to let them know I was done and heading home. I was beat, and I still had a crap ton of homework to do before the week started.

Ugh and we needed to grocery shop this week. I probably should have made a list before I went out, but I'd do it tonight and maybe bribe one of the guys into going with me after school on Monday. That triggered thoughts about actual homework and what projects I needed to get ahead on, followed by the fact that Bryan and I had been given actual homework for our assignments this next week.

We were going to be working in finance. I wasn't sure whether the prospect excited or terrified me. Probably both. It was a lot to absorb, particularly because the prospectus they'd given me had to be eight hundred pages.

Archie had flipped through it and then grinned almost crookedly before offering to bring over the latest stockholder's projections from their last meeting.

And here I thought he loved me. He'd laughed so hard at me.

Ass.

Speaking of asses, I needed to call Rach. She'd been ducking my calls the last three days. That, or she hadn't come up for air from her latest conquest. I probably shouldn't think of them that way, but I was still bummed about her and Skylar.

Not that I was the one who needed to be made happy in that situation.

Still, I was worried about her.

Coop's car was in the lot, and so was Ian's bike, but Jake's SUV and Archie's Ferrari were both absent. I grabbed my phone after I parked, but Trina was standing out in the cold, arms tucked around herself without a jacket, and I frowned.

Worse, her eyes were red-rimmed like she'd been crying, and her face was all kinds of splotchy.

I shoved out of the car in a hurry. "What's wrong?" Worry threaded through me. "What happened?" I would have given her a hug, but she backed off and glared at me, nostrils flaring even as she sniffed. It was like she couldn't make up her mind whether she was angry or sad.

"Is it true?" she demanded.

So we were playing the vague game. I closed the door to the car and nodded toward the apartment. "Is what true? And it's freezing out here, do you want to come over?"

"No," she snapped and stomped forward, more angry tears gathering in her eyes even, as she sniffled. "I want to know if it's true."

"Okay," I said, blowing out a breath. "You're going to have to be more—"

"Are you fucking cheating on my brother?"

The accusation hit me like a brick. All the air in my lungs squeezed out. "Trina…"

"Are you?" Her voice pitched higher. "Noah told Jenny and Mandy that you're a whore. Everyone at the high school knows it… How could you do that to him?"

"I'm not—"

She swung before I could even finish the sentence and I barely got my arm up in time, but too many years of taking Maddy's slaps made me wary of another one. Trina flailed with her other hand, and I dropped my keys to catch her arm.

"Trina…stop it."

Then she shoved me back to the car, and while Trina and I were closer in height, she had a lot of anger behind her.

"You're as bad as your mother!" she screamed this time, and the tears fell in earnest. "She screwed my dad, and now you're screwing up my brother."

Shock slapped me harder than she could have, and my stomach cramped. "Sis," I tried again, because tears ripped through her words like a record screech.

"Don't. Call. Me. That." The flailing turned to half slaps against my arms as I fought to keep her from actually landing any real hits.

"Stop it," I ordered, and this time, I shoved her backward. I didn't want to hurt her, but she was too damn angry and not listening. "I mean it, Trina."

She bounced forward and shoved me into the side mirror on the car.

"I hate you," Trina cried. "I hate you. I hate you, and I hate your mother. You're nothing but a…"

"Trina!" I dodged another flail, and this time, I grabbed both of her forearms and shoved her against the car. "Stop. It."

I had to raise my voice over hers, and even then, all it did was leave her shaking and crying.

"C'mon, Sis, stop. Listen to me…please?"

"Why?" She choked and coughed as snot ran from her nose and tears soaked her face. "Why would you do that to him?"

"I'm not," I told her.

"Yes you are. There are pictures of you kissing Jake and Archie. I didn't believe them. I *defended* you, and they showed me pictures."

"I didn't say I wasn't with Jake or Archie or even Ian."

The admission shut her up.

She gawked at me.

"Then you're telling me you're a slut?" For someone who had been so furious just seconds earlier, disbelief populated her tone.

I swallowed. "No," I said, and chose my next words carefully, but I also leaned my weight into her to keep her pinned, because I really didn't want to get hit in the face. This was already a nightmare. "I'm telling you I'm not cheating on Coop. I love Coop, I would *never* hurt him that way."

Trina stared at me, fat tears rolling down her reddened face. "How can you make out with other guys and it not be cheating?"

"Because I know about it," Coop said from somewhere behind me. Trina jerked to look past, and I let go of her, even as I released a breath and backed up. "Frankie's not Dad, Sis. She didn't lie or cheat or stab anyone in the back. She didn't walk away from her family. She's not cheating on me."

There was an inflexible note in his usually patient voice, one that seemed to strike a chord with Trina, and she flinched. "But there are…"

"Trina," I said before she could bring up the pictures. When Coop closed his hand over mine, I threaded my fingers with his. The class ring I'd worn all day seemed heavier somehow, like the anchor I hadn't realized I needed until just now. "I promise. I know what you were told, and I know what you're thinking. You've made that clear. Yes, I'm dating all four of them, and they all know."

"We're doing more than dating," Coop said, tugging me closer. "We're together. All of us and Frankie."

The earlier disbelief dissolved into incredulity as she stared at her brother. "Wait…*you're gay?*" Before either of us could say anything, she shook her head. "No, you'd have to be bi." She scrubbed a hand over her face, then glanced back and forth between us. "I don't understand. I thought… He said Frankie was a whore."

"Who said?" Coop asked in a deceptively mild tone, and I shook my head.

"It doesn't matter."

"I disagree," he countered. "It matters very much, because if it's who I think it is…"

Fuck.

There was going to be blood.

"That's not important right now," I said, elbowing Coop and then holding out my free hand to Trina. "Come inside? Please? It's freezing out here, and we can talk."

Her face had gone from splotchy red with tears to beet red, and she darted her gaze away from me. "How can you be nice to me?"

"'Cause she's Frankie, Sis. Now come on before I focus too hard on the fact that you called my girlfriend a slut and go burn all those Barbies you have hidden in the back of your closet."

Outrage blossomed on Trina's face. "Don't. You. Dare." But she moved, and when I grasped her hand in my free one, she clung to me.

Well, whatever worked.

The conversation with Trina left me drained. Coop took her back to his apartment after he made sure their mother was there. I offered to go with him, but he told me he would handle it. Ian had kept his distance while Trina was in the apartment, but there was no way he hadn't gleaned a good chunk of the story.

Trina had been yelling again. She and Coop both looked like hell when they left. Well, more Trina looked miserable and Coop grim. He'd given me a very thorough kiss before he took his sister home.

Ian had wanted to wait for Archie to get back, but he also intended to go have dinner and talk to his parents. Jake had warned us his mother had figured it out and that she suggested we tell everyone.

After the incident with Trina? Yeah. I got it.

"I could go with you," I offered.

But Ian had shaken his head. "Angel, let me deal with any initial fallout. They love you. But they need to understand that I love you and that this isn't a negotiation."

Guilt eating away and my focus shot, I pulled the kitchen apart to clean it, emptying the various dead takeout boxes from the fridge and making a shopping list.

At least I had a coupon app to go with the coupons in the sale paper. Another text to Rachel went unanswered, and I called her to leave a message as I grabbed my keys.

"Hey, if I don't see and hear that you're alright tomorrow *before* school, I'm going to camp out on your porch. Call me. I'm worried." I hesitated a beat, then added, "And feeling neglected. If she's that hot, I want pictures."

Jacket on and keys in hand, I ran into Archie as I let myself out. He grinned. "Hey, babe, where are you running off to?"

Despite the grin, he gave me a critical once over. I didn't even ask. I'd bet money Ian had texted Jake and Archie so they knew what was going on. "Grocery shopping," I told him. I also had the trash bag to toss, so he snagged that and then hooked his arm through mine.

"I'll drive, if you want," he offered, and I chuckled.

"I need more groceries than we can load in the Ferrari. Besides, you're not a fan of grocery shopping.”

“Maybe not,” he said easily. “But I’m a huge fan of you.”

I didn’t groan as he left me at my car with a quick kiss and jogged the trash over to the dumpster. Archie in a grocery store was a disaster. He hated grocery budgets.

He strolled back over to the car and grinned at me. “You don’t have to look like that, babe. I know how to behave.”

“Uh huh.”

Thirty minutes later, we were having an argument on the cereal aisle.

“We do not need both of those,” I told him. “Not to mention, I have a coupon and a buy two get one free for this one.”

Archie eyed the box I had versus the name brands he had. “Hard disagree. That crap tastes like cardboard, even with the milk. And I know for a fact that Jake prefers this brand and so do I.”

“But they’re smaller boxes…”

“So we get more.”

And I tilted my head back to stare at the ceiling as he added more to the cart. “Archie, they cost more.”

“They taste better, of course they cost more.”

“How are you a genius at so many things and so very bad at this?” I grabbed the boxes I’d intended to buy and put them back.

Even with the strain of the brand names, and the extra boxes, the budget would be all right, I’d just scale back on a couple of other things. The guys were all throwing money into the grocery shopping fund.

“Babe, I’m not bad at shopping.”

“We have a grocery budget…”

“It’s a guideline,” he told me as he took charge of the basket and started walking.

“No, it’s a *budget*. It keeps us from spending a small fortune on groceries. If you spend too much one week, you don’t have enough for the following. It’s basic economics."

Pivoting, he gave me a smile. "You're going to hit me for this, and I want you to know I say it with absolute love and adoration…"

Arms folded, I raised both eyebrows.

"I respect your budget, and I believe every word you say."

"But?" I dangled that word out there, because there had to be a but on that sentence.

"But," he said with a grin and spread his arms, "I'm a fan of enjoying the things we can, and one of the things we can enjoy is whatever the hell we want to eat. You have your grocery budget, and I will respect it. And I have mine that will fill in all the gaps, so you never have to worry about coming up short next week."

It was almost like he was patronizing me, and at the same time… "You just paying for everything makes it hard to keep us all equals."

"Again," he said, a smile tugging at the corners of his mouth and his eyes soft. "Hard disagree."

"Oh, this should be good," I murmured and started pushing the cart myself, but he caught it to hold it still, then began to load everyone's favorite Pop-Tarts—a ridiculous amount.

Now he was just making a point.

"I'm glad you like my reasoning before I've even said it."

"Yeah, we're not all the way there yet, so get on with it, Standish."

His grin grew, if that were at all possible. "Finances don't make people equal. Never have. Never will. All money does is pay for comfort. It doesn't keep you warm at night or hold your hand when you need it. It doesn't push you to be a better person or challenge your patience."

He snagged the cart and tugged it forward, and I moved with it until we were face to face again.

"It definitely doesn't teach you how to do your own laundry or make you realize just what you've been missing. My equals? They fill in the other parts of me. They balance me out. That, Miss Curtis, is spelled F-R-A-N-K-I-E."

"Wow."

"Good, right?"

I laughed. "You kind of ruin it when you pat yourself on the back."

"No," he murmured, dipping his head to kiss me. "I don't."

No, he really didn't.

Still… "This doesn't mean the budget is off. "

"I'd never presume," he murmured. "So should we skip the ice cream, since we're spending so much on this?"

"Now you really want me to hurt you."

"I'm just trying to keep us on budget."

Yep.

I admit it.

I hit him.

He still laughed and pinched my ass in retaliation.

Ugh. The budget died long before we reached the register, but he killed me when he picked out the chocolate ice cream cake and it was really hard to argue with it.

Jake was there when we got home and helped us offload everything. I carried a pint of my ice cream off to eat in the living room while the engineers debated on how to fit everything in the fridge. It was damn amusing.

My phone buzzed.

Rachel

> I'm alive. No need to threaten mayhem or bodily harm. The boys not fulfilling you? You read the new books yet? If not, then go do that. Should cure your boredom. Give you all kinds of ideas for them. Talk to you tomorrow.

My mouth dropped open. But before I could fire off a response, another image filled the screen.

Oh, she was adorable. Rachel held a baby cuddled up to her chest and the message said,

Rachel

> Meet my niece. She made an unexpected
> appearance, and I forgot my phone. My bad.
> You know you're my favorite bitch. Xoxo

My squeal pulled Jake and Archie's attention.

The fact that they blanched at the picture cracked me up. Well to be fair, Archie blanched, Jake just looked amused.

"Huh, there's another Rachel running around in the world," he said. "That's…either really really cool or kind of terrifying."

Archie snorted. "I'm going with terrifying. Mostly because Frankie looks way too excited."

"She gets to be an aunt and play with a baby," I said and rolled my eyes. "Of course, I'm excited. I kind of want to do that someday."

There was a distinct pause, and I caught them both staring at me.

"Some. Day." I enunciated the words clearly. "As in, sometime in the future, distant. Not any time in the next five years."

"So, five-year plan?" Jake asked.

"Five-year plan," Archie agreed, and I groaned. Archie couldn't live on a grocery budget, but a five-year plan?

Still…

That baby was cute.

I sent Rachel back heart eyes emojis. That definitely helped lift the mood of the day.

Then I remembered I still had homework.

Fuck.

Chapter Twenty-Three

I'D NEVER FORGET ABOUT YOU

COOP

I left for school before everyone else on Monday. Archie would run interference with Frankie, but I wanted to catch that smoky little fuckweed before school started. I knew just where he and his smelly little shits would be hanging out off-campus.

A win-win because they couldn't smoke on school grounds, so their little dumpster playground was also out of bounds for school rules. Jake slid into the car next to me before I even got it started, and I side-eyed him. "To be perfectly clear, I can handle the little asshole."

"Not a doubt in my mind," he said as he set his backpack on the floor and pulled his seatbelt on. "I'm just tagging along for the ride."

I blew out a breath. It had taken me most of the evening and then some to settle Trina and Mom. The whole damn thing had been one ugly conversation after another. One where we'd ended up finally having to call Dad in to join us for, and damn, Mom put him on the spot.

Trina had figured out the Maddy affair, and I had no idea how. But she had blamed Mom for some backwards ass reason. Like it was Mom's fault Dad had to go and have an affair with Maddy. Some of the psychology I got—Trina wanted her family back. Her sense of security and her self-confidence had gotten all tied up in the divorce. She was also lashing out at me because I was going to leave "too."

It had been a really long night. Trina was staying home with Mom today, and they discussed real therapy, not just for Trina but maybe for the whole family. All the therapy I needed was beating up the little fuck who not only took pictures of Frankie with all of us, but had gone out of his way to use them to hurt my sister.

I still hadn't ruled out burning a couple of her prized Barbie dolls. Nothing that had gone down justified her physically assaulting Frankie.

Nothing.

If I got nothing else through my sister last night, that had better have sunk in. Funnily enough, Dad passed off the bruises on his face as something related to a racquetball accident with his friends. I let it go because while the initial urge to rearrange his face had passed, I couldn't say it was gone all the way.

"Ease up on the steering wheel grip," Jake drawled. "You want your hands loose for this. Too much tension in your shoulders and arms, you run the risk of an injury."

"Har har."

"Not kidding," he said. "I brought the first aid kit for your hands and tape to protect your knuckles. I also grabbed a clean shirt and fresh jeans from the stash at Frankie's, in case you get too much blood on you."

The fact that he said it with a straight face penetrated the hot bubble of tension boiling the air around me. I slanted a look at him. "You're taking this very calmly."

"I got to pound some of my feelings out into Reed's face," he mused. "I'm fine with you handling this one. You look like you could use it. You need me to tag in, just say the word. Otherwise, I'm your alibi."

Ten minutes later, I pulled into the row of industrial buildings and storefronts that lined the far side of the grocery store parking lot. It was less than a five-minute walk from the school, but with more than enough distance to not be in danger of violating the rules.

Jake was a half-step behind me.

"Coop," he warned. "Knuckles."

"I'm good. I'm calm."

I was very calm. I also had gloves in my pocket. When I pulled them out and began tugging them on as I walked, Jake let out a soft laugh. We crossed between the buildings and followed the L around to where Noah "dead man" Auburn and his friends were laughing away in their cloud of blue smoke.

"Go the fuck away," Jake said when the three guys with Noah looked up at us. At least the guy my sister had wanted to date had the brains to blanch at our arrival. I sailed right through the smoky cloud and caught the cigarette dangling from his mouth and flicked it.

"Hey!" Noah complained, but my hand locked on his jaw as I kept walking him back away from the smoke and any potential help from his friends shut him up. Jake would get rid of the friends.

"No need to be so excited to see me," I told him as I kept him going, feet stumbling until he hit the side of the building. "You put out the kind of invitation you did, you had to know we were showing up."

"Um…" one of the guys behind me said.

"Did I stutter?" Jake asked.

The sound of feet on pavement moving away answered that question.

Noah's eyes widened.

"I don't know what the fuck you're doing…" Dude had balls, I'd give him that. He was still sputtering with my hand on his face, so I just tightened my grip until he shut up.

"I don't endorse violence," I told him in a calm voice. I hadn't been lying about being calm. I was not raging or furious.

Not at the moment.

I had a purpose here and a message to deliver.

When Noah tried to speak again, I flexed my fingers against his face. The pressure contorted his mouth, and tears flashed into his eyes.

"Better, now you're paying attention. This is the point where I speak and you listen. You apparently didn't hear us when we told you to steer clear of my sister. Not only did you not listen, you decided to take pictures of our girlfriend and then use those as leverage to hurt Trina. This is not acceptable on any level. Are you following this conversation?"

He made a grunting sound.

"A simple nod or a shake of your head will do. This is not a difficult question."

Noah gave a little jerk of a nod.

"Now, in addition to trying to hurt my sister, which is a no go, let us be blunt. You attempted to use my sister to hurt our girlfriend, because you were lashing out at us. Yes? Or no?"

The kid cut a look past me, but resignation crawled into his eyes. Yeah, there was no help back there. I applied a little more pressure until Noah groaned and reached out to latch onto my wrist like this would save him.

"Yes," he squeezed out. "Stupid idea."

"On that, we agree." I let go of his face, and he let out a choked breath and stared at me.

"Man, I was just—"

I slammed my fist out, and the satisfying crack of his cheekbone echoed through the alcove between the buildings where I'd pinned him. I didn't give him time to drop before I plowed my other fist into his gut. When he went down this time, bile and blood spattered the pavement as he retched.

Deep breaths. Deep cleansing breaths tucked the edges of my temper back as I paced a half-circle around him.

"What was your first mistake?" Might as well make it an object lesson.

"Telling your sister," he wheezed.

"Ehhh." Jake made a buzzing noise from where he stood. "Wrong answer."

I hauled the guy back up and shoved him back against the wall. One arm braced against his chest to keep him place. I ignored the additionally vile scent of sour vomit accompanying the smoke clinging to him.

"One strike. What was your first mistake?"

Noah gave me a wild-eyed look, then again at Jake, like that was gonna help him, but he finally sagged again. "The pictures of your girlfriend?"

"You don't sound certain," I mused. "Do you think that was your first mistake or not?"

Sucking in a painful gasp of air, Noah nodded. "Deciding to get even with you by using her and your sister was my first mistake."

"Ding ding ding," Jake said. "We have a winner. What do you know, he can be taught."

"I don't know," I said, still studying him. Sweat dotted the other guy's forehead, and his breath came in sharp little huffs. His throat bobbed as he swallowed. "What were second and third mistakes?"

"Taking the pictures and showing them to your sister."

Close enough.

"Do you feel like a big man now? Does that get you off? Making girls cry?"

"Fuck," Noah swore, grimacing. "No. I just—you fucking humiliated me, man. Treated me like dog shit."

"Yeah, we didn't scrape you off, we just made some rules clear. Rules you apparently struggled to follow. Then you made it worse…and I'm not okay with that."

"What do you want me to do?"

"I don't know," I admitted. "You're going to walk real carefully for a while. You don't look at Frankie. You don't even think her name. If I see your phone or the phones of any of your friends pointed in her direction, I know who I'll be looking for."

Jake cracked his knuckles for emphasis.

Noah swallowed again, then licked his lips as I took a step back.

"As for my sister…"

"I'll forget I know her," Noah promised, hands up.

"And you're going to apologize," Jake said. "Publicly. You're going to own up to being a big bag of dicks. No details. You take full responsibility. You don't tag her, and you should probably steer clear of anything resembling a date until you figure out how to treat a girl right."

"Are you for fucking real?" Noah seemed to rally, and I chuckled.

"As real as it gets, or do you want me to be the less than reasonable one you deal with?" Jake asked.

I cocked my head to the side as the calculations went across Noah's expression. His face was starting to swell, and I was pretty sure I'd at least fractured a bone there. He was still pale and sweaty.

"Fine, what the fuck, man… I'll forget your sister, your girlfriend. I'd really like to fucking forget all of you."

"I'm sure you would," I told him. "Unfortunately for you, we have friends in your grade and the juniors. Trina's gonna be at this school next year, and I'll know if you go anywhere near her or anyone else. So…you just think about what stories you want us to hear."

I gripped his shoulder before I slammed my fist into his stomach again. The kid folded over my arm.

"I don't want to talk to you again, Noah. We clear?"

"Crystal," he wheezed.

With that, I let him drop and then backed away.

"You should probably get a move on. The bell rings in thirty."

Pivoting, I walked away from the little ink-stain and stripped off my gloves as I walked.

"Not bad," Jake said as he fell into step. "You were *really* calm."

"I told you I was."

He chuckled and slung an arm over my shoulder. "You need to change your jacket."

I glanced down at the blood on the front. Fuck.

"Yeah."

I stripped it off and put it in the trunk along with the gloves. It was frigid outside, but I had on a long-sleeved shirt. It would do.

Once we were back in the car, Jake rolled his head from side to side. "Feel better?"

I thought about it. "Yeah," I said. "I do. I'm glad he decided to be reasonable."

Jake invited me to join him and Frankie at the gym for her first "boxing" lesson, but I'd had to focus a little more on Trina and Mom over the course of that week. Not that I didn't want to spend the time with Frankie. I'd managed to slip back over a couple of nights and steal into her bed after she was already asleep, whether it was Jake, Bubba, or Archie sleeping in there.

We were still waiting to hear from the attorney on what was going on with Frankie's so-called trust. Archie didn't trust it at all. Neither did I. But he had more resources for handling that one, so I just kept tabs on it.

Trina had gone to her first therapy session with Mom, and I'd been waiting at home for them with dinner. Not that Sis wanted anything to eat. She'd basically grunted at me and vanished into her room, without her phone.

She was still grounded from it, since Mom took it away after everything that happened. There was no mistaking the tired around the edges as Mom sat at the table with me. "You didn't have to bring us dinner." The chastising seemed almost perfunctory, the tired in her voice betraying her.

"I know. I wanted to be here for both of you. I know that can't be easy."

"No," she admitted. "But your father showed up and he put some effort in, so maybe this will work."

"I hope so, but I really want Trina to focus on her and you to focus on you." 'Cause, honestly, fuck Dad.

"Sweetie," Mom said as she started to stand, and I waved her back to the table. "I was going to get the wine."

"I can open it," I told her and got the bottle out from the fridge.

"We're not going to discuss how well you can do that."

"Just like we don't discuss the first time I got drunk," I said over my shoulder as I worked the corkscrew in. "Or the second."

She sighed. "You always told me when you and the boys planned to drink. Usually, you all stayed at Archie's and you had Frankie with you at least until last summer."

That had me giving her a look. "What does Frankie being there have to do with anything?"

"She kept you boys in line. Most of the time, you thought twice about every decision if she was there. You have since you were a little boy. Last summer, not so much…"

Yeah, we had gotten a little stupid over the summer. I couldn't argue that. I poured her glass of wine and then carried the bottle and glass over to the table. "Mom," I said as I sat down opposite her. "I'm fine. I'm good. I'm worried about Sis. I've been worried about her for a while but this…"

"I never wanted you to know," she said abruptly, and I frowned. "Your father told me that you found out. He also told me you hit him."

"Apparently not hard enough." Why the fuck was he telling Mom that?

"Don't get mad," she said, though it was a little fucking late for that. "He wanted to apologize to me…and it's the first time since everything happened that he apologized for making choices that hurt me."

Huh.

"And choices that hurt you and Trina."

I didn't really have a comment on that, so I just pulled the lasagna open and started dishing it out to her and to me. I'd picked it up from the one Italian restaurant I knew she liked. Garlic bread too.

"Coop, look at me."

I met Mom's gaze.

"I'm sorry."

"You have nothing to be sorry about, Mom…"

"I do," she argued with me, then raised a hand to stop my disagreement. "I do. Because I leaned on you pretty hard after I threw your father out."

It was the first time we'd tackled this particular subject. He'd left, that I'd always known. And the fights, those had started over an affair. But I hadn't known the finer details.

Part of me hadn't wanted to know. I'd gone to Frankie's to get away from it, sometimes taking Sis with me to spare her.

"But I did that, and that's on me. You didn't have to be my sturdy boy and prop me up, and you did it anyway."

"You're my mom," I told her, as if it summed it all up. "You weren't the one who messed up."

"We all mess up in different ways, and don't look at me like that, Cooper. I'm not excusing his choices. I'm not even comparing them. I'm just saying that I also made some questionable ones. Now…we didn't really talk about this Frankie thing that night."

I took a bite of the garlic breadstick and eyed her. Eating at least kept me from saying anything snappy, and I preferred to listen to everything said before I formulated a response. But the crap with Noah and Trina this week had left me on edge. So far, the little shit had done exactly as instructed, and Trina even admitted he'd apologized to her over a text message and that was the last contact she'd had from him.

I'd let it go.

"I'm not comfortable with it," Mom said. "The idea all of you boys are having that mature a relationship with one girl. I don't know if it's fair to you or to her."

After dipping the breadstick in the sauce, I took another bite.

"That said, I also don't know that it's unfair because all of you are being honest with each other, and I have to admit I'm not entirely sure how you're all doing that. Talking to boys at your age was hard enough, and even now, after everything or maybe especially because of everything, your father and I never seem to be able to get our point across easily. At least until this thing with Trina." She frowned. "He seems very determined."

"Okay," I said around the bite of food I chewed. "I'm glad he's being there for you guys. Sis loves him, and I think she feels his absence more than we do."

"She's younger," Mom admonished me. "She's a daddy's girl and it's hard for her, especially now that she knows. Part of why I never wanted either of you to know. Another fail on my part…"

"Mom," I said and shook my head. "Stop it. You're human. Maybe you didn't hang the moon and you can't catch a star, but you're still the best mom ever. You're human. You're allowed mistakes."

"So are you," she said softly.

"Frankie's not a mistake. What we have…it's never been a mistake. It's always been her, it's always going to be her."

"But can it really be that serious or that invested if she can't commit to one of you?"

"We're not asking her to," I said simply. "I know she's committed to me. I know she loves me. I know exactly how important I am to her. Just like I know how important the guys are. And she's… She makes everything better, Mom. She makes me better. She makes them better. We're stronger together. All of us."

"I don't understand that." She sounded almost sorrowful. "I want to understand, baby, so I can be there for you." She took a sip of her wine, then licked her lips as she shook her head. "I'm so worried this can't possibly work. Someone always gets hurt…especially if she decides one of those other boys is better for her. Not that you're not perfect…"

I chuckled. Honestly, this was a way better reaction than I'd hoped for, so I could roll with it. "None of them can be a more perfect me."

Mom eyed me.

I spread my hands. "Seriously, Archie's awesome, Jake's got skills, and Bubba's not bad, but none of them are me. None of them have my history with her. They can't do for her what I can. Just like I can't be them."

Staring at me, Mom swirled the wine in her glass. "I don't know what I did right with you, baby, but I hope this works out the way you want it. I love Frankie too, and I want you both to be happy."

"Right back atcha, Mom."

A couple of days later, I ran into Archie and Bubba in the parking lot. We didn't always arrive home at the same time, but I'd been running deliveries and they'd both had plans or work. Course, Archie had probably been building something or plotting the takedown of the civilized world with his grandfather.

Still, it was amusing, right up until we let ourselves in the apartment. The lights were on in the living room. Text books were open and laptops abandoned. Hell, the television was even on, and Tiddles sat atop the television stand, staring at the characters moving on the screen.

A second later, a soft cry echoed through the apartment, and I grinned. "Hell yes," I said, dropping my shit and tossing my keys. "See you boys later."

With that, I headed straight back to the bedroom and pushed the door open. Not only was it unlocked, it wasn't even closed all the way. Frankie sprawled on the bed with Jake's face buried between her thighs, and I grinned.

Closing the door behind me, I announced, "Player three entering the game."

Her laughter and his was all the welcome I needed.

Chapter Twenty-Four
YOU MAKE LOVING FUN

FRANKIE

It had been a long week in some ways and blown past me in others. Ian and I were working on new songs, even though we hadn't heard anything from the producers about the demos he'd submitted. Most of the time, I blocked out that we were waiting to hear so I didn't throw up from anxiety. There were so many things we were waiting on. Including submitting our acceptances to the various programs.

Archie and Jake continued to be secretive about their project, and Coop had been tied up with his family. I wanted to be there for him more, but I also didn't want to get in the way and they needed to focus on them. If not for the fact that Coop kept showing up to sleep with me, I would probably chase him down.

The weird thing about being so busy—we were all busy—we still managed to find time for each other. Not as much as before, sometimes it was just all of us hanging out rather than one on one, but we made the time. When Jake sprang going to the gym with me to work on my boxing, I'd actually been excited.

We went to the gym he and the team used, which I left me with a flicker of doubt. It was hard not to since what happened with some of the other guys on the team. But Jake promised it would be fine. It was more than fine. There were a few other guys there doing weights and stuff, but other than calling out greetings, they totally ignored us.

I mean like utterly ignored, didn't even look in our direction. Course, Jake stripped down to just shorts and taped his hands, and I forgot why the hell we'd come here, too.

"Um, do I need to change?" Not totally drooling. Yet. But *damn*.

He grinned, sweeping a look over me. Since he'd said gym, I'd worn a tank top, sports bra, and yoga pants. It was too frigid for shorts, but I could strip down further if he needed me too. "Damn, Baby Girl, don't tempt me."

Yeah, so that thing about there being other people present? I didn't really care anymore. I slept with Jake near nightly and showered with him several times a week, but there was just something panty melting about him standing in the middle of the chilly gym in nothing but a pair of workout shorts and nothing else.

It was a *good* look.

"Okay." I did my best to not sound disappointed. Pretty sure he wasn't buying it.

"Be good, Baby Girl. I promise I'll make it worth your while."

I cocked my head as he began taping up my knuckles. "What if I don't want to be good?"

The corners of his mouth curved into a dark little smile, and a shiver traced up my spine. "I can work with it. I'm getting the feeling you enjoy the idea of being bad. But I'm not completely caught up on all your extracurricular reading material."

I grinned. "I knew you were reading them."

"Because I told you," he murmured, then kissed the tip of my nose before inspecting my hands. "Okay, we're gloving you up, but don't think just because you have those on you can go nuts."

"Define nuts?" I bounced on my feet and jabbed at the air. "Is that when you and I go toe to toe in the ring?"

Amusement flickered in his pale blue eyes as he swept me from head to toe. "Baby Girl, the only place you and I will ever go toe to toe is full contact wrestling. You can spar against me, and I'll hold the punch mitts for you and I'll make sure you can land a hit that will hurt. But I'm never punching you back, Baby Girl. That's just a hard limit for me."

The gleam in his eyes went from humor to wicked teasing, and a shiver chased up my spine. "Interesting," I said, and bumped his hip with mine. "We should talk about these limits more."

"Happy to," he agreed with a light slap to my ass. "But first, we're going to work on your stance and punch, then the follow through. When we're done, I want you to know how to break someone's nose if you have to."

"Not their jaw?" I was only half-teasing.

"Nose is easier, and it will half-blind them with pain," he said and moved right up behind me, hands on my hips as we stood in front of the speed bag. There weren't a lot of mirrors where we were standing, so it wasn't like I could meet his gaze as he tightened his grip on me and stepped right up until the erection he was sporting pressed against my ass. "And you're being a bit of a tease, Baby Girl. Don't think I'm not paying attention."

I glanced back and up at him. "I told you I didn't want to be good."

He grinned. "Give me an hour, and I'll give you whatever you want."

A shudder had my nipples tightening and my thighs clenching. "Promise?"

"Oh yeah." He winked. "Now…let's do this."

I blew out a shaky breath and then rolled my shoulders. I could do this. "I'm all yours."

He let out the faintest of groans, then nipped my ear. "You will be."

I really wasn't sure who won the game of one upmanship here, or if there even were any winners. Either way, I was down to keep playing. For the next hour, though, Jake dialed up the punishment as he drilled me on how to throw a punch. It wasn't that I didn't know how, I'd thrown my fair share. But as Jake pointed out, I didn't train to fight people who were bigger than me.

Guys, as a rule, were all bigger than me. So the way I hit them had to take into account height and weight differences as well as circumstances. Essentially, if I was close enough to hit them, they were too damn close and could hurt me worse. First rule was always to get away. Second rule was to hit them hard enough to let the first rule come into play. Third rule, make a lot of noise while employing the first and second rules.

Despite the way he patiently walked me through everything and then worked with me to get my speed up, an undercurrent of dislike threaded through him. We went longer than an hour. In between giving me pointers, he demonstrated hits on the speed bag next to mine. We went until sweat soaked through my tank and my arms were spaghetti.

"And now I remember why I hate sports," I complained as he peeled the gloves off my hands.

"You're going to hurt more tomorrow, Baby Girl, so we'll make sure we rub those arms tonight."

"Oh, massage?" I perked up. I might not like going to other people for full body massages, but the guys were awfully good with their hands.

Chuckling, he untaped my knuckles and then pressed a fresh bottle of water into my hands. I'd already drunk a full other one. Despite having dressed for the workout and that the gym was all kinds of chilly, I was still hot and I needed a shower.

Badly.

That and the droplets of water skating down Jake's chest were utterly lickable.

Hey, I focused for the last—I checked the clock on the wall—ninety minutes. He slid a hand against my nape, and I grimaced. "I'm all sweaty."

"I like you all sweaty," he murmured and tugged. Then his mouth was on mine. I forgot all about the sweat and the burning muscles as I wrapped my arms around his neck. The stroke of his tongue demanding entrance had me pushing up on my toes. Desire kindled and adrenaline flooded my tired system. Nipping my lower lip once, he sucked on it before he lifted his head and stared at me from half-lowered lids. "You did fantastic, Baby Girl. You were so good for me."

I grinned. "I like this reward system."

"I'm a little partial to it myself." Then he gave me another kiss, and I groaned. "But we have to go home first," he whispered. "And we have homework."

"Blegh."

He laughed at me.

The meanie.

Still, I got one more kiss in before we pulled apart and he dragged on his sweatshirt and jeans. Apparently, we weren't showering here. I glanced toward the locker room and then away, but not before Jake caught me.

"Don't tempt me," he growled.

I made a face, but I was still smiling. It couldn't be any riskier than the library, right?

I flicked a look to the three guys still working out on the weight benches studiously ignoring us. "Next time?"

Huffing laughter, he snaked an arm around my waist and dragged me back against him. "Definitely," he said against my ear. "Though you're playing with fire if you want to do it here."

"I trust you," I reminded him, and his groan sent another shiver through me.

"You're killing me."

"You love it."

"Hmm." But the fact that he squeezed my ass and then gave me another kiss was all the answer I needed. We grabbed protein shakes on the way home, for hydrating and muscle recovery, and also damn tasty. Once we got back, I half-expected Jake to follow me into the shower, but he'd snuck one on his own.

Wrapped in a towel, I stared at him in the living room where he had his phone in his hand and wore just boxer shorts.

Definitely as lickable as he'd been at the gym.

"Did I do something to offend you?"

He glanced up and grinned slowly at me. "What's a matter, Baby Girl? You got an ache?"

Eyes narrowing, I squinted at him. "I thought I was a very good girl."

"I don't disagree," he murmured, sending another message before setting the phone down with the open textbooks. He had the television on to something, but I couldn't care less what he'd been watching. "But you also said you wanted to be bad."

"So I'm getting punished for being good?"

Chuckling, he folded his arms, and if not for the fact that his muscles were all corded and tense, I'd have worried. But no, this was a game. Jake was fucking with me instead of actually fucking me.

"Are you feeling neglected, Baby Girl?"

Yes. This was a game.

"It's okay," I soothed him and let the towel loosen and fall. "I've got new toys that'll fix the problem. Go ahead and get started on the homework."

I pivoted and headed back up the hallway.

Four.

Three.

Two.

Jake scooped me up before I even reached the door. He dumped me on the bed and then half-pinned me as he leaned down, nose to nose. "Toys? You really want to go the toys route?"

"That or I can call Coop. I'm sure he'd be happy to talk me through it."

Eyes flashing, Jake chuckled, and his beautiful, sensuous mouth pulled into a grin. "Who do you think I'm waiting on? He's doing his last delivery and then he'll be home." Nipping my jaw, he traced a path to my ear. "Good girls get good rewards. Think you can wait that long?"

Oh.

I groaned and arched my hips because he was already nestled right between my thighs, and that sexy chest of his that had been torturing me for the last couple of hours was hot against my breasts. Jake's grip on my wrists was gentle, but he had both of my arms pinned next to my head and his smile grew.

"No, my baby girl is a little too wound up and impatient, isn't she?" Sympathy filled his tone as he nuzzled a kiss against my throat, and I couldn't help but squirm as he pressed his hips into mine. The slow grind was making me crazy.

"She was good, but she's seriously considering bad was the way to go."

"Fine," he said, huffing out a sigh as he straightened. "Let's just take the edge off, shall we? I'm sure I can keep you busy for at least twenty minutes. What's the going record right now?"

"For what?" The damp tousle of his hair was doing really good things for him, and so were his very smooth cheeks. Someone had shaved.

"For most orgasms in that time frame? I think it was four. Might be five." He slanted a look at me, and his grin grew. "Shall we go for six?"

"Six…?" But the thought stuttered out as he released my wrists and slid down my body. I was so wound up, it only took the pressure of his mouth on my clit and his hands spreading me wide to trigger the first orgasm. His laughter had me arching up and digging my toes into the bed, but Jake settled my legs over his shoulders and glanced up at me.

"Settle in, Baby Girl. We're hitting six before Coop hits that door…"

I was crying by the time we hit number five, and Jake was absolutely ruthless in pushing me right up to and over the edge. At some point between orgasms three and four, he'd slipped lubed fingers into my ass and had begun to stretch me, and that just made me hungry for more. Jake let me writhe on the bed as I ground against his mouth.

Six was right there, when the door shoved inward and Coop stared at us.

The grin on his face was wide, and his eyes were hot when he focused on me. Honestly, we hadn't had this kind of time in a while. Not where it was just the three of us playing. Not since we'd been back. We'd come close, but not like this.

Coop shoved the door closed. "Player three entering the game."

The comment was just so out there and unexpected, I burst out laughing. Jake's laughter against the inside of my thighs sent another spark through me as he hooked his fingers, and then I was gasping as I came and tears spilled. Coop swallowed the gasps with a kiss, and I clung to him as Jake eased away from me.

Everything ached and I couldn't possibly still be trembling, but Coop dragged me up into his kiss and held me there suspended before he settled me back against the bed and then stroked a hand down my face. "You have a preference?"

I laughed. The last time they'd asked me that, my whole brain had stuttered. Right now, my brain was drunk on Jake, but not so much I wasn't eager for Coop to have made it. "We were waiting on you," I told him, and his grin grew.

"Aww, that's 'cause I'm your favorite."

I laughed. "You all are."

"I can live with that," he said with a wink and dragged his shirt off. Oh, he was pretty to look at. Jake slid his palms up along my thighs and tugged my attention to him.

"What do you want, Baby Girl?"

Pushing up on my elbows, I dragged my gaze from Jake to where Coop finished stripping and licked my lips. I kind of wanted everything, and at the same time, I didn't want to have to decide. Then again…

I crooked my finger at Jake and he crawled up to me, then his mouth closed over mine as I wound my shaking arms around him. Everything trembled. Quivering muscles made it hard to maneuver, and tasting myself on Jake just reminded me of how much pleasure he'd just poured into me. With very little urging, he rolled over, and then I was straddling him.

A laugh broke free as I shook, trying to grip him and get him in place.

"I think you broke her," Coop murmured from behind me as he settled his hands on my hips and helped me slide down onto Jake. He hissed, and so did I, at the contact. But I leaned my head back against Coop's shoulder and laughed.

"Not broken…just happy…and oh that feels good."

Jake thrust up once, and then Coop was easing me forward to rest my hands on Jake's shoulders. He helped balance me when my arms threatened to fold. The stroke of Coop's hand down my back to my ass had me arching my back.

"You sure?" The question came from both of them. It was written in Jake's eyes, even as Coop whispered it.

"Oh yeah," I said, and a giggle escaped me. "I need your massive cock, Coop."

With a laugh, Jake thrust up. "Just his, Baby Girl?"

"No, I need your magical cock almost as much as your delightful tongue."

That had him fisting my hair and dragging me in for a kiss, even as our hips rocked, but Coop slowed us both when he pressed two fingers against my ass and spilled more lube along the crease. We needed to practice this more, but at the same time, I was aching for him to just push in. Even if he was huge.

I could handle it.

I kind of felt like I could handle anything.

Between biting kisses and loving pets, they eased me between them, and then Coop was pressing inside. The stretch had me gasping as Jake went totally still and stroked my hair as he whispered encouragement.

Coop only eased forward a little before he began to rock, and he let out an almost pained groan. "So fucking tight…" The ragged words left me almost boneless, and I relaxed as he filled me all the way. Then he was kissing my shoulder, and I forgot anything but how it felt to be impaled between them.

I don't know who started the motion, but it was all sensation and heated kisses, sometimes pulling me forward or back. They traded me between them like they'd been practicing it and took me apart so expertly, all I could do was hold on as they found their rhythm. Jake came first, following me as I spasmed around them and clenched down. Coop followed so swiftly after that, then we collapsed together in a tangled, sweaty heap and I never wanted to move again.

I didn't think I could.

Even softening, they felt so huge inside of me, and the faint stirring of desire tugged at my belly. I would never get used to this, and I kind of liked that I wouldn't.

"Fuck," Coop whispered. "Now I have to move."

A giggle escaped and then another. Jake stretched his arm out and thumped him, but Coop just laughed, and when he pulled out, we were all gasping. He didn't go far, rolling onto the bed next to us, and I turned my head to meet his gaze while I still sprawled over Jake.

"I totally kicked ass at fight training," I told him.

"I bet you did," he whispered, and brushed his fingers down my cheek.

My eyes were heavy, and the soft, deepening of Jake's breathing had me lifting my head.

"Shh," Coop murmured. "He dozed off. It's only nine. We can nap, then clean up before round two."

"Round two?" Oh, he'd piqued my interest.

"Definitely round two," he answered. "I missed all the foreplay, I should get that turn, don't you think?"

Reaching over, I traced my fingers over his face. "You okay?"

Kissing my fingertips, he whispered, "I'm okay. It's hard, Mom, Trina. Dad. The whole mess. But I'm okay."

"I'm here for you."

"I know you are."

Jake rumbled beneath me, and I smiled. "Jake's here for you, too."

"Yeah," Coop said, then leaned over to kiss my nose. "Lie still and I'll go get a washcloth for you, but you should try to sleep. I think we might be pulling an all-nighter."

"Oh, cramming for a test?" I teased.

"I'll be cramming something." Then he was off the bed and walking out of the room naked. I let out a little sigh, and Jake trailed his fingers up my spine.

"He's okay, Baby Girl."

"I hope so, I worry about him."

"That's why he's going to be okay."

They weren't wrong about the all-nighter.

Worth it.

Chapter Twenty-Five

IN YOUR EYES

Me

Are you back this week?

Rachel

Yep. Sorry I've been spending a lot of time at the hospital.

Me

You don't have to be sorry. I just worry about you.

Rachel

I'm fine, you control freak.

Me

Don't pretend you aren't enjoying the fact that I'm missing you.

Rachel

You have a point. You free later this week? And want to do me a favor?

Me

I can be, and it depends on the favor.

Rachel

And here I thought you missed me.

Me

LOL I also know you.

Rachel

Fair point. I'm working on a project, and I need to borrow your bod. Totally safe and clean. Promise. I'll pick you up, or you want to just drive over?

Me

Your place?

Rachel

To start… Oh and wear pretty lingerie.

Me

Why?

Rachel

You'll see.

∞

The days seemed to be flying by. Maddy had all but vanished after the meeting at Wittaker's office. Her attorney had forwarded the trust details, and I'd gone to a meeting with Archie where we learned that the trust itself had an attorney. Maddy had no signing power over the trust, she was just legally tied to it until I turned eighteen. The trust had indeed been set up by my grandparents—plural, not singular.

The trust attorney would not speak to me directly until when and if the legal emancipation finalized or I turned eighteen. Really not useful. As for the actual terms of the trust, those had been sketchier. My age was a factor, as was my academic status, but the trust attorney had been deliberately vague with Wittaker. Something in his demeanor told me this wasn't normal.

Archie pointed out that as the recipient of the trust, it was on those who set up the trust to make sure I was aware of all the terms. Since Maddy dropped this like a bomb and that attorney was being cagey, that suggested there was either something to hide or this was some kind of trap.

"Paranoid," Wittaker commented. "But not undeserved. I can send them a strongly worded letter advising them to provide this information or we will sue." He glanced at me. "Or we can wait until after your court date in March."

"What if the emancipation itself breaks some rule of the trust? Or if I choose the wrong school? Or maybe if I got my ears pierced at the wrong age? Do I even care what it is?"

"I can't answer that question for you. From what you've said, you don't know that much about your grandparents."

"I didn't even know there were two of them. Like I said, I only ever met my grandmother, and that was exactly once and she barely even spoke to me."

"William and Anne Grayson." Wittaker said their names like I should know who they were, but it was Archie who frowned.

"Seriously? Maddy Curtis is a Grayson?"

"Apparently," Wittaker stated. "The information on her family was buried. She legally changed her name at twenty-one, and when you were born, she was a Curtis—her mother's maiden name. The designee on the trust is Francesca Curtis. You're named after your great-grandmother."

I had no idea how I was supposed to feel about that.

"Why didn't that come up in the background you did on her before?" Archie asked. And he had a point.

"It did, but it was excised from the report before it reached me. An oversight that has since been corrected."

"Edward." Archie's expression turned grim, but Wittaker's expression didn't shift.

"I'm afraid I can't disclose that. However, all the excised information has since been restored. I have a better idea of your mother's history now, if you want to have it."

Did I?

"I don't know right now. Honestly, I want less to do with her, not more, and this feels like a lot more."

"I can understand that. I'll hold onto it, and when you're ready, you tell me and I'll make sure you have it."

"What about the labs?" Archie asked. "Any movement with them?"

"At the moment, no, but I have contacted an attorney in New York who will handle our filings there, and they are going to begin the process of the suit. It might take time, but unless your mother is willing to give us the information, we may very well have to sue to get it. The lab manager seemed willing to cooperate, but their corporate owners are less flexible and more willing to make us force their hand."

"You know, it's like a puzzle I didn't want. This is all about the past. The trust. The DNA test. All of it. What if I just don't need to know?" I glanced at Archie. "I know who I am. I know where I am. I know where I want to go. Do I need to know what came before?"

"It's up to you," Archie told me, even as he spread his hands. "If it were me, I'd want to know. What I know can't bite me in the ass."

"Well, that's not entirely true. Some things you knew about still bit you in the ass. But I get your point. I just hate wasting more money on this…"

Still, the corner of his mouth kicked up. "Do you want to know, babe? Do you want to have all lingering questions settled so she has zero power over you? Not even information?"

I really did. At the same time…

"Then we keep going." He linked his fingers with mine. "We'll figure it out."

"What are we doing?" I asked as I followed Rachel through her house toward her bedroom.

"A project I've been meaning to talk to you about, but you texted last week about Valentine's Day and what to do for the boys and I have some thoughts." Rachel guided me through what might cheerfully be described as clutter and chaos to the hallway where her room was.

The last couple of times I'd been here, I hadn't seen her family but I had heard them. Today, one of her uncles was yelling across the house to her cousin about some game they were playing.

"They've never heard of headsets or discord or manners," she added as her uncle yelled out an obscenity and her cousin laughed.

"How many of you live here? And it's not like I haven't heard the word fuck before."

"It feels like too many somedays, but yeah, I'll bet you've heard it," she teased and winked as she pushed open the door to her room and let me in. Like before, it was cluttered, but cheerful with colorful blankets and pillows. There was even new art on the wall, and I grinned at a photograph of the two of us taken at the homecoming dance. "I know it ended up being a shitty night, but we look fucking fantastic right there."

It was from the dance floor, and I could make out Coop's arm and Archie's. I was pretty sure Jake was somewhere behind me, just out of frame. "We really do look great, and I love it. You don't have to get a different one."

"Cool." She moved over to her desk and flipped her laptop open. "C'mere, I want to show you something."

On the screen were pictures of woman in panties and a corset. She was kneeling amidst some flower petals, and it looked amazing and erotic. "Wow," I said as I set my bag down and leaned against the chair she perched on. "What are these?"

"My hobby."

"Your hobby is hot girl pics? I think the guys have that 'hobby' too, but that's not what they call it."

Rachel pinched me and laughed. "You're funny." Head tilted back, she motioned to the screen. "I took this picture." Tabbing through, she showed me a few more. They were all beautiful and tasteful, but it was the same woman. Definitely erotic with teasing angles and ample curves, but nothing quite pornographic.

"Holy shit, for real?"

With a little shrug, she tabbed to a different set of photos. "Been doing it for a couple of years. Mostly for friends, sometimes for model friends. Started out as a whim more than anything…but…"

"But nothing, are you going to go to school for photography?"

Laughing, she shook her head. "Not a lot of money in that. And this is… well, it's kind of just my thing. I like keeping it personal."

Personal.

And she was sharing it with me. "You're really talented."

"Thank you." A hint of a blush flushed her cheeks. "However, I'm not showing you these to fish for compliments. This is my idea for your Valentine's Day gift for the guys."

"You want to do shots of me like this?" I glanced back at the screen, and Rachel gave a little shrug.

"You're stunning. I've got a couple of corsets, and we can find something else. You can even do it in a T-shirt and panties if you want. Seriously, the pictures should reflect you as much as the aesthetic. I can do your makeup and help with the hair. It might take us a couple of sessions, and then we can pick out our favorites… I can do some touch-ups, not that I think you'll need it, and we can either print and frame them, or you can just give them access."

I dropped to perch on the edge of her bed and stared at the laptop screen, then at her. When I didn't answer right away, she swiveled to face me.

"If you hate the idea, we don't have to do it. You just seemed stressed about what to do for Valentine's."

"Well, that's more because Valentine's Day is like candied hearts, goofy cards, and waiting for all the chocolate to go on sale the next day, then making myself sick on it." I'd never had a boyfriend before, much less four. "It feels kind of stressful. Like I should make it special for them, but it's not like their birthdays where I can just focus on one of them so…yeah…I guess I am stressing."

"So like the idea? Hate the idea?"

I studied her and my gaze dipped to the fresh set of hickeys, and I rubbed a hand over my face. "Fuck, I don't know, Rachel. I think the guys would love them and you obviously take really good shots, but I have no idea if I could pose for something like that without laughing my ass off." The women in those pictures looked so intense and kind of earthy. That just wasn't me.

"So you laugh, that's you. This isn't about making you look like someone else. It's about revealing another side of you or maybe just a deeper look at you. The confidence you have now is just…stunning. You've always been a looker, but those boys, as much as they irk me at times, have been good for you."

"You like them," I told her as I flopped back on her bed and stared at the ceiling. She abandoned her chair and crawled over to lay on her back too. Rachel had star patterns on her ceiling. I bet they were cool when the lights were out.

"I do," she admitted. "But we don't discuss that. It's more effective if I'm the friend they need to be wary of so they don't do something stupid again and hurt you."

"They're not going to," I told her, and she linked her arm with mine.

"Frankie, honey, I love you, but guys are dumb. They do dumb shit all the time. They mess with your head, and they turn things inside out. They can be the best and worst thing that ever happened to you."

The vehemence in her voice had me cutting a look at her sideways.

"What's his name? I'll ask Jake to go kick his ass. He likes beating up jerks."

"Whose?" But the flicker in her expression there held just the barest hint of guilt. "Fuck," she said with a sigh.

"You don't have to tell me," I promised, squeezing her arm. "But now I'm more worried about those hickeys. You kind of go through girls like tissue paper, and if you're going to throw guys in…" Though… "I thought you didn't like guys."

"I don't, as a rule. I don't. Most of them are too controlling, and I prefer vag and boobs. Not going to lie. But there are some guys…"

I bit my lip and glanced over at her, and Rachel sighed.

"I promise, I'm fine," she told me and met my gaze. "I'm working on figuring things out. But I don't want to get into it right now. Let me focus on you? It helps to get out of my head."

I studied her for a beat. "I adore you, you know that, right?"

"The feeling is mutual. I promise, I'm not running away and obsessing over my crush on you to keep myself safe from feelings elsewhere." She made a face. "Or at least I'm mostly sure, because I'm ninety-nine percent certain you're never going to throw those guys over for me."

The corner of my mouth curved. "Only ninety-nine percent sure?"

"Well, they are guys and I am me, so there's always a chance, however remote." Humor filled her eyes, and I chuckled. "See, there's always hope. Now, tell me about what's got you all tangled up, because that boudoir photography idea is killer and I know those guys would lose their minds. Tell me everything, and I'll see if I can help you figure it out."

And just like that, I told her everything. Maddy. Eddie. The DNA tests. The secret trust. The mysterious grandparents. Trina. Carly. Alicia. Jake's sisters. The fact that Ian wouldn't tell me what his parents said, just that he was handling it and it would be fine. He asked me to trust him, and I was. I told her about the music we'd been recording and the fact that we were all still waiting to hear back on what the producers thought. And that I was terrified I might have screwed up his chances. Finally, I told her about Harvard and the other colleges.

By the time I finished, my throat ached and I swiped away the tears I hadn't even realized had been falling. "I shouldn't be crying about any of this, life is pretty awesome…"

"Awesome doesn't mean stress free," she murmured. "Good stress is still stress, and, honey, you're living with four guys. I think you should get a fucking medal because you haven't killed them."

I laughed, wiping away more of the tears as I sat up. "They're not so bad. I mean…they have their moments. Archie is *never* going to accept a grocery budget. He orders in even on nights we're supposed to be cooking, and I think he finds mac and cheese a personal affront."

"I shouldn't ask, but now I have to know… Why do you say that?"

"Because I used to stock it. It's cheap and good food for an emergency. It's also filling, and you can make it with just water, no butter or milk, though it is kind of gross that way, it's still better than nothing."

"Uh huh." Rachel eyed me. "And?"

"And the boxes keep disappearing from the kitchen. If he shops with me, they vanish from the cart. If I do manage to get them home, they disappear from the cupboards. I actually hid two boxes in my dresser the other day. So far, he doesn't seem to have found them. But…yeah, those are not things that make me too crazy. Coop and Jake both know how to do chores. Ian's learning to cook, and so is Archie. He built the robotic vacuum, and then he and Jake just built a litter scooper that's better than the one they sell…"

Rachel laughed. "He's building toys to do chores."

"Right?" I spread my hands. "It's adorable and aggravating and…my life is good. And in a couple of weeks, I'll be going to court and hopefully severing my last tie to Maddy."

"It's still a lot," she said and rubbed my back. "Ice cream? Epic fail videos?"

"Oh my god, yes."

Our lives took on a new rhythm. One that definitely helped with the stress. Twice a week, I went to the gym with Jake and worked on my punching. It was fun. Archie tagged along once, and he actually got Jake into the ring to spar. That was highly entertaining. Archie also had more skills than he'd let on.

Ian and I still worked on music, and he had me playing more than three chords on the guitar. Coop continued to spend more time with his family, but we'd taken Trina to the movies and we'd had Trina come over to my place, too.

It was still a struggle for her, but when I told her I had a therapist too, she'd lost some of her defensive edge. The fact that his dad was showing up at the apartment was grating on him, and honestly, I got that. I still couldn't believe Maddy had done that. While I didn't actively avoid going over there if I knew his dad was going to be present, I had no idea what to say to him.

Mr. Standish was bad enough, and I'd only seen him once recently when I'd been at the office. He'd stopped by a meeting Bryan and I had been attending. When he'd taken the time to talk to Bryan and me, I kept it polite and to the neutral topic of the internship. At least I could tell him honestly that I'd been enjoying some of our work.

We were in research and development for two weeks because it covered so many areas, and the labs were just cool. Suddenly, I could see exactly what Archie would be doing when he came to Standish to work. Though, I refrained from bringing that up.

The guys surprised me on the morning of Valentine's with roses and breakfast in bed, followed by the invitation to go out on a date with all of them that night after they picked me up at Standish. Apparently, they'd taken a vote, and Valentine's—like Christmas—was a group holiday going forward.

Archie got me a locket heart and key charm for my bracelet. Ian gave me a musical note pendant on a chain necklace. Jake found the most adorable stuffed cat that looked exactly like Tiddles and my very own pair of boxing gloves in cherry red. Coop held up a jar of candied hearts with a coupon book attached to the front. "There's chocolates, too," he promised. "But I didn't think you'd want to eat those for breakfast."

I laughed, but the coupon book made me laugh harder.

It had coupons like redeem for one orgasm. Redeem for a cock to blow. Redeem for foot massage. Redeem for an evening of pampering. A lot of other sexual favors were included in the various offers, but my favorite one was the last one.

Redeem for whatever you need.

"Dammit," Archie said. "Outdone by something you probably could have made in elementary school."

I swatted him and laughed, even if my face was red. "He could not have offered me a cock to blow in elementary school."

"No, but I could have in junior high," Coop said with a wink, and I grinned. "Besides, don't get your panties in a twist, Archie. I just happen to know how to be the favorite."

That got him playfully pummeled by Jake and Ian. However, I hugged my cat, my jar of candies, my necklace, and my charm. "I love them all, don't be silly."

They were still grinning when I reached for my phone.

"Which reminds me, I need to give you your gifts."

"You didn't have to get us anything, Baby Girl. We have you as our Valentine." Jake gave my foot a squeeze, and Ian grinned.

"That was smooth, man." Ian fist bumped him.

"Thank you, I liked it."

I rolled my eyes, but opened the password protected file on my phone and uploaded the whole set to the shared cloud they'd set up over Christmas. Each of their phones pinged, and I traded my phone for my coffee and stared as they tabbed through.

"Holy shit," Coop said and jerked his gaze up to me.

Archie's mouth formed a wide smile. "I like the red…"

"When did you do this?" Ian asked, his eyes hot as he glanced at me.

"Who the fuck took these pictures?" Jake demanded, the growl in his voice sending all kinds of delicious shivers through me. The look he pinned on me should not have turned me on. While overprotective Jake used to annoy me, possessive Jake just turned me into mush.

"You don't like them?" I played innocent, and Coop turned away smothering a snicker, while Archie just lifted a brow.

"Oh, we just want to know who has been looking at you wearing next to nothing, babe. Because Jake's going to have some feelings on that subject."

"Like you fucking don't," Jake snapped.

It was Ian biting back a smile this time, though he did give me a bit of side-eye. "They look professionally done."

"Just give me a name, Baby Girl. I love them. I'll have to thank them, in person."

"You do not fool me, Jacob Benton," I teased, and I could kiss Rachel. She was right, this really was the perfect gift for them. Something they could all enjoy, and I'd had a blast doing it. I'd done pictures in their boxers and in their T-shirts, as well as a few in a corset and lace panties. I'd even dug out a couple of the sets they'd given me for Christmas that I hadn't had occasion to wear.

The pictures were fun and playful, and she'd kept the cosmetics to a minimum. She'd also started telling me a little about the *guy* she'd been experimenting with, but stressed it was only an experiment and she wouldn't call it dating.

She wouldn't even call it benefits, yet.

To say she'd been close-mouthed and sparse would be an understatement.

"I'm not trying to fool you," Jake murmured. "I really do want to have a chat with whomever this was…"

"Well, I think she can handle you, but you have to promise to be nice."

"She," Jake repeated, his frown easing.

Coop let out a laugh. "Rachel took these?"

"I don't know that that's much better," Archie said. "Some of these are hella sexy. Though I gotta say, babe, you wear my boxers better than I do."

"Rachel's got a good eye," Ian told me, and then gave me a kiss. "Thanks for these, Angel. You didn't have to."

"I know but it was fun, and I wanted to give you guys something special."

As much fun as it was, the morning wasn't waiting for any of us. They had to get to school, and I had to get to my internship. The bubble of happiness floated with me on the drive in. Jake took me since the guys decided to trade out to minimize how often anyone of them were late, and even when I said I could drive myself, they insisted.

When I'd tried to argue that I would be fine, the strain around Archie's eyes had squeezed my heart, so I left it alone. "We'll all be here to get you," Jake promised as he gave me a kiss.

"You guys never told me where we were going…"

"Karaoke," Jake warned with a grin. "Dinner and karaoke. Then all of us back to the apartment, and everyone is crashing out in the living room. I'd say sex was on the table, but since Archie and Bubba haven't mastered the open sharing, we'll have to settle for cuddling. And maybe some sneaking off for seven minutes in heaven."

I burst out laughing at that mental image. He meant it, too.

Valentine's Day at Standish, even in the R&D areas, proved to be a lot of fun. Flowers were delivered all day long. There were small boxes of chocolates on everyone's desks. There was even a heart-shaped box on mine, and Bryan handed his over.

The heathen didn't like chocolate that much. Oh well, more for me. We grabbed lunch at the deli down the street, and the place was hosed down in Valentine's hearts. It made me laugh, particularly when all the cold cuts were heart shaped, so I took pictures to send to the guys.

Bryan did not *believe* in Valentine's Day. He waxed poetic about how Valentine was Santa Claus and the whole greeting card company nature of it. I kind of tuned him out when he really warmed to the topic. Back at the office, we split up to work with different R&D staff. I got to hang out in the robotics area, where they were working on rovers for space missions.

I pretty much blew up Archie's phone at every single chance. His amusement at my excitement had me sticking my tongue out at him. But it was cool. They had to take all kinds of stuff into account, and there were so many different pieces that went into making the group work. It wasn't just tech or design. There was someone managing all their projects and keeping them on track. There was someone who coordinated with other groups. Another person interfaced with their government liaisons.

They even showed me a test model of one they'd actually sent to Mars. It had failed. But they'd learned a lot from the data it sent back.

Standish really did have their fingers in everything.

Not long before the end of the day, I headed up for my weekly debrief with the HR rep. They liked to go over our experiences and to keep a finger on the pulse of it all. It made sense. I usually sent an email to our advisor at the program too for the same reason.

When I let myself into the conference room, I froze.

"I'm sorry," I said to Mr. Standish. "I thought this is where I was supposed to be."

I started to back out, but he took a step toward me and raised his hand. "You are supposed to be here, Frankie. I'm doing this week's check-in with you."

"Why?" The question slipped out as I stared at him. Mr. Standish raked a hand through his hair and then motioned to the table.

"Because at the end of the day, your internship is with my company. This program is highly regarded, and you are one of our top candidates. I'd like to get a feel for what you think so far, and if any of the divisions have interested you."

My gut cramped. I did not want to have this conversation with him, but at the same time… "I like the research and development stuff. It's been fascinating." I moved toward the table and set my backpack down, but I didn't sit.

Mirroring my posture, Mr. Standish stood on the other side of the table from me. "Are you interested in studying engineering? I was thinking the marketing or the educational materials might have held more interest for you."

"I don't know that much about engineering other than building rovers for Mars sounds cool, and I love watching Archie build stuff." I wanted to add, *remember Archie, your son? The one who does love engineering?*

"He's always been creative," Mr. Standish said. "Driven, too. Took apart a vintage car when he was ten because he wanted to understand how the engine worked. He'd ordered all the equipment he would need. It was a mess and it took weeks for him to put it back together, but I thought that was more defiance because I'd grounded him for tearing the car apart." Mr. Standish frowned. "I suppose I should have told him I was proud, but he was forever destroying things without regard for the time and investment. I wanted him to learn the value of it."

Wow. I didn't think I'd heard him put together that many words in a sentence before.

"Then again, that's Muriel's influence. She doesn't value anything that she can't replace for a more expensive brand. At least when he was with my parents, it seemed to help…" He tapped his knuckles against the table. "But that's not the important part here."

"Your son isn't important?" What was wrong with him?

"My relationship with Archie is complicated."

"Then uncomplicate it." Was I really trying to fix this? "I can't stand my mother." The words just came out. "I think I hate her most days. I still love her and that makes it worse, because I hate her for her choices and for always choosing *everything* but me."

Mr. Standish stared at me, his expression growing grim.

Fine. Maybe I was severely overstepping and I was about to lose this internship. Whatever.

"He deserves better than you and your wife. He's so fucking awesome, and I don't understand how you can't see it."

"I see it," the older man said with a sigh. "It's not his fault that we don't get along. It's never been his fault. It wasn't his fault when Muriel set out to trap me in marriage, or his fault that my parents punished my hubris by making me agree to stay in the marriage if I was going to make the changes I did. I gave up a lot for him."

He rapped his knuckles against the table.

"And I blame him for it. But it was never his fault. I'm not the best father. So I did the best I could by keeping my distance."

"Well, that all sounds kind of shitty." What else was I supposed to say to that?

"It was a choice. I can't change it. I can only try to face what the results of those choices are. It's part of why I wanted you to have this internship. When I saw your name on the list…I wanted you here. I've wanted to have this conversation with you for a while, but things weren't working out. The dinner was a definite disaster. I should have realized you'd bring Archie, because you two have become such good friends."

"Wait, why did you want to talk to me about it?"

"Archie was right about a few things. Before he turned eighteen, divorcing Muriel wasn't an option. It is now. I've fulfilled the prenuptial agreement. She'll receive a tidy sum, and we'll both have our freedom."

"Again, *why* do you want to tell me this? I get it, you're engaged to Maddy. Good luck with that. But that's not my problem anymore."

"Maddy and I have known each other a long time, Frankie," he said. "A long time. We actually knew each other back in school."

What?

"We were close…practically engaged. We had a disagreement one night, and I went out and met Muriel." His expression didn't change an inch. If anything, he seemed carved from stone as he revealed these deeply personal and frankly disturbing details.

"Okay. Great. You used to know Maddy. More lies. So happy to know." It was kind of nauseating actually.

Mr. Standish sighed and circled the table toward me. "I'm saying this badly, and you'd think after the months having to prepare, I would be able to handle this. But Maddy…Maddy wanted me to wait. and then she wanted to repair the damage done with you, but I don't see that happening any time soon. She's had nearly eighteen years to set this to rights, and if she isn't going to, then I have to."

My heart slammed against my rib cage as he narrowed the distance, but I took a breath when he stopped one chair away.

"I'm not a good man. In many ways, I've been a fairly terrible and selfish one. I cheated on her, and then I married another woman. I cheated on that woman with Maddy. Then Maddy punished me by not telling me she was pregnant when she left. I hadn't seen her in years before we moved here. I think Muriel knew she was here and it was why she chose the place. Her own personal little bit of vindictive punishment."

I was still back on the *cheating on Muriel and Maddy being pregnant* part.

"You cheated on Muriel by sleeping with Maddy?"

He let out a long sigh. "Yes. I'm your father. I've wanted to tell you since she provided me with the proof. She told me of course, after we reconnected… but I needed the evidence, and she had the DNA tests done… I'm aware this is a lot for you, and I've tried to…"

I was pretty sure he said other stuff after that, but I didn't hear it.

"I can't stay here," I mumbled, grabbing my bag and turning.

"Frankie…"

When he tried to grab my arm, I flinched away.

"Don't."

None of this made sense.

None of it.

I yanked the door open and charged out of the office. The elevators kind of blurred ahead of me, and I kept jamming the down button until the doors dinged and opened. Inside, I pressed the button for the lobby, jabbing it frantically, and as the doors closed, I met Mr. Standish's gaze.

No.

Not possible.

What the fuck just happened?

Edward Standish was my father?

* * *

Frankie and the boys will return in *Trials and Tiaras*.

To keep up with Heather and all her series join her reader's group:

Https://www.facebook.com/groups/HeathersPack/

Afterword

Well, if you need a minute. Go ahead and do that. Grab some water. Maybe coffee. If it's late and you were planning on sleeping, I hear breathing exercises are good.

Yeah, so I'll wait.

Please don't have damaged your Kindle or phone or other reading device. Do you need to check to make sure it's okay? Yes? Okay. I'll wait.

If you're still here, I'm hoping all is well. If you're asking did you just read that ending? Well, then the answer is also—yes. Sorry about that.

I promised you in the last book that their holiday in Colorado was very much needed and I think now you know why. Is this a curveball? Absolutely.

Do I hope you'll trust me and return for Trials and Tiaras? Also yes. This series has truly taken on a life of its own. Frankie and the boys have become friends and in some ways family. I talk about them like they're very much real people and I've been thrilled by how many of you have responded to them in the same way.

Their journey is far from over. I told you in the last book that happily ever after is a work in progress and I maintain that. They're a unit, they can handle what life throws at them and they are adapting and shifting around in the relationship as they all find their footing in this dynamic. Curveballs and sucker punches are not the end of the road. Bad Meatloaf was always a problem that needed to be addressed and we always knew they'd come back around.

Thank you again for being on this journey with me. I am so excited to see where we go next. Fair warning, the gloves are off in the next book.

xoxo

Heather

About Heather Long

USA Today bestselling author, Heather Long, likes long walks in the park, science fiction, superheroes, Marines, and men who aren't douche bags. Her books are filled with heroes and heroines tangled in romance as hot as Texas summertime. From paranormal historical westerns to contemporary military romance, Heather might switch genres, but one thing is true in all of her stories—her characters drive the books. When she's not wrangling her menagerie of animals, she devotes her time to family and friends she considers family. She believes if you like your heroes so real you could lick the grit off their chest, and your heroines so likable, you're sure you've been friends with women just like them, you'll enjoy her worlds as much as she does.

Follow Heather & Sign up for her newsletter:
www.heatherlong.net

Also by Heather Long

UNTOUCHABLE

Rules and Roses

Changes and Chocolates

Keys and Kisses

Whispers and Wishes

Hangovers and Holidays

Brazen and Breathless

Trials and Tiaras

Graduation and Gifts

Defiance and Dedication

82ND STREET VANDALS

Savage Vandal

Vicious Rebel

Ruthless Traitor

Dirty Devil

ALWAYS A MARINE SERIES

Once Her Man, Always Her Man

Retreat Hell! She Just Got Here

Tell It to the Marine

Proud to Serve Her

Her Marine

No Regrets, No Surrender

The Marine Cowboy

The Two and the Proud

A Marine and a Gentleman

Combat Barbie

Whiskey Tango Foxtrot

What Part of Marine Don't You Understand?

A Marine Affair

Marine Ever After

Marine in the Wind

Marine with Benefits

A Marine of Plenty

A Candle for a Marine

Marine under the Mistletoe

Have Yourself a Marine Christmas

Lest Old Marines Be Forgot

Her Marine Bodyguard

Smoke & Marines

BRAVO TEAM WOLF

When Danger Bites

Bitten Under Fire

BOOMERS

The Judas Contact

Deadly Genesis

Unstoppable

Chance Monroe

Earth Witches Aren't Easy

Plan Witch from Out of Town

Bad Witch Rising

Her Elite Assets

Featuring:

Pure Copper

Target: Tungsten

Asset: Arsenic

Fevered Hearts

Marshal of Hel Dorado

Brave are the Lonely

Micah & Mrs. Miller

A Fistful of Dreams

Raising Kane

Wanted: Fevered or Alive

Wild and Fevered

The Quick & The Fevered

A Man Called Wyatt

Going Royal

Some Like It Royal

Some Like It Scandalous

Some Like It Deadly

Some Like it Secret

Some Like it Easy

Her Marine Prince

Blocked

HEART OF THE NEBULA
Queenmaker

Deal Breaker

Throne Taker

LONE STAR LEATHERNECKS
Semper Fi Cowboy

As You Were, Cowboy

MADISON, THE WITCH HUNTER
Every Witch Way But Floosey's

MAGIC & MAYHEM
The Witch Singer

Bridget's Witch's Diary

The Witched Away Bride

Mongrels

Mongrels, Mischief & Mayhem

SHACKLED SOULS
Succubus Chained

Succubus Unchained

Succubus Blessed

SPACE COWBOY
Space Cowboy Survival Guide

WOLVES OF WILLOW BEND
Wolf at Law

Wolf Bite

Caged Wolf

Wolf Claim

Wolf Next Door

Rogue Wolf

Bayou Wolf

Untamed Wolf

Wolf with Benefits

River Wolf

Single Wicked Wolf

Desert Wolf

Snow Wolf

Wolf on Board

Holly Jolly Wolf

Shadow Wolf

His Moonstruck Wolf

Thunder Wolf

Ghost Wolf

Outlaw Wolves

Wolf Unleashed